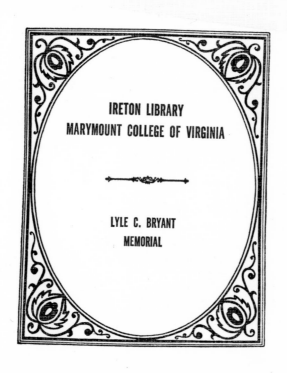

The
Twenty-Ninth Day

Other Norton/Worldwatch Books

Erik P. Eckholm
Losing Ground:
Environmental Stress and World Food Prospects

Erik P. Eckholm
The Picture of Health:
Environmental Sources of Disease

Denis Hayes
Rays of Hope:
The Transition to a Post-Petroleum World

The Twenty-Ninth Day

Accommodating Human Needs and Numbers to the Earth's Resources

Lester R. Brown

A WORLDWATCH INSTITUTE BOOK

W·W· NORTON & COMPANY· INC·
New York

Copyright © 1978 by Worldwatch Institute
Published simultaneously in Canada by George J. McLeod Limited,
Toronto. Printed in the United States of America.
All Rights Reserved
First Edition

Library of Congress Cataloging in Publication Data
Brown, Lester Russell, 1934–
The twenty-ninth day
"A Worldwatch Institute book."
Includes bibliographical references and index.
1. Human ecology. 2. Natural resources.
3. Population. 4. Environmental policy. I. Title
GF41.B76 1978   301.31   77–27823
ISBN 0 393 05664 3 cloth edition
ISBN 0 393 05673 2 paper edition
1 2 3 4 5 6 7 8 9 0

*To Brian and Brenda
and the world in which they and their generation will live.*

Contents

Preface   xi

1. Introduction   1

2. Ecological Stresses I: The Dimensions   12
   Carrying Capacity: The Concept   13
   The Tragedy of the Commons   15
   Overfishing: The Oceanic Commons   17
   Deforestation: Cutting Too Many Trees   23
   Overgrazing: Eroding the Protein Base   27
   Overplowing: Moving onto Marginal Land   33
   Pollution: Overloading the Ecosystem   37

3. Ecological Stresses II: The Consequences   45
   The Loss of Cropland   46
   Oceans: The Ultimate Sink   50
   Endangered Species   54
   Environmentally Induced Illnesses   57
   Inadvertent Climate Change   61
   Natural Disasters: The Human Hand   65
   Reflections on Carrying Capacity   67

4. Population: Understanding the Threat   71
Arithmetic and Dynamics   72
A Problem of Many Dimensions   75
A Double-Edged Sword   78
Trends of the Seventies   79
Countries Achieving Stability   82
The Tragic Rise in Death Rates   86
Population Stabilization: A New Urgency   92

5. Energy: The Coming Transition   97
Energy and Social Evolution   98
Middle East Dominance   100
Petroleum: A Transitory Era   102
Nuclear Power: A Dead-End Street?   108
The Case for Conservation   113
Returning to Coal   116
Turning to the Sun   118

6. The Food Prospect   128
The Past Quarter-Century   129
The North American Breadbasket   135
Land and Water   139
The Energy Dimension   143
The Green Revolution   145
Rising Yields: An Interrupted Trend   149
The Protein Bind   152
Toward Century's End   156

7. Economic Stresses   161
Diminishing and Negative Returns   162
Global Inflation: New Sources   169
Capital Scarcity   177
Labor Productivity   182
Unemployment: A Growing Social Ill   184

The Changing Growth Prospect 188

8. Wealth Among Societies 192
Global Distribution of Wealth 193
The Dimensions of Poverty 198
The Global Politics of Scarcity 202
Commodity Cartels: OPEC and Beyond 205
Technology: A Global Commodity 208
Drawers of Water, Hewers of Wood 214
Calls for a New Order 217

9. Wealth within Societies 220
The National Distribution of Wealth 221
The Role of Planners 223
The Role of Technology 229
Countryside versus City 232
Land Distribution: Social Significance 235
Ecological Deterioration and Income Distribution 237
National versus International Inequities 239

10. The Inevitable Accommodation 241
Coming to Terms with Nature 244
The Inner Limits 247
The Limits of Technology 250
The Analytical Gap 253
The Economic Dilemma 259
The Basic Political Choice 263
Social and Political Stresses 267

11. The Elements of Accommodation 272
Stabilizing World Population 273
The Energy Transition 278
Recycling Raw Materials 282
Reform in the Countryside 285

The Changing Roles of Women   289
Redefining National Security   293
Coping with Complexity   296

12. The Means of Accommodation   299
A Planetary Bargain   300
Long-Term Global Planning   305
The Role of Government   310
Individuals and Organizations   314
Education and the Media   320
A Social Transformation   322

Notes   327
Selected References   345
Index   351

Preface

The purpose of this book is to shed some light on the interaction of the world ecological, economic and social systems, a topic of central interest to me and my colleagues at the Worldwatch Institute. Our goal is to analyze important global issues and bring them to the attention of busy decision makers at all levels, whether political leaders establishing national priorities, foundation officers allocating research funds or young couples deciding whether to have a child. We hope this book will be a useful source of information for those working for a world that is ecologically sustainable and socially just.

The book draws on a wide range of personal experiences including formal education in both the natural and social sciences, a youth spent farming with my brother, a year spent living in villages in India, a decade with the U.S. Department of Agriculture during the Kennedy-Johnson era, and five years with the Overseas Development Council. The early part of the decade with USDA was spent in researching and writing on world agriculture and the remainder in managing the Department's technical assistance programs in some forty countries. This latter position involved extensive travel, much of it in the countryside of the Third World where many of the problems addressed in this book were then beginning to surface.

The Twenty-Ninth Day is by no means a final work. It should be viewed as part of an ongoing process, of a continuing effort to understand a set of complex interrelated global issues. It is part of a continuous flow of Worldwatch Papers and books. Indeed, some of the material in this book has been taken from my own earlier Worldwatch Papers.

Completion of a book of this scope leaves the author indebted to many people. At various points along the way Patricia McGrath, Frank Record, and Christopher Flavin assisted with the research and analysis. Macinda Byrd helped gather research materials. Marion Frayman, Blondeen Duhaney, and Joanne Senechal typed the manuscript as it evolved through several drafts.

My debt to Kathleen Courrier, who edited the manuscript, is uncommonly large. Her contribution went far beyond that of editor as she added texture and color to my prose. At times it was difficult to tell when editing ended and writing began.

Each of my colleagues—Erik Eckholm, Denis Hayes, Kathleen Newland, Colin Norman, Linda Starke, Bruce Stokes, and Frank Record—reviewed the manuscript at least once. Among those outside the Institute who reviewed the manuscript and offered helpful suggestions are Robert O. Anderson, George Brockway, Kent Collins, Peter Cott, Anne de Castillo, Gail Finsterbusch, James P. Grant, Martin McLaughlin, Donella Meadows, Rufus Miles, David Poindexter, Andrew Rice, Rafael Salas, Joyti Singh, and Tarzie Vittachi, Isaiah Frank, Carl Gerber, Ronald Ridker, and Roger Sant reviewed portions of the manuscript. I am grateful to all these individuals for their time and advice. As is always the case, the final product is one for which I, the author, bear the responsibility.

The Worldwatch Institute has provided a fertile environment in which to do the book. The Institute, which effectively began operation in 1975 was incorporated by Erik Eckholm, Blondeen Duhaney, and myself. It is governed by an international Board of Directors chaired by Orville L. Freeman. Other

members include Robert O. Anderson (U.S.), Charles M. Car-
gille (U.S.), Carlo Cipolla (Italy), Edward S. Cornish (U.S.),
Hazel Henderson (U.S.), Anne-Marie Holenstein (Switzerland), Abd-El Rahman Khane (Algeria), Elizabeth McCor-
mack (U.S.), Larry Minear (U.S.), I. G. Patel (Vice-Chairman,
India), Andrew E. Rice (U.S.), Walter O. Roberts (U.S.),
Rafael M. Salas (Philippines), and Lynne G. Stitt (U.S.). Officers are Felix Gorrell, Treasurer; Blondeen Duhaney, Secretary; and myself, President. Funding is provided by several
foundations, UN agencies, U.S. government departments, and
private contributions.

I am indebted to The Kettering Foundation for the primary
financial support for the book and for their early vote of confidence in the Institute. Kent Collins, Vice President for Exploration and Development, was extraordinarily supportive
throughout. Additional support for the book came from the
UN Fund for Population Activities, the Council on Environmental Quality, and the Agency for International Development through the Population Information Program of George
Washington University. The general funding provided the Institute by the Rockefeller Brothers Fund, the Edna McConnell
Clark Foundation, and Robert O. Anderson, also aided in the
completion of this book. At this broader level, both my colleagues and I are grateful for the generous multi-year launching
grant approved by the trustees of the Rockefeller Brothers
Fund three years ago that brought the Institute into existence.
We are particularly grateful to the RBF President, William
Dietel, who helped found the Institute, and to Gerry Barney,
our project officer.

The Twenty-Ninth Day

1

Introduction

The French use a riddle to teach schoolchildren the nature of exponential growth. A lily pond, so the riddle goes, contains a single leaf. Each day the number of leaves doubles—two leaves the second day, four the third, eight the fourth, and so on. "If the pond is full on the thirtieth day," the question goes, "at what point is it half full?" Answer: "On the twenty-ninth day."[1]

The global lily pond in which four billion of us live may already be at least half full. Within the next generation, it could fill up entirely. Occasional clusters of lily leaves are already crowding against the edge, signaling the day when the pond will be completely filled. The great risk is that we will miss or misread the signals and fail to adjust our lifestyles and reproductive habits in the time available.

A careful reading of the signals indicates that pressures on the earth's principal biological systems and energy resources are mounting. Stress is evident in each of the four major biological systems—oceanic fisheries, grasslands, forests, and croplands—that humanity depends on for food and industrial raw materials. Except for croplands, all are essentially natural systems, little modified by humans. In large areas of the world, the pressure of growing human demands on these systems has reached the point where it is impairing their productive capacities.

Discussions of long-term economic growth prospects in recent years have concentrated on nonrenewable resources, especially minerals and fossil fuels. They have been undergirded by the implicit assumption that because biological resources were renewable they were of little concern. In fact, both the nonrenewable and renewable resource bases have been shrinking. The earth's biological systems form the foundation of the global economic system. In addition to food, biological systems provide virtually all the raw materials for industry except minerals and petroleum-derived synthetics.

The oceanic food chain, yielding some 70 million tons of fish per year, is humanity's principal source of high-quality protein. Not only do fisheries provide animal protein for direct consumption, but the less palatable species are converted into fishmeal and fed to poultry that produce meat and eggs.

Forests provide not only lumber, still a universal building material, but for fully a third of humanity, firewood as well. They are the source of the newsprint for the daily newspaper and of other paper. In short, the housing, education, and communications sectors depend heavily on forests for raw materials.

The earth's grasslands are a rich source of protein, from

which comes most of the world's meat, milk, butter, and cheese. In addition they sustain the draft animals that till a third of the world's croplands. They are also the source of leather for the footwear and leather-goods industries, and of wool, one of the oldest and most highly prized fibers of the clothing industry.

Croplands produce an even greater range of products. They supply food, industrial raw materials such as rubber, and a variety of fibers, alcohols, starches, and vegetable oils. The contribution of cultivated crops to the global economy is far greater than the one-tenth of the earth's land surface that they occupy.

Four billion human beings with rising aspirations exert great pressure on these biological systems, often exceeding nature's long-term carrying capacity. The productivity of scores of oceanic fisheries is falling as the catch exceeds their regenerative capacity. In a protein-hungry world, overfishing has recently become the rule, not the exception. Forests are shrinking before the onslaught of the firewood gatherer, the land-hungry farmer, and international timber interests.

As the number of cattle, water buffalo, sheep, goats, and camels increases apace with human populations, the earth's grasslands are being overtaxed. Denudation, soil erosion, and desert encroachment result. Croplands, too, are under pressure. The frontiers have largely disappeared. Fallow cycles everywhere are shortening, and farmers seeking land are being forced up steeply sloping hillsides and onto less fertile soils.

In many ways the natural biological systems on which humanity depends function like a philanthropic foundation operating on a fixed endowment. If a foundation has an endowment of a hundred million dollars that earns 6 percent yearly, it can safely disburse six million dollars per year indefinitely. If, however, overly enthusiastic project officers begin disbursing the foundation's resources at ten million dollars per year, this level of grants would steadily consume the foundation's financial assets. Eventually the foundation would lose its productive assets and close its doors. So too with biological systems. In neither case can the offtake exceed the regenerative capacity for long.

The deterioration of biological systems is not a peripheral issue of concern only to environmentalists. Our economic system depends on the earth's biological systems. Anything that threatens the viability of these biological systems threatens the global economy. Any deterioration in these systems represents a deterioration in the human prospect.

The deterioration of ecological systems through human abuse is not new. Overcutting and the subsequent decimation of forests by humans date back to the earliest civilizations in the Middle East. What is new today is the scale and speed at which biological resources are being impaired and destroyed.

Although these recent trends cannot long continue, how much time it will take to face up to the problem and to arrest the biological deterioration is unclear. Re-establishing a stable relationship between humanity and the natural systems that support human life will perforce preoccupy political leaders during the years and decades immediately ahead.

The adjustments we must now make in consumption patterns, in population policy, and in the economic system if we are to preserve the biological underpinnings of the global economy are profound; they will challenge fully both human ingenuity and the human capacity for behavioral change. Unfortunately, a second equally momentous change—namely, the shift from nonrenewable to renewable energy sources—will compound the difficulties of making the first.

It has long been known that world oil production would eventually turn downward, as it already has in the United States, but until recently few cared because it was assumed that the future economy would be powered largely by nuclear power, by energy "too cheap to meter." But with each passing day, the nuclear dream fades further.

With the projected downturn in oil production only ten to fifteen years away, there is little time in which to convert the economic system from oil to renewable energy sources. The conversion should have been launched decades ago, but the promise of nuclear power lured planners and political leaders down what now appears to be a blind alley.

The impending shift in energy sources is certain to transform the economic system, but nowhere more than in the energy-wasteful United States. As energy analyst Denis Hayes has indicated, the effort required to transform the U.S. energy system will dwarf that involved in the space race. In terms of political commitment and the mobilization of resources, he believes, it is more comparable to the national effort made during World War II.[2] Indeed, President Carter has described this effort as the moral equivalent of war.

Recognition of the coming energy transition coincides with the appearance of signs suggesting that the world has entered a new economic era during the seventies. During the quarter century following World War II, the global output of goods and services nearly tripled. Never before had energy and food supplies been cheap and abundant enough to permit such rapid economic and population growth. Nor will they likely ever be again.

Two events ushered out the era of cheap energy and surplus food. The massive Soviet wheat purchase in the summer of 1972, the largest ever made by any country, brought the era of chronic food surpluses to a close. The Arab oil embargo and the subsequent quadrupling of oil prices in late 1973 brought down the curtain on the era of cheap energy.

The new era now emerging defies description. The gradual acceleration of economic and population growth that characterized the industrial era may have ended. Growth rates of both apparently peaked sometime in the late sixties or early seventies. Both now appear to be slowing. Yet, the growth dynamic that is so much the stamp of the industrial era has shaped our institutions, values, and priorities. Indeed, the contemporary social order is its offspring.

The seemingly inevitable slowing of economic growth during the closing quarter of this century will put the question of how to more equitably distribute wealth on the political agenda everywhere. Both within and among societies, the issue seems certain to exact a heavy claim on the time and energy of political leaders. Indeed, a more equitable distribution of material wealth may be one of the keys to managing many population and resource problems.

As the earth's various carrying capacities are exceeded, attitudes and policies may change overnight. In some places, particularly in relatively poor countries, population growth now acts as a double-edged sword, expanding the demand for a given biological resource even as it reduces production. Although Malthus warned that population would tend to expand faster than food supplies, he failed to tell us that population growth can actually destroy productive capacity when it generates a demand for biological resources that exceeds the regenerative capacity of natural systems. When this point is reached, crises can emerge suddenly, with little warning.

The most immediate symptoms of ecological stress are physical—deteriorating grasslands, soil erosion, or climate modification. At the next level, the stresses manifest themselves in economic terms—scarcity, inflation, unemployment, and economic stagnation or decline. And finally, the stresses assume a social and political character—hunger, forced migration to the cities, deteriorating living standards, and political unrest.

The need to adapt human life simultaneously to the carrying capacity of the earth's biological systems and to the limits of renewable energy sources will require a new social ethic. The essence of this new ethic is accommodation—the accommodation of human numbers and aspirations to the earth's resources and capacities. This new ethic must above all arrest the deterioration of man's relationship to nature. If civilization as we know it is to survive, this ethic of accommodation must replace the prevailing growth ethic.

Even as human pressures on the earth's natural systems have mounted, the interdependence of societies has deepened. Economic or political decisions made within a given country may affect far more people outside that country than within. The overnight devaluation of a major currency immediately affects export prospects and employment levels in scores of countries. The daily news reminds us that few matters of energy, food, climate, and finance are strictly domestic affairs.

The traditional independence of Americans, who could draw on a continental storehouse of raw materials and who live in one of the world's strongest economies, is being affected in unexpected ways. From the time of the United States' birth as a nation, its invulnerability has been epitomized by the capacity of U.S. farmers to provide American consumers with abundant cheap food. Yet, suddenly in 1973 food prices took off, and surprised and upset Americans found themselves sharing food scarcity with consumers in the one hundred or more countries that import food from the United States.

The Soviets may have fared even worse. To maintain consumption levels without stringently rationing food, the Soviet government imported some 30 million tons of grain, dwarfing in scale even India's food imports. When the Soviets turned to the world market, they discovered that only the United States, their principal political adversary, could rescue them.

Clearly, resource scarcities are altering the global power structure. From the onset of the Industrial Revolution, if not from the Age of Exploration, political power accrued in those countries that controlled capital and technology. Now, almost overnight, this power is being diffused. Scarcities of raw materials, especially of energy, are causing shifts in political power toward those countries that control raw materials. Nonindustrial powers such as Saudi Arabia and Iran must be considered ranking powers today. Venezuela's new-found oil wealth enables it to exercise considerable influence in Latin America, in some instances to supplant that of the United States. Canada's rich endowment of raw materials has given it new economic and political clout to wield in its dealings with the United States.

The shift in the global power structure during the seventies reflects the redistribution of economic power more than shifts in military power. Thus, countries heavily dependent on imported food and energy are particularly vulnerable and insecure, as Japan's economic turmoil during the energy crisis made clear. The rising U.S. dependence on Middle East oil translates into Middle East influence on U.S. foreign policy. The vulnerability associated with this energy dependence strikes some as greater than that associated with foreign military threats. Indeed, for many countries national security can no longer be defined primarily in military terms.

Increasingly, threats to national security are more ecological and economic. A rapid population growth rate can destroy a country's ecological system or social structure more effectively than a foreign adversary ever could. Potential Indian or Chinese aggression jeopardizes Bangladesh far less than does flood-producing deforestation in neighboring Nepal and India. For some countries, encroaching deserts may pose a greater threat to national security than invading armies. For many industrial economies, the projected depletion of oil reserves may now be a more serious threat to security than any likely military aggression. The decision by major oil-exporting countries to reduce production to conserve dwindling oil reserves may disrupt the U.S. economic system far more than any likely military action.

As disturbing as the discontinuities of the seventies are, the myopia of those officially charged with analyzing and preparing us for the future is even more unsettling. Biologists who see and understand the deterioration of the earth's biological systems were not able to link it to the performance of the economic system. Conversely, economic and political decision makers failed to grasp the relationship between biological and economic systems. Communications between economics and ecology are virtually nonexistent, in part because ecological principles and economic theory share so little common ground. Economists tend to think in terms of unlimited exponential growth and to place great faith in "technological fixes," while biologists tend to think in terms of closed systems, of natural cycles and of carrying capacities. Economists see specialization as a virtue and as a source of efficiency, while ecologists perceive it as a risk and a threat to the stability of systems.

The analytical breakdown is not confined to any particular area. Experts failed to anticipate the energy crisis, food shortages, double-digit global inflation, the abrupt alteration of the international political structure, the collapse of major fisheries, the astronomical climb in world wheat prices during the early seventies, and a global economic slump unmatched since the Great Depression.

That our world is changing rapidly few deny. But our record in anticipating the future during the seventies has not been anything to write home about. This shortcoming was acknowledged by Walter Heller, former Chairman of President Kennedy's Council of Economic Advisors, in his Presidential address to the American Economic Association when he said, 'We [economists] have been caught with our parameters down."[3]

Many, economists among them, admit that economics may no longer be able to explain the workings of the economic system. Arthur Okun, former Chairman of the Council of Economic Advisors, greets this prospect by lamely claiming that economists understand what is happening at least as well as anyone else does.[4] Economist Alan Coddington is less hopeful; he thinks that economists might contribute most by remaining silent, at least until they had something worthwhile to say.[5] At any rate, the problem is not an occasional breakdown or shortcoming in analytical capacity, but an overall loss of confidence. It is not just that the least able are stumbling, but that the finest minds are missing the mark so widely.

We now confront the prospect that the complexities of the modern world might exceed our analytical capacities. We must now also ask whether existing political institutions can effectively manage deepening international interdependence. Perhaps more important, are we capable of creating and managing the political institutions we need?

In recent years, considerations of economic growth have focused on the physical constraints upon economic activity, on the outer limits. In those immediately to come, the inner limits posed by political processes, social institutions, and the capacity for behavioral change may figure more centrally. For example, the shortsightedness of political leaders who must survive from year to year or from term to term do not readily mesh with the time horizons of long-term social goals such as reforestation, energy conservation, or population stabilization. Tangible and measurable physical limits are hard to ignore, but the social limits imposed by humans are hard to identify and even more difficult to measure. They may be almost as difficult to push back as the natural or physical constraints.

In the third quarter of this century, man conquered space. Hundreds of millions representing every nationality thrilled at the sight of American astronauts walking on the moon. But in the last quarter, the earth is destined to again become the technological frontier as food becomes scarce and energy costlier. Circumstances indicate a return to basics on the human agenda—food, energy, and population.

The social changes that must be compressed into the next two decades promise to be profound as measured by any historical yardstick. Each of us will be affected. Arresting the deteriorating relationship between ourselves, now numbering four billion, and the earth's natural systems and resources will affect what we eat, how much we pay for housing, and how many children we have. Some will view the changes in prospect with alarm, even in doomsday terms. Others, including the author, believe that the problems outlined in this book are manageable but that managing them satisfactorily will require an exceptional exercise of political will and human ingenuity.

2

Ecological Stresses I: The Dimensions

The concept of carrying capacity is familiar to biologists, ranchers, and wildlife managers but not to economic advisers and political decision makers. Even the biologists who developed the concept usually apply it only locally. Curiously little attention has been paid to the carrying capacity of biological systems by national governments, and the subject has been almost entirely ignored at the global level. Only with the preparation of the documents for the 1977 UN Conference on Desertification did the term begin to creep into the vocabulary of UN officials.

The daily news frequently carries accounts of what happens when biological carrying capacities are exceeded. Extensive deforestation in the western Himalayas leads to record floods and destruction in Pakistan. An earthquake in the Peruvian Andes wreaks damages far greater than those suggested by the Richter scale reading, because extensive deforestation paved the way for massive earth and rock slides following the initial tremors. The price of soybeans multiplies as the global fish catch declines. A dust storm in northeastern Colorado closes schools for two days because the growing world demand for wheat led farmers to plow marginal lands that should have been left in grass.

These consequences of excessive pressure on biological systems are not intended. Nobody wanted the North Atlantic haddock fishery to collapse. The combined claims made by fishing nations simply overtaxed it. But, if the deterioration or outright destruction of local biological systems like this one continues, the number of humans the earth can ultimately "carry" will fall off sharply.

Carrying Capacity: The Concept

The carrying capacity of a natural biological system is determined by its maximum sustainable yield, and this in turn is the product of its size and regenerative powers. The latter varies widely. Grasslands and forests in humid areas have greater regenerative capacities and hence greater carrying capacities than those in semi-arid regions. The maximum sustainable yield of biological systems, which can be expressed as a percentage of stock, may vary from a few percent of growth to well over half; but it cannot be exceeded indefinitely without reducing the system's carrying capacity.

A natural grassland can support a set number of cattle or a somewhat larger number of sheep; a fishery will supply the protein needs of a certain number of people; and the forest surrounding a village will satisfy the firewood needs of a given population. If the number of livestock or of people dependent on these biological systems becomes excessive, then the biological system will slowly be destroyed. If the trees regularly removed from a forest exceed its regenerative capacity, then the forest will eventually disappear. If the offtake from a fishery exceeds its regenerative capacity, stocks will dwindle and it will eventually collapse. Where herds grow too large, livestock will decimate grazing lands; as erosion exacts its toll, these pastures will turn into barren wastelands.

Weather, disease, or other changing natural conditions can also reduce the carrying capacity of biological systems. Prudence suggests leaving a margin of safety; otherwise, a drought or outbreak of plant disease can spell disaster. Such was the case in the Sahelian Zone of Africa when nomadic tribes lost entire herds of cattle and goats during the prolonged drought.

Perhaps the most easily understood example of carrying capacity is that applied by ranchers. Ranchers know that if they carry too many cattle on their land, the range slowly deteriorates and the cattle become emaciated. Eventually, part of the herds may be lost through attrition or the forced selling of breeding stock for slaughter. Successful ranchers can peg rather precisely the carrying capacity of their land, and they allow a small margin of excess capacity so that their herds can survive the lean years. They understand the costs and risks of overstocking. Aside from being forced to sell breeding stock in poor years, they recognize that if they overstock for years on end they will slowly destroy their own grasslands and the carrying capacity of their ranches.

The concept of biological carrying capacity is of central importance: human existence itself depends on the output of fisheries, forests, grasslands, and croplands. The natural productivity of the first three is, for the most part, out of human hands. The productivity of the earth's vast semi-arid and arid grasslands can be raised, but the principal techniques for doing so require water and fertilizer and are energy-intensive. Any effort to convert natural systems to controlled systems invariably involves heavy expenditures of energy, something that will likely become prohibitively expensive as the earth's oil reserves run out. Occasional cases of successful tree or fish farming notwithstanding, no economical way of greatly enhancing the productivity of these systems on a global scale has yet been discovered.

The fourth biological system—croplands—is a natural system fundamentally modified to satisfy man's needs. From the beginning of agriculture until the present, humans have sought to improve both the genetic potential of the originally domesticated crops, particularly cereals, and the techniques of cultivating them. The great growth in human numbers since agriculture began testifies to the success of these efforts. Of the four biological systems, the earth's croplands have by far the greatest potential for future growth in productivity.

The three biological systems that remain essentially in their natural state are being adversely affected by the pressures born of excessive demand. In some situations, the pressure put on a biological system can be controlled—witness the case of the individual rancher who owns and carefully tends a piece of land. But when resources are held in common (as are the woodlands surrounding a village), controlling the offtake may prove impossible. The shrinkage of carrying capacity is exacerbated by what has been called the "tragedy of the commons."

The Tragedy of the Commons

The inherent tragedy associated with the common use of common resources was first articulated by an English political economist, William Forster Lloyd, in 1883, in a pamphlet entitled "Two Lectures on the Checks to Population."[1] In his monograph, Lloyd considered the problem posed by the village green —perhaps relying on his observations of the very village green that still adjoins Oxford University, where he was then lecturing. He pointed out that a common grazing area worked well as long as the number of cattle did not overtax the land's carrying capacity, ruining the pasture and reducing the number of cattle it would sustain. According to Lloyd, the herdsmen using the green might agree that it would be in the interest of all to reduce the number of cattle to that which could be supported indefinitely. But the individuals had no incentive to remove *their* cattle. If a particular herdsman decided to cut down his herd to ease the pressures, others would not necessarily follow suit. Thus, the sum of individual decisions to maximize gains would be to place far more cattle on the green than it could sustain.

Lloyd's pamphlet received little notice. His idea, however, has been called back into circulation as carrying capacities are exceeded in one way or another. In particular, Garrett Hardin applied it to the contemporary world in an article in *Science* in 1968 entitled "The Tragedy of the Commons."[2] Hardin contended that the commons today is nothing less than the earth itself. Since then, political scientist William Ophuls has taken the concept farther.[3] He points out that today the commons includes the earth's atmosphere, water, outer space, upper atmosphere, oceans, and biological cycles. On our global commons, the individual herdsmen may be whole nations, multinational corporations, or individuals.

In an increasingly interdependent world, local tragedies of the commons can have global consequences. As the demands for wood for use as fuel and for other purposes increase in developing countries as a result of population growth, deforestation spreads. As the effort required by villagers to reach the receding forests mounts, they are eventually forced to burn animal dung for fuel, reducing the amounts available for use as fertilizer. In turn, local food production falls off, and world food prices rise as ever more local shortages are offset with food imports.

The solution to the tragedy of the commons is to limit the collective claim on common resources to a sustainable level and to find a just and enforceable way to adjudicate claims. At the international level, conventions are needed to regulate the catch from oceanic fisheries. So too are regulations restricting the waste oil that ocean-going tankers can discharge. If the worldwide use of aerosols is not restricted or banned, the protective layer of ozone surrounding the earth may be irreversibly depleted. The energies of diplomats are consumed increasingly by efforts to cope with the tragedy of our earthly commons, to work out the regulations, the conventions, and the treaties that will protect and preserve it.

Overfishing: The Oceanic Commons

Throughout most of human history there were far more fish in the oceans that we could ever hope to catch. Indeed, the fish in the seas seemed as plentiful as those in the New Testament parable. But recently, as human numbers moved toward four billion, the global appetite for table-grade fish such as salmon and tuna approached and, in some cases, exceeded the regenerative capacity of fisheries. Overfishing led to shrinking stocks and declining catches.

Between 1950 and 1970, fish supplied more and more of the human diet as the technological capacity to exploit oceanic fisheries expanded. During this two-decade span, the catch more than tripled, climbing from 21 to 70 million tons.[4] At nearly 70 million tons in live weight, it averaged some 18 kilograms (1 kilogram equals 2.2 pounds) per person annually, well above the annual yield from the world's beef herds.

At least 90 percent of the world fish catch comes from the oceanic commons. The remainder is produced in fresh water, mainly in inland lakes and streams. Two-thirds or more of the catch is eaten directly by humans, while the remaining third is consumed indirectly in the form of fishmeal fed to poultry and hogs.[5]

The importance of fish in diets varies widely by country.

Among the larger countries, fish figure most prominently in the diets of the Japanese and the Soviet people. As population pressure built up during the late nineteenth and the twentieth centuries, the Japanese were forced to turn to the oceans for animal protein and to devote their limited land resources to rice production. As a result, they evolved a fish-and-rice diet with an annual fish consumption per person of thirty-two kilograms, the highest of any large country.[6]

The Soviet Union, hard pressed to expand its livestock industry adequately, began some two decades ago to mine the oceans for animal protein. It has invested heavily not only in fishing fleets but also in floating fish-processing factories and in sophisticated fishing technologies that enable its fleets to locate and take fish in all waters. Consequently, Soviet consumers now each eat an average of ten kilograms of fish a year, nearly double the American level.[7] In the United States fish compose an important part of the diet, but direct consumption averages only about six kilograms per capita (compared with about one hundred kilograms of meat and poultry).[8]

World fishing fleets have expanded enormously since World War II. Investment in fishing capacity multiplied severalfold as the industry adopted sophisticated fishing technologies such as sonar tracking. Between 1950 and 1970, the catch increased by an average of nearly 5 percent yearly, far outstripping population growth and sharply boosting per capita supplies of marine protein. But in 1970 the trend was abruptly and unexpectedly interrupted. Since then the catch has fluctuated between 65 and 70 million tons, clouding the prospects for an ever-bigger catch (see Figure 2-1). Meanwhile, world population growth has led to an 11-percent decline in the per-capita catch and to rising prices for virtually every edible species. Many marine biologists feel that the global catch of table-grade species may be approaching the maximum sustainable limit. If the "tragedy of the commons" befalls more fisheries, the world catch will decrease even further.

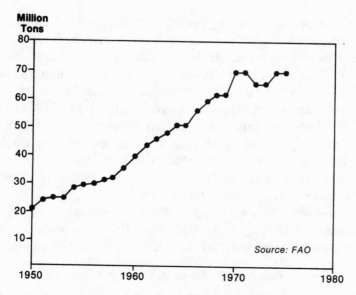

Figure 2-1. World Fish Catch, 1950-75

The northwest Atlantic fishing area, extending from Rhode Island northward to the southern coast of Greenland, is a microcosm of world fisheries. Accounting for 5 percent of the total world fish catch, its 350-year history makes it one of the world's oldest oceanic fisheries. The catch of this biologically rich region totaled 1.8 million tons in 1954 and increased steadily until 1968, when it reached 3.9 million tons. It then dropped by 18 percent to 3.2 million tons in 1970, where it has remained even though the number of countries fishing in the region and investments in fishing capacity have continued to rise.

The catch of several individual species peaked in the late sixties. Fishery experts attribute the declines since then to overfishing. The haddock catch reached a high of 249,000 tons in 1965 and then fell steadily until by 1972 it amounted to only one-seventh of its earlier level. The catches of cod, halibut, and herring peaked in 1968; but all have dropped substantially since then, with declines ranging from 40 percent for herring to over 90 percent for halibut.[9]

The decline of the northwest Atlantic fishery is mirrored in the northeast Atlantic, a region that has supplied Europe's tables with fish for centuries. An analysis by D. H. Cushing of the fisheries in this region indicates extensive overfishing. Overfishing, according to Cushing, has reduced the catch below the maximum sustainable yield in twenty-seven of the region's thirty fisheries. In the majority overfishing has been moderate to heavy (see Table 2-1).

Overfishing is not limited to the North Atlantic or to older fisheries. Beginning in the late fifties, Peru's fishing industry expanded spectacularly. By the late sixties, Peru had emerged

Table 2-1. Extent of Overfishing in Northeast Atlantic Fisheries

Species	None	Slight	Moderate	Heavy
Cod	N.E. Arctic[1]	W. Scotland	Faroe	North Sea Irish Sea Bristol Channel
Haddock		Faroe W. Scotland		N.E. Arctic North Sea Irish Sea Bristol Channel
Whiting	North Sea			Irish Sea Bristol Channel
Saithe		Iceland	North Sea	
Plaice	North Sea		Irish Sea Bristol Channel English Channel	
Sole			Bristol Channel English Channel	North Sea Irish Sea
Herring		W. Scotland		North Sea Irish Sea Celtic Sea

[1]With the present pattern of exploitation.
Source: D. H. Cushing, *Nature*, November 25, 1976.

as the world's leading fishing nation, almost entirely on the strength of its vast offshore anchovy fishery. The increase in the nation's anchovy catch was matched by the growing demand in the affluent industrialized world for high-protein feed for poultry and pork production (about 90 percent of all fishmeal is mixed into poultry feeds, with hog rations accounting for the remainder). Peruvian fishmeal found eager buyers in Europe, Japan, and the United States, and it temporarily replaced copper as Peru's number-one export.

During 1972 and most of 1973, anchovies were scarce in the traditional offshore fishing areas. No stir followed immediately since thinnings of the anchovy population had previously been associated with slight temperature changes in the Humboldt current (el Niño). Considerable evidence, however, shows that heavy annual catches of between 10 and 12 million tons in the late sixties and the early seventies seriously depleted stocks (see Figure 2-2).

According to a 1970 UN-sponsored study by an international team of biologists, the maximum sustainable yield of the Peruvian anchovy fishery is roughly 9.5 million tons per year.[10] Since the catches in 1967, 1968, 1970, and 1971 all exceeded this level, the collapse of the fishery during the early seventies should not have been a surprise. Since the 1972–73 debacle, when the catch dropped to a few million tons, the Peruvian government has controlled fishing rigorously in an effort to restore the fishery's productivity. As of 1977, these efforts had met with little success.

Although some of the potential for extracting food from the sea remains untapped, dramatic growth in the world fish catch of the sort that occurred between 1950 and 1970 looks like a thing of the past. Fish farming has been practiced for thousands of years and has been widely discussed for the past decade, yet it still accounts for only a minute share of world fish consumption. Only by turning to unexploited species such as krill, the shrimp-like crustacean found in massive quantities

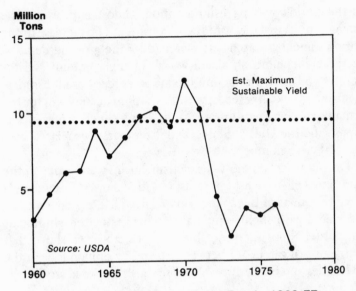

Figure 2-2. Peruvian Anchovy Catch, 1960-77

off the coast of Antartica, will it be possible to markedly expand the world catch in the foreseeable future. Whether krill will ever become an important food source will be influenced by consumer acceptance and by the energy requirements of developing a food resource so distant from areas of consumption. As human populations expand further, per-capita supplies of preferred species will likely fall further. Higher prices and growing international competition for available supplies appear inevitable.

Overfishing, frequently discovered only when the catch begins to decline in a sustained fashion, has become a pervasive global problem. Catches of most of the thirty-odd leading species of table-grade fish may now exceed maximum sustainable levels; in other words, the species' regenerative capacities cannot sustain even the levels of the present catch. As growth in the world catch slows and in some cases declines, the large

Soviet and Japanese populations are especially vulnerable. Deprived of oceanic sources of protein, they will likely have to offset declines by importing more feedgrains and soybeans to expand indigenous poultry and livestock production. Taking such a tack will place additional pressures on exportable grain supplies, but the only alternative is belt-tightening.

The oceans have long been considered a major potential source of food, but the hope that humans could turn to the oceans for food as pressures on land-based food resources mounted is being shattered. Indeed, as the world fish catch levels off or drops, pressures on the land are intensifying.

Deforestation: Cutting Too Many Trees

Four billion people now depend on the earth's forests for firewood, lumber, newsprint, and a host of less essential products. Firewood is used primarily for cooking, but in mountainous communities such as Afghanistan or Bolivia, it may be the only means of fending off the cold.

Villagers in the poor countries where firewood is used for cooking are decimating local forests. The average villager requires between one and two tons of firewood each year, and expanding village populations are raising firewood demands so fast that the regenerative capacities of many forests are being surpassed (see Table 2-2). Under the population onslaught, forests recede farther and farther from the villages until entire regions and countries are eventually deforested.

While firewood is a principal energy source only in developing countries, wood is a primary building material everywhere. Vast tracts of forests are cut to secure the lumber used to build houses, schools, churches, offices, shops, bridges, railroads, factories, and storage facilities. But even though the forests are being decimated, most of humanity is poorly housed: the need to house some 64 million new inhabitants each year, coupled with the need to replace existing housing, is raising total claims

Table 2-2. Fuel Wood Consumption in Tanzania, Gambia, and Thailand

	Fuel Wood Consumption Per Capita (tons/year)	Fuel Wood as Share of Total Timber Consumption (percent)	Fuel Wood Users as Share of Total Population (percent)
Tanzania	1.8	96	99
Gambia	1.2	94	99
Thailand	1.1	76	97

Source: Adapted from Keith Openshaw, "Wood Fuels the Developing World," *New Scientist*, January 31, 1974.

on many remaining forests to an unsustainable level.

A third major pressure on the earth's woodlands comes from the demand for paper. It is the feedstock of modern industrial societies, in which more people are employed in offices than in factories and on farms. In a bureaucratic, nonindustrial city like Washington it is the principal raw material. It is the common medium of both mass and interpersonal communication everywhere. As the share of humanity that is literate expands, the demand for newsprint expands even more rapidly than population. The pressures of these rising demands are further aggravated by a lack of paper recycling facilities in principal consuming countries.

Forests have proved to be one of humanity's most valuable economic resources and in consequence one of the most heavily exploited. If cutting is excessive, forests shrink, and their capacity to satisfy human needs diminishes. Most of the Middle East and North Africa and much of continental Asia, Central America, and the Andean regions of South America are now virtually treeless. In the denuded areas, wood and wood products are scarce and expensive. What is worse, the remaining forested area in all these regions except eastern Asia is shrinking.

Almost every country undergoing rapid population growth is

being rapidly deforested. Forests that once covered a third of
the total land area of Morocco, Tunisia, and Algeria, for example, had been reduced to scarcely a tenth of their original area
by the mid-twentieth century. Despite the major reforestation
programs that are under way throughout North Africa, the net
loss continues unabated. At least a third of the grassy savannah
in sub-Saharan Africa was once forest. Successive aerial surveys
of the Ivory Coast's dense rain forest show a reduction in
forested area of 30 percent between 1956 and 1966.[11] In
Nigeria, the shrinkage of the forests prompted one forester to
talk about "timber famine before the end of the century."[12]

Deforestation threatens all ecological systems and undermines the fertility and stability of soils. Over the past generation, the Indian subcontinent has been progressively deforested; as a result, the soil's ability to absorb and hold water has
diminished, and flooding has become more frequent and more
severe. Deforestation has taken its greatest toll in the Himalayas and in the surrounding foothills where the subcontinent's
major river systems—the Indus, the Ganges, and the Brah-
maputra—originate. Hans Rieger, a German economist working in Nepal, reports that "the destruction of the forests is
progressing more rapidly every year and that the country is
likely to be all but totally denuded by the end of the century."[13]

Portions of India's Deccan plateau that were largely forested
twenty years ago have now been put under the plow, and
satellite pictures of Java indicate that only 12 percent of this
once-lush island now has tree cover. In the watersheds of Indonesia's Solo, Brantas, and Citarum river systems, forest cover
is well under 10 percent. The acceleration of soil erosion in
several watersheds has been documented by an Indonesian
ecologist, Dr. Otto Soemarwoto, who notes in particular that
the silt load of the Citarum increased by a factor of seven over
a recent three-year period.[14]

Satellite photographs of the Philippines show that deforestation is far more advanced than official statistics reveal, with the forest cover probably less than a fifth of the country's land area —a far cry from the 33 to 50 percent commonly assumed. In Northern Thailand, forests are being decimated at an estimated rate of 5 to 7 percent a year.[15] This deforestation rate and the projection of a 3-percent annual rate of population growth indicate that Thailand has trouble in store: intensive, controlled irrigation will be most needed just when upstream erosion and an irregular water flow will frustrate effective management downstream.

In Latin America, deforestation is proceeding at a record rate as population grows and incomes rise. Firewood is becoming scarce in the Andean countries. Brazilian agriculture is expanding at the expense of the forests, whose shrinkage contributes to soil compaction and erosion. Petroleum exploration in Ecuador destroyed 50,000 hectares (1 ha. = 2.47 acres) in a five-year span. Venezuela lost one-fifth of its forested area between 1961 and 1970. Chile is being deforested at the rate of 60,000 hectares each year, while Mexico annually loses 350,-000 to 500,000 hectares of forests.[16]

Areas such as the Middle East, which were densely settled ages ago, have long been treeless, and many countries are now following the example of the older Middle Eastern civilizations —desecrating their landscapes, perhaps irreversibly. As the French philosopher Chateaubriand put it, "The forests come before civilization, the deserts after them."[17]

A review of the state of the world's forests provides no grounds for optimism. In the landmark work on land degradation, *Losing Ground*, Erik Eckholm notes that Western Europe has "achieved a reasonable balance between the ecological need for forests and other land uses, but it is a balance maintained in part by large imports of wood and wood products," principally from Scandinavia, the Soviet Union, and tropical Africa. Similarly, Japan "is now protecting its steeper slopes from deforestation," but doing so means importing timber from Southeast Asia and elsewhere.[18] Only North America, Scandinavia, and the Soviet Union appear to have both relatively satisfactory forest-management programs and sufficient forest resources to cover domestic needs.

In early 1977 the *Economist,* in an article on "Sweden's Coming Timber Shortage," described the extent to which future export demand for Sweden's forest products would be outstripping the regenerative capacity of forests. Two UN studies have "forecast expanding demand for timber products soon running ahead of what Sweden will have available for cutting. Since Sweden supplies 30 percent of Europe's timber and 60 percent of its pulp, the repercussions for Europe's construction and paper industries could be severe."[19] Even in lushly forested Scandinavia, the pressures of ever-growing global demand appear to be overrunning the sustainability of forests at the existing intensity of management.

Although deforestation jeopardizes future supplies of firewood, lumber, and newsprint as it contributes to soil erosion, flooding, and silting, little is being done to reverse existing trends. A United Nations study reports that only 10 percent of the area destroyed by slash-and-burn agriculture in Brazil has been reforested. In Colombia, only 1 percent of the land deforested each year is replanted.[20]

Wood shortages and the ecological problems deforestation causes have led many governments to resolve to reforest their lands. Unfortunately, as Eckholm points out, "the annals of the past few decades are littered with ambitious national forestry plans unfulfilled by governments either unwilling or incapable of backing their schemes with sufficient money and political commitment."[21]

Overgrazing: Eroding the Protein Base

On every continent the area in grass exceeds that planted to crops. The products grown on the 2.5 billion hectares of grassland play an important role in the food, energy, and industrial sectors of the global economy. Grasslands supply protein in a variety of forms, energy in several forms, and numerous raw materials for industry. The ruminants supported by grasslands —beef and dairy cattle, water buffalo, camels, goats, and sheep —supply most of the world's meat and milk. As humanity's demand for protein has risen in step with population and affluence over the past generation, pressures on grasslands have increased markedly.

Besides supplying protein for human consumption, grasslands are a source of energy for agriculture. Just as the firewood from forests provides cooking fuel for close to one-third of humanity, so the roughage from grasslands provides the fuel for cultivating that one-third or more of the world's cropland that is tilled by draft animals. In addition, the world's grasslands indirectly supply leather for footwear and other goods. They are the source of wool, a staple fiber of the world's textile and clothing industries, and of the tallow rendered by the meat packing industry and used in various industrial products and processes.

Endowed with complex four-stomach digestive systems, ruminants can efficiently convert grass and other types of forage into products humans can use. Each of these species, most of which eat roughage rather than grain or other feed concentrates, provides some of the vast quantities of meat and milk humanity consumes. According to livestock specialist Harlow Hodgson, even in the United States where vast tonnages of grain are fed to livestock, roughage still accounts for 63 percent of the feed units fed to dairy animals and 73 percent of those fed to beef.[22] Elsewhere, of course, these figures are far higher.

The one-fifth of the earth's land surface on which forage for ruminants and other animals is produced is a cornerstone of the global economy. Integral parts of both the world food and the world energy economies, these grasslands and the 2.7 billion domesticated ruminants they support—1.2 billion cattle, 1 billion sheep, 400 million goats and 130 million water buffalo— also represent an essential source of raw materials for industry.[23] Their production potential and their condition directly influence the prospect of feeding our still-expanding population and of further expanding the global economy.

The amount of range vegetation that can be removed by cattle each year varies widely. Where rainfall is heavy and the species are hardy, well over half of the annual growth can be removed, but where it is exceedingly light only a small fraction of the grass or other vegetative matter can be safely removed without damaging the stand. If more than this is removed year after year, the grass slowly dies out and leaves the bare earth exposed to the elements. A rancher can occasionally alter and substantially improve the productivity of grasslands by seeding them with non-indigenous grasses or, where moisture is abundant, by fertilizing them. But the maximum number of cattle that the land can carry is determined by natural factors usually beyond the rancher's control—by soil fertility, temperature, and the amount and seasonal distribution of rainfall.

Together, population growth and rising affluence are taxing the world's grasslands at a time when overgrazing is already commonplace. Because the best grasslands are gradually being converted into croplands, most remaining grasslands are either concentrated in arid or semi-arid regions or are located on land that is too steeply sloping to be farmed. As ecosystems, semi-arid and steeply sloping grasslands are among the most fragile, capable of surviving only if grazing is carefully controlled.

Even in agriculturally advanced regions, overgrazing is widespread. Recent analyses of the conditions of U.S. grazing lands leave no room for complacency. Reporting in 1975 on the sixty-six million hectares of range it manages, the Bureau of Land Management (BLM) found half the area to be in only "fair" condition—meaning that the more valuable forage species had been depleted and had been replaced by less palatable plants or by bare ground. Another 28 percent was in "poor" condition; stripped of much of its topsoil and vegetative cover, it produced only a fraction of its forage potential. Five percent of all BLM-controlled land was deemed in "bad" condition: with most of its topsoil gone, it could support only a sporadic array of plants of little worth. The twenty million hectares of land in "poor" or "bad" condition, an area equal to that of the state of Utah, was damaged primarily by overgrazing.[24]

In densely populated regions such as Western India, Pakistan, Nepal, northern China, North Africa, the Middle East, and the Andean regions of South America, severe overgrazing has already led to serious erosion. Over the past thirty-five years, human and livestock populations on the edges of the Sahara have multiplied rapidly, nearly doubling in some areas. Human populations in Mali, Niger, the Sudan, Algeria, and Ethiopia are now expanding at the rate of fifteen- to twentyfold per century. Overgrazing and deforestation brought on by new population pressures have encouraged the Sahara Desert to expand along its southern fringe from Senegal to the Sudan.

As human and livestock populations retreat before the spreading desert, "ecological" refugees place heavy demands on new fringe areas, exacerbating land degradation and perpetuating a self-reinforcing negative cycle of overcrowding and overgrazing in ever-wider areas. When the inevitable drought sets in, as one did in the late sixties, deterioration turns into disaster—for the humans who perish by the hundreds of thousands, for the livestock that die in even greater numbers, and for the once-productive land that is destroyed. If reliable information were available, it would undoubtedly show that cattle production in parts of the Sahel collapsed during the early seventies much as Peruvian anchovy production did.

Over time, climatic changes and the ecological stresses that lead to denudation may be reinforcing each other with devastating effect. Unless the desertification process is reversed, Africa, which has the highest birth rate of all the continents, may lose a part of its food-producing capacity. Meanwhile, the vastness of the Sahel and the delicate social problems involved in getting the proud nomadic inhabitants to alter their living habits pose formidable obstacles.

Overgrazing is now commonplace in the tier of North African countries that border the Mediterranean. But it is by no means limited to the Saharan fringe. Overgrazing is now rampant on the East African plateau from Ethiopia and Somalia to Tanzania and is damaging the region's rich grasslands. In *Losing Ground,* Eckholm observes that "Barren, desert-like environments have been created by centuries of overgrazing and wood gathering over huge areas of the Middle East from the Mediterranean coast of Israel all the way to Afghanistan —areas that were once at least moderately vegetated." In many instances the process is irreversible. As Eckholm notes, "some such lands would recover if the constant pressure of overgrazing, which is the norm in virtually every Middle Eastern country, were removed. But others have been permanently downgraded by erosion and, in more extreme cases, dune formation."[25]

Unfortunately, the overgrazing in these countries is severe. A UN report on the Middle East prepared for the Conference on Desertification in the fall of 1977 reported that "although the natural rangelands in the north of Iraq are able to support 250,000 head of sheep, in actual fact they contain about one million head. Similarly, the arid and semi-arid natural rangeland zones in Syria contain three times the amount of livestock they can support." The author of the report, Professor Ibrahim Nahal, further notes that "this heavy pressure on the natural rangelands is one of the main reasons for the deterioration of the plant cover and the rapid progress of desertification."[26]

The area available exclusively for grazing in western Rajasthan in India shrank from thirteen million to eleven million hectares between 1951 and 1961, while the population of cattle, sheep, and goats jumped from 9.4 million to 14.4 million. Chronically overgrazed for several decades, extensive areas of northwest India today appear barren and lifeless—and the livestock population continues to grow.[27]

The role of grazing lands in supplying food, principally live-stock products, is well understood. What is less widely under-stood is that grasslands or woodlands used for grazing also provide fuel for tillage in the form of forage for draft animals. In most developing countries precious cropland cannot be de-voted to the production of grain for draft animals, so these animals must survive largely on foraged roughage.

Cattle populations can harm grasslands severely. But goats can wreak even more damage, destroying trees and shrubs as well. In countries such as Pakistan where vegetation is fast disappearing, goats have learned to climb trees in search of greenery. The wire-service photograph carried in American newspapers of a dead goat lodged in the crotch of a tree provided graphic evidence of the deteriorating Sahelian ecosys-tem during the drought-stricken seventies. K. K. Panday, a Nepali agricultural engineer, frankly addresses the situation: "What we cannot ignore any longer is the fact that the size of the ruminant population is simply too high for the prevailing fodder situation. The policy and action of conducting an ani-mal Family Planning Programme would not be objectionable and impracticable now. The shortage of fodder is affecting the whole ecology of man and his animals."[28]

In many communities in many countries, forage for livestock grows scarcer by the day. If agriculture were modernized and mechanized in these countries, the pressure on grazing areas would abate somewhat. Indeed, when U.S. agriculture was mechanized a generation ago, some twelve to sixteen million hectares of cropland once used to produce feed for horses was converted to the production of food.[29] But, with petroleum supplies dwindling and fuel prices climbing, the prospect for even limited small-scale mechanization is dimming perceptibly unless fuel can be diverted from less essential uses such as private automobiles.

In some areas supporting draft animals has become well-nigh impossible, and draft animals too emaciated to draw plows are becoming common sights. Now that the hope of replacing water buffalo or bullocks with tractors has been deferred in many poor countries because of rising fuel costs, overgrazing both directly threatens the supply of livestock products and indirectly threatens food production by imperiling draft animals.

Overgrazing is not new, but it is now in evidence to some degree on every continent. Deterioration that once took centuries is now being compressed into years by population growth. Populations are, in effect, outgrowing the biological systems that sustain them.

Overplowing: Moving onto Marginal Land

As world population gradually expanded after the development of agriculture, farming spread from valley to valley and from continent to continent until by the mid-twentieth century the frontiers had virtually disappeared. Even while the amount of new land awaiting the plow shrank, the growth in demand for food was expanding at a record pace. Coupled with the uneven distribution of land in many countries, these trends gave birth to a land hunger that is driving millions of farmers onto soils of marginal quality—lands subject to low and unreliable rainfall, lands with inherently low fertility, and lands too steep to sustain cultivation.

Over the millennia, farmers have devised special techniques for farming land that could not otherwise sustain cultivation. In mountainous regions, the use of terrace agriculture stabilizes soils and protects them from erosion. Centuries of laborious effort have gone into the construction of elaborate systems of terraces that work quite well in older settled countries such as Japan, China, and Nepal and in the Andean regions once inhabited by the Incas. But over the past generation explosive Third World population growth has forced farmers onto steeply sloping areas, and there has not been sufficient time to construct terraces. Where mountainous land is not terraced, it erodes severely and soil accumulates in the valleys in streams, irrigation canals, and reservoirs. As the erosion progresses, such land must be abandoned. Gradually, the productive capacity of both the mountainsides and the valleys is impaired.

In the vast semi-arid regions in which rainfall and moisture are inadequate to sustain continuous cultivation, systems of alternate-year cropping have evolved. Under these systems, land lies fallow in alternate years to accumulate moisture; all vegetative cover is destroyed during the fallow year, and the land is left covered with dust mulch that curbs the evaporation of soil moisture. The crop produced the subsequent year can draw on two years of accumulated moisture. This practice would lead to serious wind-erosion if strip cropping were not practiced simultaneously; the alternate strips planted to crops each year serve as windbreaks for the fallow strips.

In low-rainfall areas, continuous cropping would be catastrophic. Indeed, it proved so in the U.S. Great Plains during the Dust Bowl era of the thirties and in the Virgin Lands of the Soviet Union during the sixties. Except where land can be irrigated, the basic natural constraints on cultivation under low-rainfall conditions cannot be altered substantially. Where rains are light, the use of strip cropping has permitted farmers to crop land that otherwise would not sustain cultivation.

In the tropics, fallowing is used to restore fertility. Stripped of their dense vegetative cover, soils in the humid tropics quickly lose their fertility. In response to these conditions, shifting cultivation has evolved. Farmers who practice shifting cultivation clear and crop land for two, three, or possibly four years and systematically abandon it as its fertility falls; they then move on to fresh terrain and repeat the process. These cultivators return to the starting point after 15 to 20 years, by which time the soil fertility has regenerated sufficiently to again support crop production for a few years.

Over time, shifting cultivation, strip-cropping, and terracing have enabled farmers slowly to expand agriculture into areas where conventional agriculture would not survive. Without these specialized techniques, the earth's capacity to support humans would be far lower than it is. Although these practices have withstood the test of time, in some areas they are now beginning to break down under population pressure.

Taking agriculture uphill is often a losing proposition. As a UN study of Latin American agriculture indicates, land with slopes up to 30 degrees is being cultivated, and the consequences of such acts of desperation are harrowing: "Throughout the Andes acute examples of gullying and sheet erosion are commonplace sights and frequently cropping occurs right up to the edge of rapidly advancing gullies." In a study of soil erosion in Latin America, Hilaria Valladares Antica associated falling potato harvests with soil erosion in the Peruvian Andes, the region that gave the world the potato.[30]

German geographer Robert Schmid describes a situation in Nepal that is similar to Peru's: "During the last century man in search of more arable land had greatly extended the terraced fields. Increasingly, the farmers had to be self-sufficient and therefore marginal land was taken into cultivation. . . ." The farming of increasingly marginal land, Schmid goes on, combines with progressive deforestation, as trees are felled for wood and branches lopped from remaining trees for use as animal fodder, until a cycle of soil erosion and deterioration is set in motion. "On the permanently farmed fields the soil showed signs of exhaustion and the yields declined slowly."[31]

Schmid's account resembles those of others who have witnesed the deterioration of hill agriculture in Iran, Pakistan, north India, and Ethiopia. The Nepalese government estimates that the country's rivers now annually carry 240 million cubic meters of soil to India.[32] This loss has been described as Nepal's "most precious export." During the Ethiopian famine of 1974, a foreign ambassador in Addis Ababa described the origin of the problem in graphic terms: "Ethiopia," he said, "is quite literally going down the river."[33]

Mounting population pressures in the humid tropics and in other areas where shifting cultivation is practiced also contribute to soil deterioration. According to researchers of the Food and Agriculture Organization (FAO), "There is abundant evidence in certain regions of Venezuela that, with growing population pressure, the fallow period is becoming increasingly shorter so that soil fertility is not restored before recropping. This leads to a fall in the organic content and the water-holding capacity of the soil. Soil structure deteriorates and compaction becomes more common. . . . In other words, with the population of modern times, formerly stable shifting cultivation systems are now in a state of breakdown."[34]

Students of African agriculture refer increasingly to that continent's "cycle of land degeneration." In *Losing Ground,* Eckholm notes that "where traditional technologies persist—due either to the lack of proven alternatives or to the failure to reach farmers with new methods—deterioration of the land begins as soon as human numbers in a local area surpass the level shifting cultivation can support."[35] Geographer Barry Floyd describes the soil deterioration under way in densely populated western Nigeria as "some of the most spectacular examples of soil erosion 'bad land' topography to be seen in West Africa." He describes the severity of soil erosion and the formation of deep gullies across the land and notes in summary that "soil deterioration and degradation in terms of the progressive loss of nutrients and breakdown of structure is well nigh universal due largely to overfarming and primitive destructive methods of cultivation."[36]

Accounts of soil deterioration and loss like those about Venezuela and Nigeria could be repeated by the score to illustrate further how mounting population pressure and poor farming techniques are combining to subvert basic life-support systems. Pressures associated with the growing demand for food affect more than the humid tropical and subtropical regions where the fallowing systems of shifting cultivation are breaking down. The world's other principal system of fallow agriculture —that used in the semi-arid wheat producing regions of North America, Australia, and the Soviet Union—also shows signs of stress. The land in fallow in the United States has declined by nearly one-half during the seventies—a fact that has led Kenneth Grant, head of the Soil Conservation Service, to warn farmers that severe wind erosion and dust-bowl conditions could result. He cautioned farmers against responding to the lure of record wheat prices and short-term gains that would sacrifice the long-term productivity of their land.[37]

Anyone who has traveled across Africa, up and down the Indian subcontinent, or around Latin America sees firsthand the consequences of extending cultivation onto land that should either be left in its natural state or cultivated only with special techniques. One need not be a trained agronomist or a prophet to see the grim future that continued abuse of the earth's meager soil resources entails.

The mantle of topsoil covering the earth ranges in depth from a few inches to a few hundred feet. Over much of the earth's surface it is only inches deep, usually less than a foot. Nature produces new soil very slowly, much more slowly than the rate at which humans are now removing it. Thus, once topsoil is lost, a vital capacity to sustain life is diminished. With soil as with many other resources, humanity is beginning to ask more of the earth than it can give.

Pollution: Overloading the Ecosystem

The burden of excessive human claims on the earth's biological systems is being aggravated by yet another human excess, the generation of waste. Just as felling too many trees can overtax the regenerative capacity of forests, creating too much waste can overtax the earth's waste-absorptive capacity. The absorption of waste is an important natural function of the earth's ecosystem. Indeed, in the complex web of plant and animal life, one organism's waste is another's sustenance. But when waste is excessive, it becomes pollution.

Pollution is more than a mere nuisance. It can impair and even destroy the productivity of local biological systems. It can ruin forests, crops, and fisheries; eutrophy fresh water lakes and streams; destroy whole species of plants and animals; impair human health; break up the ozone layer; impede the exchange of oxygen and carbon dioxide between the oceans and the atmosphere; and even damage clothing, buildings, and statues. Pollution increases along with global economic activity—national efforts to curb it notwithstanding.

Among pollution's many origins are the burning of fossil fuels, the discharge of industrial waste, and the use of agricultural chemicals. The synthesis of new chemical compounds that are not readily biodegradable and the introduction into the ecosystem of heavy metals extracted from beneath the earth's surface pose special threats. The current scale of pollution, the long-lived nature of synthetic chemicals and radioactive waste, and the indestructibility of heavy metals make it an international problem, an expansion of the "village commons" problem to the global level.

Hundreds of new synthetic compounds that cannot readily be broken down by micro-organisms are being brought into use each year without a thorough investigation of their environmental impact. As Dr. John Wood, Director of the Fresh Water Biology Institute, notes, "the further the chemists get from natural chemicals the greater the danger" of environmental disruption becomes.[38] Among the long-lived synthetic chemicals that are life threatening are chlorinated hydrocarbons (including pesticides such as DDT). In 1962 Rachel Carson drew public attention to twelve pesticides that might be potentially hazardous to animals and humans—DDT, malathion, parathion, dieldrin, aldrin, endrin, chlordane, heptachlor, toxaphene, lindane, benzene hexachloride and 2,4-D. Since then the use of each has been regulated, and some have been phased out.[39]

The threat of this family of compounds to the survival of numerous species of birds and fish and to human health has been well established. But another newer group of long-lived synthetic chemicals, the polychlorinated biphenyls (PCBs) may pose an even greater threat to humans. An outbreak of a disfiguring skin disease affecting more than a thousand Japanese was traced to a batch of rice oil heavily contaminated with PCBs. Monkeys exposed to the compound have experienced a sharp increase in miscarriages and have borne sickly infants. Rats have developed liver cancer after sustained exposure to PCB, a laboratory finding that has prompted Dr. Renata D. Kimbrough of the Center for Disease Control in Atlanta to warn "that PCBs may be a low-grade carcinogenic agent in man."[40]

The heavy metals that are mined and used for various industrial purposes (including lead, mercury, arsenic, cadmium) are often part of natural systems, but they occur in very minute quantities. It is only when the amount becomes excessive that various animal and plant species are threatened. One of the first hints of the extreme toxicity of heavy metals came in the early fifties in the small Japanese coastal town of Minimata. Mercury poisoning resulting from the discharge of effluent wastes by local industry spread from fish to fishermen and their families. Hundreds of people were poisoned. A few years later Swedish ornithologists observed that some species of birds were fast disappearing. Mercury from pulp and paper mills was responsible.[41]

Such experiences are not confined to industrially advanced countries. As part of its industrialization effort, the government of Malaysia in 1971 established an industrial park, the Perai Industrial Estate on the Sungei Juru River. The Consumers Association of Penang has measured high levels of mercury, cadmium, chromium, and lead in the industrial effluent canals which flow into the river. Fish kills have become common, and fishermen now claim that more than 30 species of fish have disappeared from the river.[42]

Pollution attends industrialization wherever it occurs. If Johann Strauss were entitling his famous waltz now, he might better call it the "Brown Danube." A Czechoslovakian environmentalist reports that "a dozen years ago we could swim in the Danube. Today the river is so dangerous it is illegal to swim in it."[43]

The Rhine river "is becoming Europe's sewer." The world's busiest waterway, it is also the dirtiest. Billions of dollars spent to clean it up have failed to offset the ill effects of continuing rapid industrial growth in Germany, Switzerland, and France. The city of Rotterdam found the Rhine becoming so polluted that it could no longer purify it sufficiently and was forced to turn elsewhere for drinking water.[44]

A conference of biologists convened in April of 1977 to discuss the future of the Chesapeake Bay talked of a "biological nightmare." One participant reported that "both synthetic and naturally occurring toxicants are entering the bay in progressively greater proportions." Robert J. Huggett, who chaired a task force on toxic substances, concluded that "the time may be approaching when the chemistry of the bay will be controlled by man rather than by nature." Dr. J.L. McHugh, former Director of Fisheries for Virginia, insisted on focusing on causal factors rather than symptoms, emphasizing that efforts to save the bay would "be in vain unless population is curbed."[45]

While scientists have long recognized the effects of pollutants on rivers, lakes, and the oceans, the effect of pollutants on the upper atmosphere is only beginning to be understood. Professor Michael B. McElroy, Director of Harvard's Center for Earth and Planetary Sciences has joined a swelling body of scientists who believes that "atmospheric ozone is threatened by certain air pollutants" and that this is leading to an increase in solar ultraviolet radiation. According to McElroy, the challenge "is to clarify the exact biological consequences of serious ozone depletion, and to figure out how to prevent such an environmental disaster."[46] If the ozone layer is being progressively depleted, it could affect all biological processes and all forms of plant and animal life.

Public attention has focused on the relationship of skin cancer incidence and ozone depletion. Harvard dermatologist Dr. Thomas Fitzpatrick believes that one of the severe forms of skin cancer, malignant melanoma—"a medical tragedy at least as fatal as breast cancer,"—is definitely linked to ultraviolet radiation. He testified before a congressional committee that the incidence of malignant melanoma "is rising rapidly in all countries at a rate of between 3 and 9 percent per year" and that "death rates from the disease have doubled in the last 15 years."[47] Although this short-term rise may be due more to increased sunbathing and to changing dress habits, it is indicative of the consequences of a marked depletion in the ozone layer.

Ozone depletion has many possible causes: among them are the release of nitrous oxide by SSTs, the release of the fluorocarbons used in aerosol spray cans (mainly Freon in the United States and Eskimon in the Soviet Union), and the release of nitrous oxide from the soil as a result of the heavy use of nitrogen fertilizer. SSTs can be banned if governments are willing to abandon the supersonic military aircraft as well as commercial transport. So can aerosol spray cans. What to do about the third source of ozone depletion, the heavy use of nitrogen fertilizer, assuming further research confirms this linkage, is a far more complicated matter.

Pollution has many dimensions and many consequences. Air pollution is now so concentrated in many industrial countries that it affects crop production. According to a recent U.S. Congressional study, "The impact of air pollutants on crop productivity is becoming increasingly apparent. A 1974 field experiment in Riverside, California, for example, found that yields of crops exposed to pollution were markedly reduced when compared to those of the control crops." The experiment provided precise but disturbing data. "For alfalfa there was a 38 percent decline in production; for black-eyed beans, 32 percent; lettuce, 42 percent; sweet corn, a phenomenal 72 percent; and for radishes a 38 percent reduction." In California alone, air pollutants cause an estimated 25 million dollars worth of crop damage yearly.[48]

The impact of industrial air pollution on agriculture can be felt and measured far from the fields adjacent to industrial plants. Grape production in upper New York State is threatened by polluted air carried eastward from factories and automobiles in heavily populated industrial regions in northern Ohio and Indiana. Dr. Trenholm D. Jordan, an agricultural specialist in Chautauqua County, reported that yields of the Ives variety of grapes used in red wines had fallen from four or five tons per acre to two tons. Both the yield and sugar content of wine and table grapes are reduced by air pollution. Dr. Jordan reported that Concord grapes were "seriously affected all over the East."[49]

Even proverbially durable trees are vulnerable to air pollution. Pollution-related damage to forests has been reported in such dissimilar climates as those of southern California and western Poland. One report indicates that "A comparison of annual ring growth in similarly aged groups of ponderosa pines in the San Bernardino mountains of California during the relatively unpolluted 30 year period between 1910 and 1940 and the more polluted years between 1944 and 1974 showed that after adjusting for climate variability, 20 board feet of merchantable wood was produced per tree between 1910 and 1940, whereas only five board feet were produced between 1944 and 1974."[50]

The term "acid rain" is rapidly becoming a part of our daily vocabulary. When sulfur-bearing fossil fuels are burned, sulfur dioxide is formed. Some of it further oxidizes to form sulfur trioxide. As the hot fumes from electrical power plants move up the stacks and into the atmosphere, the sulfur trioxide reacts with atmospheric moisture to form sulfuric acid. This then returns to earth as acid rain, the effects of which on plant and animal life can be devastating, if not deadly. It can also discolor paint, corrode metal, erode marble statues, and deteriorate boat canvas and clothing.[51]

One report by the U.S. National Academy of Sciences cites specific studies in Sweden and northern New England that correlate reductions in forest growth with acid-rain levels.[52] Now that this causal relationship has been discovered, the estimated 100-fold increase in the acidity of rainfall in the eastern United States in recent decades ought to give Americans pause. Scandinavians are already deeply concerned. Both Sweden and Norway have recorded enormous increases in the acidity of rainfall in recent decades—they are regularly doused by rain saturated with acidic pollutants released in the heavily industrialized Ruhr Valley in Germany and in Great Britain.

Fresh-water lakes are particularly vulnerable to acid rain. In literally thousands of lakes in Scandinavia, the northeastern United States, and southeastern Canada, some species of fish have disappeared entirely. A 1976 Cornell University survey of 217 lakes in the Adirondack Mountains of New York State showed 51 percent of these lakes to be highly acidic. A generation ago virtually all were alive with fish, but, the survey showed, 90 percent are now barren.[53]

At least one industrial country, the United Kingdom, has managed to visibly improve its environment. Blessed with a stable population and a slow rate of industrial growth, it has reversed the process of environmental deterioration. While air quality continues to deteriorate in Washington, D.C., where pollution alerts sometimes remain in force for several days, the air in London is now far cleaner than at any time in recent history. Eighty percent more sunshine reaches London now than in 1955—the year the first Clean Air Act was passed.[54] While the Rhine gets dirtier and less fit for fish year by year, the once filthy Thames is undergoing a remarkable rebirth. Leonard Santorelli reports that "some 83 species of fish have now been identified in the Thames estuary and its first salmon in 141 years was caught in 1975."[55] Although a small measure of Great Britain's progress may be Scandinavia's sorrow (progress may be due to tall smokestacks that release pollutants into atmospheric air currents), this encouraging effort does indicate that environmental deterioration can be arrested.

Relationships between pollution and the productivity of biological systems need further study. Gaps in knowledge exist because pollution has reached destructive levels so recently that neither the time nor the resources needed to examine pollution's immediate impact, much less its longer-term effects, has been mustered.

The earth's waste-absorptive capacity is a prime economic resource. It is also a finite resource. When the amount or nature of waste generated exceeds the amount that the natural system can handle, the system cannot function properly. Overburdening the earth's waste-absorptive capacity, all but inviting malfunctioning, involves far-reaching and perhaps even incomprehensible costs.

3

Ecological Stresses II: The Consequences

The consequences of overtaxing the earth's carrying capacity are invariably negative, destructive, and costly. They range from the loss of cropland to the inadvertent modification of climate. Virtually all such ecological stresses are likely to intensify as human numbers and aspirations increase further. Only some of the more obvious physical consequences of exceeding nature's thresholds are dealt with in this chapter. The economic and social manifestations of biological abuse are addressed in later chapters.

The Loss of Cropland

Three of the excesses described in the preceding chapter—deforestation, overgrazing and overplowing—all contribute to one of the most serious ecological stresses—soil erosion and the loss of cropland. All countries, rich and poor, suffer some soil erosion. The loss of cropland, wherever it occurs, affects the world food outlook.

Roughly one-tenth of the earth's thirteen billion hectares of land surface is cropland. On this land the indigenous forest or grass cover has been replaced with the selected plant species that best serve human needs. The human prospect is closely tied to the size and condition of this cropland base, which is the foundation not only of agriculture but of civilization itself. Thus, both the outright loss and abandonment of cropland—through either severe erosion or conversion to nonagricultural uses—and the deterioration of soil fertility through erosion deserve careful attention.

Each year some of the world's cropland goes out of production. It is paved over, strip-mined, eroded, and left to dry out when irrigation water is diverted to other purposes. Deserts and cities encroaching on cropland on every continent are claiming uncounted millions of hectares each year.

While governments keep careful statistics on the development of new areas for human settlement, on irrigation and drainage projects, and on other attempts to bring untilled land under cultivation, they have relatively little solid information on the actual loss or deterioration of cropland. As yet, this vital part of the human life-support system is not systematically monitored on a global basis. Until the United Nations Environment Program, which has made this one of its principal concerns, is able to gather data on cropland loss and degradation systematically, analysts and economic planners will have to make do with sketchy data.

H. N. Le Houérou reports that the northern tier of African countries is losing one hundred thousand hectares of range and cropland each year to the Sahara as the desert creeps north-ward.[1] A UNESCO study from the Sudan reports that the southern boundary of the Sahara "has shifted south by an average of about 90 to 100 kilometers during the last seventeen years."[2] In effect, this movement is slowly shrinking the agri-cultural resource base of the Sudan, squeezing the expanding population of nomadic herdsmen and farmers into an ever-smaller geographical area.

Similar trends are under way in North America, though for different reasons. Canada, the second ranking exporter of ce-reals after the United States, is losing large chunks of its best cropland to urban sprawl and other nonfarm uses. According to the Science Council of Canada, "Between 1966 and 1971, four hundred thousand hectares, or almost one-tenth of the improved farmland in southern Ontario, was lost to agricul-ture."[3] Canada's total harvested area remains constant only because the loss of prime agricultural land is being offset by the addition of marginal land in lower-rainfall areas. This substitu-tion helps explain why grain yields in Canada no longer seem to be increasing. The Science Council found that "an es-timated one-half of the farmland lost to urban expansion is coming from the best one-twentieth of our farmland. The farmland which normally might be considered to replace this loss is almost invariably in regions with poorer soil and a less favorable climate."[4] Another study concludes that the agricul-tural land requirements associated with a doubling of Canada's population will reduce the area of premium farmland by one-third, putting "urbanization in direct confrontation with agri-culture."[5]

The United States shares the problems of land loss with its neighbor to the north. In the United States, the production base is shrinking because the area of agricultural land being lost exceeds that of the new land being brought under the plow. As

David Pimentel and his colleagues reported in *Science*, "Each year more than one million hectares of arable cropland are lost to highways, urbanization and other special uses." They go on to note that this "loss is partially offset by the addition (primarily through irrigation and drainage projects) of five hundred thousand hectares of newly developed cropland per year."[6] These trends do not suggest that the United States and Canada will themselves experience food shortages, but they do suggest that the world's ever-growing dependence on the North American export surplus is risky.

India too is losing precious farmland. A report by the Indian government to the United Nations Conference on Human Settlements in 1976 projects "an increase in the use of land for non-agricultural uses . . . from 16.2 million hectares in 1970 to 26 million hectares by the end of the century."[7] If the pattern for other countries holds in India's case, this growth in nonagricultural land use will be at least partly at the expense of cropland. As in Canada and elsewhere, it will likely be the more productive cropland that is surrendered to nonagricultural uses.

Cropland losses are being particularly hard-felt in populous lands. In Egypt, an estimated twenty-six thousand hectares of the best cropland along the Nile is being lost each year to cities, roads, factories, and military installations.[8] In Japan, where "the spread of industry into former farming areas in the vicinity of large cities has reduced the land available for agricultural production by about 6 percent during the sixties," the situation looks even worse.[9]

Apart from the loss of cropland, soil erosion on remaining cropland is undermining land productivity. A natural process, soil erosion as such is neither new nor necessarily alarming. Soil is continuously being formed by the weathering of rocks, and it is continuously eroding. Indeed, geologists sometimes casually refer to soil as "rocks on their way to the sea." But when erosion outpaces the formation of new soil (something like one hundred years is required to form an inch of topsoil), inherent soil fertility declines.

It is the rate of soil erosion that distinguishes the current era. In vast areas the topsoil being lost through erosion exceeds that being formed by nature. Soil scientists analyzing the relationship between soil loss and formation calculate the T-factor (or tolerable rate of soil loss), which ordinarily varies from 1 to 5 tons per acre. In a survey of Wisconsin soils, 70 percent were found to have a soil loss greater than the tolerable level. On these soils with a T-factor of 3.6 tons, the actual loss was 8.4 tons, more than double the tolerable rate.[10] The annual loss of agricultural topsoil in the United States has been estimated by Pimentel at thirty tons per hectare or some three billion tons per year. Three independent studies help put this loss into perspective: they indicate that, other things being equal, U.S. corn yields have declined by an average of "four bushels per acre for each inch of topsoil lost from a base of 12 inches of topsoil or less."[11]

Concerns over the loss of topsoil in the United States are escalating. Luther Carter writes in *Science* that "the erosion of croplands by wind and water remain one of the biggest, most pervasive problems the nation faces." The problem persists because "in the calculations of many farmers, the hope of maximizing short-term crop yields and profits has taken precedence over the longer term advantages of conserving the soil."[12] The Iowa-based Council for Agricultural Science and Technology reports that as of the mid-seventies "a third of all cropland was suffering soil losses too great to be sustained without a gradual, but ultimately disastrous, decline in productivity."[13]

Early declines in natural fertility may be compensated for by the heavy use of fertilizer, as in the American Midwest, but over the longer term even this will not suffice. According to UN estimates, erosion robs Colombia of 426 million tons of fertile topsoil each year, a loss equal to thirty centimeters of soil on 160,000 hectares.[14] Colombia's topsoil is relatively thin, and the nation can ill afford to see it washed away. A United Nations report on Mexico indicated that "an estimated 150 to 200 thousand hectares have been rendered unusable by erosion."[15] In Pakistan, progressive deforestation has led to severe soil erosion and loss of cropland. At some point these losses in Colombia and other severely affected countries may begin to overwhelm the efforts to expand output.

Thus far efforts to step up the productivity of the world's cropland base by applying more fertilizer, expanding irrigation, adopting new technologies, and investing in land improvement still more than offset the loss and degradation of cropland, so world food production continues to grow. But in some individual countries, the negative forces now nearly equal or even exceed efforts to expand food supplies. Per-hectare grain yields in Nigeria and Nepal have declined steadily for more than a decade as agriculture has moved onto marginal land and as soil erosion has worsened.[16] The growing dependence of scores of countries on North American food shipments reflects in part the deterioration of local food systems.

The disturbing trends emerging in the world food economy during the seventies indicate that national governments may have to take much stronger action than heretofore to preserve agricultural land. Failure to do so could lead to unprecedented food scarcity and food price inflation. The urgent need for such action is heightened by the rising cost of "land substitutes" such as energy and fertilizer, and by the scarcity of water.

Oceans: The Ultimate Sink

The oceans that cover two-thirds of the earth's surface are the common heritage of all. They constitute an integral part of humanity's life-support system—supplying both food and oxygen. The long oceanic food chain, with microscopic plants at the bottom and choice table grade fish at the top, supplies

humanity with vitally needed high-quality protein. Thus, pollution jeopardizes human nutrition as well as marine life.

Long too vast for humans to fathom, oceans were also long
thought to be too vast for humans to harm. But the scale of
human activity is now such that it can damage the seas irrevo-
cably. While it is not in humankind's interest to discharge
more waste than the oceans can absorb, the benefits to the
individual polluter (whether a country or a corporation) so
outweigh the costs that there is little or no incentive to exercise
restraint. The tragedy of the commons is now the tragedy of
the world's oceans.

A major source of human food, the oceans have become the
planet's ultimate waste receptacle, the passive recipient of staggering amounts of industrial, agricultural, and municipal
wastes. Thousands of waste products—some highly toxic—are
polluting the oceans from which life first sprang. Oil, chemical
effluents, lethal gases, radioactive wastes, junk metal, trace
elements, organic wastes from humans and animals, automobile exhaust products, pesticides, detergents, and other wastes
are routinely dumped into the sea. Hydrocarbon pollution—
the legacy of offshore drilling, routine oil-tanker operations and
the growing number of wrecked oil tankers—is getting out of
hand. Over ten thousand oil spills in U.S. navigable waters
were reported by the U.S. Coast Guard in 1975 alone.[17]

In July of 1976, a huge fish kill covering over a thousand
square miles was found off the New Jersey coast. Microbiolo-
gist Pat Yanaton reported that the ocean "was completely dead
—starfish, eels, lobsters, all sizes of crab—everything was
dead."[18] Apparently, decomposing sewage sludge from New
York and other adjoining municipalities was responsible.

Such disasters should not come as a surprise. An article in
the *Marine Pollution Bulletin* in 1973 reported that concentra-
tions of chromium, copper, lead, nickel, and zinc were "10 to
100 times greater near waste disposal areas" than in other
waters in the Atlantic Ocean off New York. Robert S. Dyer,

an oceanographer with the U.S. Environmental Protection Agency, reported finding traces of plutonium off both the Atlantic and Pacific coasts of the United States. The plutonium had leaked from some of the 114,500 barrels of radioactive waste materials dumped into the oceans by the U.S. government between 1946 and 1970.[19]

Shortly before Christmas of 1976, the oil tanker *Argo Merchant* ran aground forty-three kilometers off the coast of Nantucket and forty-eight kilometers from Georges Bank, one of the world's richest fishing areas. The spill of over seven million gallons of oil became the largest ever recorded in U.S. waters, surpassing the Santa Barbara oil-well blowout off the California coast in 1969.

Efforts to investigate the effect of oil spills initially focused on cleanup efforts, but now they are concentrating on the longer-term biological consequences. To this end, the prevalence and distribution of various marine organisms—birds, fish, sea mammals, or phytoplankton—are being watched. But these indicators alone provide only a limited understanding of the overall impact of oil spills. Biological researcher Erick Schneider of the Environmental Protection Agency argues that the impact of spills on organisms themselves needs to be examined and that the most useful indicators of marine health are "feeding, growth, reproduction, metabolism and behaviour" patterns.[20]

Approximately a million tons of oil seep into the seas from freighters, tankers, and offshore drilling rigs each year. Several million more tons of crude oil products in the forms of gasoline solvents and waste crankcase oil also pollute the oceans. Since the presence of surface oil interferes with the flow of light and oxygen in the sea, oil can render waters at least temporarily uninhabitable. Both the quantity and the variety of oceanic pollutants are multiplying so fast that their individual and combined effects on the marine biosphere cannot be precisely gauged. But it is clear that oceanic pollution has reached alarming proportions, is global in scale, and is a growing threat to oceanic food resources.

Fish have virtually disappeared from some of the more defiled rivers and coastal zones of the industrial countries. The once-rich oyster beds of Raritan Bay, New Jersey, have been almost obliterated. The shrimp harvest of Galveston Bay in the Gulf of Mexico shrank by more than half between 1962 and 1966. The shad catch in Chesapeake Bay, estimated at fourteen million pounds in 1890, has averaged only three million pounds in recent years.[21] In the United States, over half the human population and 40 percent of all manufacturing plants are clustered next to estuaries and coastal waters. City sewage, little of which is treated, is the major pollutant, followed by industrial effluents and agricultural chemicals.

Pollution has seriously damaged the valuable sturgeon industry of the Caspian Sea. Similarly, many of Japan's once-great fisheries such as Tokyo Bay, Osaka Bay, and Hiroshima Bay are now "dead seas," and the Inland Sea may soon die. Commercial fishing has been banned by national regulatory agencies in numerous offshore areas where fish manage to survive but where contamination with PCBs, mercury, oil, and numerous other compounds have rendered the fish unsafe for human consumption. Perhaps even more serious, the ever-swelling tide of waste discharged by humanity into the oceans could threaten the phytoplankton that form the foundation of the oceanic food chain. Whether the death of the phytoplankton would jeopardize the earth's oxygen supply as well is not certain. But, as Nöel Mostert asks in *Supership*, "If the seas don't breathe or if they breathe asthmatically and imperfectly, what else in our environment will struggle for breath?"[22]

Before long, humanity must choose between preserving the oceans as a food source and using them as a waste receptacle. Over the longer term they simply cannot be both. Clearly, oceanic pollution is worsening, and the oceans are bound to deteriorate further before existing trends can be reversed.

The basic conflict inherent in efforts to maintain oceanic health is a conflict between short-term desires and profits versus the long-term maintenance of biotic integrity. In weighing the pros and cons of oil drilling off the U.S. east coast, biologist George Woodwell notes that "the controversy over the prospect of oil wells on fishing grounds embodies one of the classic conflicts of our time—the confrontation between the demands of an oil-hungry industrial system and the need to preserve a basic living resource."[23] As Thor Heyerdahl, a lifelong observer of the oceans, puts it, "Today more than ever before mankind depends on the welfare of this marine plankton for his future survival as a species. With the population explosion we need to harvest even more protein from the sea. Without plankton there will be no fish."[24]

Endangered Species

The creation of new forms of life and the extinction of old ones is the essence of evolution. Over the two billion years or so since life first emerged on earth, more species have evolved than have disappeared. Accordingly, the web of plant and animal life has grown incredibly complex and interlinked. Although not all species have been identified and catalogued, biologists estimate that as many as ten million plant and animal species may coexist in the world today.

Climate and other natural forces have always influenced evolution, but during the modern era humans have become an evolutionary force. Unfortunately, the human contribution is negative, furthering the extinction of species. In recent decades, more plant and animal species have been destroyed than have evolved. The number of extant species is now declining, and the diversity of life is diminishing apace.

The more nostalgic dimensions of this problem usually capture public attention. The loss of a large and visible species of wildlife is heart-rending, but it is cause for another kind of concern. If too many species are lost, the complex biological web could begin to unravel. The extinction of any species of fauna or flora can become a tear in the whole cloth of life. No species exists in isolation: all animals depend directly or indirectly on plants for food, and plants depend on soil microorganisms to cycle nutrients. Each species, whether found in only one river or on every continent, serves a particular function. All land and marine plant species, for example, employ photosynthesis to convert solar energy into chemically bound energy that humans and other animals need.

All life forms support other life forms. Micro-organisms aid in the decomposition of organic matter. Some birds feed on insects whose numbers could otherwise become excessive. Ruminants concentrate plant materials into forms that humans can eat, but ruminants cannot perform this task unaided. They depend upon the micro-organisms that live in their complex series of stomachs. Micro-organisms also break down crude organic material in the soil, returning its carbon to the atmosphere as the carbon dioxide that plants need. Thus, numerous species of micro-organisms turn the carbon cycle on which all life depends.

The threats of extinction take three forms. One is by contact with artificially made or artificially concentrated compounds that interfere with life processes. For those micro-organisms in the soil that cannot tolerate an acidic environment, the change in soil chemistry resulting from "acid rain" can be lethal. Similarly, the release into the atmosphere of carbon from coal and oil alters the composition of the air we breathe. Oceanic pollution endangers both fish, a major protein source, and the marine micro-organisms that supply atmospheric oxygen.

A second threat to the survival of species is the physical destruction of natural habitats. Destroying the homes of such animals as the Bengal tiger, the Ceylonese elephant, or the Indonesian orangutan could turn these species into zoological rarities. At worst, it could lead to their extinction. The hunting of wild animals poses yet another threat—whether they be leopards for pelts or whales for food.

Preserving a particular form of life is seldom merely a matter of instituting a ban or quota on the killing of certain forms of wildlife prized by hunters, tailors, or furriers. Rather, the issue strikes at the heart of modern materialism and at human reproductive habits. Increasingly, ecologists hold that efforts to preserve endangered species are futile unless they are combined with efforts to preserve entire ecosystems. "The principal destructive process at work now," ecologist Norman Myers notes, "is modification or loss of species' habitats, which arises for the most part from economic development of natural environments."[25] To adopt this view is perforce to question present-day population policies and the pursuit of material wealth by those whose basic needs have been met.

If Myers's surmise is correct, we must now decide who should bear the cost of preserving the threatened species, most of whose habitats are in low-income countries in the tropics. As complex politically as it is economically, this issue is far from being satisfactorily resolved. Myers notes, for example, that designating extensive tracts of wild land as parks or preserves puts the poorer countries in the position of subsidizing efforts to preserve the earth's biotic integrity.

Others, Thomas Lovejoy among them, believe that common sense now argues against trying to save all forms of threatened life and that humans ought to concentrate on helping the fittest survive. Since saving everything is impossible, the reasoning goes, net losses would be minimized if the species whose prospects look bleakest were left to die. Once this decision is made, concentrating all available energies and resources on the most important (ecologically and economically) of those that remain might pay off. According to Lovejoy, the result of growing pressures on ecosystems is "impoverishment of the biota of the planet, a reduction of its ability to support man and other forms of life." The problem of endangered species, says

Lovejoy, is "not, therefore, a hypothetical one as many may wishfully believe; biotic impoverishment is an irreversible process that has profound consequences for the future of man."[26] These analyses underline the urgency of the need to address this problem systematically at the international level, preferably within the United Nations.

Environmentally Induced Illnesses

Environmentally induced illnesses, here defined as those illnesses caused directly or indirectly by human alterations of the environment, now rank high among the worldwide causes of human suffering. They also include some of the world's leading sources of death and illness, among them cancer, heart disease, and schistosomiasis. Collectively, these diseases hit those of all ages and cut across geographic regions. However, some of them affect primarily the rich and others primarily the poor.

Some illnesses are the by-product of human efforts to expand food supplies, others of the increased burning of high-sulfur fossil fuels in industrial societies. Still other environmentally induced illnesses originate in modern materialistic lifestyles typified by both underexercising and overeating. Although these diseases are present in epidemic proportions in some countries, the origins of many of them are not well understood even by the medical community, much less by the public at large.

Cancer, the scourge of the industrial countries, may be the most feared of all industrial diseases. The pain, the suffering, the lingering death, and the knowledge that few recover from it unscathed make cancer one of the worst illnesses known. Epidemiologists in the United States estimate one of every four Americans now living will contract some form of cancer, and many will die of it.[27] Cancer now claims the lives of more children under fifteen years of age in the United States than does any other disease.[28] Fully three-fourths of all cancer may be environmentally induced—the result of an unsound diet, smoking, breathing polluted air, exposure to certain industrial chemicals, or even some of the drugs doctors prescribe.[29]

During the modern era, some fifty thousand new compounds have been synthesized. Only a minute percentage of these have been tested for either their carcinogenic or their mutagenic effects. The compounds that cause cancer may thus number in the thousands. Work places, factories, homes, and public places are often permeated with chemical compounds that are alien to nature and thus to the environment in which human life evolved.

The synthesis and widespread environmental dispersal of new chemicals that are now the hallmarks of an industrial society bring with them health hazards that may not be identified as such for years or even generations. Dr. David Rall, Director of the National Institute of Environmental Health Sciences, testified before the U.S. Congress, "New forms of energy production, expanded uses of known energy sources, greater development of the chemical process industry and, particularly, the petrochemical industry (the United States now produces the equivalent of the body weight of each American in plastics each year), all pose the real threat of releasing toxic chemicals into the environment." He illustrated his point by noting the recent discovery that vinyl chloride, biochloromethyl ether, methyl butyl hetone, and sulfuric acid mist "are not theoretical threats, but known causes of illness and death." He then went on to add that "the latency period (time from initial exposure to effect) associated with such categories of disease as cancer and genetic disorders often ranges from ten years to two or more generations." Therefore, he argued, we must begin now to search for potential causative agents, otherwise, "we may be exposing a significant proportion of our population to irreversible deleterious effects."[30]

Some synthetic chemicals affect the immunological system, some the reproductive system, and others the central nervous

system. The accidental substitution of polybrominated biphenyls, a fire retardant, for magnesium oxide in a large batch of
livestock feed in Michigan led not only to the death and
wholesale slaughter of hundreds of thousands of farm animals
but it also affected the health of unknown numbers of Michigan residents. When one thousand Michigan farm residents
were given physical examinations and the results compared
with the health profiles of a similarly sized Wisconsin control
group, "an unusual number of neurological, behavioral, joint
and gastro-intentional problems, including memory loss, mus-
cular weakness, coordination difficulties, sleep problems, arthri-
tis-like symptoms, diarrhea and abdominal pain," were discovered in the Michigan group.[31] Dr. Irving Selikoff, who
conducted the study, also reported abnormalities of the white
blood cells and impaired immunological functions in the
affected population.

The discharge of heavy metals into the environment poses
health problems everywhere. Mercury, cadmium, and lead are
perhaps the most common of these culprits. They have been
linked to the deaths of many and to the illnesses of hundreds
or even thousands of people in countries as diverse as Iraq and
Japan.

Occupational health hazards can be traced back not only to
synthetic materials and heavy metals, but to numerous other
factors as well. An estimated one million American workers
have handled asbestos in one form or another—as insulation,
as automobile brake linings, or as filters for beer and wine.
Epidemiologists estimate that these asbestos handlers will be
twice as likely as the rest of the population to contract terminal
cancer.[32]

In *The Picture of Health*, a book analyzing environmental
influences on health, Erik Eckholm identifies miners as one of
the most widely afflicted occupational groups. He notes that "8
to 10 percent of U.S. coal miners suffer from black lung disease,"[33] and that silicosis, another respiratory disease, is even

more prevalent worldwide. The World Health Organization (WHO) reports that "of all occupational diseases, silicosis is the major cause of permanent disability and mortality and is the most costly in terms of compensation payment."[34] In Bolivia, 23 percent of the large force of tin miners suffer from silicosis, as do 14 percent of all Colombian miners.[35]

Heart disease has reached near-epidemic proportions in modern industrial societies. A leading cause of debilitation and death in industrial societies, it plagues males in particular. Where obesity is common, diets are too rich in animal fats, and lifestyles are sedentary, coronary arteries can become clogged, often causing heart attacks in mid-life. A product of the social environment, heart disease is likely to remain a leading cause of illness and death unless diets are simplified and regular exercise is incorporated into daily living.

One of the worst of the environmentally induced illnesses in terms of the number of people affected is schistosomiasis. A disease virtually unknown in industrial societies, it now afflicts an estimated two hundred million people (nearly as many as live in North America) in Iran, Iraq, the Nile River Valley, nearly all of Africa, Southeast Asia, mainland China, the Caribbean, and the northeastern coast of South America. According to one estimate, about seven of every ten rural inhabitants of the Nile River Valley suffer from the disease. Its increasing incidence has been closely associated with irrigation expansion over the past few decades combined with inadequate sanitation facilities: the shift to perennial irrigation made possible by new reservoirs created an ideal habitat for the waterborne snails that carry schistosomiasis. Yet, responding to pressures to produce more food, political leaders in poor countries continue to construct new irrigation projects with the certain knowledge that the disease will spread.[36]

Not even the best-trained epidemiologists can say what future health trends will be, but certain tendencies seem evident. For example, because time lags between exposure to carcinogens and the development or detection of some of its forms involve years or even generations, cancer is likely to continue to increase in incidence and severity as long as the number of new and potentially carcinogenic compounds being released into the environment increases.

Humankind's capacity to survive and function has evolved over two million years within a particular biochemical environment. Humans are now altering that environment with only the vaguest understanding of the consequences of their actions. It is increasingly evident that future health and well-being will depend more on prevention and less on cure. A surgeon operating on a cancer victim cannot possibly guarantee the patient's complete recovery. No prescribed treatment for repairing the damage caused by a severe heart attack is consistently successful. The only effective strategy may be to mend our ways and simplify our lifestyles. Otherwise environmentally induced illnesses of our own making may simply replace the traditional threats to human health.

Inadvertent Climate Change

Climate and climate change have always affected humans, but only recently have humans acquired the means to influence climate. As a 1975 study by the national Academy of Sciences reports, "While the natural variations of climate have been larger than those that may have been induced by human activities during the past century, the rapidity with which human impacts threaten to grow in the future, and increasingly to disturb the natural course of events is a matter of concern."[37] The Academy study went on to note that "these impacts include man's changes of the atmospheric composition and his direct interference with factors controlling the all-important heat balance."

The earth's heat budget equals the amount of energy it receives from the sun minus the amount reflected or radiated into space. If this delicate balance is altered so that the earth receives more or less heat than it has in the past, the earth's climate will change. If it receives much less, a new ice age will begin. If it receives or retains a great deal more, the polar ice caps will melt—raising the oceans and submerging vast tracts of land and coastal cities.

The earth's absorption and reflection of heat can be altered in many ways. At the local level, the shift from forest to field altered this capacity, as did that from field to desert. The deforestation of vast areas, either as a result of clearing land for agriculture or of cutting firewood, can influence local climates measurably. Conducted on a large enough scale, deforestation could change the global climate as well.

The chief worry emerging among the meteorologists and geophysicists who study the earth's heat balance is that increases in the amount of carbon dioxide in the atmosphere will promote a "greenhouse effect." Carbon dioxide does not reduce incoming solar radiation, but it does absorb some of the heat that is re-radiated. Thus, any rise in the CO_2 in the atmosphere would cause the atmospheric temperature to increase.

At present, vast tonnages of carbon that have been sealed under the earth in fossil fuels for long geological epochs are being released into the atmosphere. Since the beginning of the Industrial Revolution the burning of fossil fuels has raised CO_2 levels in the atmosphere by an estimated 13 percent, and, as a 1977 study by the National Academy of Sciences projects, a four- to eightfold increase in atmospheric CO_2 can be expected within the next two centuries if heavy reliance on fossil fuels, principally coal, continues. According to the Academy study, "Our best understanding of the relation between an increase in carbon dioxide in the atmosphere and change in global temperature suggests a corresponding increase in average world temperature of six degrees Centigrade or more with polar temperature increases of as much as three times this figure."[38]

This increase in average temperature of 6 degrees Centigrade or 11 degrees Fahrenheit would be accompanied by an increase in humidity and in precipitation. If the temperature rise led to even a five-degree warming of the upper 1,000 meters of ocean water, simple expansion would raise the sea level by about one meter. In the preface to the Academy study, co-directors Philip H. Abelson and Thomas F. Malone, indicate in the study's principal conclusion, that "the primary limiting factor on energy production from fossil fuels over the next few centuries may turn out to be the climatic effects of the release of carbon dioxide." In relating the findings of their study to public policy, they report that averting a wholesale warming of the earth "will require a carefully planned international program and a fine sense of timing on the part of decision makers."[39]

The carbon dioxide factor, coupled with the air pollution that is also associated with the burning of fossil fuels, may accelerate the global shift to solar energy sources. The direct use of sunlight, wind power, and water power do not raise atmospheric CO_2 levels. Nor does the burning of wood, unless it contributes to deforestation.

Another potential influence on climate is that of airborne dust, the most common and easily recognized of man-made pollutants that affect climate. Dust is generated by virtually every human activity from suburban driving to tilling the soil. Meteorologist Helmut Landsberg estimates that, along with world population, the amount of dust in the atmosphere has doubled since the thirties, despite the absence of major volcanic eruptions.[40] Other sources estimate that the amount of dust or particulate matter being discharged into the atmosphere is now increasing by about 4 percent per year. Since particulate matter in the atmosphere tends to scatter incoming radiation and to reflect it back into space before it reaches earth, particles form what amounts to a layer of insulation, reflecting the sun's rays away from the earth and thereby lowering the planet's temperature.

Another source of climatic change is thermal pollution, as weather forecasts for major cities remind us daily. Temperatures within the inner city commonly range from a few to several degrees higher than those of the adjacent countryside. So far, the clearly measurable thermal effects remain largely localized, but the continuing growth in fossil-fuel use could eventually lead to global temperature increases. A 1977 Ford Foundation–sponsored study, *Nuclear Power: Issues and Choices*, reports that electric power generation can both directly and indirectly contribute to a warming of the earth. "The most serious potential environmental impacts from greatly increased power generation are changes in global climate. The thermal output of both coal and nuclear power plants contributes directly to the long-term heating of the atmosphere. A much more immediate atmospheric heating problem, however, results from the carbon dioxide produced when coal is burned."[41]

Apart from the inadvertent modification of climate, deliberate attempts to alter the climate are becoming increasingly common. Chief among these are efforts to increase rainfall where water supplies are inadequate. Some rainmaking technologies have proven at least occasionally successful. In fact, cloud seeding was the issue behind a clash between the states of Washington and Idaho during the drought ridden early months of 1977. Washington officials, who had hired a rainmaking firm to seed clouds moving inland from the Pacific, were accused by Idaho's political leaders of "cloud rustling."[42] This relatively tame skirmish raises the prospect of meteorological warfare as countries that are hard-pressed to expand food supplies begin to compete for available rainfall.

That humans could inadvertently or intentionally alter global climatic patterns is now beyond doubt. That there are a number of possible counteracting influences that need investigating is also clear. However, whether the world would be "better" if it were warmer or cooler is a moot question: existing agricultural systems and settlement patterns have evolved in a particular climate, and climatic changes of any sort can only disrupt those systems. Efforts to feed the mushrooming global population have prompted farmers to till ever-dryer areas—such as the USSR dryland wheat areas and lands surrounding the Sahara Desert—where even a slight shift in rainfall could cause crops to fail. More generally, even an average temperature decline of one degree in the northern latitudes could reduce the growing season by two weeks. Even minor reductions in temperatures in the northern hemisphere could lead to a southward shift of the monsoon belt in both Africa and Asia. In both cases, agricultural output would shrink, adversely affecting the well-being and survival prospects of hundreds of millions of people.

Natural Disasters: The Human Hand

When under stress, natural systems become highly susceptible to injury. Then minor or routine events can become major catastrophes. Moderate floods of a seasonal nature can assume calamitous proportions and devastate human life, crops, and livestock. A drought that would normally be a hardship becomes a disaster. A minor earthquake can leave the local economy in ruins.

One case study of the human contribution to natural disasters was undertaken by Kenneth Hewitt, who describes the extensive damage a relatively minor earthquake of 5.5 on the Richter scale caused in the mountains of northeast Pakistan. According to Hewitt, earthquake damage was far greater in deforested areas. The rockfalls and landslides that followed the quake did as much harm as the quake itself: "Farms and villages in the steep-walled tributary valleys and narrows of the Indus suffered mainly from the terrible rain of boulders following the tremors. The results were more like bomb damage.

Landslides were also a major factor in the destruction of irrigation channels and terraces here." Not only is the damage
worse, but it is often irreversible, as Hewitt emphasizes:
"Moreover, landslides are a particularly bad way for terracing
to go. The entire solid element is swept away, sometimes directly into a streambed and downstream before it can be recovered. It probably ended up in Tarbela Dam, a huge irrigation
and power project some 120 kilometers down the Indus. Since
sedimentation is the major problem in the economic lifetime
of the reservoir, agricultural productivity was thus diminished
at both ends."[43]

Increasingly, "natural" catastrophes are brought on at least
in part by humans. Even when disasters are not triggered by
human activities, they can be exacerbated by them. As Hewitt
says, "the number of natural disasters and the degree of damage in general have increased in this century," and since "there
is no reason to suppose that nature is becoming more severe,
the origin must be sought in changing human activities."

In many cases, the events that lead up to or constitute a
natural disaster intertwine so subtly that the ultimate effect of
a given activity or action is hard to predict. Overpopulation in
a particular watershed may foster deforestation, which in turn
can cause floods that destroy crops and that bring on food
shortages, hunger, and political instability. In another similar
watershed, overpopulation may lead to soil erosion, the silting
of a hydroelectric reservoir, and power shortages in a city downstream.

Nature does not always work alone to create disasters.
Human activities can set in motion chains of events that only
seem natural. Industrial expansion and overplowing can, for
example, serve to increase the amount of dust in the upper
atmosphere. As a result, rainfall patterns change and food
production falls. Eventually, the international balance of payments and political relations among countries are affected. In
short, the causal relationships between human and natural

activities are open-ended, and new stresses on the earth's eco-system pose complex economic and social issues.

Reflections on Carrying Capacity

The number of deer that a given area can support can be calculated rather precisely. So too can the number of lions that can coexist in an East African game reserve. But calculating the number of people that the earth can safely sustain is a far more complex undertaking. While all deer of the same size consume similar amounts of forage, material consumption among humans varies widely. National averages may vary by a factor of twenty or more, and individual consumption levels may vary by a hundredfold. Although the earth can support far more people with simple lifestyles than people with affluent ones, poor people almost always aspire to live as the rich do.

Calculating the earth's population-sustaining capacity is made even more complicated when technological advances are taken into account. Prior to the development of agriculture, the earth supported an estimated ten million people, no more than the number living in London or Afghanistan today. The 400-fold increase in world population since agriculture evolved was made possible by technological and social progress. But just as mankind has ingeniously enhanced the productive capacity of the natural system, so too people can impair or destroy it, either out of greed or out of ignorance. Examples of human overreaching have already made history. The population of the Fertile Crescent of the Tigris-Euphrates was probably far greater a few thousand years ago than it is today. North Africa, once the granary of the Roman Empire, can no longer even feed itself.

In those countries where the ecological stresses on food systems are greatest, the deterioration may shortly override efforts to raise output. According to an FAO study, "Overcropping, soil erosion, and declining soil fertility due to shifting cultivation and shortening fallows are major factors in the large-scale migration from the Andes to the neighboring lowlands."[44] Among the countries in which the ecological deterioration of food systems could soon lead to a downturn in food production are El Salvador, Haiti, Nigeria, Ethiopia, Afghanistan and Nepal. Arthur Candell, writing of the ecological undermining of the Haitian economy, reports that "the land produces less and less each year, while population soars. . . . The eroded and leached mountain soil can no longer support tree growth."[45]

The human excesses recited thus far reflect both the growth in human numbers and in individual consumption. A global population that grows at 2 percent multiplies seven times per century. If the demands generated by rising affluence during the postwar period are added to those associated with population growth, the growth in global consumption from 1950 through the early seventies comes to nearly 4 percent per year. If such a rate is sustained for a century, it leads to an increase of fiftyfold. The earth's biological systems cannot handle growth of such proportions. Nor can human ingenuity and technology fully compensate for the collapse of natural systems.

Biologists have long been aware of this incontrovertible fact. In their analyses of biological systems, they often refer to an S-shaped growth curve that describes various long-term biological growth processes including, among others, the growth of various animal populations introduced into new environments and the gains in productivity of a corn field as new technologies are applied (see Figure 3-1). The S-curve usually measures time on the horizontal axis and population size or yield on the vertical one. It generally shows growth increasing slowly at first, then more rapidly until the trend becomes almost vertical. At some point it then begins to slow and bend to the right as various constraints cause it to level off. The point at which progressive acceleration halts and progressive decel-

**Population
Size or Yield**

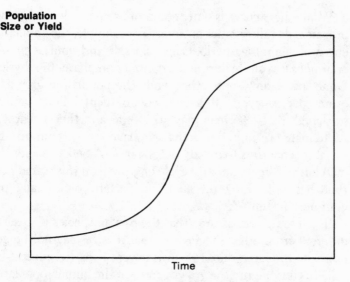

Time

Figure 3-1. The S-Shaped Biological Growth Curve

eration begins is called "the point of inflection."

The S-shaped or logistical curve describes equally well the growth of a population of fruit flies in a laboratory jar, or yeast in a petri dish, or deer set loose on a previously uninhabited island. It describes neatly the growth of lily leaves in our lily pond. In the laboratory petri dish, the impediment to growth may be the accumulation of waste produced by the micro-organisms. On the island where deer roam, hormonal changes associated with crowding may limit reproduction. In the lily pond, the availability of surface area for capturing sunlight is likely to be the constraining factor. As Dr. Jonas Salk points out, this curve describes the growth pattern of many, though not all, populations confined to a limited area.[46] Initially, the curve climbs exponentially as the population doubles at short and regular intervals. After a period, constraints that can be perceived as environmental feedback begin to slow the growth in numbers.

While the S-curve is quite common, some biological growth processes do follow other patterns. For example, the population curve of lemmings periodically expands and contracts, with enormous loss of life during the contraction phase. Biophysicist Donella Meadows notes that while the population growth of some species levels off as the environmental limits are approached, that of others may go too far and then collapse.[47] As humans we must hope that we have the wisdom and the social mechanisms to avoid "overshooting." Salk observes that man has yet "to complete a cycle of growth on this planet" and thus has not "fully revealed the pattern biologically programmed in him."[48]

It is tempting to assume that the human species is, after all, different from other species and that its size may not be governed by the same rules to which lower forms are subject. But is it? In the long run the growth curve of the human population may not be very different from that of the fruit flies in the laboratory jar, or most other biological organisms in a finite environment. The principal difference may be that human ingenuity has postponed the horizontal flattening of the curve. In the case of humans, feedback from the social environment to the organism may take the form of rising unemployment, of UN projections of growing food deficits in densely populated countries, or of warnings such as those sounded by the Club of Rome's studies. The recent slowing of human population growth suggests that the inflection point on the world population growth curve was passed several years ago. If so, it may mean that our accommodation to the earth's limited capacities and resources has already begun.

4

Population: Understanding the Threat

Human-like creatures have existed for some sixty thousand generations, but only during the last generation have human numbers grown by 2 to 3 percent per year. Rates of this order have come into effect so recently that their impact has not yet been adequately assessed. Few of the world's political leaders understand that a population expanding at a seemingly innocuous 3 percent per year will multiply nineteenfold within a century.

The lack of understanding of the arithmetic of exponential population growth is compounded by a lack of appreciation of the many dimensions of the population problem. One could fill a small library on the relationship between population growth and food but search in vain for a single article detailing the relationship between population growth and inflation or overgrazing. This traditional food focus notwithstanding, population growth intensifies almost every important problem with which humanity wrestles today.

When world population passed the four billion mark, it reached a level beyond which further growth assumes a disturbing new character.[1] While population growth has always contributed to growth in demand, it is now beginning to reduce the productive capacity of some local biological systems by promoting the consumption of the resource bases themselves. As awareness of this new reality permeates public consciousness, the need to stabilize population will take on new urgency.

Arithmetic and Dynamics

Population analysts have devised dramatic means to alert humankind to the consequences of continuing rapid population growth. Concerned demographers have calculated the time remaining until we reach standing room only. Biologists have calculated the number of centuries that population growth at current rates would take to yield a human mass greater than that of the earth itself. An imaginative physicist extended this projection even farther into the future, calculating when the expansion of the human mass would exceed the speed of light. No effort will be made here to devise yet another way of dramatizing the consequences of continuing population growth. The intent is simply to outline the historical and projected trends as briefly as possible.

Before agriculture developed, population growth was imperceptible. The preagricultural era, characterized by both high death and high birth rates, was a precarious period in human existence. Had it not been for high fertility levels, humanity might well have perished during this two-million-year span. After agriculture developed, increases in the food supply led to substantial population increases. As population pressures mounted, so did the impetus to innovate in agriculture. Agri-

cultural innovations in turn permitted further increases in population, setting in motion a self-reinforcing cycle that still
turns.

The twelve thousand years between the birth of agriculture
and the advent of the Industrial Revolution were marked by
gradually accelerating population growth. The Industrial Revolution further accelerated this growth. Besides giving rise to
new economic opportunities, advances in industrial technology
supported the continued evolution and expansion of agriculture. By the outbreak of World War II, the annual population
increase had reached 1 percent. The burst of scientific innovation and economic activity that began during the forties substantially enhanced the earth's food-producing capacity and led
to dramatic improvements in disease control. The resulting
marked reduction in death rates created an unprecedented
imbalance between births and deaths and an explosive rate of
population growth. Thus, while world population increased at
2 to 5 percent *per century* during the first fifteen centuries of
the Christian era, the rate in some countries today is between
3 and 4 percent *per year*, very close to the biological maximum.

The time now needed to add a billion people to the earth's
population has become incredibly short. It took two million
years for human numbers to reach one billion. The second
billion took only one hundred years. Successive billions came
even faster. At the present rate of increase, the sixth billion will
require only a decade. If the present growth rate were to be
maintained until this time next century, only a year would be
needed to add one billion and a mere four years to add the
present world population (see Table 4-1).

No country can seriously entertain the thought of sustaining
population growth at 3 percent or more per year for long. Such
a rate in a country of 17 million people, such as Algeria in 1975,
would result in a population of 323 million a century hence.
If Indonesia's current population growth rate of 2.1 percent
continues, in a century its population will reach 1.1 billion, or
a quarter of the present world population. Mexico's population,

The Twenty-Ninth Day

Table 4-1. Time Required to Add Each Successive Billion to World
Population, Past and Projected

	Years	Year Reached
First billion	2,000,000	1830
Second "	100	1930
Third "	30	1960
Fourth "	15	1975
Fifth "	11	1986
Sixth "	9	1995

Source: United Nations.

now growing at more than 3 percent annually, will exceed that of China and the Soviet Union combined within the next century if its growth is not slowed.

The purpose of these illustrative extrapolations of national populations is not to show what population size will be a century hence. Clearly no country could ever sustain a ten-, fifteen-, or twentyfold increase in population size, as they suggest. Rather, they underscore the urgency of formulating appropriate national population policies. The contrasting economic futures of countries with widely disparate population growth rates is obvious. Satisfying basic human needs is a relatively simple task where population is growing slowly, if at all. It will be far easier to feed, shelter, and employ people in societies where population is essentially stable, as it now is West Germany and the United Kingdom, than in societies where it is multiplying at a prodigious rate, as in Algeria or Mexico. A long-term projection by governments of the ecological and social consequences of their current population policies could be instructive.

In 1976 the world birth rate (the number of births per thousand population) was 28, and the death rate (the number of deaths per thousand population) was 12. The excess of births over deaths of 16 per thousand yielded a population growth rate of 1.6 percent annually. In that year, world population increased by 64 million—the difference between 112 million births and 48 million deaths—and births exceeded deaths by a margin of nearly five to two.[2]

Most of the world's population growth occurs in preindustrial societies. Two countries, China and India, are now contributing 9 and 12 million respectively to the annual increase. (China's population of 800 million is substantially larger than that of India, but its estimated birth rate is much lower.) Some of the comparatively small poor countries add more to the world's annual population gain than larger rich ones do. Mexico, for example, now adds more people to its population each year than the United States does. Similarly, Brazil adds 2.9 million additional people a year, while the Soviet Union grows by only 2.3 million.[3]

The world's population today is a young one. Half of the people in the less developed world have not yet reached their nineteenth birthdays, while the median age in the more developed countries, where people are more evenly distributed among age groups, is thirty-one. In many poor countries, more than 40 percent of all people are under fifteen years of age; in Nigeria and Peru the figure is 45 percent, and for Pakistan 46 percent.[4] In societies with such age structures, the youth dependency ratio—the proportion of infants and children to economically active adults—is high. Moreover, the number of entrants into the job markets in these countries will soon soar.

A Problem of Many Dimensions

Although the population problem is multidimensional, public attention has focused on the food dimension. In part this reflects the impact of Thomas R. Malthus's classic work, *An Essay on the Principle of Population*, published in 1797. Malthus's influence on demographic thinking has lasted both because his thesis is simple and because other aspects of the population problem have not been adequately investigated. Although his belief that population tends to increase geometrically while food supply increases arithmetically has not withstood the test of time, his broad contention that population growth tends to press against food supplies has held up.

Population studies unrelated to food have been pursued mainly by demographers who have clarified those human aspects of the population equation that can be quantified. These analysts have measured population sizes, rates of growth, age and sex composition, and fertility levels; and they have devised techniques for building models and for projecting population trends. This single-minded focus on demographic analysis has, however, not been matched by attention to many other consequences of population growth—consequences that might properly concern economists, ecologists, meteorologists, political scientists, urban planners, and other specialists. Perhaps because the implications of population growth embrace so many disciplines, they have been the focus of almost none.

The food dimension of the population threat remains paramount. Yet in their Malthusian mindset, population analysts often neglect the ecological manifestations of the problem discussed earlier. In addition population growth contributes to economic stresses. It fans inflation by creating resource scarcities. It raises unemployment by increasing the number of job seekers faster than jobs are created. Where it outstrips economic growth, it pushes down living standards.

The social effects of population growth are also devastating. In particular, population growth undermines efforts to spread literacy, to improve health services, and to provide housing. While more than five centuries have passed since Gutenberg invented the printing press, one-third of the world's adults cannot read. Although the percentage of illiterates in the world declined between 1950 and 1975, the number of adult illiterates increased from seven hundred million to eight hundred million.[5] As the number of youngsters of school age continuously swells, many poor-country governments are quietly abandoning the goal of universal compulsory education.

Rapid population growth and the lack of family-planning services directly affect health at the family level. When too many children are born too close together, the health of both mothers and children is jeopardized. Women become victims

of what Dr. Derrick B. Jellife describes as the "maternal depletion syndrome." After two decades of uninterrupted pregnan-
cies and lactation women in their mid-thirties are haggard and
emaciated, and appear to be in their fifties. As researchers Erik
Eckholm and Kathleen Newland point out, such women are
"Undernourished, often anemic, and generally weakened by
the biological burdens of excessive reproduction," they "become increasingly vulnerable to death during childbirth or to
simple infectious diseases at any time," and "their babies swell
the infant mortality statistics." Some of the most graphic data
on the effect of family size on infants in poor countries come
from Rwanda: 20 percent of the fifth-born die within the first
year of life; but for those born ninth and after, 40 percent die
during the first year.[6]

With the real costs of lumber and land rising as demand
pressures mount, adequate housing eludes more and more of
the world's people. Population growth also promotes crowding,
which can give rise to international political conflicts. At the
individual level, untrammeled growth can lead to the loss of
individual freedom and to the loss of privacy.

The many consequences of population growth bespeak both
the complexity and the urgency of the problem. In effect, the
population problem is not one but many. Its many facets often
interact, amplifying each other. Some dimensions of the population problem are economic, some are social, some are ecological, and some are political, but nearly all have one thing in
common: they can be expected to get much worse before they
get better.

A Double-Edged Sword

Always a drain on food and other resources, population growth
in some situations acts as a double-edged sword, simultaneously
increasing demands and reducing supplies. This double-edged
effect can readily be seen in fisheries, forests, and agriculture.
As long as the demand for firewood and lumber is lower than

the sustainable yield of the forest, population growth has no impact on production; but once the demand exceeds the sustainable yield, then population growth begins to eat away the productive resource base itself. In economic terms it consumes the principal as well as the interest.

The two-way cut of population growth also affects agriculture. As population expands so does the demand for food, and consequently, the demand for cropland. But population growth simultaneously generates other demands for land: residential construction, transport systems, and recreational areas, to cite a few. Whether population growth leads to urban encroachment on Canadian cropland or to village encroachment on Indian cropland, the effect is the same—reduced food output.

The task of meeting basic human needs is also compounded by the double-edged effect. In those poor countries with high population-growth rates, ever more of the available capital must be spent on food, shelter, and other basic survival needs, leaving ever less for health care, education, and culture. Thus, population growth not only multiplies the number of people who desire and need these social essentials, but it also reduces the resources available to satisfy them.

The double-edged effect of population growth is no longer a unique phenomenon. It can be seen in the grasslands of East Africa, the mountainous valleys of Java, and in the fisheries of the Pacific. On its current scale, it introduces a new and disturbing element into the population-resource calculus. Determining carrying capacity precisely is difficult enough when the resource base is fixed; but when it is shrinking, the calculations are far more complex.

Trends of the Seventies

While the arithmetic of rapid population growth is as frightening as ever, there is now some hope that population growth can be tamed. Some time around 1970, the rate of world population growth reached an all-time high and then began slowly to subside. In 1970, human numbers grew by an estimated 1.90 percent. The most recent data show a marked decline since then to 1.64 percent in 1975 (see Table 4-2). In most of the world, the decline reflected falling birth rates and a global trend toward smaller families. But in some low-income, food-deficit countries, rising death rates also came into play.

Growth in world population, the excess of births over deaths, fell from an estimated 69 million in 1970 to 64 million in 1975, despite a substantial increase during those years in the number of young people of reproductive age. More than anything else, this progress reflects the widening availability of family-planning services—including both contraception and abortion—and the growing desire to use them.

Although all of the widely used contraceptives, such as the pill, IUD, or condom, had existed prior to 1970, their relative importance has changed significantly. Use of the pill, promoted by both publicly supported clinics and commercial distributors, has increased on every continent. At the same time, the early seventies saw a shift toward greater reliance on male sterilization. Vasectomies became more popular in the United States during this period, with the number performed during the early seventies temporarily surpassing that of the more complex and costly female-sterilization operations.[7]

While contraceptive use patterns changed, abortion laws were liberalized. At the beginning of 1971, 38 percent of the world's people lived in countries where legal abortions were easy to obtain. By 1977, this figure stood at 64 percent, nearly two-thirds of the world. Few social changes have ever swept the world so quickly.

Table 4-3. World Population Increase, 1970 and 1975

	1970	1975
World Population (billions)	3.59	3.92
Rate of Annual Increase (percent)	1.90	1.64
Annual Increase (millions)	69	64

Source: Worldwatch Institute (Worldwide Paper 8).

The global slowing of population growth during the seventies has been concentrated in three geographic regions—Western Europe, North America, and East Asia. Between 1970 and 1975, the population growth rate fell by almost one-half in Western Europe and by a third in North America and East Asia. Western Europe, with 343 million people, cut its annual population growth from .56 percent in 1970 to .32 in 1975—a reduction without precedent for a large geographic area. North America and East Asia had populations of 236 million and 1,005 million, respectively, in 1975. North America's growth rate of .90 percent in 1970 fell to .60 percent in 1976.[8]

No achievement is more impressive than the dramatic reduction of population growth in East Asia. Influenced heavily by China's massive efforts to curb births, the region's growth rate declined from 1.85 percent in 1970 to 1.18 percent in 1975. The estimated reduction in the Chinese crude birth rate from 32 (per thousand of total population) to 19, or 2.6 points per year, is the most rapid ever recorded for a five-year span, exceeding the earlier reductions of nearly 2 points per year achieved by Taiwan, Tunisia, Barbados, Hong Kong, Singapore, Costa Rica, and Egypt. This pronounced fall-off in East Asia should come as no surprise, since virtually every country in the region has a dynamic and highly successful national family-planning program.

The other two Asian sub-regions—South Asia (principally the Indian subcontinent) and Southeast Asia (the region from Burma to the Philippines, including Indonesia)—have brought their population growth rates down slightly. Within South Asia, India's birth rate inched slowly downward, while a more marked decline took place in tiny Sri Lanka. The decline in Southeast Asia reflects modest declines in Thailand, Indonesia, and the Philippines, where family-planning programs seem to be gaining momentum during the mid-seventies. Reports from Indonesia in 1977 indicated remarkably widespread receptivity to family planning in Bali and much of Java.

In some geographic regions, the growth rate has changed

little in either direction since the turn of the decade. Although a few countries in Latin America, Eastern Europe, Africa, and the Middle East have measurably reduced their high birth rates, the declines have either been offset by a continuing decline in the death rate or been too small to affect the regional averages. Among the smaller countries, Costa Rica and Panama have brought down birth rates most effectively. Among the larger ones, Colombia's progress has put it into a leadership position, while Mexico's recently launched family-planning program is barely beginning to show results. Brazil indirectly abandoned its pro-natalist policy in 1974 when it announced "that family planning should be available to all couples who want it, as a human right, not as a part of a policy to reduce rates of growth."[9]

Within Europe the trends contrast sharply between West and East. In 1970 the birth rates in the two regions were close, sixteen and seventeen, respectively. During the next five years, however, Western Europe's rate dropped below fourteen while that of Eastern Europe increased slightly, ending the period at eighteen. During the early seventies the Eastern European birth rate had been slowly declining, but as pro-natalist policies were adopted in Poland, Czechoslovakia, and elsewhere, the rate turned sharply upward in the mid-seventies and more than offset the preceding decline.

Fertility trends in the two principal regions in the Western Hemisphere differed sharply too. While the U.S.–Canadian birth rate fell from eighteen to less than fifteen, that of Latin America changed little, ending the period at thirty-six. Although they had populations of almost identical size in 1950, Latin America now adds four times as many people each year as North America does.

Countries Achieving Stability

As of 1976, six countries—East Germany, West Germany, Luxembourg, Austria, Belgium, and the United Kingdom—

had stable or declining populations. Interestingly, none of these countries was among the lengthening list of those with an explicit policy of stabilizing population. Rather, economic, social, and demographic forces converged to bring births into balance with deaths.

In 1969, East Germany became the first country in the modern era to achieve an equilibrium between births and deaths. East German women enjoy high levels of employment and education, and relatively few of them are of reproductive age. In West Germany, the second country to bring its population growth to a standstill, the number of births fell below deaths in 1972. There, the birth rate of eighteen in 1966 dropped steadily before leveling off at just under ten in 1975 —perhaps the lowest birth rate on record (see Figure 4-1).

Low birth levels in West Germany reflect changes in attitudes toward childbearing and family size; the West Germans

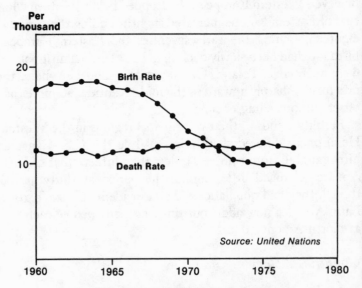

Figure 4-1. Birth and Death Rates in West Germany, 1960-77

themselves call the demographic trend "Der Pillenknick," or "the pill pinch." An estimated one-third of all West German women use the pill, while a majority of the remainder rely on other contraceptive techniques. A poll taken in West Germany in 1974 showed that 4 percent of adults wanted no children, 3 percent wanted one child, and 69 percent desired two children. A recent repeat of the same poll, which put the corresponding percentages at 7, 14, and 57 percent, helped to explain why the birth rate has dropped so low.[10]

The populations of two smaller countries, Luxembourg and Austria, also ceased to grow during the seventies. The United Kingdom and Belgium reached population equilibrium in 1976, bringing to six the total of countries with essentially stable populations. All six countries that have thus far brought population growth to a halt are European. All six enjoy high levels of income, support high levels of education and employment for women, and provide easy access to contraceptives. Collectively, they contain 152 million people, or nearly 4 percent of world population. Although this is a small percentage, it represents an important step toward the eventual stabilization of world population (see Table 4-3).

Several other countries have birth rates that are now dropping below fifteen, falling steadily, and approaching a balance

Table 4-3. Countries at or Near Population Stability, 1976

Country	Crude Birth Rate (Per Thousand)	Crude Death Rate (Per Thousand)	Annual Rate of Population Change (Percent)*	Annual Change in Population (Numbers)
East Germany	11.9	14.0	− .21	− 35,280
West Germany	9.8	11.9	− .21	− 129,150
Luxembourg	10.9	12.6	− .17	− 612
Austria	11.6	12.6	− .10	− 7,500
United Kingdom	12.1	12.1	0	0
Belgium	12.4	12.2	+ .02	+ 1,960

* Excludes both emigration and immigration.
Source: United Nations.

with death rates. France and Italy, as well as several smaller European countries such as Sweden, Norway, Denmark, the Netherlands, and Switzerland make up this group. The United States, one of the world's four most populous countries, has also pulled its birth rate down below 15. Virtually all of the remaining industrial countries—Australia, New Zealand, the nations of Eastern Europe, the Soviet Union, Japan, and Canada—have birth rates between 15 and 20.[11]

How many other major industrial countries will actually follow the two Germanys and the United Kingdom to population stability remains to be seen. A number are clearly moving in that direction. The U.S. birth rate remains low even as large numbers of young people move into the reproductive age bracket. The growing preference among Americans for small families was dramatically illustrated in a survey conducted in 1975 among wives aged eighteen to twenty-four, which indicated that 74 percent planned to have either one or two children. Eight years before, only 45 percent expressed such a preference.[12] If fertility simply remains near its current level for the next decade, then it should begin to drop as age groups with fewer constituents reach reproductive age.

Japan's age structure and the Soviet Union's resemble that of the United States. The Japanese birth rate, which fluctuated within a narrow range around nineteen from 1970 to 1974, dropped to seventeen in 1975 and to sixteen in 1976. A survey conducted every two years by Japan's Population Problems Research Council shows that the number of children most Japanese women want is dropping sharply. As recently as 1971, only 33 percent wanted to have two children; but, by 1974, 40 percent felt that two was the right number, and the percentage of Japanese desiring three or more meanwhile decreased proportionately.[13] The tendency of younger women to opt for smaller families at a time when fewer people are entering the reproductive years may lead to a dramatic fall in the birth rate in the years ahead, moving Japan quickly toward population stability.

The weightiest demographic unknown in industrial countries does not involve the Western countries and Japan, where the trends appear somewhat predictable, but Eastern Europe and the Soviet Union. During the late fifties and sixties, the trends toward declining birth rates followed remarkably parallel courses in the Soviet Union and the United States. In recent years, however, the Soviet decline seems to have leveled off, while that in the United States has continued.

How long the political leadership in Eastern Europe will want to follow the strong pro-natalist policies adopted in recent years if resource scarcities continue remains in question. When food scarcity forced the Polish government to attempt to raise food prices during the summer of 1976, it encountered widespread resistance of the sort that had unseated earlier governments. It had to rescind partially the price hikes in order to avoid civil disturbances.[14]

Almost all the East European countries face food problems resembling Poland's. Along with the Soviet Union, most have become heavily indebted to Western banks in recent years as they have found themselves living beyond their means. Glaring housing shortages in Czechoslovakia can only be aggravated by pro-natalist policies. At some point, policy-makers must reconcile pro-natalist policies with pressing needs. For example, Soviet planners may begin to link population policies to their country's massive and uncomfortable dependence on food imports after poor harvests. Demographic problems within the Soviet Union are further complicated by the wide differences in fertility levels among ethnic groups, differences that have become politically sensitive. Birth rates in the Russian Socialist Republic are comparable with those of Western Europe, while those in some of the less developed Soviet Socialist Republics, such as Tadjikistan, Turkmenia, or Kirghiz, are higher than those of India's more progressive states.

Controversial issues cloud the future of both population policies and fertility levels in Eastern Europe. Nonetheless, given the prevailing social trends, birth rates will probably not rise appreciably. Any change is more apt to be registered as a decline.

The Tragic Rise in Death Rates

The seventies have witnessed sporadic rises in death rates in many poorer countries. Neither war nor epidemics, but hunger and nutritional stress are to blame. World grain reserves were quickly depleted between 1972 and 1974, and food prices climbed accordingly, often leading to a rise in nutritional stress in poor countries after short harvests due to droughts or floods.

Death rates provide the most readily available statistical indicator of severe nutritional stress. Whenever food scarcities develop, the weaker members of society, usually infants and the elderly among the lower-income groups, suffer most. Although they are not necessarily discriminated against, they are invariably least able to withstand the acute physiological stresses of near starvation. Available data indicate that the brunt of global food scarcity during the seventies has been borne by the poorest and weakest members of these societies.

Some of the countries most severely affected by food scarcity have never had even a census, much less a system of registering births and deaths that yields reliable monthly vital statistics. But despite the time lag involved in assessing the demographic impact of food scarcity and soaring food prices, data for several countries are now becoming available. Such data give a crude approximation of the human toll in a world where food reserves are inadequate at best, where food is scarce and distributed unevenly, and where population growth is still rapid.

The point of this analysis is not that hunger is new. Indeed, chronic and seasonal hunger form an integral part of the social landscape in many countries. What is so disheartening is that the postwar trend of gradual improvement in per-capita food consumption and the associated rise in life expectancy has been arrested and reversed in a great many developing countries.

Scarcity is global in an integrated world food economy, but the most severely affected countries are the poorer ones. In Bangladesh, the impact of global food scarcity has been particularly harsh. Twice during the seventies food shortages have been followed by severe nutritional stress and loss of life. The first of these shortages occurred in 1971–72, when the crop was adversely affected both by the insurrection and by bad weather. In 1974–75, extensive flooding put the rice harvest far below expected levels and well below the minimum needed. The flooding, among the worst in the country's history, may have been in part the product of deforestation in the Nepalese and eastern Indian watersheds where two of Bangladesh's principal rivers originate.

Like most poor countries, Bangladesh does not have the means to assess precisely the impact of food shortages on its population. However, as part of its research program, the International Cholera Research Laboratory has for ten years kept meticulous demographic records for Matlab Bazar, the district in which it is located. With an almost entirely rural population of 120,000, Matlab Bazar is in many ways typical of Bangladesh as a whole (see Table 4-4).

Using the data for this district, a Ford Foundation demographic analysis of the impact of Bangladesh's war for independence indicates that the actual loss of life in combat was rather small compared with the number of lives claimed by hunger. The subgroups that shouldered the highest risks "were the very young and the very old." Per-capita cereal consumption, which averaged about 15 ounces per day during the sixties, probably fell to a near-starvation level of 12 ounces in 1972. The death rate in Matlab Bazar climbed from an average of 15.7 per thousand for the 1966–70 period to 21.3 in 1971/72.[15] If, as the Ford report suggests, Matlab Bazar is representative of

Table 4-4. Crude Death Rate in Matlab Bazar, 1966–67 to 1975–76

Year	Deaths per Thousand
1966–67	16.0
1967–68	17.2
1968–69	15.7
1969–70	15.1
1970–71	14.6
1971–72	21.3
1972–73	16.4
1973–74	14.6
1974–75	20.0
1975–76	18.2

Source: International Cholera Research Laboratory.

Bangladesh as a whole, then there was a nationwide increase in deaths of some 400,000.

In 1972–73, Bangladesh's rice crop was again poor. But in 1973–74, a bumper-crop year in most of the world, it recovered strongly. In 1974–75, the harvests fell again, this time to well below the levels required to meet national needs.[16] A Bangladesh representative at the 1974 World Food Conference in Rome held a press conference imploring the international community to come to his country's aid. But because additional food-relief exports would further raise food prices in the supplier countries, the response was both belated and inadequate; consequently, the death rate in Matlab Bazar climbed again, reaching 20.0 in 1974–75.[17] If this increase above the base period is again extrapolated to the entire country, it yields an increase in deaths above normal of 330,000. In 1975–76 the food situation improved, but not enough to bring the death rate back down to the pre-crisis norm. This time hunger claimed some 192,000 lives.

The most recent data available on mortality for Bangladesh are those compiled in the Companiganj district by a Johns Hopkins University medical team. These data for food-short 1975 show a death rate of 24.0 in a district that the team estimates to have had a normal death rate comparable to that of Matlab Bazar.[18] Whether the statistics for Matlab Bazar or the grimmer data for Companiganj are used to estimate the nationwide increase in deaths, it is clear that hunger has twice during this decade exacted a heavy human toll in Bangladesh.

India's poor 1972 harvest came in after food-production efforts slackened following the successful introduction of the high-yielding dwarf wheats during the late sixties and early seventies. Indeed, India had been able to feed an estimated 8 to 10 million refugees from Bangladesh during 1971 and early 1972 from its record food reserves. But when the monsoon failed in the summer of 1972, India found that it had used up its food reserves to aid Bangladesh, while the Soviet Union had secretly tied up most of the world's exportable wheat supplies —leaving little for India or anyone else. Unable to import all the food it needed, the Indian government stood by helplessly while food consumption dropped sharply. The poorer states, heavily dependent on rainfed production of sorghum, millet, and wheat, were the most severely affected. Death rates climbed sharply in Bihar, Orissa, and Uttar Pradesh in 1972.

In the poverty-ridden state of Uttar Pradesh in northern India, the death rate climbed from 20.1 in 1971 to 25.6 in 1972. If this rise reflects nutritional stress, as the available evidence suggests, then the fall in food consumption claimed 493,000 lives. In the smaller states of Bihar and Orissa, the data for 1972 imply that the excessive deaths totaled 235,000 and 101,000, respectively. In these three states alone, deterioration in the food situation claimed an estimated 829,000 lives (see Table 4-6).

More than anything else, the experience of 1972 taught the Indian government that it had to assume the responsibility for feeding its people. The United States, with its reserves depleted and food prices climbing at home, could no longer be counted on to launch massive rescue efforts in emergencies. And with the price of wheat soaring and the cost of a rescue

Table 4-5. Crude Death Rates in Three States in India, 1970–72

	1970	1971	1972	Increase in 1972 over 1971	Additional Deaths in 1972
	(DEATHS PER THOUSAND)				
Bihar	14.1	14.2	18.3	4.1	235,000
Orissa	16.4	15.5	20.0	4.5	101,000
Uttar Pradesh	21.6	20.1	25.6	5.5	493,000

Source: Indian Ministry of Health and Family Planning.

effort increasing accordingly, the international community expressed little interest in bailing India out. As a result, roughly a million lives, mostly those of children, were lost.

Outside Asia, the sheer numbers of people caught in the often fatal food squeeze were fewer, but the plight of the hunger-stricken groups was, if anything, worse. In Haiti, population growth generated unbearable pressures on the land and led to the loss of soil and the abandonment of cropland. This deterioration in the food-resource base was brought into public view by a drought. By mid-1975, the Haitian Government estimated, 300,000 people faced starvation conditions. By mid-July, CARE, supported by AID, was feeding 120,000 in the threatened areas.[19] Because Haiti is small and close to the United States, the rescue operation was relatively simple and the Haitian people survived the famine threat with a minimal loss of life.

Food-emergency countries that are more remote than Haiti from the North American breadbasket have fared less well. Population pressure on the fragile desert ecosystem has been steadily gathering force in the African countries that border the Sahara. On the southern fringe of the Sahelian zone, a prolonged drought beginning in the late sixties and continuing into the seventies brought the deterioration of land and food supplies into painfully sharp focus. The six countries most seriously affected by the African drought—Senegal, Mauritania, Niger, Upper Volta, Chad, and Mali—together contained 22 million people, a large segment of them nomadic herdsmen wholly dependent on their cattle, goats, and camels for their livelihood. As the drought intensified, the nomads sought to sell whatever emaciated animals remained, but for countless thousands the loss of livestock was total. The animals on which they had depended directly for food and indirectly for milk, wool, and meat to exchange for basic staples in the marketplace were gone.

With no means of support and no food, people capable of eking out an existence in the harshest of environments were forced into feeding camps. The deserts were moving southward and, along with the grasslands, the nomad's traditional way of life had been destroyed, perhaps permanently. The once-proud nomads had become "ecological refugees." In all the Sahelian countries the nomads, who represent an important segment of the population in each, suffered most. Thousands made it to camps so weakened that they died before they could be revived. Many never made it to camps, perishing en route.

The Sahelian crisis had fastened its grip well before the outside world finally began to take notice in mid-1973. Many of the Sahelian people were in such desperate straits that only a massive airlift of food saved them. By the time relief arrived in the more remote areas, tens of thousands either had already died or were too weak to recover. In an appearance before a U.S. congressional committee after a tour of the Sahelian zone, Professor Michael Latham, a Cornell nutritionist, testified that the number of lives lost was probably somewhere between 100,000 and a quarter of a million; but, he said, no one will ever know for sure.[20] Some observers give lower estimates, but the human toll was enormous in any case.

To the east an equally grisly crisis was unfolding in the mountainous kingdom of Ethiopia. There, the famine became even more serious as efforts were made to keep it a secret from the outside world. One of the most costly, life-consuming cove-

92: The Twenty-Ninth Day

rups in history, the Ethiopian disaster eventually claimed an estimated two hundred thousand lives and the throne to which the late Emperor Haile Selassie, one of the world's longest-reigning monarchs, had clung for forty-seven years.[21]

Somalia fared only marginally better. At one point in early 1975, a quarter of a million Somalis swelled relief camps. During one four-month period, twelve thousand of them, mostly children, died.[22]

This period of deterioration in the seventies contrasts sharply with the preceding twenty years of food surpluses and excess production capacity. When massive famine threatened India in 1966 and 1967 following two consecutive monsoon failures, the United States responded by shipping a fifth of its wheat harvest to India two years running. But, even with the stock rebuilding of 1976 and 1977, the United States no longer has the food resources to launch such a massive relief effort without arousing inflationary fears at home. Neither does any other country—hence, the tragic rise in death rates.

Population Stabilization: A New Urgency

United Nations projections show world population increasing from the current four billion to some 10 to 16 billion before eventually leveling off.[23] From a purely demographic point of view, these projections are quite sound. But when viewed in the larger picture of ecological stresses (even those associated with current population levels), technologies, and social structures, they do not hold up. Signs of stress on the world's principal biological system—forests, fisheries, grasslands, and croplands—indicate that in many places these systems have already reached the breaking point. Expecting these systems to withstand a tripling or quadrupling of population pressures defies ecological reality.

One way to put into perspective the prospect of a doubling of the world population over the next generation, or at all, is to make a list of countries that could conceivably support twice their present numbers. (The reader is urged to do so.) Including all those countries able to meet even the most basic needs associated with population growth—food, water, and energy— the list is remarkably short. For the great majority, a doubling of population will yield ecological, economic, and political stresses that may well prove unmanageable.

The hunger-induced rise in death rates in the poorest countries during the seventies is likely to impress on governments of the affected countries the risks of continuing on the current demographic path. Now that world food stocks have been rebuilt somewhat since the early seventies, it has been widely assumed that the higher death rates were a side-effect of a temporary, self-correcting situation. But were they? Is the world likely to be able to maintain food stocks that are sufficient to avoid rises in food prices? Or will this be hindered, or even prevented, by continuing rapid population growth? If adequate food security cannot be maintained, governments of food-deficit countries may be forced to rethink population policy. Indeed, some already are doing so.

Political pressures to slow population growth mount as population-related stresses become more evident. In India, economic planners have impressed on the political leadership the virtual impossibility of raising living standards unless the population growth curve is quickly flattened. The record of the past decade has been one of running hard simply to stand still as rising world prices for oil and wheat put India on an economic treadmill.

In Mexico, one of the early manifestations of population stress was rising unemployment. Political leaders became alarmed when they realized that even the rather impressive 7 percent annual economic growth Mexico enjoyed simply was not providing enough jobs for the new entrants into the labor force. Coupled with the return to food-deficit status after the dramatic food gains during the sixties, the unemployment rate induced an abrupt turnabout in Mexican population policy. By late 1973, the government had abandoned its pro-natalist stance and launched a nationwide family-planning program.[24]

The Chinese government has demonstrated an awareness of the risks and deleterious consequences of continuing population growth in a country containing one-fifth of humanity. Anxious to preserve the meager hard-earned gains in per-capita food consumption and social services, the Chinese leadership has applied the demographic brakes vigorously.

Concern over the population problem manifests itself in various ways and at various levels in different parts of the world. In the United States, concern over continuing population growth is most acute at the local level; many American communities are now actively resisting further growth. In Japan, mounting evidence that pollution is undermining human health is generating concern among ordinary citizens and government officials alike. So, too, is Japan's growing dependence on external supplies of food, energy, and industrial raw materials. In the Netherlands, similar circumstances have helped to raise awareness of population pressures and, apparently as a consequence, to decrease the Dutch birth rate sharply. In Egypt, the leadership was jolted into implementing family-planning measures when it was calculated that the population increase in the Nile River Valley during the period the huge Aswan High Dam was under construction would totally absorb the gains in food production the dam would make possible.

Perhaps the most surprising development in thinking about population has taken place in Canada, where deepening concern about future resource supplies is influencing public discussion and opinion. Many Canadians are disturbed by the recent loss of the traditional exportable energy surplus, a loss that occurred as domestic needs soared. Agricultural planners, alarmed at the sacrifice of Canada's most fertile cropland to urban sprawl, fear the nation's exportable food surplus may also dwindle. A recent study by the Science Council of Canada suggests trying to limit the end-of-century population to 29 million, an inarguably modest increase over the current 22 million.[25] If such analyses lead a country as richly blessed with resources as Canada to further curb its comparatively modest population growth, how would similar studies influence population policy in less well-endowed countries?

The goal of national population policies has shifted in several countries during the seventies from slowing population growth to stabilizing population. Among the governments seeking zero population growth are those of India, China, Mexico, and Bangladesh. Some governments are now setting dates by which they want to achieve population stability.

Those who attended the UN Conference on Population at Bucharest in 1974 resolved that all couples have the right to plan their families and that governments must accept responsibility for ensuring that all have the means to do so. Four years have passed since the conference, but the world is far indeed from achieving that goal. In a 1977 paper, Bruce Stokes reported that "More than half of the world's couples go to bed at night unprotected from unplanned pregnancy."[26] Unfortunately, few governments and few citizens have a thorough understanding of population issues. As more governments comprehend the dynamics and consequences of population growth, more will enact effective population policies on the basis of that knowledge. More could also be expected to educate their people on the adverse effects on the immediate family when too many children are born too close together.

A few governments with a grasp of the social consequences of continuing population growth—including China, Singapore, Barbados, and Costa Rica—have launched vigorous programs to slow population growth. Others have acted, but not vigorously enough. India was one of the first countries to recognize the population problem officially, but its success in implementing effective family-planning programs has been limited. As a result, the Indian government in 1976 found itself publicly considering the use, as a last resort, of compulsory sterilization after three children.

The legislature of Maharashtra, an Indian state with fifty-four million people, passed with just one dissenting vote a bill calling for the compulsory sterilization of all males with three or more living children. Furthermore, the bill proposed compulsory abortion of any pregnancy that would result in a fourth child. The Maharashtra State Minister of Health predicted that "the rest of India will follow our lead. They are watching and waiting. All developing countries with limited resources will have to think of this matter."[27] During the national elections in March of 1977, public resentment of this heavy-handed approach to family planning contributed to the downfall of the ruling Congress Party.

The great risk is that other governments, having delayed too long in adopting family-planning programs, many also consider compulsory measures to restrict family size. Like the Indian government, they may begin to grasp the impossibility of coping with a population that multiplies ten to twenty times per century. At least a score of countries, with population growth rates of 3 percent or more per annum face a nineteenfold population increase within a century if their current rates hold. Some, such as Algeria and Mexico, already have a quarter-century of such growth behind them and a great deal of momentum as they enter the second critical quarter. If they delay too long before implementing effective family-planning programs, such countries will be forced to cope with mass migration into neighboring countries, compulsory limitation of family size, or loss of life on a scale experienced during the seventies by Bangladesh, India, and Ethiopia.

The key to the speedy adoption of appropriate population policies in the poorest countries is likely to be the realization, squarely faced, that the only genuine choice governments have is not whether population growth will slow, but how. Will it slow because birth rates fall quickly? Or will the sporadic rises in death rates witnessed during recent years continue as food-producing systems deteriorate and food scarcities intensify?

5

Energy:
The Coming Transition

Early in 1974 American motorists found themselves sitting in long lines at service stations waiting for gasoline. Some were angry and frustrated, others waited in resignation for their turn at the gasoline pump. Half a world away wheat farmers in North India sat in line at the local petrol station with five-gallon fuel cans waiting for a delivery of gasoline for their irrigation pumps. Many held their place in the queue for days, but the gasoline never came. The shortage of irrigation fuel reduced the wheat harvest by a million tons, enough to feed six million Indians for one year. For American motorists and Punjabi wheat farmers, the energy crisis was a reality.

The harsh winter weather of early 1977 found the United

States with a shortage of natural gas, a principal fuel used for both household and industrial purposes. An uncommonly severe winter coupled with the lack of an effective conservation program had let to critical shortages in several northeastern and midwestern states. As factories were forced to close, an estimated 1.8 million workers were laid off, adding to already widespread unemployment.[1] Schools were closed, and stores cut down their business hours.

These graphic illustrations of shortages in the United States and India should not be viewed as rare, random events. Rather, they should be seen as advance warnings of an unfolding crisis of vast proportions, one that is certain to shake the foundations of the global economy. The effect of energy shortages on food production in India and industrial output in the United States illustrates the link between energy supplies and economic activity.

Energy and Social Evolution

The evolution and structure of present-day society is intimately linked to the amount and form of energy we use. The technological advances that have permitted the accelerated extraction of the earth's available fuel to serve human needs have affected not only human social evolution but the human relationship to natural systems as well. Over the past generation cheap energy has shaped the global economic system and helped triple the output of goods and services. It may also have raised expectations of material consumption to unrealistic levels.

It is against this backdrop that the energy crisis of the seventies, a crisis of both supply and price, acquires significance. The world is not running out of energy, but it is running out of oil. The fivefold increase in the price of oil during this decade heralds the end of the cheap energy era. It may also signal the end of rapid growth in the consumption of material goods. Coming at a point in history when part of humanity lives in affluence while part cannot satisfy even basic physical needs, the end of cheap energy poses difficult political issues both within and among societies.

The amount of energy at our disposal shapes not only the nature of our economic system but our individual lifestyles as well. For most of the human tenure on earth, energy use was limited to the two or three thousand Calories each person consumed daily as food. The first major advance in exploiting additional sources of energy, aside from the domestication of fire itself, followed the development of agriculture when early farmers learned that they could harness animals for draft purposes. In effect, this discovery permitted them to use animals to convert roughage into a form of energy that could augment limited human muscle power. Along with irrigation and other technological advances, harnessing draft animals to work the soil enabled some peoples to produce small food surpluses and set the stage for the emergence of the first cities.

Several millennia were to pass before the next energy breakthrough, the invention of the steam engine during the nineteenth century. Capable of burning coal as well as wood, the steam engine put another major source of energy at the disposal of humans and paved the way for the emergence of contemporary industrial society. The two centuries following James Watt's successful effort to harness steam power were to bring in quick succession the internal-combustion engine, the electric generator, and the nuclear reactor.

A society with scant energy resources must of necessity live close to the land, since there is not enough energy to process and transport food as well as produce it. Conversely, energy-rich societies tend to be highly urbanized. Cheap energy, particularly the cheap oil of the postwar decades, fostered the growth of a socioeconomic system markedly different from any in the past. It has given birth to such historically novel concepts as planned obsolescence. So, too, it has permitted the evolution of "throwaway societies" whose trash heaps dwarf the Pyramids. It has contributed to the manufacture of new "needs" on Madison Avenue. It has helped sanction consumption as an end in itself—witness prices for electricity that encourage profligate consumption by reducing per-unit prices for those who consume more.

Today humanity consumes the energy equivalent of eight billion tons of coal per year, or two tons per person, not including wood and cow dung. Per capita consumption by country varies widely from a few hundred kilograms in India, Angola, or Ethiopia to as much as twelve tons in the United States.[2] Widely varying levels of energy use help explain sharply contrasting lifestyles among societies and classes. In poorer societies such as Ethiopia, few have access to electricity or own automobiles, and there is almost no heavy industry. In parts of East Africa, the Indian subcontinent, and the Andes, even traditional energy sources such as firewood and forage are now scarce. Indeed, in parts of Africa and in parts of the Andean countries of Latin America, some farmers even do without draft animals.

Middle East Dominance

As oil has become the principal energy fuel, the world has become heavily dependent on preindustrial societies of the Middle East for its fuel supplies. Unlike traditional energy sources such as firewood, water power, or forage for draft animals, which are available locally, oil reserves are heavily concentrated in one geographic region (see Table 5-1). With more than half of the world's proven reserves of oil and scarcely 2 percent of its people, the region is able to export vast quantities, supplying most of the world's import needs.

Only a small fraction of the world's more than 160 countries are self-sufficient in energy. The vast majority import some, if not most, of the energy they use. Japan imports 99 percent of all the petroleum it burns. Prior to the discovery of oil in the

Table 5-1. World Proven Crude Oil Reserves by Region, 1977

Region	Billions of Barrels	Percent of Total
Middle East	326	55
Africa	61	10
E. Europe, USSR, and China (est.)	101	17
United States	31	5
Other Western Hemisphere	36	6
Far East and Australia	19	3
Western Europe	25	4
Total	599	100

Source: *Oil and Gas Journal*, December 27, 1976.

North Sea, Western Europe bought 96 percent of its petroleum on foreign markets.

Scarcely a dozen countries control the energy lifeline of the global economy. Among these are Saudia Arabia, Iran, the United Arab Emirates, Kuwait, Iraq, Libya, Algeria, Nigeria, Venezuela, and Indonesia. Thirteen oil exporters have joined forces within the Organization of Petroleum Exporting Countries (OPEC) to form a commodity cartel.

The influence of OPEC has been bolstered by the depletion of some of the older fields. The Ploesti oil fields of Rumania no longer come close to satisfying even Rumania's needs, much less those of its European neighbors, as it once did. Gone too are the days when the United States exported oil.

U.S. dependence on imported oil is steadily increasing. Meeting more than 40 percent of U.S. needs in 1977, imports could easily exceed half of consumption by 1985. Prior to 1970, the relatively modest gap between U.S. demand and production was filled largely by oil coming from elsewhere in the Western Hemisphere, principally Venezuela. As the import gap widens, a growing share will have to come from more distant sources such as the Middle East and North Africa.[3]

As the historical transition from wood to coal to oil has progressed, and as energy consumption has risen, the energy interdependence among countries has climbed steadily. In 1925, only 14 percent of the world's fossil fuels moved in international trade channels. By the late sixties, this share had passed 30 percent, and it is now approaching 40 percent.[4]

As the share of petroleum crossing international boundaries rises, the importing economies become more vulnerable. The fourfold increase in oil prices that occurred between late 1973 and late 1975 disrupted economies everywhere. It also contributed to the deep global economic recession of 1974 and 1975; in the most severely affected countries, especially the poorer ones, the production of goods and services actually declined.

The world oil market has shifted abruptly during the seventies from a buyer's to a seller's market. Three factors are responsible. One is the realization that the world is rapidly depleting its oil reserves. The second, closely related, is the awareness by oil-exporting countries that they must get as much as they can for their dwindling oil reserves now if they are to secure their long-term economic future. Lastly, the lack of oil substitutes has contributed to the strong seller's market. This transformation of the oil market also reflects a growing conviction by both buyers and sellers that the remaining years of the oil era may be numbered.

Petroleum: A Transitory Era

The petroleum era began just over a century ago in 1859 when Colonel E. L. Drake started drilling for oil near Titusville, Pennsylvania, using a rig powered by horses. His enterprising venture was given a big boost by the Civil War, which severely reduced the supply of whale oil that was widely used at the time for cooking and as a fuel for lamps.[5] Cheap and more easily transported than coal or wood, petroleum quickly caught on as a fuel, and production increased steadily. By 1900, the oil industry had established itself on the American scene. From the turn of the century onward, U.S. petroleum production continued to grow, interrupted only by the Great Depression. But the dramatic expansion in oil production during the forties and fifties tapered off in the late sixties, and came to a halt in 1970.

After peaking at ten million barrels per day (3.6 billion per year) in 1970, U.S. oil production then began to decline, reversing a century-long trend. By 1977, it had fallen to 2.8 billion barrels per year (see Figure 5-1). The gap between continuously rising demand and plummeting production has been filled by imported oil. Although the United States can afford to import massive quantities of oil, the economic repercussions for less wealthy oil-importing countries have been severe.

The fall-off in petroleum production in the United States, until recently the world's leading oil producer, foreshadows a similar downturn at the global level. Some idea of when this

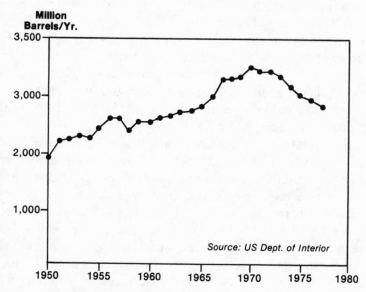

Figure 5-1. U.S. Crude Oil Production, 1950-77

drop may occur can be derived from two sets of estimates of world oil reserves—proven reserves and ultimately recoverable reserves. Proven reserves are customarily defined as those that can be recovered with current technology and prices. Ultimately recoverable reserves include allowance for new discoveries and for improvements in the technology for extracting oil through secondary and tertiary means, and are invariably much larger than proven reserves.

Proven reserves consist largely of oil that can be obtained through primary means (i.e., from natural pressure existing in oil-bearing structures). Secondary recovery involves pumping water or gas into a geological formation to maintain reservoir pressure and force the oil out. (In the United States this technique accounted for about one-third of all oil production in 1975.) Tertiary recovery involves the use of heat or chemicals to reduce the viscosity of oil, thereby increasing the amount of oil that can be recovered after primary and secondary means have been exhausted.

The estimates of reserves most widely relied upon are those produced by the *Oil and Gas Journal*, which bases its figures on consultation with both governments and oil companies. In 1976 the *Journal* estimated world proven crude oil reserves at 599 billion barrels.[6] Estimates of ultimately recoverable reserves have tended over the past decade to converge around 2,000 billion barrels (see Table 5-2).

These rather abstract global totals are more meaningful when translated into per-capita terms. Proven reserves amount to 150 barrels for each person now alive, while ultimately recoverable reserves come to 500 barrels per person. When refined, a barrel of oil will yield forty-two gallons of gasoline, fuel oil, jet fuel, and other products. The gasoline yield of the refining process is usually just under half of the total. An American with a large automobile that averages ten miles per gallon and that is driven ten thousand miles per year requires just over forty barrels of oil per year. At this rate, an individual's

Table 5-2. Estimates of Total World Ultimately Recoverable Reserves
of Crude Oil from Conventional Sources

Year	Source	Billion Barrels
1942	Pratt, Weeks & Stebinger	600
1946	Duce	400
1946	Pogue	555
1948	Weeks	610
1949	Levorsen	1500
1949	Weeks	1010
1953	MacNaughton	1000
1956	Hubbert	1250
1958	Weeks	1500
1959	Weeks	2000
1965	Hendricks (USGS)	2480
1967	Ryman (Esso)	2090
1968	Shell	1800
1968	Weeks	2200
1969	Hubbert	1350–2100
1970	Moody (Mobil)	1800
1971	Warman (BP)	1200–2000
1971	Weeks	2290
1975	Moody & Geiger	2000

Source: *Energy: Global Prospects 1985–2000.*

share of remaining oil would be exhausted in just twelve years.
This assumes, of course, that all ultimately recoverable reserves
will materialize, that the world's remaining reserves are shared
equitably, that there is no further increase in population, and
that no oil is saved for future generations.

Given the current world consumption levels and the estimates of oil reserves, it is possible to make various assumptions
concerning future consumption trends and to estimate when
all oil reserves will be exhausted. For example, if consumption
were to continue to increase at the explosive rate of 7 percent
per year as it did during the sixties, then world reserves would
dry up within twenty years. In reality, consumption is not likely
to increase this fast, so the date of exhaustion is probably
farther off.

There are two key reference points in the rapidly changing

energy situation. One is the point at which the growth in production begins to slow. The other is the point at which production begins to decline. As production begins to slow, the growth in demand may substantially outstrip production and lead to severe shortages. Both a U.S. government analysis of the world energy economy and an analysis undertaken by an international group of experts headed by Professor Carroll Wilson of MIT suggest that a serious supply-demand imbalance of energy will occur as early as 1981.[7]

In summarizing his group's findings, Professor Wilson said the world "must drastically curtail the growth of energy use and move massively out of oil into other fuels with wartime urgency. Otherwise, we face foreseeable catastrophe." He went on to say that the "end of the era of growth in oil production is probably at the most only fifteen years away."[8] U.S. Secretary of Energy James Schlesinger sounded a similar note at a meeting of the eighteen-member International Energy Agency in late 1977. Unless the Western industrial countries implement effective measures to conserve energy and to develop alternatives to oil, he warned, the United States could face "a degree of political and social unrest" even worse than in the thirties. To this he added that "on the solution of this problem rests the future of our free societies."[9]

The decline already under way in the United States will be followed by downturns in other oil-producing countries. The Soviet Union may lose its exportable surplus of oil within a matter of years, leaving Eastern Europe wholly dependent on the Middle East and other sources for all imports. An estimate made by the U.S. embassy in Djakarta indicates that if all Indonesia's future energy needs are supplied by oil and that if no new reserves of oil are found, then that country will be importing oil by 1985. While neither of these conditions is likely to materialize, this calculation does indicate that oil will not long occupy the key position in the Indonesian economy that it now does. As production begins to fall in some of the older oil fields, the pressures on other oil fields will mount. Once the process begins, a snowball effect takes hold and a market psychology of scarcity comes into force. If the alternatives to oil are not comparably cheap and abundant, then the nineties may witness not only the end of the petroleum era, but also the end of the profligate economic system it has spawned.

The sobering reality of oil depletion is only beginning to permeate public consciousness. Until recently, technology held out two promising alternatives, one of which was the extraction of oil from oil shale. Many believed that the oil that is tightly locked in oil shale or heavy tar sands could be readily extracted. But the seventies have brought discouraging setbacks that shattered this hope. The effort to develop the vast oil shale deposits in Colorado and Wyoming has been abandoned by many private companies because of the cost. So too, many firms that hoped to "mine" the Athabascan tar sands, once touted as containing more oil than the oil fields of Saudi Arabia, are shelving the notion. Only the Canadian government, using public funds, remains heavily commited to developing the tar sands. *Business Week* summed up the situation nicely when it described shale oil as "a researcher's dream and an economist's nightmare."[10]

As long as even the smallest amount of oil is produced, the depletion of reserves is inevitable. The day when the wells go dry cannot be avoided; it can only be postponed, with luck until viable alternatives are developed.

The transition to the post-petroleum era, whatever it may turn out to be, promises to be difficult. The more time available to make the transition, (i.e., to develop the technologies and make investments on a scale sufficient to maintain at least the essential economic activities), the better. If through wasteful lifestyles we hasten the transition unnecessarily, then our children will judge us harshly. Indeed, we ourselves may even live long enough to regret our wasteful ways.

Nuclear Power: A Dead-End Street?

The prospective end of the petroleum era used to be small cause for worry, for the simple reason that nuclear power was waiting in the wings. The first controlled nuclear reaction, achieved in a laboratory three years before the first atomic bomb was detonated in 1945, held out the hope that the enormous amounts of energy released in a nuclear reaction could be used to generate electricity.

The hope was a bright one. The U.S., British, French, and Soviet governments moved rapidly to translate this vast new source of energy into electrical power. By the mid-fifties, all four countries were successfully operating nuclear power plants. Today a score of countries have nuclear reactors.

Denis Hayes sums up the situation concisely: "By 1977, the world's 204 commercial reactors had a combined capacity of 94,841 megawatts of electricity—up more than tenfold in ten years. Planned additions would quickly multiply that capacity almost eightfold to 569,544 megawatts, derived from 682 reactors. By the end of the century, fifty or more countries could have a combined generating capacity of more than 2 million megawatts."[11] Hayes goes on to add that "Global nuclear development was initially spurred by the belief that fission would provide a cheap, clean, safe source of power for rich and poor alike. However, the dream of 'electricity too cheap to meter' has foundered under a heavy burden of technical, economic, and moral problems—some of which appear to be inherently unsolvable."[12]

At least six obstacles or problems beset nuclear power: the risk of a reactor meltdown or other accident; the dangers of nuclear materials falling into the hands of terrorists; the lack of a satisfactory technique for disposing of nuclear waste; the possibility that nuclear weapons will proliferate; the long-term inadequacy of fuel supplies; and the cost of nuclear power, including the costs of waste disposal and of decommissioning worn-out plants. The difficulties inherent in dealing effectively with any one of these obstacles, much less with all of them collectively, help explain why the nuclear dream is fading.

One of the earliest fears associated with the development of nuclear power was that a major catastrophe would occur. Thus far none has, and few lives have been lost. Yet the possibility of catastrophe is beyond dispute; the safety debate is about the probability. Should a major calamity involving heavy loss of life ever occur, public concern would quite likely force authorities to shut down all nuclear power plants. Under such circumstances, of course, a nuclear-based economy would collapse.

The possibility that terrorists will resort to the use of crude atomic bombs grows ever more likely. Indeed, this possibility now troubles even some traditional proponents of nuclear power such as David Lilienthal and Hans Bethe. Scarcely a day passes without news from somewhere in the world of guerrillas or political dissidents using bombs, kidnappings, or aerial hijackings to achieve political ends. Once the possibility of nuclear materials falling into the hands of terrorists becomes credible, such groups will be able to hold for ransom not merely the passengers of an airliner but the inhabitants of an entire city or the political leadership of an entire country. Such credibility will give even those who only *claim* to have "nuclear devices" potentially enormous political leverage.

Perhaps even more to be feared is the political response to the terrorist A-bomb threat. Terrorist threats could force those in power to choose between safety or even survival on one hand and individual freedom on the other. Confronted with possible annihilation, many people may well voluntarily surrender individual liberty in exchange for a stronger guarantee of protection against nuclear terrorism. Such a hard bargain could lead to the rise of police states and to degrees of surveillance and repression unknown in most societies.

While the possibility that terrorists might acquire nuclear

materials poses some profound political questions, disposing of nuclear waste raises equally profound moral questions. All radioactive materials are biologically injurious. Unlike chemical wastes, radioactive wastes cannot be neutralized, except at high cost in a high-neutron-flux process. In fact, the release of large amounts of radioactive material into the earth's ecosystem could endanger the genetic integrity of the human and other species. Even the United States, the first nuclear power, has not yet developed a strategy for waste disposal. A group of experts sponsored by the Ford Foundation declared in its 1977 report that "the United States must greatly improve the management of its rapidly growing accumulation of nuclear wastes and decide soon on the strategy for its disposal," and that "Given that radioactive waste generated by nuclear power plants may emit dangerous amounts of radiation for up to 500,000 years, the long-term consequences must also be considered."[13] The moral question at issue is whether our generation has the right to risk the health and well-being of future generations in order to satisfy its own needs.

The close relationship between nuclear power and nuclear weapons poses a particularly thorny problem at the international level. The Ford-sponsored study had this to say: "In our view, the most serious risk associated with nuclear power is the attendant increase in the number of countries that have access to technology, materials, and facilities leading to a nuclear weapons capability." The spread of nuclear power almost inevitably means that nuclear weapons will pass into more and more hands. At some point, the social risk associated with the proliferation of nuclear weapons will no doubt exceed any possible benefits associated with nuclear power.

The adequacy of fuel supplies for nuclear reactors is also questionable. For many years Westinghouse, one of the two principal vendors of nuclear reactors, sold fuel contracts to supply uranium oxide along with its reactors. In September of 1975, it announced that it could no longer honor its contracts because its uranium supplies could not cover its commitments.[14] (Spot prices at the time were far above those specified in the contract.) Between the early and middle seventies, uranium prices climbed fivefold from 8 to 40 dollars per pound.[15] Proven world uranium reserves are not extensive and are concentrated in even fewer hands than the exportable supplies of oil. The principal suppliers are the United States, the Soviet Union, South Africa, and Australia. Moreover, Australia is an uncertain and reluctant supplier; its labor unions have in the past refused to handle uranium because they believe its use constitutes a threat to political stability and to the environment.

In addition to the political and moral problems surrounding nuclear power, its economic viability is now being questioned. Donald Cook, a leader in the electric utility industry and board chairman of American Electric Power, the largest U.S. utility, said in the fall of 1975 that "an erroneous conception of the economics of nuclear power" sent U.S. utilities "down the wrong road," and that "The economics that were projected but never materialized—and never will materialize—looked so good that the companies couldn't resist it."[16] Cook was not alone in reading the economic handwriting on the wall. Hayes reports that "Annual United States reactor orders, which reached a peak of 36 in 1973, declined to 27 in 1974, and plummeted to 4 in 1975," and that "Cancellations and deferrals outpaced new reactor orders in the United States by more than 25 to one in 1975."[17] The net effects of these decisions by utilities amounted to a moratorium on the expansion of nuclear power.

In early 1977 the results of an international survey of nuclear power published in the *Economist* showed that the timetables for nuclear power "are in shambles."[18] The Energy Research and Development Administration (ERDA) has dramatically lowered its projections of nuclear power capacity for the year

2000. In 1974, ERDA projected that nuclear-generated electricity for the end of the century would reach 1,250,000 megawatts. In July 1976 these estimates were revised downward to 450,000 to 800,000 megawatts. Two months later the figures were further reduced to 380,000 to 620,000 megawatts.[19] In August 1977 West German Minister of Technology Hans Mattholfer startled outsiders when he predicted that his country would adopt a five-year moratorium on nuclear power-plant construction.[20]

As nuclear plants age, corrosion, fuel leaks, component fatigue, and other problems of aging occur. The time reactors must be shut down for repairs appears to increase with both age and size. In the United States, commercial reactors operated at 42 percent of capacity in 1973, 48 percent in 1974, and 45 percent in 1975. Similarly, the *Japan Times* has reported that, on the average, one-half of Japan's reactors had been shut down every day for some reason or another during a six month period in 1975. In addition, since older reactors contain high levels of radioactivity, repairs are slow. Frequently, great numbers of workers have to participate in the repair of a single plant so that no single worker is exposed to the maximum permissible radiation levels. Finally, the worn-out nuclear plant must be dismantled—an exceedingly costly operation, the expense of which is not being borne by those deriving the current benefits from the reactor.

The obstacles discussed above represent a formidable array of barriers that will, at a minimum, slow the spread of nuclear power. They raise serious questions as to whether nuclear power will ever fulfill the mission its proponents set for it. It may well be that the use of nuclear power, which was to replace fossil fuels, will reach its zenith even before the worldwide use of fossil fuels peaks.

The Case for Conservation

The prospective downturn in world oil production some time within the next fifteen years or so provides a compelling argument for a crash effort to conserve energy. Every barrel of oil saved buys additional time for the global economy to make the transition from oil and gas to renewable energy sources. Opportunities for conserving energy appear most impressive in the United States, where current lifestyles could be more or less maintained with only half the energy now used. Stated otherwise, more than half of U.S. energy use is wasted.[21] Indeed, the United States wastes more fuel than the poorest one-half of humanity uses, and international pressures to conserve this wasted energy will mount as world petroleum reserves dwindle.

The critical dimension of the energy transition is time. The essential question is how the world will produce food, heat homes, power factories, and transport people and goods as petroleum production wanes. Even if an ambitious program to harness renewable energy sources were already under way, energy crunches would still occur as petroleum fell off, since bringing new energy sources into large-scale commercial use takes years or decades.

The overriding rationale for conserving energy in general and petroleum in particular—to buy time—is not the sole rationale. As fuel costs rise, so do returns on investments in energy conservation, and investment opportunities exist at both the individual and corporate levels. In the United States, for example, one of the most profitable investments a homeowner can make is in home insulation—the savings in heating costs (and, where needed, in air-conditioning costs) will often equal the original outlay within three to five years. In addition to the immediate savings on fuel, property values rise when home insulation or solar collectors are installed, since home fuel bills fall. Few other investments offer comparable payoffs.

One of the least visible energy wastes is in the mismatch that often exists between energy sources and end uses. Most of the energy used is low-grade energy. Amory Lovins reports, "In the United States today, about 58 percent of all energy at the point of end use is required as heat. . . ." Although about three-fifths of this total is used at temperatures below the boiling point of water, it is often produced with high-grade (very high temperature) heat in the form of electricity. Electricity satisfies 13 percent of U.S. end-use needs, but it accounts for 29 percent of U.S. fossil fuel use. Lovins concludes, "Plainly we are using premium fuels and electricity for many tasks for which their high energy quality is superfluous, wasteful, and expensive. . . ." Further, "Where we want only to create temperature differences of tens of degrees, we should meet the need with sources whose potential is tens or hundreds, not with a flame temperature of thousands or a nuclear reaction temperature equivalent to trillions—like cutting butter with a saw."[22]

Opportunities to save energy and money saturate virtually every human economic activity. But few appreciate the profitability of energy conservation. Potential buyers and builders could benefit enormously from access to economic analyses that incorporate both current energy costs and those projected over the estimated lifetime of a home, an office building, or an automobile. If home builders and home buyers understood the long-term costs of electricity or fossil fuels better, they could make wiser investments—investments that would include far more insulation and solar collectors.

The cheapest energy available today in the advanced industrial societies is waste energy. A given investment in conservation will produce far more energy than a like investment in new energy sources. Stated in terms of oil, the investment in conservation that would save a barrel of oil per day is scarcely half that required to add an additional barrel per day of production capacity. At a time of capital scarcity, it makes little sense for oil companies to invest heavily in new production capacity when far less spent on capturing waste energy would yield better returns.[23]

The automobile will increasingly become the target of energy-conservation efforts. While the world automobile population has grown to such a point that rush-hour traffic jams are daily occurrences in cities the world over, the years of its continuing growth are numbered. If people exercise foresight, the automobile population will probably begin to decline well before petroleum production does. If they do not, they may end up investing in cars for which there will be no fuel. Indeed, some of the more durable cars now being marketed may still be on the road when oil production begins to fall. As this reality begins to penetrate public consciousness, sales may begin to drop. Yet, people's attachment to their cars will die hard. In the United States, where the love affair with the automobile resembles a marriage, a population of 215 million people own more than 100 million licensed motor vehicles. Every American could go on a Sunday drive without anyone sitting in the back seat.

American automobile owners will soon have to brace themselves for a jolt: gasoline prices are scheduled to rise steeply in the years ahead as domestic prices move toward the international level. Although the price of a gallon of gasoline in the United States rose from less than forty cents to sixty-three cents between 1972 and 1977, it is still far below the price charged in the United Kingdom, West Germany, or Italy, where stiff taxes raise prices and encourage conservation (see Table 5-3). Indeed, in both the United Kingdom and Italy the tax on gasoline exceeds the cost of the gasoline itself. As U.S. gas prices approach those prevailing in other industrial societies, frugality in gasoline use will become a necessity as well as a virtue.

Oil-exporting countries have repeatedly argued that world oil prices should be raised to encourage conservation. Even though countries such as Iran currently have a wealth of oil,

Table 5-3. Gasoline Taxes and Retail Prices in U.S. Dollars per Gallon
(Regular Grade), 1977

	Tax	Price (incl. tax)
France	1.01	1.67
West Germany	.84	1.40
Italy	1.48	2.05
Japan	.51	1.67
U.K.	.55	1.09
U.S.	.12	.63

Source: U.S. Department of Energy.

their leaders foresee the day when supplies will be exhausted, and they are loath to squander oil for nonessential uses.

Environmentalists, joining with oil suppliers, economists, and scientists, argue persuasively for the conservation of dwindling energy supplies. The production of energy from any source disrupts the environment to some extent:the more energy used, other things being equal, the greater the pollution of air and water and the more land, water, and other resources claimed by the energy sector.

Among the many reasons for conserving energy, the most compelling one is that the world does not yet have adequate alternative sources of energy clearly in sight as the liquid fossil-fuel era closes. If the transition to the post-petroleum era is to be reasonably smooth, every effort must be made to stretch remaining oil reserves as far as possible. Yet from the way many adults in the more affluent societies live, one could easily get the impression that all were childless, so little is their commitment to saving energy for the next generation.

Returning to Coal

During the twelfth century, peasants in northeast England discovered that the hard black rocks found along the coast would burn. The search for a supply of these "sea coales" eventually led to the discovery of outcroppings of coal and later to the excavation of vast subterranean deposits of this hot-burning rock. In the eight centuries that have intervened since its discovery in England, coal has been mined continuously.

A chemically bound form of solar energy, coal was the foundation upon which early industrial society was built. With its discovery, society had at its command a vast new source of energy to do its work. As more and more uses for coal were devised, energy use per capita edged upward in the industrial societies. Historically, coal production increased rather gradually. By 1900 it had reached 700 million tons per year, and by 1915 it had reached 1.3 billion tons.[24] Growth then began to slow as petroleum came into use in the western industrial societies. But after World War II and the rapid expansion in electrification and industrialization outside the Western industrial countries, production again surged upward.

Although coal was the principal source of fuel in early industrial societies, oil had several attractive features. It is easier to transport, cheaper to extract, and relatively clean burning. As the twentieth century progressed, oil captured a growing market share, until by 1970, oil rivaled coal as an energy source. Since then oil has become more popular than coal, but as the date approaches when world oil production will begin to fall, coal's value is being reassessed. Recognizing that world coal reserves are several times larger than oil reserves, governments are beginning to encourage the substitution of coal for oil and natural gas wherever it is feasible, but especially in the generation of electricity.

While petroleum can be used to power tractors, trucks, cars, and other motor vehicles, coal must be converted into synthetic liquid fuel before it can be used in motor vehicles. Consequently, advanced coal conversion research is now receiving priority attention in government-financed energy programs. Progress to date has been slow, and all indications are that the production of synthetic fuel, while it has been technologically feasible for decades, will be very costly. If its cost is prohibitive, the private automobile could soon become far less common than it is today.

World coal production currently totals 2.7 billion tons, just under 30 percent of world energy production—8.16 billion tons in coal equivalent.[25] Although the Soviet Union and North America possess the bulk of the world's coal reserves, coal is found in quantity everywhere except Latin America and Africa. Thus the supply and availability of coal bode well for its expanded use. Other factors, however, may constrain coal use. Strip-mining of coal may be prohibited in rich agricultural regions such as the American Midwest. The water required in mining operations and in land reclamation after strip mining may not be available in some locales. Moreover, health officials worry about the dangerous air pollution associated with the burning of coal.

The problems that greatly expanded coal use could entail are legion, but the most formidable may be the buildup of carbon dioxide in the earth's atmosphere as discussed earlier. Fear of the effect of carbon-dioxide buildup on the earth's heat balance alone should prompt governments to consider energy sources with less troubling impacts—and to appreciate the ecological soundness of solar energy in its many forms.

Turning to the Sun

Prior to the fossil-fuel era, the sun provided directly, in one form or another, all the energy people used. Even today, at the peak of the fossil-fuel era, renewable energy sources derived from natural systems and cycles powered by the sun account for about one-fifth of world energy use.

The sun's energy can be captured either directly or indirectly. Some indirect means, such as using firewood for heating and cooking, have been used for hundreds of thousands of years. Some direct means, such as using photovoltaic cells that convert sunlight into electricity, are ultra-modern. Aside from direct sunlight, which can be captured either with solar collectors or through photosynthesis, the other principal solar sources are water power and wind power.

Ancient though the use of firewood is, this "poor man's oil" is still the principal fuel for close to a third of mankind. According to a United Nations study, wood accounts for three-fourths of all energy used in East, Central, and West Africa. In South and Southeast Asia, the firewood share ranges between 40 and 50 percent.[26] World Bank economist P. D. Hendersen estimates India's annual firewood use at 130 million tons or about 180 kilograms per person. Henderson writes that "India's forests should be counted as an energy resource. Unfortunately, it seems probable that they are becoming gravely depleted because of the past and present extent of felling firewood."[27]

Industrial countries, too, are using wood for energy. Sweden obtains some 7 percent of its energy from wood.[28] Rising fuel bills are causing Americans, particularly those living in rural areas, to return to the use of woodburning stoves and fireplaces. But while oil and wood reserves are both being depleted simultaneously, the latter can, with proper management, be restored, while the former cannot.

One of the simplest uses of sunlight is to heat water and buildings. Solar collectors used to heat water are highly efficient and in many situations are already economically competitive with traditional energy sources. As the price of oil continues to rise and as mass production of solar collectors reduces their cost further, they will find more buyers. A study sponsored by the U.S. government reported in late 1976 that solar heating can now compete economically with electricity (although not with oil and gas) in the heating of newly built, well insulated, one-family houses throughout the country.[29] As of early 1977, an estimated two million solar water heaters had been sold in Japan.[30] Solar water-heating units are also being marketed on a significant scale in Israel, Australia, and the United States.

The use of direct sunlight to heat buildings was well understood by the ancients, as evidenced by the building designs of
the Pueblos and of the Indus civilization at Mohenjo Daro.
The heating and cooling systems in these structures were passive systems: they relied solely on a building's design and on its
orientation to the sun. In contrast, the more complex modern
solar heating and cooling systems rely on fans, air ducts, and
heat exchangers. In this relatively new field of technological
endeavor, there is ample room for improvement in the early
designs. Even so, recent U.S. studies indicate, solar heating and
cooling is fast becoming competitive with traditional heating
systems.

One of the more novel techniques for harnessing solar
energy is through solar thermal power plants. The "power
tower," which consists of a large field of mirrors focused on
a boiler supported on a tower, utilizes mirrors that can be
adjusted to the angle of the sun and that focus an intense
amount of energy on a boiler. The boiler, in turn, generates
high-pressure steam, which powers a turbine that produces
electricity.

The French linked a small prototype of a thermal power
plant into the national electricity grid in January 1977.[31] Two
thermal power plants of a much larger scale are now under
construction in the southwestern United States. Some U.S.
utilities are planning to combine thermal power plants with
existing gas- or coal-fired power plants, using the existing generators, turbines, and condensers for both. When the sun is
shining, the steam would be generated with concentrated sunlight; at other times fossil fuels would be burned.

One of the first forms of solar energy to be harnessed me-
chanically was water power. While the Romans used water
wheels to grind grain, water power in the modern era has been
converted into electrical power, a highly mobile form of energy. Although using water power may mean constructing
reservoirs that could inundate good farm land, displace wildlife,

or force humans to resettle, water power is nonetheless among the cleanest sources of electricity available.

In some areas of the world, the hydroelectric power potential has been thoroughly exploited; in others, it has not been tapped at all. Virtually all the electricity used in Egypt, Ghana, and Paraguay is generated by water power from such great rivers as the Nile, Volta, and Paraná. But most of the potential of the Mekong River system remains untouched, and the hydroelectric potential of the rivers originating in the Himalayas has scarcely been assessed, much less developed. Indeed, Nepal could be a major exporter of electricity, helping to electrify the villages of northern India.

Hydroelectric sources satisfy at least part of the electricity needs of most countries.[32] A few, such as the Netherlands, have no hydroelectricity or the potential for such, while Paraguay (richly endowed with rapidly descending rivers that produce more electricity than it needs), sells its surplus to neighboring Brazil.

Besides possessing large-scale hydroelectric projects like those found on every other continent, China has installed tens of thousands of small generators in local streams.[33] Although the share of electricity so generated is small, losses in transmission are also small, since the power is used locally. A U.S. Army Corps of Engineers study of the U.S. potential for small-scale hydroelectric generation, prepared at the request of President Carter, uncovered some forty-eight thousand untapped dam sites in the United States. Fitted with turbines, these existing dam sites—including recreation reservoir dams, flood-control dams, water-supply dams, irrigation dams, and old mill sites—would produce nearly as much electricity as currently generated from nuclear power at a cost far lower than that for fossil-fuel–burning power-plants.[34] In addition, environmental disruption would be negligible, since these dams are already in place.

Wind power, like water power, can be utilized directly by

mechanical means or indirectly through the generation of electricity. The technology for capturing the energy in wind has been known for centuries. The picturesque windmills that dot the Dutch countryside are legendary, and the windmills of sixteenth-century Spain found their way into Cervantes's *Don Quixote*. During the early twentieth century, windmills were commonplace in rural America, where they were used primarily for pumping water for both household and barn use. Once numbering in the millions in the Great Plains, they are still used rather extensively to pump water for cattle at well sites on remote rangelands.

As the need to develop alternatives to oil has grown pressing in recent years, engineers have begun to see wind not only as a direct source of energy to be harnessed for pumping water or grinding grain but also as a means of generating electricity. Dr. Wendell Hewson, Chairman of the Department of Atmospheric Sciences at Oregon State University, estimates that the wind contains twenty times more available energy than hydropower does.[35]

Hewson's enthusiasm for wind power is shared by Dr. William Heronemous of the University of Massachusetts, who envisages farms of giant windmills. Such a windmill farm could have perhaps twenty towers, each of which would stand 125 feet tall, be equipped with 200-foot blades to catch the wind, and could supply the electrical needs of a small town.[36] An early prototype erected with funds from the U.S. Energy Research and Development Administration is now operating in Sandusky, Ohio.

Wind power can also be put to work on a small scale by individuals. Wind generators for homes can be purchased for from four thousand to ten thousand dollars. As Congressman Henry Reuss of Wisconsin has suggested, homes with wind generators could be tied to large electrical grids with two-way linkages.[37] Whenever the electricity produced by a home generator exceeded that required by the homeowner, it could be

fed into the system and be metered and credited to the individual's electricity account. During lulls, the home system would
draw from the larger grid. A New York tenement with a small
wind-powered generator is already feeding surplus electricity
into the grid of Consolidated Edison, the local electrical utility.[38]

Wind power does have drawbacks. No more predictable
than the winds themselves, it would entail the use of electrici-
ty-storage systems or coal-fired generators as backup measures.
Its use is also hard to justify economically where air currents
are weak. However, a large part of the United States—the
Rocky Mountain States, the Great Plains, New England, and
the East Coast—does have wind power potential. In addition,
wind power does not pollute either air or water.

For coastal homes and communities, tidal power, which can
be utilized as the tides flow into and out of partially enclosed
coastal basins, represents a potentially economical energy
source. The world's first tidal-electric plant, which consists of
twenty-four units with a generating capacity of 10,000 kilowatts each, began operations in the LaRance estuary in France
in 1966. Another prime site for the development of tidal-
electric power is in the Passamaquoddy Bay on the U.S.-
Canadian boundary in the Bay of Fundy. Long considered but
as yet unbuilt, the plant proposed for this location would have
thirty generators of 10,000 kilowatts capacity each and would
be slightly larger than the French prototype.[39]

Tidal power does not represent a large source of untapped
power, but as geologist King Hubbert points out, there are
"many social advantages and few disadvantages to the utilization of tidal power wherever tidal and topographical factors
combine to make this practicable."[40] The technology for converting moving water into electricity is essentially the same as
that traditionally used in hydroelectric installations. Thus, little
new research is needed to exploit tidal power.

An even more novel source of oceanic energy is that embodied in waves. Of all the potentially renewable energy sources, wave motion may be the least studied. Like tidal power, wave power can be used to operate electrical generators; but the mechanism for capturing wave power is somewhat more complex than that used to capture tidal power. At present the British, ideally situated as an island country, are in the forefront of efforts to convert wave power into electricity.

One energy source receiving public notice of late is the solar energy captured by plants. An estimated o.1 percent of all the solar energy striking the earth is captured by plants through photosynthesis. Roughly half of this energy is used by the plants for their metabolism, leaving one-half in plant materials that humans can use. The energy embodied in the earth's biomass is estimated at roughly fifteen to twenty times the amount of all commercial energy used in the world today.[41] Some of this, of course, is found in the oceans, where it is not readily accessible.

One form of biological energy that has traditionally been wasted in industrial societies is waste itself. The organic material that composes a large share of urban garbage is combustible, although it is seldom uniform enough to yield a steady flow of heat. Yet, in cities like St. Louis, where a seventy-million-dollar plant has been constructed to burn the city's garbage along with local coal, waste-disposal problems are being solved as energy for electricity is being created.[42]

Still another form of organic waste that contains a valuable energy component is cow dung. An estimated sixty-eight million tons is used directly as fuel each year in India, much as buffalo chips were burned by the early settlers in the U.S. Great Plains.[43] However, key nutrients that could be used as fertilizer are lost in direct burning, and much of the energy resulting from burning in open fires is wasted. A more efficient approach is to convert the cow dung and other organic wastes into methane through anaerobic fermentation, which leaves a rich organic residue that can then be used as fertilizer. Small biogas plants employing this process and designed for local use are becoming increasingly popular in several Asian countries: China has an estimated 4.3 million biogas plants in operation.[44] Interest in biogas plants at the family and village levels in India has expanded sharply since the 1973 oil-price rise.

The U.S. Federal Power Commission has granted an Oklahoma company permission to use interstate pipelines to market annually 820 million cubic feet of gas produced from feedlot waste.[45] Some studies indicate that U.S. feedlots with a thousand or more head of cattle can profitably invest in a methane-generation plant, while other more optimistic studies indicate that methane production might even be economical for herds of a hundred. If so, many of the nation's dairy herds could produce gas along with milk.

An indirect source of solar energy with almost endless possibilities is the energy crop. Although tree-farming for production of lumber, wood pulp, or firewood accounts for only a minuscule share of the world's forest products, it is well established in some areas such as the southeastern United States. Kelp, which grows rapidly on nutrients available in the ocean, can be converted into methane; and a U.S. Naval Research project on the West Coast is experimenting with oceanic kelp production.[46]

At least one country plans to produce organic materials for conversion into alcohol for use as automobile fuel. Allen Hammond writes in *Science* that "The Brazilian Government has launched a bold program to replace much of that country's imported oil with ethyl alcohol produced from sugar cane and other crops." The admittedly ambitious goal of producing enough ethanol to supply one-fifth of its gasoline needs by 1980 rests on the Brazilian government's proposal to build seventy new alcohol distilleries and to plant an additional 500,000 hectares to sugar cane. Brazil's plan to obtain nearly all its automotive fuel from alcohol by 2000 makes it one of the few countries to have charted a path to the post-petroleum era.[47]

Brazilian scientists and government officials are now debating the relative merits of sugar cane versus manioc (also known as cassava) as the raw material from which to distill alcohol. Sugar cane produces vast quantities of energy per acre, but since it is a seasonal crop that must be quickly processed, sugar distilleries could operate less than half of each year. Manioc would provide a steady year-round supply of raw material for the distilleries, but it lacks the photosynthetic efficiency of sugar cane. In either case, only 2 percent of Brazil's cropland, *Science* reports, would be sufficient to produce enough ethanol to replace the imported petroleum that now accounts for the bulk of national automotive fuel consumption.

As efforts to reduce dependence on imported oil gain momentum, different countries will look to different substitutes. Countries situated in the higher latitudes are favored with wind resources; mountainous countries have falling water; tropical countries can produce organic materials for fuel throughout the year, and countries in desert areas have an abundance of sunlight. The exploitation of indigenous energy resources may lead to a new self-reliance and a new security of energy supply. It may also lead to a far greater diversity of energy sources than exist today. According to Denis Hayes, "Brazil's large ethanol program, India's gobar gas plants, and the Middle East's growing fascination with solar electric technologies can all bode well for the future of renewable energy sources."[48]

That the human energy future is fraught with difficulty there is no doubt. Oil is being rapidly depleted, nuclear power may never materialize, and the heavy use of coal may lead to unacceptable climatic changes. Charles Hitch, President of Resources for the Future, asks in the annual report: "Are the hazards of coal . . . any less than those of nuclear fission? The more deeply I look at both coal and fission—our only competitive present options—the more I am convinced we should not rely on either of them for any longer than necessary. They present a no-win choice."[49]

Clearly, there is no single well-defined path to a post-petroleum, potentially non-nuclear world. While countries can and should exchange knowledge and share technology, it is clear that each will have to chart its own transition. Energy strategies should reflect the mix of indigenous energy sources, both those already existing and those that can be developed. For more affluent countries such as the United States, Canada, or Japan, curbing energy waste may be the cheapest way to obtain energy. In developing countries, national reforestation efforts may be central to any effective transition to alternative sources. Most transition plans will likely embody a variety of efforts designed to eliminate waste energy, to improve the energy efficiency of all economic sectors, and to develop the numerous sources of renewable energy.

6

The Food Prospect

The world food economy has undergone a basic transformation during the seventies. Not only did the world have huge surplus stocks and excess production capacity at the beginning of the decade, but it also appeared that both would be around for a long time to come. Suddenly in 1972 and 1973, they disappeared and the whole world was struggling to make it from one harvest to the next. Global food insecurity was greater than at any time since the war-torn years immediately following World War II.

Although grain stocks have been partially rebuilt in the late seventies, the global balance between the supply and demand for food remains delicate. The precariousness of this balance is illustrated by the extreme sensitivity of commodity prices to weather reports. The forecast of rain in western Kansas can send wheat-futures prices down the daily limit on the Chicago Board of Trade. A report that the Indian monsoon has started three weeks later than usual can send wheat prices up the limit. When the balance of supply and demand is so delicate, a crop shortfall in a key producing country can set off a wave of global inflation. In poor countries, where rising food prices can push death rates upward, it can also have a demographic impact.

Most of the factors contributing to the transformation of the world food economy are inherent in efforts to expand food production in a world where the four basic biological systems are under stress, where returns on some agricultural inputs are diminishing, and where land is inequitably distributed. Systemic stresses are reflected in the decline of the fish catch, the encroachment of deserts on farmland, and widespread soil erosion (especially in Third World countries). The growing scarcity of firewood in the countryside of the Third World is forcing more and more villagers to burn the cow dung they once used to fertilize their crops.[1]

The Past Quarter-Century

The third quarter of this century saw unprecedented gains in world food output. Between 1950 and 1975, the world grain harvest nearly doubled, climbing from 685 million tons to 1.35 billion tons.[2] At any other time in history such an advance would have meant more for all. Unfortunately, population growth also expanded at a record rate during this period, increasing by almost two-thirds.

Worldwide, per-capita grain production increased some 31 percent from 251 kilograms (1 kg. = 2.2 lbs.) in 1950 to 328 kilograms in 1971 (see Figure 6-1). Despite the return to use of idled U.S. cropland during the seventies, world production in 1977 averaged only 324 kilograms per persons. As the seven-

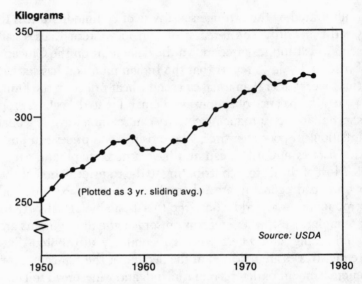

**Figure 6-1. World Grain Production Per Person,
1950-77**

ties unfolded, farmers were hard pressed to keep pace with the growth in human numbers. Fishermen were finding it even more difficult. The world fish catch per capita peaked in 1970, a year before the postwar rise in per capita grain production was interrupted. Reaching a high of eighteen kilograms per capita, it has fallen 11 percent since then.[3]

These global food averages conceal wide variation in performance by individual countries. Those governments that have combined sound agricultural and population policies have realized impressive gains in per-capita food consumption. Others have managed both so poorly that food production per person has fallen precipitously. Between 1950 and 1975, per-capita grain production fell by half in Algeria and by a third in Honduras. During the same period, per-capita grain production in the Ivory Coast nearly doubled, and in China it rose by more than 20 percent.[4]

Throughout most of the period since World War II, the world had two major food reserves: stocks of grain held by the principal grain-exporting countries and cropland idled under farm programs in the United States. Some 20 million hectares out of a total U.S. cropland base of 140 million hectares was held out of production to support prices.[5] Together, grain stockpiles and the U.S. cropland reserve provided security for all humankind, a cushion against any imaginable food disasters.

As recently as early 1972, this dual reserve seemed more than adequate for the foreseeable future, but then the growth in global demand for food began to outstrip production. Adverse weather brought the longer-term deterioration in the food situation into public view. Food reserves disappeared almost overnight.

In 1961, the combination of reserve grain stocks in exporting countries and the production equivalent of the idled U.S. cropland equaled 112 days of world grain consumption. In 1969 they totaled 93 days. Shortly thereafter they began to fall precipitously—to 60 days in 1972 and to 39 days in 1973 (see Figure 6-2). All of the idled cropland was released for production by 1974, entirely eliminating this portion of the reserve.

In 1976 the rarity of simultaneous record grain harvests in three of four leading food producing countries—the United States, the Soviet Union, and India—led to a modest rebuilding of stocks for 1977. An average or better harvest in 1977 further contributed to stock rebuilding, raising reserves for 1978 to the equivalent of 54 days of consumption. But even this exceedingly encouraging development guarantees only a minimal level of food security. Far less than the margin of 90 to 110 days that prevailed in the early 1960s, the reserves are below those held in 1972, when poor harvests in the Soviet Union, India, and several smaller countries wiped out the world's food surplus so quickly.

The decision in 1972 by Soviet political leaders to offset crop

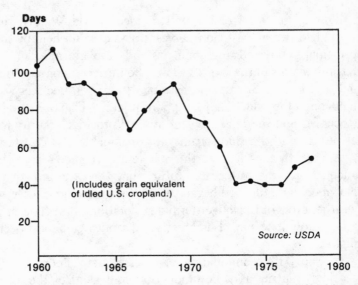

Figure 6-2. World Grain Reserves as Days of World Consumption, 1960-78

shortfalls with imports has injected another element of instability into the world food economy. Aside from the additional pressures on exportable grain supplies, the vast year-to-year fluctuations in the Soviet grain harvest sometimes exceed the annual gains in the world grain crop. Wide swings in the size of the Soviet harvest that were once absorbed entirely within the country must now be absorbed elsewhere. The Soviet decision to import may not be irreversible, but neither will it be easily turned around. It has facilitated the expansion of Soviet livestock herds and poultry flocks, which has in turn raised consumer expectations and appetites.

Yet another source of global food insecurity and instability in the mid-seventies is the near-total dependence of the entire world on one region—North America—for its exportable food supplies. Since the Great Plains wheat-growing regions of the two countries are affected by the same climatic cycles, complete reliance on these two countries is even riskier than it first seems.

The high costs of food-price instability take many forms—economic, political, and social. Consumers, particularly the poor, obviously suffer. Most families cannot easily adjust to wide fluctuations in food prices. Nor can producers easily decide how much to plant and how much to invest in agricultural inputs when prices fluctuate constantly. When grain prices soar, livestock and poultry producers get trapped in tight temporary binds that can drive the less financially secure into bankruptcy.

Violent vacillations in food prices complicate economic planning for governments too. Unstable food markets wreak havoc with foreign-exchange budgets, particularly those of countries heavily dependent on food imports. They also undermine efforts to combat inflation. Indeed, soaring food prices have contributed heavily to the global double-digit inflation of the mid-seventies.

Food insecurity derives not so much from production failures as from the relentless growth in demand. Virtually all countries with falling per-capita food output are those with populations multiplying at the rate of fifteen- to twentyfold per century. The record global growth in demand for food, for some 30 million additional tons of grain per year in good weather or bad, is fueled both by the unyielding growth of population and by growing affluence, with the former accounting for two-thirds or more of the annual growth. Each year the world's farmers and fishermen, already straining to feed some 4 billion people, must attempt to feed 64 million more people.[6] Each day 178,000 new faces appear at the breakfast table.

Since consumption per person remained close to the subsistence level during most of human history, population growth long generated nearly all growth in food demand. Only since World War II has rising affluence become an important factor at the global level. In countries such as West Germany, where population growth has ceased, and in Japan, where population growth is negligible compared with income growth, increases in food consumption derive almost entirely from income rises.

At the opposite end of the spectrum are the poorer countries such as India, in which per-capita incomes are rising by a pittance, if at all, and in which population accounts for almost all growth in food consumption. In Brazil, the rapid population and economic growth of the past decade have together created one of the most rapid overall increases in demand ever experienced in any country. Despite its food-production potential, Brazil has become one of the Western Hemisphere's largest cereal importers.

In the poorer countries, the average person can get only about 180 kilograms of grain per year—about a pound per day. With so little to go around, nearly all grain must be consumed directly if minimal energy needs are to be met. But as incomes rise, so do grain-consumption levels. In the wealthier industrial societies such as the United States and the Soviet Union, the average person consumes four-fifths of a ton of grain per year. Of this, only 90 to 140 kilograms is eaten directly as bread, pastries, and breakfast cereals; most is consumed indirectly as meat, milk, and eggs.[7]

In effect, wealth enables individuals to move up the biological food chain. Thus, the average Russian or American uses roughly four times the land, water, and fertilizer used by an Indian, a Colombian, or a Nigerian. (This ratio is not likely to widen appreciably, since the lower limit on consumption is established by the survival level and the upper limit by the human digestive system's capacity to consume animal protein.)

The dominant change in dietary habits since midcentury has been the dramatic increase in the consumption of livestock products among the affluent in both rich and poor countries. This trend has been most pronounced in the United States, where consumption of beef and poultry has more than doubled over the past generation. In the northern tier of industrial countries—stretching eastward from Britain and Ireland and including Scandinavia, Western Europe, Eastern Europe, the Soviet Union, and Japan—dietary patterns compare roughly with those of the United States a generation ago. The demand for livestock products is rising with incomes, but few nations can meet this growth in demand using only indigenous resources. Most must instead rely at least partly upon imported livestock products or else import feedgrains and soybeans to produce these products.

The North American Breadbasket

Prior to World War II, all geographic regions except Western Europe exported some grain. North America was not the only exporter or even the leading one (see Table 6-1). Both Eastern Europe, including the Soviet Union, and Latin America were major exporters, the latter exporting even more grain than North America. But following World War II the pattern of world grain trade changed beyond recognition. Asia developed a massive deficit, most of it accounted for by Japan, China, and India. Africa, Latin America, and Eastern Europe (including the USSR) also became food-deficit regions. Traditionally dependent on imported grain, only Western Europe remained

Table 6-1. The Changing Pattern of World Grain Trade[1]

Region	1934–38	1948–52	1960	1970	1976[2]
	(MILLION TONS)				
North America	+ 5	+23	+39	+56	+94
Latin America	+ 9	+ 1	0	+ 4	− 3
Western Europe	−24	−22	−25	−30	−17
E. Europe and USSR	+ 5	—	0	0	−27
Africa	+ 1	0	− 2	− 5	−10
Asia	+ 2	− 6	−17	−37	−47
Australia and N.Z.	+ 3	+ 3	+ 6	+12	+ 8

[1] Plus sign indicates net exports; minus sign, net imports.
[2] Preliminary estimates of fiscal year data.
Source: Derived from FAO and USDA data and author's estimates.

relatively stable through the period. Its imports rarely moved outside the twenty-to-thirty-million-ton range.

Dependence on North American food has climbed sharply during the seventies. The list of food-deficit countries has lengthened until today it reads like a UN roster, encompassing most of the world. Those countries with significant exportable surpluses can be numbered on the fingers of one hand. The United States and Canada exported 56 million tons of grain in 1970, but by 1976 exports had climbed to 94 million tons. North American farmers now produce a surplus sufficient to feed nearly all of India's 600 million people or half of the Soviet Union's 250 million at their much higher consumption levels.

North America today has a near monopoly of the world's exportable grain supplies, a situation without precedent. The reasons are manifold, but principal among them are rapid population growth and agricultural mismanagement in the food-short countries.

The most potent force to reshape global trade patterns in recent decades is population growth. A comparison of population and food trends in North America and Latin America reveals the devastating effect of unfettered growth. As recently as 1950, North America and Latin America had roughly equal populations—163 and 168 million, respectively. But while North America's population growth has slowed markedly since the late fifties, Latin America's has increased explosively. Several larger countries such as Brazil, Mexico, Venezuela, and Peru have population growth rates of 3 percent or more per year. If the North American population of 1950 had expanded at 3 percent per year, it would now be 341 million instead of 236 million. Eating at current food-consumption levels, those additional 105 million people would absorb virtually all exportable supplies, leaving North America struggling to feed itself.[8]

Unfortunately, many of the Third World countries plagued with rapid population growth have managed agriculture poorly. Social forces that have concentrated land holdings in the hands of a few have crowded a majority of the farm population onto a small area of land, or even worse, off the land entirely. Consequently, both land and labor are grossly underutilized. In country after country, the persistence of malnutrition and growing national food deficits is due more to existing social structures than to a lack of productive capacity.

While the growth of national food deficits has various causes, its effects—ever-greater pressure on North American food supplies—are always the same. Moreover, they appear to be cumulative. Literally scores of countries have become food importers since World War II, but *not one new country has emerged as a significant cereal exporter during this period.* The worldwide shift of countries outside of North America from export to import status is a well-traveled one-way street.

The extent to which importers rely on outside supplies is also growing. The list of both industrial and developing countries that now import more grain than they produce is lengthening. Among those that now import over half of their grain supply are Japan, Belgium, Switzerland, Saudi Arabia, Lebanon, Libya, Algeria, Senegal, and Venezuela. Other countries rapidly approaching primary dependence on imported foodstuffs include Portugal, Costa Rica, Sri Lanka, South Korea, and Egypt.[9]

In simplest terms, most national food deficits exist because the surpluses produced in the countryside are no longer sufficient to feed the swelling urban population. Between 1950 and 1975 the urban share of world population, boosted by massive rural-urban migration in the Third World, increased from 29 to 39 percent. In effect, this record rate of urbanization was made possible by North American food surpluses. Although the United Nations projects a continuation of this trend, with the world becoming 49 percent urban by the end of the century, the difficulties associated with expanding food production and with generating the requisite surplus in the countryside seem certain to slow this trend.[10] In some countries, urbanization could come to a halt.

The growth in dependence on North American food cannot long continue at the recent rate. Aided by the return of 20 million hectares of idled cropland to production during the mid-seventies, North American farmers have nearly doubled grain exports over the past decade. But future gains will not be so easy to realize, and the world should not count on a repeat performance during the next decade.

In mid-July of 1975, the Canadian Wheat Board banned further exports of wheat until the size of Canada's harvest could be ascertained.[11] Similarly, the United States yielded to political pressures generated by rising domestic food prices and limited grain exports to the Soviet Union and Poland in the late summer and early fall of 1975. Levied in 1972, in 1974, and again in 1975, such restrictions on exports are becoming routine. More unsettling, these export controls were adopted in 1974 and 1975, despite the return to production of the previously idled U.S. cropland. In many ways the situation is analogous to that of a general who commits his fresh reserves when he sees the tide of battle running against him only to discover that, having done so, he is still losing the battle. In the world food economy, U.S. reserves of idled cropland have been thrown into the fray but in themselves have proved insufficient to replenish depleted world food stocks quickly.

As the seventies draw to a close, the international community must at least prepare for the possibility that the food scramble of recent years may not be temporary. Most of the slack appears to have gone out of the world food economy, leaving the entire world in a vulnerable position. Consequently, the U.S. and Canadian governments could someday find themselves in the uncomfortable position of having to decide who would and would not get North America's extra food in time of scarcity. In effect, the two governments would be operating a global food-rationing program. Although they have not consciously sought this responsibility, they must now reckon with it.

The scarcity of food at prices low-income consumers can afford traces back to the scarcity of land, water, and energy. While shortages or cost increases of any of these basic food-producing resources can disrupt world food production seriously, all three have become scarce in the past quarter-century.

Land and Water

Until about 1950, expansion of the cultivated area accounted for most of the growth in the world's food supply.[12] Since then, the stork has outrun the plow. As population has continued to grow, cropland per person has declined, until today there is less than half a hectare for each of the earth's four billion inhabitants. The growth in the total area devoted to agriculture has slowed markedly, and the food supply continues to grow only because farmers have managed to increase the land's productivity.

Most good cropland is already being worked. Little, if any, fertile new land awaits the plow in North America, Europe, or Asia. Most North African and Middle Eastern countries cannot significantly expand the area in crops without developing new sources of irrigation water. The only remaining regions with well-watered, potentially arable land yet to be exploited are the southern Sudan, the tsetse-fly belt of sub-Saharan Africa, and the vast interior of Brazil. Nonetheless, to view Africa and Brazil as vast unexploited repositories of fertile farmland would be a serious error. Much "potentially" tillable land lies in the tropics, but farming tropical soils entails exasperating difficulties associated with maintaining both soil tilth and fertility.

One problem is that in the tropics a disproportionately large share of the available nutrients reside in the dense vegetative cover. Once the land is cleared the nutrients often leach, and the soil's fertility declines. Moreover, when cleared soils reach high temperatures, organic matter oxidizes rapidly, and the soil sometimes becomes so compacted that it can no longer be cultivated. Another difficulty is that before large new areas in sub-Saharan Africa can be farmed, the tsetse fly—the carrier of the cattle-killing disease trypanosomiasis—must be eradicated. And, further, in the Sudan and Brazil, heavy investments in roads, marketing systems, credit institutions, and technical advisory services are needed before the new land can be brought into use. In sum, estimates of how much additional land can be brought under the plow are plentiful, but most are of little use because they fail to specify the costs of making additional land productive. Meaningful estimates must take into account the relationship between the cost of the food that could be produced and the price people could afford to pay for it.

While unexploited fertile land is scarce, the lack of fresh water may prove an even tougher constraint on efforts to expand world food output. In countries as widely separated as Mexico and Afghanistan, a shortage of fresh water acts as the main inhibitor to the expansion of the area planted to the high-yielding wheats. In the Soviet Union, a lack of fresh water is frustrating efforts to expand feed-grain production for Russia's swelling livestock herds.

Competition for water among countries with common river systems has become increasingly fierce. Protracted negotiations were required to allocate the waters of the Indus River between India and Pakistan; conflicts between India and Bangladesh over the rights to use the Ganges surfaced in 1976. Competition is also keen between Israel and the Arab countries for the waters of the Jordan. Only with painstaking negotiations were the Nile River waters divided between the Sudan and the United Arab Republic. The distribution and salt content of the Colorado River waters are matters of constant dispute in U.S.–Mexican relations.

As new irrigation options are exhausted, the link between

bread and water becomes increasingly obvious. Irrigation has played a major role in expanding the earth's food-producing capacities. Irrigated agriculture supplied the surplus food and the impetus for social organization in Mesopotamia and ancient Egypt. Indeed, so gentle, punctual, and perfectly synchronized with the natural growing season is the flood of the Nile that Herodotus once described Egypt as the "gift of the Nile."[13] Irrigation also developed early along the major rivers of southern Asia, particularly along the Indus and the Hwang Ho, or Yellow River, of China.

Although irrigated agriculture was practiced as long as six thousand years ago, only in the twentieth century did irrigation begin to cover a significant share of the earth's land surface. In 1800, an estimated 8 million hectares of the world's cropland was irrigated. By 1900, irrigation covered 40 million hectares; and by 1950, it extended over 105 million hectares. But the greatest expansion has occurred since 1950: the total irrigated area nearly doubled to an estimated 200 million hectares by 1975 (see Table 6-2). In China alone, the number of irrigated hectares has increased by more than 24 million since 1950 and now exceeds 40 million; China's vast construction effort has been achieved largely through the massive mobilization of off-season rural labor.[14]

Table 6-2. Estimated World Irrigated Area, 1900–1975, with Projections to 2000

Year	Irrigated Area	Average Annual Increase
	(MILLION HECTARES)	(PERCENT)
1900	40	
1950	110	1.9
1975	200	2.6
2000 (projected)	260	1.1

Source: *FAO Production Yearbook,* and author's estimates.

As pressures to produce ever more food intensify, national governments are being forced to consider ambitious interventions in the hydrological cycle. They are considering, among other tactics, the wholesale diversion of rivers, and rainmaking through cloud seeding. To augment the supply of irrigation water in its southern reaches, the Soviet Union is planning to reverse the flow of four Arctic-bound rivers by blocking their northward passage and constructing diversion channels.

During the mid-sixties some play was given to the possibility of desalting sea water as a means of expanding irrigation supplies. Proposals for massive nuclear powered agro-industrial complexes surfaced. Like many other dreams based on dramatic new technologies, this one fell apart. Breakthroughs in desalting technology have yet to materialize, and rising energy costs actually prohibit the use of desalted sea water for agricultural purposes.

Like per-capita grain requirements, agriculture's future water requirements escalate as diets improve. The 2.5 pounds of grain a vegetarian eats each day requires 300 gallons of water to produce. In contrast, producing 2 pounds of vegetable matter and 1 pound of beef and animal fat a day requires a total of 2,500 gallons of water. The "water cost" of a pound of beef, which includes the water used to produce grass and feed as well as that drunk by the animal, amounts to about twenty-five times that needed to produce a pound of bread.[15]

The prospect of feeding the future population adequately is pinned to the prospect of expanding the area irrigated by large-scale river systems and wells. The chance that more rivers can be harnessed appears much smaller in the final quarter of this century than it did in the one that just ended. The easiest to build of extensive irrigation projects—whether in China, India, the Soviet Union, the Middle East, Africa, or North America—have already been completed. The irrigation potential of most of the world's major rivers, including the Yellow, the Indus, the Ganges, the Colorado, and the Egyptian share of the Nile, has largely been realized. The Mekong and the Amazon remain unexploited, but the latter's vast width and broad flood plains make it virtually impossible to harness.

Opportunities for expanding well-irrigation are limited by the extent of underground water supplies and by the rising cost of the fuels needed to operate pumps. Unused potential may be greatest in the Gangetic and Indus flood plains in the Indian subcontinent, where underground water supplies are both abundant and close to the surface. In the United States, well irrigation in the Western Great Plains and in the Southwest has expanded rapidly, often to such an extent that water tables are now dropping. Thus, while the world's irrigated area expanded by 2.6 percent annually between 1950 and 1975, it will probably grow at less than half that rate for the remainder of this century.

The Energy Dimension

In addition to land, water, and sunlight, the production of food requires energy. In early agricultural systems, the principal energy input was human muscle power. Later this was augmented by that of harnessed cattle and other draft animals. The invention of the internal-combustion engine several thousand years later led to the development of the tractor. The advent of chemical fertilizers, particularly those containing nitrogen, brought another massive jump in the use of energy to produce food. While nature annually fixes an estimated 120 million tons of atmospheric nitrogen through legumes, soil microflora, and other means, humans now add some 40 million tons of nitrogen to the soil in the form of nitrogen fertilizer.[16] If fertilizer projections materialize, the artificial fixing of atmospheric nitrogen in chemical form may eventually rival that fixed by nature itself.

In terms of energy use, there are essentially three types of agriculture. The simplest, one that relies on human muscle power alone, is still practiced in some parts of the world. It is best exemplified by Mexican hoe-corn cultivation or the more traditional forms of wet-rice cultivation that involve little more than hand sowing and hand harvesting. The second, which utilizes draft animals as the principal source of energy, prevailed worldwide until World War II and is still dominant in Asia, Africa, and Latin America. The third system is highly energy intensive, heavily reliant on mechanical power, and, where appropriate, dependent upon chemical fertilizer and irrigation. Somewhat over half of all world agriculture is of this third type.

Energy is used in agriculture to raise the productivity of both labor and land. In the United States, Canada, the Soviet Union, and other countries where land has been relatively abundant and labor relatively scarce, energy has long been substituted extensively for labor through large-scale mechanization. But only over the last generation has energy been employed intensively to raise land productivity. In Japan and China, where historically land has been scarce and labor relatively abundant, the primary emphasis has been on raising the land productivity through the intensive use of labor and energy.

As the global demand for food expanded far more rapidly than the area under cultivation did, more and more energy was required to enhance the productivity of the land. From 1950 until oil prices rose sharply in 1973, the world's farmers freely substituted energy for land. In the midwestern corn belt of the United States, the energy embodied in the nitrogen fertilizer used on corn now exceeds that in the tractor fuel used during plowing, planting, cultivation, and harvesting.[17]

In a world where the principal techniques used to expand food production are energy intensive, rising energy costs thwart efforts to eliminate undernutrition. They also place farmers in an impossible bind. Most of the countless opportunities for conserving energy in modern food systems exist at the distribution end of the system. Only one-fourth of the energy used in the ultra-modern U.S. food system, for example, goes into production. The remaining three-fourths is spent to transport, process, and package the food once it leaves the farm. Commonly, food is wrapped in packages that embody more energy than the food itself does. One of the grossest inefficiencies in the food-distribution system is the widespread use of a two-ton automobile to transport ten to fifteen kilograms of groceries from the supermarket to the home. Even worse, that same two-ton vehicle is sometimes driven several miles merely to obtain a quart of milk or a loaf of bread.

The two-thirds growth in world population since midcentury was sustained by increases in food output that were in turn made possible by cheap energy. So, too, the doubling of the urban population that has taken place since midcentury reflects the availability of cheap energy. The farther people live from their food supply, the more energy is required for food transport and processing.

The Green Revolution

The term "Green Revolution" describes in shorthand the introduction and spread of high-yield "dwarf" wheats and rices in the developing countries. Originating in Japan, the dwarf wheats were introduced into Mexico via the United States, where they had increased wheat production dramatically in the irrigated wheat-growing areas of the Northwest. In Mexico, the dwarf genes were incorporated into the high-yielding wheats that were later to be disseminated throughout the world.

The defining characteristic of the high-yielding strains is their responsiveness to fertilizer. While heavy doses of fertilizer produced a heavy head of grain that tall, thin-strawed indigenous varieties of wheat cannot support, the shorter and sturdier stalks typical of dwarf wheats will not topple as heads grow heavy. The sturdy dwarf wheats can effectively use 135 kilograms of fertilizer per hectare, roughly three times as much as the standard varieties could.[18] Well managed, the dwarf varieties can easily double the yields of the traditional strains. Adapted to a wide range of growing conditions, the new wheats represent a packaging of the technologies used in the agriculturally advanced countries.

Encouraged by the adaptability of the new wheat varieties, the Rockefeller and Ford Foundations joined forces in 1962 to establish the International Rice Research Institute (IRRI) at Los Baños in the Philippines. Within years, research using dwarf genes from Japan led to the development of high-yielding rice varieties that were then quickly distributed throughout Asia. Use of the new seeds led to dramatic jumps in the productivity of local resources: grain production per ton of fertilizer and per acre of land doubled, and the productivity of the water and labor used in agriculture increased by a third.

Appearing at a time when food deficits in the poor countries were widening and when requests for food aid were pouring into Washington, the high-yielding grains were widely heralded, and their spread was rapid. In 1964–65 the area planted in Asia to the high-yielding wheats and rices totaled some eighty hectares, most of them in experimental demonstration plots. Four years later, thirteen million hectares had been planted with the new seeds.[19] Assuming that the new seeds made possible an increase in output of roughly 1.2 tons per hectare, the Asian food supply expanded by some 16 million tons, or enough to feed some 90 million people. The threat of massive famine that loomed large in Asia in the late sixties had been at least temporarily allayed.

Overall, the short-term progress in expanding food production was encouraging. When the Rockefeller team arrived in late 1944, Mexico was a hungry country forced to import much of its food from the United States. By 1967, wheat production had tripled, the average Mexican was consuming 40 percent more food, Mexico was exporting more than a million tons of grain annually, and the economy was prospering.[20]

Advances in Asia were in some cases even more dramatic than Mexico's. India doubled its wheat crop in one six-year period, a feat unmatched by any large country (see Figure 6-3). In Pakistan, the advances in wheat production were only slightly less phenomenal. While far less dramatic, rice production gains in the Philippines, Sri Lanka, Indonesia, and Malaysia were substantial.

The Green Revolution enabled many countries to cut back grain imports and enabled some to become exporters. India, riding the crest of this agricultural breakthrough, was on the verge of cereal self-sufficiency in the early seventies. Heady with success, Indian Prime Minister Indira Gandhi proclaimed that India no longer needed U.S. food assistance. In the Philippines, advances in rice production ended a half-century of dependence on imported rice.

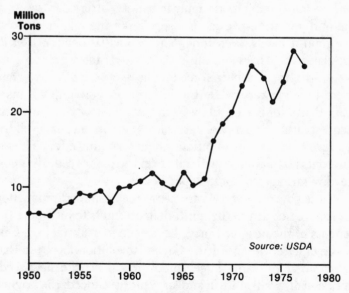

Figure 6-3. Wheat Production in India, 1950-77

Food production advances in the Green Revolution countries continue, though at a less dramatic rate. Wheat production has expanded most rapidly, while the spread of the high-yielding rices depends on expensive, time-consuming investments in sophisticated irrigation and water control. But the initial quantum jumps associated with the Green Revolution cannot be repeated. Those who were involved in its launching, such as Dr. Norman Borlaug, who received the Nobel Peace Prize for his work on the high-yielding wheats, had warned from the beginning that the Green Revolution was not a final solution to the world food problem. At most, he said, it would only buy time, perhaps ten or twenty years, in which governments could bridle population growth.[21]

Some governments used the additional time bought with the new seeds to mount effective family-planning programs, but most failed to do so. A full decade has passed since the Green Revolution took on international dimensions, and population is again outrunning food supply in country after country. As of the mid-seventies, Mexico is again importing a large share of the grain it needs, even though an estimated one-tenth of its population now lives illegally in the United States[22] (see Figure 6-4). India, too, has been forced to buy large quantities of grain on foreign markets, while the Philippines now imports more grain than ever before. Only China, which now uses the fertilizer-responsive dwarf rices and wheats extensively, has used the reprieve to launch an ambitious family-planning effort. Having halved its population growth rate over the past decade, it is now steadily raising food output per person.

While governments' efforts to capitalize on food-production gains have not stirred the spirit, their attempts to distribute the benefits of the new seeds have been even less satisfactory. One of the chief criticisms of the Green Revolution has been that it benefited primarily large landowners. Yet, the new seeds work equally well on small and large farms. Indeed, the original dwarf-germ plasm for both the wheats and rices came from

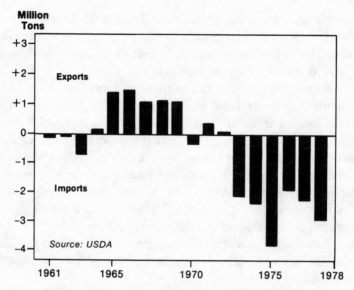

Figure 6-4. Mexico: Net Grain Trade, 1961-78

Japan, whose farms are the world's tiniest. The reason the benefits deriving from the new seeds have often fallen to the larger landholders has nothing to do with the seeds themselves. Rather, this inequity is a function of the social and political structures of the countries into which the seeds are introduced. The answer is not to prohibit the new technologies but rather to reform elitist social and political structures.

Rising Yields: An Interrupted Trend

The ancients calculated yield as the ratio of grain produced to that used as seed. For them, the constraining factor was seed-grain itself. The yield was probably very low by modern standards, reflecting the marginal nature of early agricultural ventures. Today, wheat grown in the U.S. Great Plains yields thirty kilograms for each kilogram used as seed. For transplanted rice in Japan or Taiwan, the ratio may be one hundred to one. For corn, the only cereal domesticated in the New World, the ratio often reaches five hundred to one.[23] Believed to be the last of the three major cereals to be domesticated, maize is also the highest yielding.

As agriculture spread and as more and more of the world's potentially tillable land was brought under cultivation, the focus shifted from the productivity of seed to that of land. Using yield per hectare as the principal criterion, corn remains at the top of the list in terms of productivity. The average U.S. corn yield, exceeding six tons per hectare, surpasses even the Japanese rice yield. Within the United States, the per-acre yield of corn easily quadruples that of wheat, a cereal grown largely under semi-arid conditions. Wheat yields are also low in other semi-arid wheat-growing areas such as those in Canada, the Soviet Union, North Africa, the Middle East, and Australia.

From the end of World War II until the early seventies, one of the most predictable trends in the world economy was the steady rise in cereal yield per hectare. Between 1950 and 1973, the average worldwide grain yield per hectare moved steadily upward from just under 1.04 tons per hectare to 1.77 tons per hectare (1 ha. = 2.47 acres). Beginning in 1974 the trend was interrupted as yields declined somewhat (see Figure 6-5).

Since little new land remains to be opened up to agriculture, this downturn in yield per hectare has hit the world food economy hard, contributing to food scarcity and rising food prices. The fall-off appears to be the product of several factors. The marginal quality of the once-idled cropland that was returned to production in 1973 and 1974 is perhaps the most crucial factor. In the United States, per-hectare yields of wheat, barley, oats, rye, and rice peaked in 1971; yields of corn and soybeans peaked in 1972. As of 1977 none had regained that earlier high.[24] A second factor is the high cost of energy. The sixfold increase in the cost of petroleum during the seventies has slowed the growth in the use of energy in agriculture.

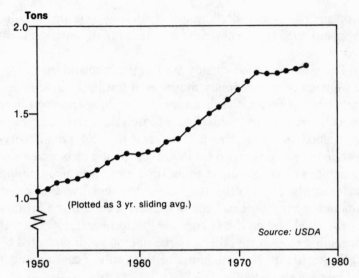

Figure 6-5. World Grain Yield Per Hectare, 1950-77

A third and closely related factor is the high cost of fertilizer. Fertilizer prices during the mid-seventies, influenced both by cyclical trends in the industry and by rising energy costs, have soared to record highs.

A fourth factor influencing the productivity of cropland is a shrinkage in the world's fallowed area. As world wheat prices rose during the seventies, the U.S. land in fallow declined from an average of sixty-five acres for every hundred acres planted in wheat during the sixties to thirty-seven acres in 1976.[25] As a result, U.S. wheat yields have fallen, and severe dust storms reminiscent of those of the thirties are reappearing in some states.

In tropical and subtropical regions, where fallowing has evolved as a method of restoring soil fertility, mounting population pressures are forcing shifting cultivators to shorten the rotation cycles. As cycles are shortened, land productivity falls. In Nigeria, where both the addition of marginal land to the cropland base and a shortening of the fallow cycle are lowering cropland fertility, cereal yields have been falling since the early sixties.

The addition of low-quality land to the cropland base, soaring energy costs, temporary shortages of fertilizer, the shortening of fallow cycles, the diversion of cow dung from fertilizer to fuel uses, and the gradual loss of topsoil through erosion have all helped interrupt the postwar rise in land productivity. While the world demand for food expands at a record rate, the difficulties of raising or, in some situations, even maintaining soil fertility are multiplying. Only by applying ever-larger amounts of fertilizer can many farmers maintain the fertility of their soils. Since the energy used in fertilizer production is becoming more costly, the large rise in crop yields projected by agriculturists for the remainder of this century can no longer be taken for granted.

The Protein Bind

The two basic yardsticks for measuring the quality of diets are calories and protein: calories measure the diet quantitatively, protein qualitatively. The several hundred million people who are chronically undernourished suffer from a shortage of calories or protein or both. Since expanding protein supplies adequately has become increasingly difficult during the seventies, protein hunger could well worsen in the years ahead.

Most of the world's high protein comes from fish, beef, and soybeans. According to marine biologists, the catch of table-grade species cannot be markedly expanded beyond current levels (see Figure 6-6). Expanding marine protein supplies thus means turning to "inferior" species. Similarly, the continuing expansion of the world's cattle herd, which now annually amounts to some forty-one million tons or ten kilograms per person, has already led to extensive overgrazing.[26] Although livestock output can be expanded amply in some countries by

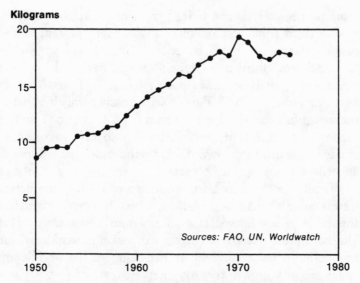

Figure 6-6. World Fish Catch Per Capita, 1950-75

improving livestock management, raising productivity of grasslands is difficult, since the world's principal grazing areas are natural or unimproved grasslands in semi-arid regions.

Other important biological constraints impede protein production in general and beef production in particular. Like the first domesticated cattle, beef cows still give birth to only one calf each year. And since not every cow bears a calf each year even in the best-managed herds, the calving rate is well below 100 percent. Thus, for every calf that goes into the market cycle at least one cow must be maintained for one full year. Herds could, of course, be sharply expanded if more cattle could be put in feedlots. But during the mid-seventies, high grain prices have reduced the amount of grain fed to cattle well below what it would otherwise be. In 1975, roughly one-third of the world's grain harvest—some 450 million tons—was fed to livestock and poultry, and this share may not expand markedly in the years immediately ahead if feed-grain prices remain high.[27]

The third principal source of high-quality protein is soybeans, a crop produced almost entirely by three countries—the United States, Brazil, and China. Between 1950 and 1975, the world soybean harvest nearly quadrupled, rising from sixteen to sixty-one million tons.[28] This growth closely paralleled that of the world fish catch, which climbed from twenty-one million tons in 1950 to seventy million tons in 1970.[29] Like the increase in the fish catch, it also reflects the enormous worldwide appetite for high-quality protein.

Within the three soybean-producing countries, production trends contrast sharply. In China, where the crop originated, the stable harvest fluctuates at around nine million tons. In the United States, where most of the expansion of world soybean production occurred and where two-thirds of the world's soybeans are now grown, the 1977 harvest reached forty-six million tons. Since soybean prices doubled in 1973, Brazil has been dramatically expanding its acreage from a small base, edging ahead of China in production in 1976.[30]

Despite strenuous efforts, none of the three soybean-producing countries has been able to increase per-acre soybean yields significantly. Attempts to raise soybean yields run up against incontrovertible biological facts: legumes fix their own nitrogen and respond only modestly to applications of nitrogen fertilizer. Yields have edged upward only grudgingly. Soybean yields in the United States, for example, have increased by a mere 25 percent since 1950, a period during which corn yields nearly tripled.[31]

In effect, farmers get more soybeans only by planting more soybeans. From 1950 to 1973, U.S. soybean acreage moved to a new high virtually every year, expanding from seven million hectares to twenty-two million hectares (see Figure 6-7). In 1973, this era of rapid uninterrupted expansion in soybean acreage and supplies was arrested, largely because the idled cropland had vanished.

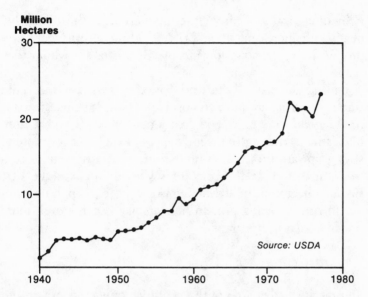

**Figure 6-7. United States: Soybean Area Harvested,
1940-77**

With one hectare in every six on U.S. farms now planted in
soybeans, it is unclear how much more land farmers can shift
to soybean production and still satisfy the expanding world
demand for other crops, particularly cereals. Yet, while the
United States cannot continue to expand soybean acreage as
it did from 1950 to 1973, Brazil could substantially expand
production. In southern Brazil, soybeans and cereals (particularly wheat) have proved to be more complementary and less
competitive than in the United States. Two-thirds of the soybeans, a summer crop, are successfully rotated with wheat, a
winter crop.[32] Consequently, Brazil can produce two harvests
per year. As a bonus, the soybeans fix soil nitrogen that boosts
the wheat crop.

Unfortunately, in parts of Brazil soybeans also compete with
table beans. The surging demand for Brazilian soybeans as
livestock feed in Japan, affluent Europe, and the Soviet Union

is bidding land away from the production of Brazilian table beans and increasing their price.[33] This in turn aggravates protein hunger among low-income Brazilians for whom they are a staple.

During the sixties, the world price of soybeans was quite stable, hovering around 110 dollars per ton. But since 1973, it has ranged from 220 to 290 dollars per ton.[34] Given the difficulties in expanding the world supply of high-quality protein, strong upward pressure on protein prices seems likely to continue unabated. If the price of soybeans (perhaps the best single indicator of the tightening world protein supply) continues to rise, reducing protein hunger may become even more difficult than it already is.

Toward Century's End

During the final quarter of this century, population growth and rising affluence are projected to double world demand for food again as they did during the third quarter. Whether these demand projections will materialize is questionable. Whether farmers and fishermen can double the supply of food is even more questionable. Indeed, the dim prospect for doing so may influence the projected growth in both population and affluence.

Four factors have contributed centrally to the near doubling of food output between 1950 and 1975: the spreading use of hybrid corn, the vast expansion of irrigation, the sixfold growth in fertilizer use, and the rapid spread of the high-yielding dwarf wheats and rices. The agricultural use of energy, including that energy embodied in fertilizer and that used for mechanical power, also multiplied rapidly during this period. Numerous other technological advances in both crop and livestock production also contributed.

Maintaining past rates of growth in food output will likely become even more difficult. Net expansion of the cropland base is likely to be even less than the rather modest expansion of the third quarter of this century. Growth in the irrigated area is projected to fall by more than half. The rate of growth in energy use will undoubtedly be far less. The potential for expanding fertilizer use is still substantial in Third World countries; but while the growth rate in these countries is almost certain to fall, the quantitative increase is likely to be quite large.

Constrained by the limits of available land, water, and energy, food production is also subject to biological limits. Whether crop production per hectare or milk production per cow, natural processes eventually conform to the S-shaped growth curve. Crop production per hectare is ultimately limited by the incidence of solar energy. The efficiency with which broilers convert feed into meat is ultimately limited by the physiology and metabolism of the birds themselves.

Selective breeding and improved nutrition of both plants and animals can push up production limits—but only so far. Some of these absolute limits are already being approached in some situations. Corn yields in the United States, wheat yields in Western Europe, and rice yields in Japan may already be well past the inflection point on the S-shaped curve.

As food supplies tightened during the early seventies, confidence in science's power to push back the constraints on food production fast enough to meet growing demands has eroded. Indeed, as Professor Louis Thompson of Iowa State University notes, the backlog of unused agricultural technology is shrinking. As recently as 1960, the average corn yield attained by farmers in Iowa was scarcely half that attained by the experiment stations. But since then, yields on the experiment stations have risen only modestly, while those attained by Iowa farmers have risen dramatically, and they now approach those achieved on the experimental plots.[35]

There is no identifiable technology about to come off the drawing board that can make possible a quantum jump in world food output comparable to that associated with the expansion of chemical fertilizer use or the adoption of hybrid corn. Two possibilities—raising the photosynthetic efficiency of key crops, and the development of cereals which can fix nitrogen —have this potential, but both await fundamental advances in biological engineering. The fact that some crops, such as sugar cane or corn, convert solar energy into chemical energy much more efficiently than others has prompted scientists to try to raise the photosynthetic efficiency of some crops through genetic manipulation. A breakthrough on this front is particularly critical to the development of energy crops as sources of automotive fuel.

The second potential advance, the breeding of cereals that can fix nitrogen, is the subject of major research programs sponsored by the Brazilian government, the Kettering Foundation, and the DuPont Corporation. Whereas increasing photosynthetic efficiency would raise productivity, developing cereals that can fix nitrogen would lead to energy savings by reducing nitrogen fertilizer uses. Some scientists contend that a breakthrough in this field would, however, be a shallow victory, since using biochemical energy to fix nitrogen would divert it from other biological tasks and lead to a reduction in yields. Yet, if the preliminary research indicating that the heavy application of nitrogen fertilizer leads to the release of nitrous oxide and the subsequent depletion of the ozone layer should be confirmed, the effort to breed nitrogen-fixing cereals could take on new urgency.

Whether these exciting advances ever materialize and become commercially applicable remains to be seen. In any event, considerable unrealized food-production potential (most of it in the Third World) can now be tapped using existing agricultural technologies.

The obstacles to realizing this food-production potential are not technological but political. Often land productivity in countries with more progressive agriculture systems is two, three, or four times that of countries with less progressive systems. For example, rice yields in Taiwan are four times those in Burma. Similarly, corn yields in the United States are two to four times those in most Latin American countries. With the bulk of the rural population squeezed onto a small fraction of the arable land area, both land and labor are severely underutilized in country after country in Latin America. Then, too, food-price policies that have a pro-urban bias and that fail to provide farmers with sufficient incentive inhibit agricultural innovation and investment.

The unrealized potential in the poor countries notwithstanding, the conditions under which the world's farmers and fishermen will attempt to expand output during the final quarter of this century are less favorable than the conditions of the past. Whether the world can expand food production is not at issue. How much it will cost to do so and how the cost will relate to the purchasing power of the world's poor are the real questions.

If the rise in food prices that results from rising real costs and scarcity exceeds the growth in purchasing power among the poor, then food consumption among the world's poor will fall. The decline in world food consumption per person since 1971 suggests that it has already begun. For those whose nutritional requirements were just beginning to be met, this reversal has been a particularly crushing blow.

A world of cheap food with stable prices, surplus stocks, and a large reserve of idled cropland may now be history. Barring some dramatic increase in the priority given family planning and food production, a future typified by more or less chronic scarcity enlivened only by occasional surpluses of a local and short-lived nature appears to be in store. The steady rise in food-production costs, a rise associated with the employment of marginal land and low-grade water resources, may make global inflation progressively more difficult to manage. At the same time, the international community's failure to respond effectively to crop shortfalls in poor countries may make severe nutritional stress and sporadic rises in death rates more common.

Progress in eliminating hunger and malnutrition is not likely unless available food supplies are distributed more equitably both within and among societies. As the demand for land, water, and energy grows in other sectors, priorities for resource use will have to be established between agriculture and these other sectors. In a world where scarcity threatens to become commonplace and where food remains basic not only to human survival but also to economic and political stability, family planning and food production deserve a higher priority.

7

Economic Stresses

Economically, the seventies have been traumatic and confusing. They have brought the first global double-digit inflation on record during peacetime and the highest unemployment since the Great Depression. Capital shortages are plaguing the citadels of capitalism and socialism alike. This unexplained coexistence of inflation and unemployment has led economists to coin a new term—*stagflation*—to describe a situation about which many of them worry but for which none can prescribe a satisfactory remedy.

Unprecedented scarcities and price hikes have given rise to "resource diplomacy"; they have profoundly altered the global political structure and accorded new power to raw-materials producers. The dramatic rise in the world price of oil, the associated convulsive shift in the global power structure, and the tripling of wheat and soybean prices caught economic and political analysts off guard.

The economics fraternity has had trouble explaining, much less anticipating, the events of the seventies—perhaps because it has lost sight of the fact that economic activity depends upon the productivity of the earth's natural systems and resources. Understanding contemporary economic stresses and dilemmas requires understanding the relationship between the condition of the earth's natural systems and the operations of the economic system. Since ecological stresses can quickly become economic stresses, we need to incorporate into our economic analyses such biological concepts as "carrying capacity" and the "S-shaped growth curve." We need to take into account not only the diminishing returns of economics but also the negative returns associated with over-exploiting nature.

Diminishing and Negative Returns

The widely held notion that investing ever-increasing amounts of capital or labor in any activity will eventually result in diminishing returns derives from early classical economics, in particular from David Ricardo's nineteenth-century writings. Ricardo's early work dealt primarily with the application of labor to land and did not anticipate some of the technological advances that enabled the point of diminishing returns to be pushed farther and farther back. His thinking, like that of Malthus, thus came under attack because his projections did not materialize in the short run. Indeed, as science and technology progressed, many came to believe that the point of diminishing returns, the day of economic reckoning, could be postponed indefinitely.

While Ricardo's preoccupation with diminishing returns was premature, it was nonetheless well-founded. The world's seemingly modest annual economic growth of nearly 4 percent since midcentury will result in a fiftyfold expansion if it continues for a century. With the global economy growing at such a rate, it should come as no surprise that each of the earth's biological systems is under growing stress and that the world's nonrenewable resources are dwindling.

A global economy expanding at 4 percent per year will eventually be forced to rely upon resources of diminishing quality. Technological advances may for a time more than offset declines in resource quality, but at some point even the most ingenious attempts to compensate for nature will no longer be adequate. During the seventies the decline in quality of additional resources has had many manifestations. One is the falling quality of new cropland. Efforts to expand sharply the global cultivated area, including the return to production of idled U.S. cropland, have led to a fall in per-hectare yields. The steady rise in crop yield per acre, one of the most predictable of postwar economic trends, has been interrupted.[1] So poor is the quality of this new land that it has apparently overridden, at least temporarily, the broad-based and continuing efforts by the world's farmers to raise the productivity of their land.

Just as the extension of agriculture onto new land runs up against diminishing returns, so do the development of water resources and the expansion of the use of fertilizer. Most of the world's good cropland is already under the plow, and most of the easy-to-irrigate sites have already been developed. Further expansion in irrigation invariably involves moving up a steeply rising cost curve, either because new dam sites are less desirable or because water tables are falling.

While the application of chemical fertilizer accounted for much of the increase in world food output since mid-century, returns on additional fertilizer use are also beginning to diminish in those areas where its use is heaviest. Crop yields increase predictably with each increment of chemical fertilizer—rapidly at first, then more slowly until they eventually level off.

With hybrid corn in the American Midwest, for example, when fertilizer is applied at the rate of 40 pounds per acre, each pound of nitrogen fertilizer yields an additional 27 pounds of corn. With the addition of the second 40 pounds of fertilizer, each pound yields 14 extra pounds of grain. For the third and fourth 40-pound increments, the additional corn produced per pound of nitrogen drops to 9 pounds and 4 pounds, respectively. The fifth 40-pound increment yields only one pound of corn per pound of nitrogen fertilizer. Since a pound of fertilizer costs far more than a pound of corn, the additional application becomes unprofitable well before this level is reached. This particular fertilizer-response curve is drawn from a 1964 experiment in Iowa. A fertilizer-response curve similar to that for corn exists for rice in China, for wheat in Western Europe, or for any other cereal grown where moisture levels justify fertilizer use. No crop is exempt from the law of diminishing returns. The breeding of varieties more responsive to fertilizer or the adoption of improved farming practices may raise the level of the curve, but they do not appreciably alter its form; nor can they push it back forever.

The shape of this fertilizer-response curve is central to any analysis of future food-production prospects, because the doubling of world grain output since 1950 is due more to the expanded use of commercial fertilizer than to any other factor. Indeed, the contribution of fertilizer may approach that of all other factors combined—improved varieties, expanded cultivated area, expanded irrigated area, improved pest protection, and better farm management.

The earliest data for both world grain production and fertilizer use are those for 1934–38 (see Table 7-1). At that time world grain production averaged 651 million tons per year and fertilizer consumption ran about 10 million tons. From then until 1948–52, fertilizer consumption increased by only 4 million tons. After 1950, growth in the cultivated area slowed and fertilizer consumption began to grow by leaps and bounds.

Table 7-1. World Grain Production and Fertilizer Use

	World Grain Production (a)	Grain Increment (b)	World Fertilizer Use (c)	Fertilizer Increment (d)	Ratio of (b) to (d) (e)
	MILLION METRIC TONS				
1934–38	651		10		
1948–52	710	59	14	4	14.8
1959–61	840	130	27	13	10.0
1964–66	955	115	41	14	8.2
1969–71	1120	165	64	23	7.2
1974–76	1236	116	84	20	5.8

Source: FAO; USDA.

During the fifties, annual fertilizer use increased by 13 million tons, while grain production increased by 130 million tons: each additional million tons of fertilizer increased the grain harvest by 10 million tons. During the early sixties, the response per million tons of fertilizer used declined to 8.2 million tons; during the late sixties it fell further to 7.2 million tons. As of the early seventies, each additional million tons of fertilizer yielded only 5.8 million tons of grain.

Clearly, the returns on the use of ever-expanding amounts of fertilizer are diminishing. Barring either a sharp improvement in the capacity of cereals to utilize fertilizer or a sharp rise in food prices relative to fertilizer, the growth in fertilizer use will begin to slow. In fact, it already has tapered off. Ranging from 7 to 9 percent between 1950 and 1970, the annual growth in world fertilizer use has fallen below 6 percent during the seventies.

Improving agricultural practices and breeding more fertilizer-responsive varieties can increase the amount of fertilizer a crop can profitably use; but as application rates rise, such gains become harder to realize. Limits on the amount of water or sunlight, for example, or the limits imposed by photosynthetic efficiency eventually curtail production. The prospect for any vast expansion in chemical fertilizer use appears dim in the United States, Western Europe, and Japan. In Eastern Europe, the Soviet Union, and China, fertilizer use could profitably be expanded somewhat, but not dramatically. In contrast, in India, Argentina, or other countries where application rates are uncommonly low, the potential for expanding production through the use of fertilizer remains high.

Although the returns on efforts to expand crop production by expanding the cropland base or by intensifying land use are diminishing in many locales, hopes run higher for this sector than for fisheries, forests, and grasslands. Where grasslands are already being used at full capacity or beyond—as they certainly are in much of Africa, the Middle East, and South Asia— efforts to exploit them further may invite ecological trouble.

Oceanic fisheries represent a clearly documented case of diminishing investment returns on a biological system. Even though overfishing has become commonplace, countries and corporations continue to invest in new fishing fleets. In its review of fisheries for 1975, the Organization for Economic Cooperation and Development (OECD) reports "that the total gross tonnage of the world's fishing vessels over 100 G.R.T. [gross registered tonnage] has grown by more than 50 percent in the six years to mid-1975."[2] During the same period the world catch did not increase at all, which means that the catch per dollar invested fell precipitously.

With energy as with food, efforts to expand supplies meet with diminishing returns. The most promising prospects for discovering new underground oil fields have been thoroughly investigated. Geological and seismic data indicate that new finds will be relatively meager compared to past discoveries. New finds are invariably located in more remote and inhospitable spots. Off-shore drilling, which accounts for a substantial and growing share of the total oil-exploration effort, can cost several times more per barrel than drilling on land.

The prospects of further developing various other sources

of energy are equally lackluster. The shift from wood use to coal use was highly desirable in economic and technological terms. Similarly, the progression from coal use to oil reflected the technological, economic, and environmental advantages of oil rather than the scarcity of coal. In contrast, embracing nuclear power as oil supplies dwindle would apparently entail no important advantages of any kind and would involve grave risks. In short, no other energy source is likely to be as cheap and efficient during the foreseeable future as oil was during its heyday. Direct solar energy, wind power, water power, and biological fuel sources may all be more costly, and the diminishing returns now characteristic of oil exploration may thus come to typify the overall energy economy. Barring a miraculous breakthrough in fusion research, the global cost curve for energy will probably continue to rise throughout this century.

Another factor that diminishes returns on investments, the limits of the capacity of the earth's biological system to absorb waste, cuts across virtually every sector of economic activity. At some point, the cost of environmental damage caused by a given economic activity can exceed the value of the product itself, though neither the producer nor the consumer may know it since the larger community bears the cost. When concerned governments impose restrictions on the discharge of waste, industry will return less product per dollar invested.

The law of diminishing returns also governs the mining industry. During the first seven decades of this century, the cost of unearthing minerals generally declined as mining and extraction technologies advanced and as energy became cheap and abundant. But as mineral reserves dwindle, lower-grade ores and less accessible deposits must be mined. Even the mining of relatively abundant minerals, such as iron ore, entails the immediate prospect of diminishing returns. According to a World Bank analysis of the future prospects of the iron-mining industry, "new discoveries during the last twenty-five years of world reserves of all grades of ore are now deemed sufficient to last at least one hundred years at exponentially growing demand." But the report then adds, "increasing claims have been made on the world's reserves of high-grade ore since World War II," and "while present reserves of all grades of ore are ample, the greatest iron resources of the world are in low-grade deposits."[3] Turning to lower-grade ores or to less accessible deposits raises the energy requirements. Since oil production is now subject to similar limits, the multiplier effect can amplify the decline in mineral produced per dollar invested.

Diminishing returns in mining initially occurred in those countries that industrialized first, since their richer domestic deposits were exhausted relatively early. While these countries could turn to foreign supplies, the world as a whole obviously cannot take the same approach. Overall, technological advances in extraction and refining are not likely to offset the added costs that mining lower-grade and less accessible ore deposits entail.

Advancing technology, once expected to bail humanity out, cannot do the job alone. Indeed, returns on the research and development of better technologies may be diminishing as well. After a generation or two of intensive scientific research in, say, agriculture, physics, or medicine, the easy advances usually have been made, so comparable gains with later investments will be more difficult. Within agriculture, for example, the development of chemical fertilizer and cereal hybridization required relatively small investments of time and money, but comparable future advances in food production may be far harder to realize. In physics, splitting the atom and developing solid-state physics were landmark breakthroughs, but comparable seminal gains in the future may require the lifetime effort of thousands of highly trained physicists. Similarly, future medical advances as important as the development of vaccines and antibiotics are hard to imagine. At any rate, as the heavily funded, generation-long search for a cure for cancer shows, great leaps cannot be taken for granted.

Global Inflation: New Sources

Closely related to the diminishing returns that plague efforts to expand output in many critical sectors of the global economy is that of rising real costs. In effect, diminishing returns and rising real costs are opposite sides of the same coin. Both bear the image of the inflationary threat with which policymakers wrestle.

Inflation is as old as money. But its global character and some of its recent causes are fairly new on the scene. Historically, inflation has been a localized phenomenon, ravaging individual countries from time to time. But during the seventies, it has assumed a global dimension. The meshing of the economic cycles of the major industrial countries in the mid-seventies contributed to both inflation's spread and its record severity. With virtually all the industrial economies simultaneously on the upswing, the worldwide demand for both raw materials and manufactured goods expanded at record rate. The virulent inflation that ensued affected even the inflation-resistant United States, financially conservative Switzerland, and socialist Poland (which had clung to the belief that socialism was somehow immune to inflationary forces).

Although global double-digit inflation is unique to the seventies, it has been many years in the making. Throughout the postwar period the average rate of price increase in the OECD countries, which account for the bulk of the world's output of goods and services, has been gradually accelerating. From 1958 to 1967, the annual rate of inflation was 2.5 percent. From 1968 to 1972, it increased to 4.8 percent. By 1974 it had moved into the double-digit range, exceeding 10 percent. In 1976, following two consecutive years of recession in the OECD countries, the annual inflation rate was still running at 7 percent.[4]

Double-digit global inflation has created extreme anxiety among national political leaders who must try to cope with it. The economists whose advice national leaders seek are puzzled by the failure of all traditional inflation controls short of the sanction of wide-scale unemployment. Indeed, inflation may be the great unsolved problem of modern economics. British economist Joan Robinson doubts that a solution can be found within the context of conventional economics. Robinson describes the problem with precision, but summarizes with a disclaimer: "Economics can't answer it."[5]

Inflation cannot be cured until its causes are well understood. The causes traditionally enumerated in economics textbooks include wage increases that exceed productivity gains, excessive demand stemming from "easy" money or deficit financing, short-term supply shortages following crop failures or other supply disruptions, and "administered" prices that have an upward bias. By "administered" prices, economists mean prices that are fixed either as a result of a concentration of economic power within an industry or by a commodity-marketing board or other government body. Within the U.S. automobile industry, for instance, production is dominated by three firms, and the prices set for new models do not fluctuate with demand. The price per car is fixed, and the number of cars sold is adjusted to fit that price; annual adjustments between "model years" are invariably upward. Similarly, OPEC sets the price for oil and then markets whatever it can at that price. Like the automobile industry, it has enough concentrated market power to make set prices stick.

Organized labor may also contribute to inflation by negotiating wage increases that exceed gains in labor productivity. This inflationary practice in some countries takes the form of "productivity bargaining," negotiations that relate wage increases to gains in labor productivity. Inflation generated by excessive demand—itself a product of deficit financing or of low interest rates that lead to "easy" money and to heavy investment and expansion—can be managed rather effectively by adjusting fiscal or monetary policy. Temporary by definition, inflationary pressures issuing from short-term supply shortages caused by crop failures, embargoes, or other disruptions do not usually pose long-term problems.

Although not easily managed, these traditional sources of inflation are at least understood reasonably well, as are the techniques for coping with them. It may not be easy for political leaders to convince labor-union leaders to exercise restraint in contract negotiations or to convince powerful industries to keep the inflationary effects of price increases in mind as they price their products. But at least leaders can try; the remedy is known. Whenever inflation arising from these sources gets out of hand, slowing the rate of economic growth will usually curb it, though in recent years reliance on this technique has fostered unemployment.

Before a satisfactory solution to contemporary global inflation can be found, however, new inflationary forces must be identified. One identifiable source is rising real costs resulting from the diminishing and negative returns experienced when offtake exceeds the regenerative capacities of biological systems. Under these circumstances, the real costs of production can only rise. The reduction in grazing capacity as a result of overgrazing can, for example, boost the prices of shoes and other leather products. So, too, the cost of home building rises in step with the price of lumber. Similarly, as soil erosion thins the topsoil, production can be maintained only by using more and more fertilizer. The effect is rising real costs for food.

Turning to marginal land in agriculture or to lower grade ores in mining can also lead to rising real costs if the decline in resource quality is not offset by gains in technology. For the economist, rising real costs do not necessarily translate into inflation as long as the money supply is fixed. Nonetheless, in the less technical, popular usage and in this discussion, rising real costs are treated as inflationary.

Scarcity associated with the short-run inability to expand resource supplies fast enough to meet rapid growth in demand also engenders inflation. During the mid-seventies the rapid continuing growth in demand for all basic resources was accentuated in the short term by the unplanned synchronization of the business cycles of the major industrial economies. For the first time ever, all were in the expansion phase at the same time, which forced global demand and raw-material prices to new highs. Marginal increases of 10, 20 or 30 percent gave way to a doubling or tripling of prices for some commodities. These widespread price leaps are often blamed on the coincidental synchronization of the industrial economies, but this explanation confuses symptoms and causes. Indeed, the inflationary effects of synchronization may merely be providing a glimpse of the future, when continuously expanding raw-material supplies may be an even more difficult and costlier endeavor than it is at present.

Although the prices of many commodities have climbed abruptly, the fourfold increase in the price of oil thus far during this decade is perhaps the most dramatic and foreboding hike (see Figure 7-1). These steep rises in petroleum prices reflected OPEC's decision to "administer" prices, but the strength to make its resolution stick derived from the lack of suitable substitutes for oil, from the ability of principal suppliers such as Saudia Arabia and Kuwait to restrict production, and from the associated transformation of the world energy market from one dominated by abundance to one dominated by scarcity.

Although OPEC raised the price of oil, the organization itself is not the cause of the high oil price. Rather, the higher price is a reflection of the transition from a time of cheap, abundant energy to a future when energy will be scarce and costly. The production of North Sea oil has been fraught with unanticipated costs. The expense of transporting oil from re-

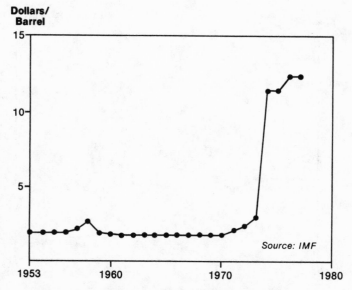

Figure 7-1. World Price of Petroleum, 1953-77

mote regions such as Central Siberia or the North Slope of
Alaska also boosted real oil costs. According to a study by the
Federal Energy Administration released in early 1977, the five-
to-eight-dollar-per-barrel cost of transporting oil from Alaska's
North Slope to the U.S. Pacific Coast is so high that if this oil
were priced at the same level as other new oil in the continental
United States, its delivered price would exceed that of OPEC
oil.[6] In fact, alternative energy sources under development do
not appear capable of seriously undercutting the OPEC oil
price.

Commodity prices of renewable resources have also increased during the seventies. The world price of wheat, for
example, tripled between 1970 and 1974 (see Figure 7-2).
Although the big jump in prices followed the massive Soviet
purchase of U.S. wheat during the summer of 1972, the Soviet
deal was merely the triggering event that brought the longer-

The Twenty-Ninth Day

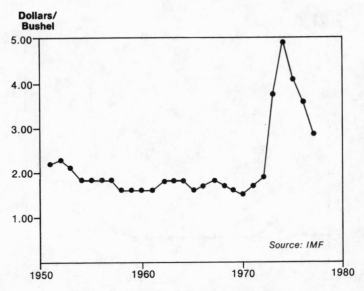

Figure 7-2. World Price of Wheat, 1951-77

term trends into focus. The growth in world demand for food during the early seventies simply outstripped the capacity of farmers to expand supplies of wheat and other commodities at historical price levels.

Matching the rises in the prices of food staples such as wheat was an equally dramatic rise in the price of soybeans, a principal source of high-quality protein (see Figure 7-3). Between 1970 and 1973, world soybean prices increased two and one-half times, and during the four years since they have shown no indication of returning to the remarkably stable historical level prevailing before 1971. The soaring price of soybeans reflects the inability of agricultural scientists to raise yields significantly, a worldwide scarcity of land on which to produce soybeans, and the deterioration of oceanic fisheries.

Like soybeans, lumber and firewood prices have doubled and in some cases tripled during the seventies. Between 1970 and

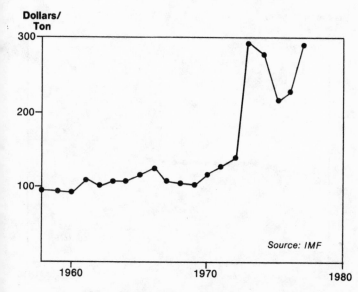

Figure 7-3. World Price of Soybeans, 1958-77

1976, the price of newsprint increased from about 150 dollars per ton to just under 300 dollars per ton (see Figure 7-4). Although the sharp climb in prices was commonly attributed to the global surge in economic expansion of the early seventies, the subsequent cessation of economic growth during the mid-seventies did not cause prices to fall. The "ratchet effect" that seems to be operating here suggests strongly that it is not the short-term shift in demand as much as the overall relationship between the level of demand and the sustainable yield of forests that counts.

Even things normally taken for granted such as land, living space, fresh water, and clean air become costly in a crowded, increasingly affluent world. Land prices required for home building have soared everywhere. Land prices in Tokyo shot up more than tenfold in the decade ending in 1972, while monthly wages rose only two and a half times.[7] "The American

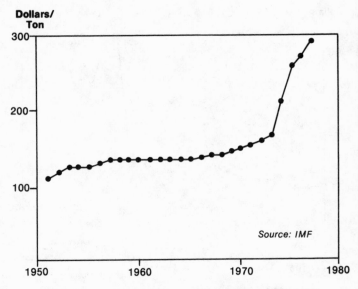

Figure 7-4. World Price of Newsprint, 1951-77

dream house has passed 50,000 dollars," the *New York Times* reported on October 23, 1976: "The milestone was marked this week when the Federal Home Loan Bank Board noted that the average price of a new home bought with a conventional mortgage in the United States during September was 50,500 dollars. The announcement presented the most striking evidence yet of how the single-family home—which since frontier days has been regarded as part of the American birthright, is becoming increasingly unattainable to millions of middle income families." Within a decade the average price for a new home in the United States had climbed from just under 30,000 dollars to just over 50,000 dollars.

Severe inflation can distort both economic and social values. It rewards speculators and penalizes savers. It can wipe out lifetime savings almost overnight or reduce those on low or fixed incomes to unexpected penury. Inflationary stresses can also aggravate social division, turning political cracks into fissures. Perhaps the ultimate threat of uncontrolled inflation is that it eventually undermines public confidence in governments and institutions and can thus pave the way for violent shifts to the radical right or left. When German Chancellor Helmut Schmidt was his country's finance minister in early 1974, he voiced his concern: "I only have to go to the years 1931 to 1933 to say that the meaning of stability is not limited to prices."[8]

Inflation has long threatened global economic health, but new sources of inflationary pressure baffle economists. While "administered prices" and what amounts to administered wages are undermining the flexibility of the economic system in general and the ability of the marketplace in particular to cope with inflation, rising real costs represent a pervasive new inflationary force. The traditional remedies of manipulating monetary and fiscal policies are no longer adequate. New remedies may not be found within economics, but rather may require new population policies and lifestyles.

Capital Scarcity

In addition to contributing to rising real costs and inflation, the diminishing returns typical of the food, energy, and other sectors of the global economy also make capital formation more difficult. Nowhere has the concern been greater than at the New York Stock Exchange, the institutional heart of modern capitalism. As James Needham, President of the Exchange, put it in the preface of a report published in late 1974, "We have become increasingly concerned about the supply and allocation of investment capital and our concerns have deepened with the realization that a capital shortage is no longer a threat for the future, but a fact of the present as inflationary pressures come to bear on the capital markets."[9]

No economic system or enterprise can grow unless it can

generate investment capital. Corporations raise capital for new investments by retaining profits, by borrowing in the financial markets (from the savings of others), or, more commonly, by doing both. Capital may be formed either through private or public means: if it is formed privately, it is derived from profits; if it is formed publicly, it is derived from taxes and other revenues. (For example, capital used for new investments in the automotive industry usually comes from retained profits, but the capital used to build the network of highways on which these cars operate comes from taxes.) All countries must be able to mobilize public or private capital or both for investment; to do so, they must make sure that production exceeds consumption. Whether a multinational corporation retains profits to construct a new factory or a rural Chinese commune uses seasonally unemployed labor to expand irrigation capacity, a portion of current production is invested to increase longer-term productive capacity. If a corporation has no profit margin or if all the labor in the commune is required to satisfy current consumption, then there is no capital formation.

The size of the prospective capital deficit is debatable. In a study published in the fall of 1975, *Business Week* pointed out that during the decade from 1965 to 1974, capital formation in the United States had amounted to 1.6 trillion dollars and that a capital requirement of an estimated 4.5 trillion dollars would be needed for the next decade.[10] The New York Stock Exchange estimated in its study that capital requirements for 1975–84 would reach 4.7 trillion dollars and that actual savings would amount to about 4.05 trillion dollars, leaving a gap of 650 billion dollars to be reckoned with over the next decade.

While the best available analyses on the projected scale of the capital deficit are those for the United States, the shortage is by no means confined to North America. Like inflation and unemployment, it afflicts the entire world. Even such efficient savers as the Japanese are running into difficulty. The centrally planned economies of Eastern Europe and the Soviet Union are collectively faced with a severe and deepening capital short-age; while borrowing heavily in Western capital markets, these nations are simultaneously scaling down their growth plans. The ailing economies of Britain and Italy also suffer from the inability to form enough capital. But if the problem is more visible in the industrial countries, it is more worrisome in the poor countries, where merely sustaining population increases requires heavy capital outlays.

The capital requirements of virtually every sector of the global economy are projected to increase sharply over the next decade. If U.S. energy consumption, for example, continues to expand rapidly, enormous amounts of capital will be needed. Because almost all prospective energy sources cost more to bring into use than traditional ones, the energy sector appears to have an insatiable appetite for new capital. Indeed, some estimates show capital requirements over the next decade to be three or four times those of the last decade. If the energy demands projected for the next decade materialize, satisfying energy requirements alone could absorb most of the capital that would otherwise be available for investment.

Agriculture too needs money to grow. The new-money needs of U.S. agriculture in 1975 were three times those of 1960, and they are growing by about 10 percent yearly.[11] Similar trends are emerging worldwide. Once the settlement frontiers are gone, all of the widely used means of expanding food produc-tion—chemical fertilizers, irrigation, and farm mechanization—are capital intensive. Reclaiming new land and developing the remaining irrigation sites will require heavy expenditures. So too will the increased use of fertilizer spurred by the exten-sion of farming onto less fertile land.

The capital requirements of the global housing industry are staggering. Faced with the need to find housing for the boom of postwar babies come of age, the United States will require an estimated 765 billion dollars between 1975 and 1985.[12] In poor countries with very high birth rates or in those centrally planned economies of Eastern Europe that have been woefully unable to satisfy even existing housing needs, the problem takes on graver proportions. The quarter-million people living on the streets in Calcutta and the countless millions living in shantytowns on the outskirts of Mexico City, Rio de Janeiro, Lima, and other Latin American cities, attest to a housing shortage of already staggering dimensions; adding sixty-four million people per year to the earth's present population of four billion will not ease capital shortages in this sector.

Besides the more traditional claims on new capital, a relatively new one—pollution control—now requires vast sums, particularly in the industrial countries. In Japan, where worsening pollution is visibly affecting human health, these claims are diverting capital from further industrial expansion. Indeed, this necessary diversion has contributed to the halving of Japan's economic growth since the early seventies.

Worldwide, investments in pollution control are particularly heavy in the paper, chemicals, and petroleum industries. Pollution-control expenditures for the U.S. paper industry grew from 93 million dollars in 1968 to 644 million dollars in 1975, a sevenfold expansion. These expenditures accounted for nearly one-third of all capital investment in the pulp, paper, and paperboard industries in the mid-seventies. According to a 1975 report in the *Journal of Commerce*, "rising capital outlays just for pollution control expenditures resulted in a marked shrinkage in funds for maintaining facilities and increased expansion in the paper industry."[13]

While the U.S. Environmental Protection Agency (EPA) must be empowered to enforce even more stringent regulation of discharged waste, this move will further raise pollution-control outlays in the future. One study indicates that the industry planned to spend 1.5 billion dollars on pollution abatement in the 1975–77 period. Merely satisfying the EPA's 1977 standards, however, would have cost 3.7 billion dollars, or 2.2 billion dollars more than the industry had earmarked for this purpose.[14] Waste is not the only environmental pollutant with far-reaching economic consequences. The noise associated with the use of modern technologies has climbed to a level where it is now a pollutant. More than a nuisance, prolonged noise at high levels can pose serious physical and psychological problems, including disorientation. Recent U.S. government regulations designed to reduce noise to a more tolerable level will require airlines to invest some five to eight billion dollars over the next five years.[15] With a population of 200 million, this proposed effort to reduce aircraft noise will cost each American an average of thirty dollars.

While numerous studies indicate that severe capital shortages impend, the issue is by no means settled. Some economists point out that, when adjusted for inflation, interest rates are not rising. This may be, but at the same time economic growth rates are slowing, perhaps indicating a reluctance to borrow at potentially higher interest rates.

Some economists argue that capital deficits never occur in the real world and that the supply of money always balances with the demand at the appropriate market price (which in the case of capital is the interest rate). While few economists would challenge this point, the fact remains that some social goals will not be met if interest rates are excessively high. If savings fail to match needs, growth will slow, unemployment will increase, and more political promises will remain unfulfilled.

Real-life capital shortages will no doubt call social goals into question. More specifically, they may bring into focus a growing divergence between traditional economic goals and evolving social goals. Capital scarcity may also prompt us to express goals in social rather than in economic terms—to value, for example, individual mobility and longevity over automobile sales and hospital construction. Indeed, one positive consequence of a capital shortage, one that might make the negative aspects more tolerable, might be a long-overdue reassessment of social goals.

Labor Productivity

People stand at the center of the modern economic system; output and consumption per person are the ultimate concerns of economics. Indeed, human economic progress is in large measure a history of the rising productivity of human labor. While land, capital, and other production factors are indispensable, their relevance rests ultimately on their contribution to the productivity of labor. The cost of capital as expressed in interest rates and the costs of land and other natural resources varies little between rich and poor countries, but variations in the value of labor, of output per person, are extraordinarily wide, often varying by a factor of 10, 20, or 30.

Prior to the machine age, the productivity of human labor was both low and unchanging. Only after World War II did labor productivity begin to rise in a rapid, sustained fashion. Economies of scale, those efficiencies associated with producing the optimum size of production units, have helped raise the productivity of labor to its present point. Improved organizational and management skills have helped raise labor productivity much as technical innovations such as the assembly line have. In recent years, electronic computers have helped make the white-collar labor force more productive in much the same way that mechanical power did for the blue-collar labor force. While other means of increasing productivity have been rather fully exploited in the industrial economies, computers and other innovations such as office copiers and pocket calculators still have much to add to productivity.

A look at the future suggests that new factors may influence labor's productivity in years to come. One of the earliest sources of increased labor productivity during the industrial era was the growing specialization of economic activity. The specialization that Adam Smith discussed and advocated two centuries ago has become a cornerstone of the modern economic system. At the beginning of the Industrial Revolution, the list of identifiable occupations—shoemaker, tailor, potter, teacher, and farmer—was relatively short; now literally thousands of recognized professions, occupations, and job specialties are widely recognized. Under way for nearly two centuries, the trend toward increased specialization in the industrialized world may now have nearly run its course in some situations. In some sectors, further specialization may contribute little to productivity. In others, particularly in assembly-line production, extreme specialization is sapping worker morale and, consequently, productivity.

The substitution of inanimate forms of energy for human muscle power may also have nearly run its course. All potential has not been exhausted, but the combination of rising energy costs and rising unemployment make the continuing substitution of energy for human labor less economical than it has been. Indeed, substitutions of labor for energy may be called for where unemployment is high. Already the historical trend of substituting energy for labor has been arrested in some sectors of industrial economies. The U.S. imposition of the nationwide fifty-five-mile-per-hour speed limit means, in effect, that labor is being substituted for energy in the transport sector. Less energy is used at the new slower speeds, but more driving time is required. The per-capita productivity of truckers, of bus drivers, and of deliverymen is being sacrificed to fuel economy. In the United States and Europe, the resurgence of bicycling among commuters represents another potential reversal of a long-standing trend toward the substitution of fossil fuels for human muscle power.

Another sector in which the substitution of energy for labor may be slowing is agriculture. In the United States, the historical decline in the number of farms and the associated growth in their average size has slowed. In North America, the Soviet Union, and Australia, the size of farm implements is also approaching the maximum that engineering and topography will permit. At the same time, home gardening, a labor-intensive mode of food production, thrives in the United States on a scale reminiscent of that of the World War II victory gardens. All these factors are likely to remain in force as long as energy costs remain high.

Besides those factors already mentioned, many others will frustrate continuing attempts to raise labor productivity, and not all such factors will be as highly visible or as readily measured as those that tend to increase productivity. Among them are the deterioration of biological systems and decline in the quality of mineral ores. Altered circumstances raise fundamental questions about future wage increases and consumption levels, since societies can consume only what they produce or purchase. The long-standing trend toward shorter work weeks may be slowed or even arrested. National initiatives to raise average output per person may involve increasing the share of the population in the active labor force. Where female employment is low, bringing more women into the labor force would expand average output; but in some societies, notably those with aging populations, doing away with mandatory retirement policies would have the same effect.

Unemployment: A Growing Social Ill

The global labor force is growing at a record rate. Young people are flooding the labor market in the poor countries, and ever more women of all ages are entering the job market in the rich ones. Governments have become accustomed to creating additional jobs by promoting overall economic growth; and, indeed, in some countries this growth long outran the indigenous labor supply. Acute labor shortages plagued northwestern Europe and Japan during the sixties and early seventies as the jobs created by record economic expansion outstripped the number of new entrants coming into the job market. However, by the mid-seventies rising unemployment had even these countries in its grip.

If new employment is to be created, there must be something to work with. For the half or so of the global labor force in agriculture, that "something" is land. From the age of exploration onward, the jobless would move to the frontiers of human settlement and could often obtain land there for the asking. In fact, this centrifugal force long saved Europe from overpopulation. As long as frontiers existed, employment could be created with trifling amounts of capital—enough to buy crude farm implements and seed. But now that land for settlement has become scarce or concentrated in a few hands, this is no longer possible without land redistribution.

As the opportunities for continuing rapid economic growth subside, unemployment spreads. During the recession of the mid-seventies, some 17 million workers, the highest number in forty years, were unemployed in North America, Japan, and in the industrial countries of Western Europe.[16] This continuously expanding corps of jobless is becoming a serious burden on unemployment and welfare funds. In many poor countries, entrants into the job market outnumber new jobs by two to one; levels of unemployment in these countries are without precedent.

India's labor force was projected to increase from 210 million to 273 million during the seventies. Although the nation is already stricken with widespread unemployment and underemployment, 100,000 new entrants join the Indian labor force each week. According to the estimates of economist Harry T. Oshima, at least 15 percent of the labor force is unemployed in Pakistan, Sri Lanka, Malaysia, and the Philippines.[17] One-third of Bangladesh's available manpower may be unemployed. Indonesia's working-age population is growing by an estimated 1.8 million annually; one-fourth of its potential labor force may now be jobless. Data for scores of other countries now show the same trend.

Looking at the developing countries as a whole, the International Labour Office (ILO) estimates that 24.7 percent of the total labor force was either out of work or underemployed in 1970. The comparable figure for 1980 is expected to approach 30 percent. Between 1970 and the end of the century, the labor force in the less developed countries is projected by the ILO to expand by 91 percent, requiring a phenomenal 922 million additional jobs (see Table 7-2). The projected growth in the developed countries, meanwhile, will be only 33 percent.

In countries with low fertility rates, young people entering the labor markets step into vacancies created by the retirement of older workers. In countries with high fertility rates, comparatively few older workers retire each year while large numbers of the young annually join the lines for jobs. Consequently, half to two-thirds of all new entrants into the job market may require newly created jobs.

If ILO projections prove accurate, the world labor force will increase from 1.51 billion in 1970 to 1.96 billion by 1985. Employing 30 million more persons per year in productive ways will require vast amounts of capital and natural resources, including energy. Since the world economy stagnated during two of the first seven years of this period, worldwide unemployment and underemployment are almost certainly rising. Unemployment at current levels—much less at future ones—is frustrating, dehumanizing, and politically destabilizing.

One of the most visible signs of rising unemployment in the developing countries has been the outmigration of job seekers.

Table 7-2. Projected Growth in World Labor Force, 1970–2000

	1970	2000	Additional Jobs Required	Change 1970–2000
	(MILLIONS)			(PERCENT)
More Developed Nations	488	649	161	+33
Less Developed Nations	1,011	1,933	922	+91

Source: International Labour Office.

In early 1973, when a national election campaign was in progress in Colombia, both major political parties opened campaign offices in New York City; their purpose, the *New York Times* reported, was to solicit votes from the estimated 80,000 Colombians residing illegally in the city.

In 1975 an estimated eight to twelve million illegal immigrants made their homes in the United States. Half or more of these uncertified workers were probably Mexican. What began as a trickle of illegal aliens crossing the U.S. border has now become a flood. While the Immigration and Naturalization Service (INS) has eight thousand employees and an annual budget of 160 million dollars with which to enforce the immigration laws, it is not equipped even to begin to cope with the problem.[18] Indeed, the INS is so overwhelmed that it will respond only to tips of groups of illegal aliens working in the United States, and makes no attempt to prosecute or deport isolated individuals. Moreover, the agency is short of funds needed to ship apprehended aliens home.

Emigration would solve unemployment problems only if those emigrating were not now competing with unemployed Americans for jobs. Indeed, the number of aliens believed to be holding jobs in the United States in 1977 approximated six million—the number of Americans out of work and actively seeking jobs.[19] Illegal immigrants also make a mockery of immigration laws and of those who wait patiently for years to migrate to the United States legally. In addition, they often collect welfare payments, adding to the burden of financially troubled cities such as New York.

In Europe, a legal migration of workers on a comparable scale has occurred between the preindustrial countries surrounding the Mediterranean and the industrial countries of northwestern Europe. As economic growth rates accelerated in Western Europe following World War II, labor shortages developed. Among other governments, those of France, Germany, the Netherlands, Switzerland, and Belgium began to invite workers from Mediterranean countries to work for an unspecified period of time. These southerners were clearly not being invited to apply for citizenship, but rather to remain in the host countries as "guest" workers. Not surprisingly, invitations issued to countries where wages were low and jobs were scarce brought guest workers in droves. By the early seventies, the migrants in Western Europe from countries such as Turkey, Yugoslavia, Algeria, Italy, Spain, Portugal, Morocco, Tunisia, and Greece numbered an estimated ten to eleven million, equaling the combined population of Denmark and Ireland. In individual countries, they made up anywhere from one-twentieth to one-third of the labor force.[20]

Since then dramatic changes have occurred. The severe economic downturn of the mid-seventies made fully employing even their native populations difficult for some industrial countries. Consequently, millions of guest workers have left for home. While this exodus has ameliorated the unemployment problem in northwestern Europe, it has only worsened that of the guest workers and of their home-country governments.

As the seventies pass, it is becoming clear that expanding unemployment constitutes one of the world's gravest social ills. As unemployment levels climb, the distribution of income within a society invariably worsens and further aggravates social inequities and political stresses. It is an issue that is certain to occupy political leaders and the unemployed themselves for some time to come.

The Changing Growth Prospect

During the seventies these several convergent factors—including diminishing returns on investments in basic sectors of the global economy, unprecedented inflationary pressures, and widespread capital scarcity—are all slowing economic growth. Growth has by no means stopped, but the global engine of economic growth is clearly losing steam. This slowdown did not originate in some sudden human failure to manage the economic system. Rather, it is rooted in humanity's relationship to the carrying capacity of biological systems and to the dwindling reserves of several key nonrenewable resources such as oil. In effect, the changing growth prospect reflects the constraining forces inherent in the planet's limited capacities and resources.

Economic expansion has slowed measurably during the seventies in Japan, the Soviet Union, the United States, Germany, France, the United Kingdom, and most other industrialized countries. Accordingly, the industrial nations have lowered their economic sights. The economic predicaments besetting the Soviet Union and Eastern Europe are reflected in their most recent development plans, which set out substantially lower growth targets, as well as reduced capital investment.

From 1966 through 1973, the global economy expanded at almost exactly 5 percent per year (see Figure 7-5). A steep

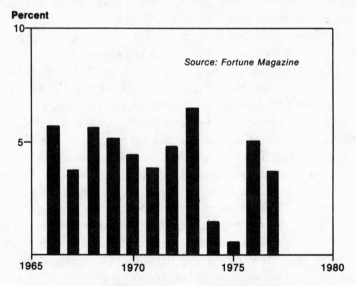

Figure 7-5. World Economic Growth Rates, 1966-77

descent from the 1973 peak brought growth down to less than 2 percent in 1974, and to less than 1 percent in 1975. The global economy resumed a respectable 5-percent growth rate in 1976 but then promptly subsided to a more modest 3- to 4-percent growth rate in 1977. The average annual growth rate of 2 to 3 percent for the past four years certainly does not in itself constitute a new trend, but when combined with the analysis underlying this book and the slower national growth projected by several key countries, it suggests a measurable slowing in future global economic growth from the levels prevailing throughout most of the postwar period.

The slowdown in economic growth, as experienced and as projected, cuts across ideological lines, affecting centrally planned and free-enterprise economies alike. Brazil, after years of a heady 9-percent annual growth, is scaling down its goals as its economy struggles with the high cost of energy and with a swollen external debt. Cornucopian promises for the future are no longer made in Cuba, where the government now projects an annual growth rate of 6 percent from 1975 to 1980, much lower than the 10-percent rate it claimed for 1975.[21] The South Korean economy, which has grown at a yearly rate of 10 percent over the past decade, is projected by the Bank of Korea to expand by only 4 percent annually for the next five years.[22] While rapid growth economies such as those of South Korea and Brazil are scaling down their plans and expectations, less robust national economies find themselves in exceedingly difficult straits. The prospect of static living standards, or even of lower standards in some countries, is not just a remote possibility. In India, real incomes have increased little since 1972.[23] In Bangladesh, rice consumption per person is less even in years of bumper harvest than it was a decade earlier.[24]

As national economic growth slows, public attention will turn to population policy and the distribution of output. As long as economies expand at several percent per year, rises in average income are assured, but when economic growth slows and that of population continues unabated, then the margin between the two may narrow or vanish. In even less fortunate countries where economic growth comes to a complete halt, even the slightest further population growth will erode living standards. Similarly, as the prospect of diminishing growth gives way to the reality, the distribution of wealth will become an even more pressing issue. As long as growth continued at a robust pace, the rich within a society could always say to the poor, "Be patient, the pie is expanding; wait your turn, your time is coming." At the international level, the "haves" could always give the "have nots" the same assurance. But when the pie is no longer expanding, or expanding only slowly, the question becomes how to divide it—a vexing issue both within and among societies.

8

Wealth Among Societies

From the Age of Exploration until quite recently those countries that controlled capital and technology have dominated international affairs. An early edge in the acquisition of wealth, of superior organizational skills, and of military technology permitted European countries to establish colonial empires. Once acquired, the colonies themselves helped bolster Europe's already dominant position further. As a result, the international order that prevailed from the Age of Exploration onward was shaped by European countries and peoples.

Only during the current decade has this long-standing international order begun to change. As the spiraling demands of four billion people began to press against the resources of our global lily pond, those countries controlling the more vital scarce resources are acquiring both economic and political leverage in the international system. The fourfold increase in oil prices in real terms has led to the most massive redistribution of wealth in history. Completely dwarfing the Marshall Plan, which involved resource transfers among industrial countries, the OPEC redistribution is primarily a transfer of resources from industrial to preindustrial societies.

In addition to the new-found power and wealth associated with the control of scarce resources, several other factors are converging to escalate concern over the distribution of wealth internationally. One of these, made possible by the improved international communications network, is the spreading awareness of the contrasts in consumption among societies. Another is the deepening economic interdependence among nations and the cooperation required to manage it. And, finally, as the global rate of economic growth slows, attention is shifting toward the distribution of income and wealth.

Global Distribution of Wealth

Prior to the Industrial Revolution, all but the ruling classes lived at or near the subsistence level. Peasants in Europe, Egypt, China, and the Andes all lived under similar economic conditions. With the advent of the Industrial Revolution, Western European living standards began to rise gradually. By 1850, consumption levels in the industrializing societies stood at roughly double those of the rest of the world. A century later, the gap had widened to perhaps ten to one. Today, the differences in living levels between the richest and poorest countries are easily twenty to one. Even though income per capita overstates on many accounts the current contrasts between rich and poor, it nonetheless crudely reflects the widening of the gap.

Much has been written about the historical forces that made

some countries rich and others poor. In the past, the subject has attracted numerous theorists who have attempted to explain the divergence in terms of a single factor—climate, religion, natural resource endowments, child-rearing techniques, soil fertility, colonialism, etc. But, individually, none of these explanations does justice to such a complex phenomenon.

The origins of the gap might be better understood if the gap itself were defined. We customarily refer to the gulf between the rich and the poor as an "economic gap" because it is most easily measured in economic terms, but it might also be described as a technological or knowledge gap. Surely, a major distinguishing characteristic of the rich societies is their capacity to develop technology and exploit global resources to raise the material living standard. But this capacity is not necessarily related to natural resource endowments, prevailing religion, or climate.

With the exception of Japan, all the countries that participated in the Industrial Revolution are countries with substantial cultural ties to Great Britain. These affinities undoubtedly facilitated the transmission and adoption of industrial technologies. Consequently, productivity in these countries began to rise rather steadily, interrupted only by war and economic recession. In other countries, productivity increased little, if at all. Once formed, this gap has tended to widen—in part because the rich countries learned to wield their economic power and the political influence it engenders to protect their privileged position.

European countries at the forefront of the age of exploration and the Industrial Revolution used their technological, economic, and military superiority to establish colonial empires. With these empires in tow, the British, French, Dutch, Portuguese, and Spanish acquired further wealth by exploiting the raw materials in the colonies. This set the stage for both the expansion of trade and further industrialization of the European powers.

Following World War II, the colonial empires were largely dismantled, with the former colonies becoming politically independent nation-states. But the newly independent countries remained economically dependent on their former masters. Some European countries, such as Belgium, had purposely avoided educating their colonial subjects so as to reduce the prospect that the colonized would ever become self-governing. Even more important, European countries adopted trade policies that discriminated against industrial imports and so perpetuated the historical pattern of exchanging industrial goods for raw materials. Then, too, heavy corporate investments in the extractive industries in the former colonies served to maintain the colonial relationship long after it had officially ended.

Recognizing the need for investment capital and technology, some former colonies tried to attract investments and to develop trade ties with other industrial countries so as to reduce dependence on the former colonial powers. Indonesia, for example, turned to both Japanese and American investors following the ouster of the Dutch. Algeria moved quickly after the French had been forced out to develop economic ties with the United States, now an important market for its oil and natural gas. While such alliances helped reduce dependence on the expelled colonial powers, reliance on industrial countries as a whole remained intact. Even as they lost their colonies, those countries in control of capital and technology increased their share of the world's productive wealth.

Regardless of what factors and circumstances served to distribute wealth, the fact remains that average incomes in countries of the modern world vary enormously (see Table 8-1). Throughout most of the period since World War II, average income in the United States was easily the world's highest; but other countries have recently begun to approach North American income levels. Incomes in the Middle Eastern countries of Kuwait, Libya, and Saudia Arabia now rank with or surpass those in the United States, partly because each of these leading

Table 8-1. GNP per Capita in Twenty Most Populous Countries, 1974

Country	Dollars
United States	6,640
Fed. Rep. of Germany	5,890
France	5,190
Japan	3,880
United Kingdom	3,360
Italy	2,770
USSR	2,300
Spain	1,960
Mexico	1,000
Brazil	900
Turkey	690
Philippines	310
People's Rep. of China	300
Thailand	300
Egypt	280
Nigeria	240
Indonesia	150
India	130
Pakistan	130
Bangladesh	100

Source: World Bank.

oil exporters has a relatively small population. Some of the leading industrial countries of Western Europe (among them, Sweden, Germany, and France) now also enjoy incomes on a par with those in the United States.

Income per person ranges from close to seven thousand dollars per year in the United States to a hundred dollars per year or less in poor countries like Ethiopia and Bangladesh. While income differences are only a crude economic indicator, they do reflect substantial differences in the consumption of goods and in access to social services.

Following World War II, the poor countries came to be known collectively as the Third World. Subject to unrelieved poverty, this group included all of Asia, Africa, and Latin America at midcentury. Government, religion, and geography separated the members of this large group, but poverty was common to all. As the years went by, the group slowly began to lose its economic homogeneity. Many so-called Third World countries were able to raise their levels of living well above the subsistence line. Some had strong leaders capable of framing and implementing wise economic and population policies. Others possessed valuable raw materials such as oil. In any event, some of those that moved ahead economically assumed economic and social characteristics resembling those of more industrialized societies. Among these were Korea, Taiwan, Hong Kong, the Ivory Coast, Brazil, Mexico, and mainland China. (Since China's economic transformation affected one-fifth of the world's population, its efforts stand out. Numerous countries have expanded production more rapidly than China, but its top-to-bottom social reforms add up to one of the outstanding success stories of postwar development.)

The oil-exporting countries have also made spectacular economic gains in recent years. The phenomenal rise in the price of oil has given the OPEC members enormous financial resources with which to underwrite development and to raise living levels. Petro-dollars have not yet wrought pronounced changes on behalf of the masses, but the resources and potential for change are nonetheless there.

The oil-exporting countries contain 260 million people. Among the more populous are Indonesia, Iran, Algeria, Nigeria, and Venezuela. For these countries, hefty oil revenues represent a particularly welcome source of finance. Other thinly populated OPEC countries with sizable oil endowments, such as Kuwait, Saudi Arabia, and Libya, are earning far more than they can absorb domestically and are therefore investing heavily abroad. Unfortunately, this surplus, totaling in the tens of billions of dollars annually, is invested almost entirely in Western Europe and North America. Only rather trifling amounts have been put to work in the poor countries.

Another small group of countries controls large shares of vital raw materials and has also quickly and impressively raised living standards. Morocco with its vast phosphate revenues and Malaysia with its tin and forest products stand out in this group.

While the Third World countries with raw materials, inspired leaders, or both have been able to hoist up their living standards and their prospects for further improvement, another group of countries remains stuck in the slough of poverty. Members of this group lack the necessary combination of resources, committed leadership, effective family-planning programs, and external assistance. Designated the "Most Severely Affected" (MSA) countries by the United Nations and the "Fourth World" by the Overseas Development Council, nearly all of these forty or so countries are Asian or African.[1] Among them are India, Pakistan, Bangladesh, Egypt, Ethiopia, Uganda, Chad, and Tanzania. With little capital per person and with a combined population of nine hundred million, most of these countries are also resource poor and dependent on imports of oil, food, and fertilizer. They have been most severely affected by the dramatic price rises of commodities.

The Dimensions of Poverty

In the Fourth World, where life for most is largely a struggle for survival, the convulsions of the international economic system during the seventies have pushed those living at the subsistence level even farther out on a shaky limb. Where nearly all personal income goes for food, pronounced rises in food prices invariably translate into increased nutritional stress and into rising death rates as experienced in recent years by Bangladesh, India, Ethiopia, and Somalia.

In this group of countries, people make do with almost nothing, personal possessions are few, social security outside the family scarcely exists, and many people receive no medical attention whatsoever. A pittance is all most can afford to spend on clothing, shelter, and fuel. The costs of education are too much for most to bear, and for want of textbooks, millions of children are barred from school.

Life in these poorer countries scarcely resembles life as lived by most in highly industrialized societies. A typical resident of a rich nation is comfortable, literate, overfed if not overweight, affluent, and acquisitive. A typical person in the Fourth World is penniless, illiterate, hungry or under-nourished, and survival oriented. Those in rich countries have a life expectancy at birth that approaches the Biblical ideal of three score and ten. In the Fourth World, millions die in infancy. In *The Picture of Health*, Erik Eckholm estimates that "thirteen million children aged five and under die each year—about thirty-five thousand a day, so many that the power of the living to comprehend the deep daily tragedy has grown dull."[2] In rich countries, economic opportunities are plentiful, and social mobility is high. In the poorest nations, economic opportunities are scarce, and societies are rigidly stratified.

The wide differences in food consumption among societies is perhaps the most troubling social disparity between rich and poor. Per-capita grain use, a useful indicator of dietary quality, varies from less than 200 kilograms per year in some countries to more than 700 kilograms in a few of the more affluent ones.

In countries on the lower rungs of the economic ladder, average grain use equals 150 kilograms per year or just under one pound per day (see Table 8-2). Where average grain consumption falls below that figure people are probably consuming starchy root crops in lieu of grain. In Nigeria, for example, the alternative staples are yams and cassava. At the upper end of the income ladder, North Americans and Russians each consume close to three-fourths of a ton of grain per year.

In nations where per-capita grain availability rises above 200 kilograms a day, the excess is usually consumed as livestock

The Twenty-Ninth Day

Table 8-2. Grain Consumption Per Capita in Twenty Most Populous
Countries, 1975 [1]

Country	Kilograms
United States	708
USSR	645
Spain	508
France	446
Fed. Rep. of Germany	441
Turkey	415
Italy	413
United Kingdom	394
Mexico	304
Egypt	286
Japan	274
Brazil	239
Thailand	225
People's Rep. of China	218
Bangladesh	203
Pakistan	171
Philippines	157
Indonesia	152
India	150
Nigeria	92

[1]Includes both that consumed directly and that consumed indirectly in the form of meat, milk and eggs.
Source: USDA.

products. Indeed, consumption of more meat, milk, and eggs is the single most pronounced change in dietary habits as incomes rise. After a point, grain consumed directly actually declines as livestock products begin to dominate diets. For example, a typical American consumes only 100 of the annual 700-kilogram total directly as bread, pastries, and breakfast cereals. The 600-kilogram remainder is fed to livestock that produce milk, butter, cheese, and eggs.

The rise of incomes in more affluent countries has led to increases in the intake of fat-rich livestock products, increases that are undesirable in terms of health. The two leading causes of death in industrial societies—heart disease and cancer—have both been linked to excessive consumption of animal fats.

Although the medical researchers investigating the relationship between fat intake and health recommend a diet that
translates into less than one half-ton of grain per person yearly,
actual consumption in affluent societies far exceeds this. Closer
to the ideal would be a simplified diet rich in whole-grain
cereals, fresh fruits, and vegetables and low in fat-rich livestock
products.

The affluent use up proportionately too much of the world's
energy, as well as too much of its food resources. While human
claims on the earth's agricultural resources seem to be limited
by the quantity of fat-rich livestock products individuals can
consume, no comparable constraints appear to limit energy
consumption. In rich and wasteful countries such as the
United States and Canada, annual energy consumption per
person may exceed ten tons of coal-equivalent. The consumption of commercial energy (excluding firewood and cow dung),
measured in coal-equivalent, totals less than 100 kilograms per
year in Nigeria, Ethiopia, Bangladesh, and some other poor
countries (see Table 8-3).

The national differences in energy-use levels reflect waste
as well as wealth. Between countries with similar income
levels, such as the United States and Sweden, energy consumption per person can vary by a factor of two to one. As
energy supplies grow shorter and costlier, the extravagant
and wasteful use of energy by the wealthy becomes more
difficult to justify. In the energy sector of the global economy at least, the traditional argument that more rapid
growth in consumption in the affluent countries would benefit the low-income countries by stimulating the international economy no longer holds.

Table 8-3. Energy Consumption Per Capita in Twenty Most Populous
Countries, 1974 [1]

Country	Kilograms of Coal Equivalent
United States	11,485
Fed. Rep. of Germany	5,689
United Kingdom	5,464
USSR	5,252
France	4,330
Japan	3,839
Italy	3,227
Spain	2,063
Mexico	1,269
Brazil	646
People's Rep. of China	632
Turkey	628
Egypt	322
Philippines	309
Thailand	300
India	201
Pakistan	188
Indonesia	158
Nigeria	94
Bangladesh	31

[1]Excludes firewood and dung.
Source: United Nations.

The Global Politics of Scarcity

Perhaps the most prominent change in the global economic
system during the seventies has been the emergence of resource shortages and their natural progeny, the politics of
resource scarcity. Price increases of two, three, or five times
in basic commodities such as oil, phosphate rock, wheat,
soybeans, bauxite, or timber have profoundly affected the
economic fortunes of both supplying and importing countries. Principal oil suppliers, for example, have acquired economic and political influence of the sort previously exerted
only by industrial powers.

Historically, the industrial powers bought raw materials in a buyer's market. Under the old dispensation, the overriding objective of national trade policies was to expand access of exports to foreign markets. The General Agreement on Tariffs and Trade (GATT) was created specifically with this goal in mind. Six successive rounds of GATT negotiations since World War II have steadily reduced tariff barriers and have stimulated world trade. More equitable access to and preferential treatment in the markets of the developed countries was the developing countries' principal demand at the three sessions of the United Nations Conference on Trade and Development. But temporary and chronic scarcities have converted many commodity markets into seller's markets, bringing to the fore the question of access to supplies. Lending special urgency to this issue is the increasing tendency of countries to limit exports of raw materials and other products. The imposition of such limits helps countries cope with internal inflationary pressures, extend the power of their depletable resources to earn foreign exchange, increase the share of indigenous processing, improve export terms, and take advantage of anticipated future price rises. But actions that may serve the narrowly defined national interest may be detrimental to the international community.

Countries with petroleum, minerals, and other nonrenewable resources are beginning to ask themselves how fast they want to exploit their resources. When potential supplies exceeded foreseeable demand and countries were eager to maximize exports, this issue was seldom raised. But today it cannot be ignored. Should world demand determine the rate at which a given resource is exploited, or should some longer-term internal-development strategy determine the rate? For example, should Venezuela's own long-range foreign-exchange needs or the short-term consumption needs of the United States determine the rate at which Venezuela exploits its shrinking oil reserves? Chances are that the two questions will not yield the same answer, that suppliers and users will not be satisfied with the same rate.

Frequently during the seventies, nations have banned or restricted the export of scarce commodities in order to cope with internal inflationary pressures. Brazil limited the export of beef in 1973 to levels 30 percent below those of the corresponding month in 1972. Thailand, a leading rice supplier, banned exports for several months in order to control domestic rises in rice prices. The United States, the chief supplier of soybeans, embargoed soybean exports in mid-1973 to keep prices down at home. Both the United States and Canada restricted cereal exports during late 1974. And as its domestic lumber prices soared, the United States also tried to get Japan to cut back voluntarily on its imports of U.S. forest products. This represented a dramatic turnabout since the U.S.–Japanese trade dialogue had heretofore always centered on increasing the United States' access to Japanese markets.

These cases raise some extremely difficult and unsettling questions. Under what conditions should a country be permitted to use trade policy, in effect, to export inflation? Should a sole or principal supplier of a particular resource be permitted to deny others access to the raw materials they need? If so, under what circumstances? Guidelines governing the terms of access to external markets and establishing penalities for countries that fail to comply have already evolved within the framework of GATT and have contributed greatly to world prosperity in the past twenty-five years. But no existing guidelines specify whether or when a country should be permitted to withhold a given resource from the rest of the world—even though restricting exports might cause hunger or lead to massive economic dislocations. If such guidelines existed, the United States probably would not have been allowed to withhold soybeans from the market as it did in mid-1973; nor would the Arab nations have been permitted to curb oil production after the 1973 Arab-Israeli War.

Launching embargoes to advance political objectives is

scarcely a new tactic. The Allies issued trade prohibitions in both World Wars. Similarly, the United States disqualified China as a trading partner for over twenty years and has excluded Cuba from its sphere of trade for more than fifteen years. But the events of the seventies make it clear that if global economic security and stability are to be maintained, international rules for determining national access to resources need to be negotiated and respected.

Commodity Cartels: OPEC and Beyond

The dictionary defines a cartel as "a combination of independent commercial enterprises to limit competition." Economics texts customarily discuss cartels as combinations of firms, but during the current decade it is nation-states that have been combining their forces to raise prices of a common export commodity. Membership may include a few countries or many. These resource cartels would not have been formed had poor countries that export raw materials remained content with a fixed or ever-shrinking wedge of an expanding global economic pie. Once these countries realized that their position as principal suppliers could be exploited through the formation of cartels, many were tempted to try.

This new era of cartels was heralded by the dramatic success of OPEC. Thirteen countries, which controlled the bulk of the oil that entered international trade channels, raised the world price of oil from $3.29 per barrel in 1973 to $11.58 in 1974. By 1976 the price had hit $12.38 per barrel, an increase of almost sevenfold over the 1970 price ($1.80) per barrel.[3] With this series of price increases began a massive transfer of wealth from importing to exporting countries. OPEC's export revenues from oil in 1973 were 23 billion dollars. With the new prices in effect, they climbed to 90 billion dollars.[4] The annual increase in revenues to this group of countries amounted to 16 dollars per person for the entire world population. It may represent the quickest massive transfer of wealth among societies since the Spanish Conquistadores seized the Incan gold stores some four centuries ago.

Reactions to the oil price increases were mixed. Economists who felt that the dwindling reserves had long been severely underpriced supported the price hikes. Political leaders in importing countries decried them. Spokesmen for poor countries with natural resources rejoiced; they saw in the increases signs of a profound shift in the international economic order in favor of raw-material exporters. President Carlos Andres Perez of Venezuela put the price rises in a Third World perspective when he said, "The increase of petroleum prices is by no means a selfish act of OPEC members for the exclusive benefit of their countries," and that the increase "represents the irrevocable decision to dignify the terms of trade, to revalue raw materials and other basic products of the Third World."[5]

Overnight, the oil-exporting countries gained enormous economic and political leverage in world affairs. Saudi Arabia suddenly joined the ranks of the superpowers. Prominent figures in the world of international finance such as David Rockefeller of the Chase Manhattan Bank and Robert McNamara of the World Bank traveled to Riyadh and Tehran. Industrial powers such as the United States found themselves pleading for oil on concessional terms, much as the poor countries had sought U.S. food.

OPEC's extraordinary and highly visible success has prompted suppliers of other raw materials to consider the advantages of collective bargaining. For them OPEC is an inspiration and a tantalizing model. Among the first to imitate OPEC were the suppliers of phosphate rock, a principal ingredient in fertilizer. Morocco, which is the leading exporter of phosphate rock, quadrupled the world phosphate price in late 1973, raising it from 14 dollars to 64 dollars per ton.[6] This action was widely considered a unilateral move, but the companies that control exports of phosphate from the United States, the second-ranking supplier, quickly followed suit. The speed with which this opportunity was seized suggests that if there was not outright collusion, there was at least parallel price action. Morocco's overall export earnings more than doubled as a result of the price rise.

The bauxite exporters have attempted to emulate OPEC. Jamaica, which supplies 60 percent of the bauxite used in the United States, has increased the levy on the ore from 2 to 13 dollars per ton. This sevenfold increase, administered in the form of a production tax on the corporations that mine Jamaica's bauxite, has sharply boosted Jamaica's export earnings. At the same time, it has raised the price of aluminum by only two cents per pound. At this new price level, bauxite is delivered to the United States at 19 to 27 dollars per ton. Alternate sources of aluminum (such as alumina clays) could not, geochemists estimate, come into play until bauxite reaches at least 40 dollars per ton. Thus, Jamaica's position is reasonably secure.[7]

Other mineral exporters have also banded together to increase mineral prices. Copper producers have united to form the International Council of Copper Exporting Countries (CIPEC is the French acronym), but this cartel has met with only limited success to date. India and Algeria have supported the formation of a cartel for iron ore; they point out that steel prices have more than doubled in recent years, while iron-ore prices failed even to rise in step with inflation. Australia, a major iron-ore exporter, has been a moderating influence in this effort. Indeed, raw-material suppliers who happen to be industrial countries are customarily less enthusiastic than nonindustrial members about cartels, making such unions difficult to organize. In part the reluctance of industrial countries may reflect their common bond with the other industrial countries most affected by rises in raw-material prices. Another factor may be that raw-material exports do not dominate their foreign-exchange earnings.

Exporters of chrome, rubber, timber, mercury, lead, and wool have either considered forming cartels or actually tried to set them up. So have the exporters of bananas, a perishable commodity. In effect, what began as the politics of oil is becoming the politics of raw materials. According to the August 1975 issue of *Fortune*, "There is no point in glossing over the gritty fact that the purpose of the nations trying to establish these cartels is to bring about a great redistribution of wealth in the world." If the materials exporters "succeed in that endeavor," the article goes on, "the days of sustained improvement in living standards in the advanced industrial countries may well come to an end."[8] Whether the latter point is tainted by paranoia remains to be seen, but that the purpose of cartels is to help redistribute wealth cannot be denied.

The likelihood that raw-material exporters will be able to bargain collectively and successfully is influenced by many factors: the number of suppliers, the ability and willingness of these suppliers to restrict exports, the availability of possible substitutes for the commodities in question, the existence of alternative sources of foreign-exchange earnings for the participating exporters, and the possibility of collective bargaining by importing countries. Whether cartels formed by countries that export commodities other than oil will succeed has been debated at length. While generalizations do not hold, the economic climate seems at present to be conducive to the formation of cartels and to their success.

Technology: A Global Commodity

As competition for physical commodities fosters interdependence among countries, so does the race for access to technology. Like food, energy, and minerals, the most advanced technologies are controlled largely by a handful of countries, and the transfer of these technologies is as politically sensitive as that of raw materials.

Technology today is a global commodity. New technologies developed in one country often have or find wide application elsewhere. The cure for polio developed in Pittsburgh is used throughout the world. Computer technologies everywhere are based on the same principles. Technological advances in air transport, communications, medicine, and metallurgy make their way around the world quickly.

Technology may be either commercial or noncommercial, proprietary or nonproprietary. Historically, the flow of technology across national borders has reflected more than anything else differences in levels of development. But as knowledge has expanded and as fields of scientific research and development have multiplied, it has become progressively more difficult for any single country, however wealthy and scientifically advanced, to remain abreast of all fields of research, much less to provide leadership. Thus, individual countries tend to specialize in particular areas, much as they have historically in international trade. In air transportation and computers, the United States leads in research and design efforts. In the field of oceanic transport, particularly in the design and construction of large ocean-going supertankers, the Japanese have no close competitors. In the field of mineral extraction, the Soviet Union has outdistanced most other countries and can now sell extraction techniques to foreign governments and multinational corporations engaged in mining.

Other countries have cornered other markets. In birth control, American medical researchers pioneered development of both the pill and the modern intrauterine device, while the widely used vacuum-aspiration technique of abortion originated in China. In agriculture, the American scientific establishment has long been in the forefront, developing many of the agricultural technologies that farmers everywhere now use. As the world's best deep-sea fishers, the Soviet Union and Japan have created new techniques of catching and processing fish. The Japanese and the French have developed the most efficient rapid-rail transportation systems and vehicles. In irrigation and desert reclamation, Israeli scientists have conducted much of the most innovative research. In satellite communications, the United States has been the pioneer.

Countries can obtain commercial technology abroad by purchasing patents and licenses or by importing high technologies. They can also invite the investments of multinational corporations or hire commercial consultants. Buying and selling technology internationally in the form of license payments and royalties (including management fees) is big business today. It has, in fact, given rise to a new concept, the "technological" balance of payments, the foreign exchange spent versus that earned in importing and exporting technology. Interestingly, the most technologically advanced countries—Japan, the United States, the United Kingdom, West Germany, and France—import the most technology, largely because they can absorb and utilize it effectively.

The United States, with its vast scientific-research establishment, has become the principal exporter of technology, steadily expanding its exports over the past decade. In 1965, the United States exported 1.26 billion dollars worth of technology in the form of licenses and royalties. Preliminary data for 1975 show that exports for that year amounted to nearly 4 billion dollars.[9]

The main current in the transnational flow of technology (licenses and patents) moves among the rich countries, often within the arteries of multinational corporations. Relatively few licenses and patents move from north to south via these giant companies—a problem for the southern poor countries since no alternative institutions are capable of transferring technology on a large scale.

Even the leaders of the centrally planned industrial economies of Eastern Europe and the Soviet Union recognize the need to further national development by securing technology from multinational corporations. Feeling the need to regulate both its exports and imports of technology systematically, the Soviet Union has created a firm to buy and sell technology from Western multinational corporations. Among this agency's more important transactions was the sale of improved mineral-extraction processes to multinational mining corporations based in the United States. In contrast, Soviet purchases of technology have concentrated on high-technology products, consumer-goods designs, and turnkey plants for producing chemicals and motor vehicles.

China, too, has imported advanced technologies from multi-national corporations. A contract with U.S.–based Kellogg Engineering, Incorporated, to build eight massive new nitrogen-fertilizer complexes has given China access to a highly sophisticated, highly efficient process for manufacturing nitrogen fertilizer.[10] By buying the plants, China is in effect buying the technology.

Among the countries that have exploited the international technology market most effectively is Japan. Between 1960 and 1970, Japanese firms entered into some 9,800 licensing agreements with foreign firms for the purchase of technology.[11] Although it still has the largest technological balance-of-payments deficit of any country, Japan now exports technology in significant quantities. Historically, Japan has often scaled down technology imported from the West and made it more labor intensive before exporting it to poor countries that have surplus labor. Indeed, a major share of Japan's exports go to the poor countries, while other industrial countries export technology primarily to each other.

In addition to licenses and patents, technology also crosses national boundaries embodied in products. The purchase of computers from IBM by the Soviet Government is an obvious effort to obtain a new technology. The purchase of commercial jet airliners from the Boeing Corporation by airlines everywhere is a means of obtaining a highly advanced air-transport technology not otherwise available. Imported pharmaceuticals

and construction equipment also exemplify technology embodied in goods.

Obtaining technology by attracting private foreign investors
is an approach that poor countries often employ. Eyeing the
latest in Wester computer technology, India encouraged IBM
to invest in computer-manufacturing facilities in India. The
Democratic Republic of the Congo, which needs tires to replace those on imported vehicles, acquired this technology
when Firestone invested in a tire factory there. In these instances, technology transfers may show up on the books as
licensing fees paid to the current firm by the foreign subsidiary.

Like bees that carry pollen, consultants and consulting firms
also carry commercial or proprietary technology across national
boundaries. Some developing countries, among them Algeria,
are effectively utilizing this source. When the Algerians began
to expropriate French energy investments, they hired a New
York Wall Street legal firm to help them negotiate. From these
U.S. lawyers they bought both financial and legal know-how,
as well as a sophisticated understanding of the Western business community. The Algerians added insult to injury, reports
Ann Crittenden of the *New York Times,* when they hired
Arthur D. Little, Inc., a U.S. economic consulting firm, to help
them prepare a speech for their representative to the UN
Special Session on Raw Materials; the delegate attacked the
existing international economic order and in the process
emerged as a Third World spokesman. Arthur D. Little's staff
pointed out that it was not asked to produce a position paper,
only to produce the analysis and data to support the position
the Algerians wished to take. But according to Crittenden,
private consulting firms "tell one country what its export industry should be, another how to plan its energy policy for the year
2000, and a third how to restructure its education system."[12]

While no sacred formula dictates how commercially held
technology moves across national borders, the international
transfer of noncommercial or public technologies has been

more or less institutionalized since World War II. In agriculture, bilateral and multilateral assistance agencies act as midwives in this transfer. So do such well-established institutions as the International Corn and Wheat Improvement Center located in Mexico and the International Rice Research Institute based in the Philippines, as well as a half-dozen more agricultural-research institutions scattered throughout the developing countries. Not surprisingly, technology generated in internationally supported institutions is usually much more accessible to the international community than that developed by national or private research organizations.

Nonproprietary technology can be acquired through various channels. Foreign technicians, either in residence or on short-term consulting assignments, are one key conductor. The United States and the Soviet Union acquired basic space technologies after World War II in this fashion when both eagerly sought German space-scientists.

Many poor countries obtain knowledge of new technology by sending students to the developed countries. Indeed, a majority of the estimated 135,000 foreign students enrolled in American colleges and universities are from poor countries. Many more are studying in other industrial countries.

Still another way of transferring nonproprietary technology is by disseminating products such as vaccines or new seeds. The World Health Organization has been instrumental in this effort, as have other UN and bilateral-aid agencies. The U.S. Agency for International Development in Ankara, for example, introduced high-yielding Mexican wheats into Turkey on a large scale. American technicians acquainted Turkish farmers with the new seeds and verified that they could grow in Turkey, while AID financed the importation of twenty-two thousand tons. Similarly, West Pakistan imported forty-two thousand tons of Mexican wheat seeds in 1967. Planted on more than a million acres, this wheat yielded enough seed when harvested to plant the country's entire acreage of wheat. The new technology, which enabled Pakistan to increase its wheat crop by 60 percent in four years, was virtually free to Pakistan, since the Rockefeller Foundation had already made the research investment in Mexico. A similar approach permitted India to double its wheat crop in just six years.[13]

In addition to hard technologies such as improved seeds, many soft technologies, particularly valuable social-science tools, are passed from nation to nation. Among these are national-income accounting, cost-benefit analysis, management techniques, and such basic industrial techniques as Henry Ford's assembly line. These technologies can easily be moved across national boundaries by both national-aid agencies and international technical-assistance agencies.

The transfer of technology from a rich country to a poor one is not always trouble free. Technologies being used in one country are often simply not appropriate for use in the other. Most technologies used in rich countries, for example, are capital intensive and designed to minimize labor use. Where capital is scarce, labor is exceedingly abundant, and markets are small, complex and costly technologies—the kind that multinational corporations frequently offer—are often of limited value.

Clearly, more and more of the new technology used in any one country originates outside that country. As technology continues to advance, research and development programs in any single country become more concentrated and specialized. For this reason and because the poor countries stand in desperate need of relevant technology, technological interdependence will likely increase further.

Drawers of Water, Hewers of Wood

The accrual of economic and political power tends to gather momentum with each successive increment. As economist Arthur Lewis points out, the tariff structure in force today in the rich countries leads them to charge, in effect, twice as much duty on imports from the poor countries as on goods they trade with each other, thus reinforcing the existing economic stratification.

The tariff structure not only discriminates against imports from poor countries, it also puts an inordinate cost on the value added by processing. Unprocessed commodities often enter industrial countries duty free, while tariffs are imposed on the same product if it has been processed. Unprocessed copper is imported free of duty, while a duty is levied on copper wire. Essentially, this duty is imposed on the value added to the commodity by processing it, which in the case of copper amounts to a stiff 12 percent.[14] Similarly, hides and skins enter the United States duty free, while leather is subject to a 4-to-5-percent tariff and shoes to an 8-to-10-percent tariff. In the European community, the tariff on cocoa beans from nonassociated countries is 3 percent, while cocoa bears an 18-percent tariff. Not only does this duty eliminate the comparative advantage afforded by the cheapness of labor in poor countries, but it also discourages industrial growth and reinforces traditional trading patterns.

Many developing countries see the improved market outlook for raw materials as an opportunity to substitute exports of semi-processed or processed raw materials for those of the raw materials themselves. They wish to abandon the "drawers of water, hewers of wood" role they have traditionally occupied in the world economy. A good example of the exercise of newly acquired bargaining power is reflected in a deal negotiated by Japan and Turkey: Japan has agreed to build a plant capable of processing 50,000 tons of ferro-chrome or alloy per year in Turkey in exchange for a million tons of Turkish chrome over an eleven-year period.[15]

The oil-exporting countries are exercising their new-found influence on the world market to attract investment in industrial capacity. If they get their way, these countries will export more refined oil and less crude oil. In effect, they will guarantee oil supplies to industrial countries in exchange for industrial technology and investment. Iran and Saudi Arabia, for example, are planning to refine more and more of the oil they export. Iran exported 300 million dollars worth of petrochemicals in 1976, "but hopeful Iranian economists predict that these earnings will have tripled by 1980 with the completion of a planned three-billion-dollar investment program." Tiny Qatar has announced plans to build a four-hundred-million-dollar nitrogen-fertilizer complex that will use local natural gas as the feedstock.[16] Virtually all the products of this complex are slated for export, since Qatar's own arid sands produce little food.

Not all investments in the OPEC countries relate to oil. Iran has launched an ambitious effort to develop its vast reserve of copper, now estimated at three billion tons, and is courting a Belgian–West German consortium that plans to invest 135 million dollars in a copper refinery.[17] Argentina, Brazil, and India are individually exploiting the periodic global scarcity of cattle hides by restricting or banning exports, thus furthering development of their domestic leather-goods industries. In so doing, they hope to shift the geographic focus of the leather-goods industry from Italy and Japan to the Southern Hemisphere.

Many preindustrial countries are discovering that they have an ecological advantage in international economic competition —unused waste-absorptive capacity. Indonesia is exploiting its ecological leeway and playing on mounting Japanese fears of domestic pollution to persuade Japanese mineral-extraction firms to ship processed rather than crude ore to Japan. To attract industrial investors from the United States, the Brazilian government has advertised in the *New York Times* its lack of environmental restrictions on waste disposal.

Without a doubt, resource scarcities are enabling preindustrial countries to attain at least some leverage on the international economic system and on the countries that import raw materials. Opportunities to use this leverage are not always immediately obvious. Once they become so, countries will not hesitate to exert the influence they possess.

Calls for a New Order

Dissatisfaction over the existing economic order runs high and wide in the Third and Fourth Worlds. As Roger Hansen notes, "For the past twenty years, and particularly since the founding of the UN Conference on Trade and Development (UNCTAD) in 1964, the world's developing countries have grown increasingly critical of major aspects of the various regimes—trade, investment, technological, monetary, and foreign assistance—which together constitute today's international economic system."[18] Those poor countries of the global South that have organized into the Group of 77 believe that each of these systems must be overhauled.

Within international trade, the developing countries are pushing for the adoption of international commodity agreements to raise and stabilize the prices of raw materials. All too often, they insist, importing countries have exploited the buyer's market that has existed historically for many raw materials. One study cites the case of the banana industry, pointing out that "the producing and exporting countries receive about 11.5 cents of every dollar's worth of bananas sold" to the consumer.[19] In effect, this means that those who own the land; who prepare the seedbed; and who plant, cultivate, harvest, and transport the bananas to dockside receive one-eighth as much as do those who transport, ripen, and retail them. In economic terms, this distribution of the "banana dollar" between producing and consuming countries can scarcely be justified. Wages of those working on the banana plantations are only a tiny fraction of the wages of those who handle the retail sales in the consuming countries. But such speculation only leads to other questions related to equity.

The developing countries strongly believe that inordinately

high tariffs on manufactured goods, which make it difficult for poor countries to export, are designed to confine them to the status of raw-material suppliers. Many poor countries feel that the industrial countries, whose average citizens earn approximately twenty times what their counterparts in poor countries do, are not providing enough development assistance. They further hold that debts should be renegotiated or rolled over, since the high cost of debt servicing now often stifles development efforts. Even more important, poor countries feel that they deserve easier access to capital markets in the industrial countries and that multinational corporations seldom invest in poor countries on terms sufficiently favorable to the host countries. Nor, they say, have multinational corporations taken pains to adapt their technologies to the needs and goals of developing countries.

The poor countries feel, quite rightly, that the international monetary system does not serve their needs well. They have relatively little voice in its management and are particularly distressed because most of the Special Drawing Rights, the new international liquidity created by the International Monetary Fund, go to the rich countries. The poor countries have long been pressing for change in the international economic order, but to little avail. International representatives of the rich industrial countries either have not been convinced that the system is inherently unjust or simply have not been willing to change it. Not until OPEC quadrupled the price of oil in a one-year period did the tables begin to turn. Then, the bargaining power of the poor countries began to appear more formidable. Besides offering other developing countries an example to follow, the OPEC countries have lent their newly acquired political muscle to poor countries trying to alter the international economic order.

The poor countries have two principal economic objectives. One is to increase their share of productive wealth by promoting a more equitable international distribution of the world's

riches than now exists. The other objective, more immediately
political, is to help draft the rules that govern the international
system. These nations want a greater voice in international
economic matters in general and in the control of such institutions as the International Monetary Fund and the World Bank
in particular.

The division of wealth among nations becomes more pressing each year. The principal difference between the current
period and years past is that more and more countries are
acquiring influence in the system. Scarcely responsive to time
and to the sporadic humanitatian impulses, the old economic
order is being reshaped by the forces of resource scarcity and
of deepening political and economic interdependence. Increasingly, the key issue appears to be the extent to which the
international redistribution of wealth will be tied to social
reforms and to the redistribution of wealth within the poorer
countries.

9

Wealth Within Societies

The past quarter-century has witnessed enormous and almost universal growth in the output of goods and services. Unfortunately, these remarkable achievements in production have not been matched by improvements in distribution. Indeed, the distribution of wealth has become even more inequitable than before in most developing countries. In some, the poorest have suffered an absolute deterioration of their living standard and are worse off today than they were a generation ago. Ironically, the widest gaps between the rich and poor now exist within the poorest societies.

Development planning in the developing countries has emphasized growth while neglecting distribution; strategies that reinforce existing inequities have been the rule rather than the exception. Planners assumed that with rapid growth everyone would be better off—that more growth meant more for all. But in fact, this trickle-down approach to development has not worked.

The social manifestations of the concentrating of wealth are far from pleasant. A World Bank report outlines the impressive gains in economic growth but then goes on to say, "Statistics conceal the gravity of the underlying economic and social problems, which are typified by severely skewed income distribution, excessive levels of unemployment, high rates of infant mortality, low rates of literacy, serious malnutrition and widespread ill-health."[1] This list could have included runaway migration to the cities, external indebtedness, social disintegration, and political unrest.

The National Distribution of Wealth

Data on national patterns of income distribution provide a means for comparing the distribution of wealth both among societies and within a given society over time. One of the simplest techniques for analyzing the distribution of wealth within societies is to compare the income of the richest 20 percent to that of the poorest 20 percent. This rather straightforward indicator reveals unbelievably wide gaps in some countries. Indeed, the income per person among the richest fifth of the population in some countries is twenty-five times that of the poorest fifth.

As a rule, income is distributed more equitably in the richer countries than in the poorer ones. Among the industrial countries, those of Eastern Europe appear to have gone farthest toward passing around the benefits of growth even-handedly. The ratio between the upper 20 percent and the lower 20 percent in Poland, Hungary, and Yugoslavia appears to be roughly three or four to one.[2] Close behind this group are the principal English-speaking countries—the United Kingdom, the United States, Canada, and Australia—where the ratio is perhaps five to one. Asia's leading industrial country, Japan, also belongs in this category. Clustered together not far behind are Sweden, Norway, and Denmark, each of which has a ratio of seven or eight to one.

Among the poorer countries, income is distributed most evenly in East and South Asia. Notable among them in East Asia are China, Korea, Taiwan, and Thailand. In South Asia, income is relatively equitably distributed in Sri Lanka, Pakistan, and India, where the ratios are roughly six to one between the highest and lowest quintiles of the population.

With few exceptions, the most inequitable distribution of income is to be found in the Middle East, Africa, and Latin America. Oddly enough, those countries whose leaders charge that international wealth is maldistributed and that a new international economic order is needed come out looking worst in these cross-national comparisons. Included in this group are Iraq, with a ratio of twenty-five to one, and Senegal, with a ratio of sixteen to one. The Andean countries, led by Ecuador (with a ratio of twenty-nine to one), have the worst income disparities of any regional group. Venezuela follows with a ratio of twenty-two to one; Brazil and Mexico have ratios of fifteen to one and sixteen to one, respectively. The only industrial country with an income disparity at all comparable is France, where the ratio between the incomes of the richest and the poorest fifths is thirteen to one.

Income distribution has improved dramatically over the past quarter-century in both China and Taiwan. Although these two countries have contrasting political systems, the improvements in income distribution have been more or less parallel —which suggests that it is political will, rather than the political system per se, that furthers equity.

While China and Taiwan were making great strides, many other countries scarcely changed at all. The United States typifies those in this group. Income is distributed today essentially as it was a generation ago. Instead of the rich getting richer and the poor getting poorer, virtually all have been getting richer while relative wealth has changed little.

Apart from simply separating groups according to income levels, there is no simple way of analyzing income disparities that is universally applicable. The traditional Marxist approach of dividing a society into industrialists and workers seems simplistic now and no longer accords with reality. Another approach, viewing class conflict in terms of urban and rural peoples, is in many ways a more useful way of reassessing national income-distribution patterns in some countries. In other societies, the more important distinction is that between the landowners and the landless.

In some countries, a wide economic gulf separates organized labor and the rest of the labor force. Labor unions organized within the embryonic industrial sector can use their negotiating strength to raise their own wages, thus encouraging industrialists to substitute capital-intensive equipment for labor and limiting the number of jobs created.

Special-interest groups are not the only agents that serve to concentrate wealth in developing countries. The relative position of low-income groups is often weakened by excessively rapid population growth. The deterioration of biological systems can also lower the productivity and income of some segments of society even while incomes rise in others. In some situations, the principal culprits may be the economic-planning commissions.

The Role of Planners

Economic-planning commissions, which help identify economic goals and strategies for achieving them, have invariably stated goals in terms of overall economic growth. The goal for the first development decade (the sixties) was, for example, a

5-percent rate of economic growth. By the late sixties, some analysts were questioning and even condemning this approach; they contended that while economic-growth objectives were commonly met and sometimes exceeded, living conditions for the poorest 40 percent were actually deteriorating. In scores of countries, two decades of development planning with its overwhelming emphasis on growth had further concentrated wealth in the hands of the already rich.

Conventional wisdom during this period held that achieving economic-growth targets and redistributing income in a socially desirable fashion were often mutually exclusive goals. The challenge to this traditional approach was led by Pakistani economist Mahbub ul Haq. "We were taught to take care of our GNP, as this will take care of poverty," he said; "but let us reverse this and take care of poverty, as this will take care of the GNP. . . . Let us worry about the *content* of GNP even more than its rate of increase."[3] Haq argued that what was needed was a selective attack on the worst consequences of poverty—malnutrition, disease, illiteracy, and unemployment.

Haq's attack on development planning grew out of firsthand experience. He had been one of Pakistan's principal planners during the late fifties and much of the sixties. He had seen income distribution in Pakistan grow ever more unfair and had the courage to speak out. Early in 1968, Haq publicly noted that industrial income and wealth were being concentrated in the hands of twenty-two family groups that together controlled two-thirds of the nation's industrial assets, 80 percent of its banking, and 70 percent of its insurance. In Haq's words, "It was evident that most of the population had remained virtually untouched by the forces of economic change since economic development had become warped in favor of a privileged minority." Haq also noted that the disparity in per-capita income between East and West Pakistan had doubled over a decade. Within a few years, this widening gap was to exert unbearable pressure on the tenuous political ties that held the two geographic wings together; it was to lead to a civil war and to the eventual creation of Bangladesh. Although the war made Pakistan's case extreme, the conditions that led to war made it only too typical of poor countries.

Some of the failures of development planning can be blamed on the technicians and economists who sit on the planning commissions. They deserve some of the blame; they have blindly championed growth and have been too quick to import technologies and economic strategies from the industrial countries. In agriculture in particular, the desire to imitate the capital-intensive, highly mechanized approach to farming has led countries with a high man-land ratio astray. But the fault is not entirely theirs. Political leaders often will not or cannot mobilize the support needed to push through reforms or enlightened policies.

All too often, densely populated, poor countries have mistakenly emulated Western industrial societies when they should have been looking to Japan, a more relevant model in almost every way. Edgar Owens of the Agency for International Development sums up the situation well: "One of the most fundamental premises of economics is that one should husband the resource which is scarce and use the resource which is plentiful. For developing countries this means labor intensive, capital saving investment. However self-evident this point may seem, it is unhappily true that most of the low income countries and international assistance agencies have been pursuing the opposite pattern—policies and technologies which are capital intensive and labor saving."[4]

Income distribution within a society is closely related to the employment pattern. If most of the available investment capital flows into capital-intensive industries, relatively few jobs will be created. A small segment of a labor force will be employed in high-paying capital-intensive industries, while large numbers will be unemployed. To quote Owens again, "either today's countries can choose high incomes for a few, the capital-intensive route, or modest but rising incomes for all producers, the labor intensive and also the Japanese route."

When unemployment rises, the distribution of income can only grow more lopsided. A revealing study of Colombia by the International Labor Organization indicates that the "bottom third of the rural population may be no better off today than in the 1930s."[5] The Colombian situation was made worse when organized labor bargained collectively to raise wages some 5 to 15 percent yearly for that small segment employed in the industrial sector. As James P. Grant of the Overseas Development Council sums it up, there "will be a sizeable group in the developing countries whose standard of living will be rising rapidly while unemployment is increasing. . . ." and "the contrast between those for whom the system is working and those for whom it is not" will grow sharper.[6]

The beneficiaries of investment and growth are selected, consciously or unconsciously, by development planners. Although sector planners in some rather poor countries, for example, skillfully deploy limited health resources for the good of the majority, those in other countries waste comparable resources or manipulate them in the name of the elite minority. Sri Lanka and Liberia illustrate the extremes of socially responsible resource management. The Liberian government built a large modern hospital on the outskirts of Monrovia; the edifice embodies the latest advances in medical science and equipment engineering, and provides excellent health care for the minute percentage of the country's population that is wealthy and resides in or near the capital. Unfortunately, constructing and maintaining such a top-notch hospital has siphoned off so much of the Health Ministry's budget that little is left to provide health services in the villages. In this case, the Liberian government's stress on the two central components of modern Western health systems—namely, training highly skilled medical doctors and building hospitals—clearly amounted to the decision to care for the few who are rich at the expense of the many who are poor. Some governments have eschewed the elitist approach Liberia favors. Sri Lanka, for example, has improved health care by training legions of paramedical workers who complement the work of a relatively small core of fully trained doctors, most of whom function in a supervisory capacity. Thus, although annual income in Sri Lanka averages only 130 dollars per person and health expenditures per person remain quite low, life expectancy at birth is now sixty-eight years (nearly as high as that for American males).[7] South Korea has followed a similar strategy. Both countries have outdistanced other low-income nations that have followed the Western approach to health care.

Perhaps the most dramatic achievements in health care have been realized in China. When Chairman Mao Tse-tung came into power in 1949, the health of the disease- and narcotic-ridden nation could scarcely have been worse. Resource-short, the new government put its money into the training of paramedical personnel. It drew recruits mainly from the countryside, trained them in nearby medical centers, and then sent them back to the villages. China's "barefoot doctors" provide first aid, give inoculations, and carry out simple health-related tasks, including the distribution of contraceptives and the performance of abortions; they refer cases that they cannot handle to fully trained doctors who are strategically located throughout the country. China's vital statistics reveal the effectiveness of China's approach to health: its life-expectancy, birth, death, and infant-mortality rates closely approach those of wealthy industrial societies.[8]

Education is another sector whose basic design can either encourage the just redistribution of income or help to maintain the social and economic status quo. A government can train a small segment of the society to a very high level, while leaving the great bulk of the population outside the educational mainstream, perhaps even illiterate. Alternatively, it can invest broadly in basic education for all.

Differences among countries in educational expenditures tell much about the objectives of educational policy. Compare, for example, the extensive use of public funds in South Korea to subsidize primary education, with Brazil's investment of the lion's share of its educational budget in university education. In 1970, two-thirds of all Korean children between the ages of five and fourteen were in primary schools, while only one-half of the same age group attended school in Brazil (where incomes are higher than in Korea).[9] Subsidizing advanced education for a fortunate few keeps power and wealth the prerogatives of the elite.

Among countries that have improved distribution while expanding output and that have upgraded social conditions while raising consumption levels, China stands out. But China's political system is unique, and those approaches that work in China may not be transferable. Other countries whose improvements in the distribution of income may have wider bearing and application than China's are Taiwan, Sri Lanka, South Korea, India, Tanzania, and Cuba.

A close look at Sri Lanka is instructive because it has been carrying out major reforms while under a democratic form of government. In 1953, the lower one-fifth of the Sri Lankan population commanded only 5.2 percent of the nation's income, but by 1970 its share had increased to 7.2 percent. Combined with the growth of the economy, this increase led to marked social gains by the lower economic echelons of society. Meanwhile, the upper one-fifth—which in 1953 had commanded 53.8 percent of the income—saw its share fall to 45 percent (see Table 9-1). The associated improvement during this period in all key social indicators reflects both the overall economic growth and the redistribution of income.

Taiwan's striking progress makes it in many ways unique among developing countries. Some countries have grown as rapidly, and yet others have redistributed income with comparable success. Brazil has also achieved an exceptionally rapid

Table 9-1. Income Received by Quintile Groups in Sri Lanka,
1953 and 1970

Quintiles	Percent of National Income	
	1953	1970
Lowest	5.2	7.2
Second	9.3	10.0
Third	13.3	14.4
Fourth	18.4	22.0
Fifth	53.8	45.0
Total	100.0	100.0

Source: Central Bank of Sri Lanka; Department of Census and Statistics.

growth, but its distribution of income has become more and more inequitable. Cuba has greatly improved its income distribution and social indicators; but its economy has not performed well, leaving it heavily dependent on aid and faced with chronic scarcities of consumer goods. Taiwan, having managed to do both successfully, deserves more attention from economic planners in other developing countries.

The Role of Technology

In recent years the term "appropriate technology" has crept into both public discussions and the literature on economic development. When applied to a developing country, the term usually refers to the appropriateness of a given technology for use where labor is abundant and capital scarce. But considerations of appropriate technology must now also take into account energy efficiency and social equity. Technologies that do not embrace these criteria as well are not likely to work over the longer term.

In government circles, technology is often assumed to be socially neutral, and hence left to be managed by market forces. But the nature of technology employed and the distribution of wealth are intimately related, though not even the existence of the relationship, much less its nature, is commonly acknowledged. In sector after sector—in health, education, agriculture, and transportation—the nature of the technology selected determines how the benefits of investment will be distributed and even who the beneficiaries will be. Yet, the selection is often an ad hoc affair, governed by the whims of the market or by efforts to blindly imitate technologically advanced economies. Where there is no systematic public evaluation, the existing political power structures are free to serve vested interests by adopting technologies that either maintain the status quo or strengthen the position of the elite minorities. Frequently, catering to such interests means investing heavily in capital-intensive labor-displacing equipment. For example, major landowners in poor countries can often more easily maintain their holdings if they can import farm equipment than if they have to deal with dissatisfied hired labor.

How the selection of technology determines who benefits from investments in a given sector is well illustrated by the case of transportation. The typical developing country has a limited amount of capital to invest in transport and a limited amount of foreign exchange with which to import transportation equipment and fuel. Some developing countries have nevertheless opted to try to duplicate the U.S. transportation system, to rely heavily on the private automobile. These countries invite investments by multinational automobile manufacturers in the production of cars that only a small segment of the population can afford. Most of the foreign exchange allotted to the transport sector in such countries is used to import fuel for private automobiles to satisfy the imprudent demands of a small elite. As Haq reports of his own country, during "the decade 1958–68, Pakistan imported or domestically assembled private cars worth 300 million dollars while it could spare only 20 million dollars for public buses."[10]

The alternative to the wholesale importation of an ill-suited system is to design a public transportation network of railroads and buses augmented by bicycles and mopeds. Taking this road would mean avoiding much of the congestion, noise, and air pollution that now fouls all too many of the world's cities. It would also reduce claims on scarce foreign-exchange reserves.

If an index of mobility were constructed for a national population, it would undoubtedly show that a system designed along the lines just sketched would give far more people greater mobility than an automobile-dominated system can provide. A sound policy under any circumstances, serving the overall social interest instead of letting outmoded transport models or commercial interests shape the system, is especially important where transportation funds are short.

Another example of how technology can turn the benefits of public monies into privilege is provided by the supersonic airliner. Most of the 2 billion dollars the United Kingdom and France together spent developing the Concorde was drawn from the public purse, but only those who take trips of at least a few thousand miles have any reason to use the plane; not even one in a hundred among the French or the British can even hope to ever book passage on the Concorde.[11] But because the Concorde was researched and developed with public funds, even the lowest-paid blue-collar taxpayer had to help finance it.

Now that the Concorde is in use, it turns out that only a continuing heavy public subsidy will keep it in the air. Its fuel efficiency, notoriously poor even by airline standards, prompted a member of the British Cabinet who had observed the Concorde under construction to describe it as "a flying fuel tank."[12] In all, it would be hard to conceive of a technology that would be more elitist and better at further skewing the distribution of income than this one, which forces the poor to subsidize the jet set.

Countryside versus City

In many countries, particularly the poorer ones, a strong urban
bias colors governmental policies. When public resources are
allocated and the terms of trade are set, cities often get a better
shake than the countryside does. Where such discrimination
exists, cities draw people from the countryside. The lure to the
city is reinforced by the advantage urban dwellers have as
consumers, since, in developing countries, farm products from
the countryside are exchanged for urban-manufactured goods
on terms that usually favor urbanites.

The circumstances that permit urban populations in developing countries to exploit their rural compatriots are similar to
those that give wealthier industrial societies the upper hand in
international economic relations. Both industrial nations and
urban populations are better organized politically and economically. Professor Michael Lipton of the Institute of Development Studies at Sussex, who has analyzed rural-urban relationships in the developing countries, describes graphically the
nature of this rural-urban conflict: "The most important class
conflict in the poor countries of the world today is not between
labor and capital, nor is it between foreign and national interests. It is between the rural classes and the urban classes. The
rural sector contains most of the poverty and most of the
low-cost sources of potential advance, but the urban sector
contains most of the articulateness, organization, and power."
As a result, the urban classes "have been able to 'win' most of
the rounds of the struggle with the countryside; but in so doing
they have made the development process needlessly slow and
unfair."[13]

Among the policies that directly affect rural-urban relationships are those dealing with food prices. Price policies designed
to provide unrealistically cheap food for city dwellers thwart
domestic food production. More broadly, urban-oriented

cheap food policies discourage private investment in food production and, hence, rural employment. The resulting distortion in the development process helps explain both the widespread dependence of Third World cities on food from abroad and the swelling flow of the unemployed into the cities.

In general, most public money in most developing countries is invested in urban projects. Quite commonly, countries with 70 percent of their populations in rural areas may allocate only 20 percent of their public sector investments to those same areas. In such situations, investment per urbanite can easily be several times as high as investment per country-dweller. This strong urban bias in public investments in social services, particularly in education and health, further enhances the attractiveness of the cities. As Lipton points out, a child from an Indian town or city is 8.5 times more likely than a village child to make it to a university. Thus, some university places are invariably filled by less talented urban students instead of more capable rural ones. Such geographical biases in educational policy deprive individuals of opportunity and nations of sorely needed talent.

Misbegotten policies and priorities ultimately entail high social costs. The pro-urban bias is leading to a syndrome, a recognizable set of related trends and events that will in the long run prove disastrous. When the countryside is starved of capital because it has lost out to the city in the unfair competition for investment, food production stagnates, new employment opportunities fail to materialize, and wholesale migration from countryside to city subsequently begins. When job seekers migrate into the cities, the food surplus produced in the countryside does not increase commensurately. Consequently, cities become increasingly dependent on imported food, most of it from North America. To purchase this food, governments must spend scarce foreign exchange. Money better spent on fertilizer or irrigation pumps, which would expand both food production and the national product while creating employment, is thus spent on food needed to forestall impending shortages. Constructive actions give way to holding actions.

Closely related to the massive movement to the cities is a rise in energy requirements. Other things being equal, the greater the distance between people and the sources of their sustenance, the greater the energy requirements to satisfy food needs. All food production requires energy, but producing food for urban dwellers requires extra energy—to process, transport, and distribute food. Beyond this, creating jobs in cities requires far more capital and energy than creating jobs in the countryside. In the countryside land is the principal form of capital used to generate employment, but in the cities new employment requires costly new equipment.

Many planners and analysts believe that the tide from the countryside to the city cannot be stemmed or even slowed. But, as some countries have demonstrated, it need not be inevitable. What is needed to curb and then reverse this ill-timed flood is far-sighted national policies that give those who live in the countryside their due. Indeed, the most effective efforts to ameliorate the problems facing cities may well be those to improve living conditions, social services, employment, and productivity in the countryside.

One of the most impressive instances of a country that has consciously shifted the terms of trade toward the countryside is China. John Gurley reports that "Over the past two decades, the government has several times raised the price at which it purchases grain from the peasants." At the same time, the price of items farmers buy has been reduced. He further notes that "for the same amount of wheat, a peasant can get 70 percent more salt than at the time of the birth of the People's Republic, and for the same amount of cotton he receives 2.4 times as much kerosene. Prices of fertilizer, fuel, livestock feed, electricity and various types of equipment have been lowered."[14] Herein may lie one of the keys to China's remarkably equitable development effort.

Land Distribution: Social Significance

While land is everywhere a prominent form of wealth, it is the dominant form in agrarian societies. To own land in these societies is to possess wealth, status, and authority. If land is concentrated in a few hands, so is income. In an analysis of the distribution of both income and land in Morocco, Oxford University Professor Keith Griffin shows how the two go hand in hand. According to Griffin, the richest 10 percent of the population consumes 37 percent of all goods and services, while the poorest 10 percent consumes a mere 1.24 percent of the total. Incomes in the upper decile average nearly thirty times those of the bottom decile. Moreover, the income-distribution pattern closely parallels the land-ownership pattern. "Sixty-nine percent of rural households own either no land or less than two hectares," Griffin states. "This group accounts for only 16 percent of the privately owned land actually cultivated. At the other extreme, 4 percent of the households own 33 percent of the land. By any standards this is a very uneven distribution of landed property."[15]

Nowhere are land and wealth distributed less equitably than they are in parts of Latin America. According to another study by Griffin, the wealthiest 1 percent of the Ecuadorian population collects 21 percent of the income, while the poorest one-half earns just over 11 percent. This finding is consistent with that of a study by the Inter-American Committee for Agricultural Development, which reports that the largest 1.5 percent of the farms cover 47 percent of the land, while 33 percent of the farms occupy 1.3 percent of the land area. The great bulk of the population consists of *campesinos* who are abysmally poor. Most live in the Sierra where, as Griffin says, "97 percent of houses are without sewage disposal, 93 percent without an electric light, and 85 percent without running water." Many *campesinos*, 30 percent of whom are landless laborers, live and die without ever receiving any medical or dental care. In effect, Ecuador has two social classes—the tiny prosperous landed gentry and the poor majority.[16]

The distribution of wealth within a society usually determines personal access to social services and to social well-being. As data gathered by a Johns Hopkins University medical team in Bangladesh in 1975 show, death rates in this Asian country correlated with landowning status. The less land a family had, the less likely all its members were to survive a food crisis. Death was a frequent visitor to that one-fourth of the population that owned no land at all. Among the landless, thirty-six of every thousand died during the 1975 food crisis (see Table 9-2). Those with three acres or more had a death rate of twelve, only fractionally higher than that for those living in Western industrial countries. Perhaps the most disturbing message of these figures is what they portend for the future as population growth further reduces the average size of landholdings and swells the landless population.

The key to who gets what and how much, landownership patterns also help determine how efficiently national land and labor resources are used and whether a country has food shortages or food surpluses. In countries for which data are available, land productivity is invariably higher on small holdings than on large ones even though small farms are often carved out of

Table 9-2. Death Rate by Size of Landholdings in Companiganj, Bangladesh, 1975

Size of Land Holding (acres)	Death Rate (per thousand)
None	35.8
.01–.49	28.4
.50–2.99	21.5
3.00 +	12.2

Source: The Johns Hopkins University School of Hygiene and Public Health, preliminary data.

lands of lower quality. One reason is that more labor is lavished on crops and livestock on family farms than on large farms dependent on hired labor, since the latter must pay the going wage.

Widespread unemployment at a time when record numbers of young people are coming of working age makes the need for land redistribution seem especially urgent. Where small farms are the norm, as they are in Japan or Taiwan, large numbers of people can be effectively employed as long as land is equitably distributed among the rural population. Where the land distribution is grossly inequitable, labor cannot be used effectively. Data from Colombia solidly support this point. Classifying Colombian landholdings as small farms, large crop-farms, or cattle ranches, Keith Griffin has found that the "man-land ratio is nearly five times higher on the small farms than on the large crop farms, and more than 13 times higher than on the cattle ranches."[17]

Preserving large landholdings intact in developing countries wracked by high unemployment can only impede the development process. Under such circumstances, both labor and land are underutilized. Productivity as well as social equity argues for land redistribution. The difficulty, of course, is in mobilizing the political support required to bring such change about. As Roger Hansen of the Overseas Development Council notes, "In many countries, land reform is both the key to the success of the rural strategy and its most formidable political obstacle."[18]

Ecological Deterioration and Income Distribution

Social analysts customarily try to weigh the impact of political and technological forces on the distribution of income and wealth. But they seldom take into account the ecological forces that now impair the productivity of biological systems and threaten the livelihood of those who depend on them. Several

categories of people come to mind—shifting cultivators, nomadic herdsmen, fishermen, and mountain dwellers. Most, but
not all, of the vulnerable live in the developing countries.

Throughout the tropical and subtropical regions, farmers
practice shifting cultivation. This technique has worked well
over the millennia, but it is breaking down as population pressures shorten the fallow cycle. As land productivity falls, so too
does the living standard of the tens of millions living in sub-
Saharan Africa and in the tropical regions of Latin America
and Asia.

Other ecological forces, especially grassland deterioration
and desert encroachment, affect nomadic herdsmen. Associated with population pressures, these forces are wreaking
their greatest havoc in Africa—throughout the broad fringe of
the Sahara and on the East African plateau—in the Middle
East, and in parts of Northwest Asia such as Iran and Afghanistan. As a UN report covering income distribution in the Middle East notes, "the continued deterioration in the rural environment and the natural rangeland zone were among the main
causes responsible for the impoverishment of the nomads, pas-
toralists and farmers in the arid and marginal areas."[19] The
consequences of ecological deterioration can be even more
severe. When a drought strikes, nomads can lose their herds
and their livelihoods. Some lose their lives. Farmers on the
fringe of the expanding deserts in Morocco, Tunisia, Algeria,
Senegal, the Sudan, or the state of Rajasthan in Northwest
India find themselves evicted from their farms by the desert's
ruthless march. Some become rural laborers; others move to
the shantytowns surrounding the cities.

Another class of ecological refugees includes the mountain
folk of overpopulated poor countries. As population pressure
has forced farmers up the hillsides in the Western Himalayas,
in the Ethiopian highlands, and throughout the Andes, soil
erosion has grown severe. As the soil washes down from the
mountains, the people are never far behind. Most of these

former farmers and their families wander into the tin-and-filth squatter settlements that circle Third World cities, and few ever find productive employment. In effect, these farmers have been disenfranchised; they have lost their natural capital.

The deterioration of fisheries from overfishing or, in some cases, from offshore pollution has also brought fishermen and those whose welfare depends indirectly on the catch to the shores of economic ruin. Fishing communities in Japan, in the United Kingdom, in the state of Massachusetts, and in the coastal regions of Peru have seen their "net income" plummet during the seventies as their fisheries have been decimated.

In the spring of 1977, the U.S. Food and Drug Administration, responding to the heavy offshore pollution, closed over 1,000 hectares (or 30 percent) of the productive clam beds off Long Island. In one community alone, an estimated 1,000 clammers were put out of work and a million-dollar-a-year clam industry collapsed.[20] In the global scheme of things, these local losses may seem small. But multiplied they make a measurable difference in human welfare.

Few wage-earners are completely exempt from the effects of population pressures or pollution (or of some combination of the two) on natural systems. As these pressures intensify, many groups will be robbed outright of income and security. Many more will be hurt indirectly. Of all the sources of growing income disparity, ecological deterioration may be one of the most difficult to remedy.

National versus International Inequities

Both within and among societies, income distribution follows an identifiable pattern. A group of the seven richest countries —the United States, the Soviet Union, Japan, West Germany, the United Kingdom, Italy, and France—together contain roughly one-fifth of world population and have an average income per person of 3,900 dollars. Five of the poorest countries—India, Pakistan, Bangladesh, Ethiopia, and Afghanistan —also contain approximately 800 million people. But average per-capita income in these five countries is 115 dollars per year.[21] The ratio of income received by the top one-fifth to that received by the bottom one-fifth stands at thirty-three to one. If adjusted for the overstatement generally accepted as inherent in international income comparisons, this gap turns out to be almost exactly the same as that within those societies where income is most inequitably distributed.

Over the past generation, new wealth has accrued where old wealth resided. Among societies, the widening difference in income levels is scarcely surprising, since nations are not subject to redress at the international level. What is surprising is the widening disparity in incomes within societies. Indeed, it is difficult to see how existing political systems can survive when the income distribution is as unfair as it now is in some poor countries.

One of the most interesting questions raised by analyses of income-distribution patterns within and among societies concerns what, if any, relationship exists between the two. At the national level, economic planners long focused on a now-disputed belief that the benefits of growth would "trickle down" to all economic and social groups. At the international level, economists still subscribe to a similar "trickle down" theory, arguing that the faster the rich countries grow the better off the poor will be. While this argument may once have been persuasive, its hold has been broken by scarcities of the energy, fertilizer, food, and other resources that poor countries must import. Rapid growth in consumption by the rich countries, with their superior purchasing power, may make these commodities even dearer and may thus deprive the poor countries of the resources they need for growth. While the need for markets for the poor countries' exports cannot be denied, the relationship between rapid economic growth in the rich countries and that in the poor ones is no longer direct and simple.

Another important question is how the international reallocation of wealth would affect the distribution of income within relatively poor countries. Public assistance available from governments and international lending agencies has customarily been provided in such a way as to maximize the rate of economic growth in the recipient countries. As a result, the transfer of wealth from donor to recipient countries has often merely made the rich in the poor countries richer, and has left the lot of the poor unchanged. Unless the international redistribution of wealth is linked in a positive way to the internal redistribution of wealth within the recipient countries, the wealth that changes hands may be pocketed by those who least need it.

10

The Inevitable Accommodation

Human needs and numbers have multiplied so quickly over the last generation that the demand for many commodities has now reached a level that the earth's biological systems cannot sustain. Since these systems can support only a limited yield or offtake indefinitely, excessive demands can be satisfied only by consuming the biological stocks themselves. Such a situation obviously cannot long continue.

Even as the excessive pressures on biological systems come into the public view, another unsustainable trend—the growing dependence of national economies on dwindling oil reserves—is surfacing with comparable drama. Like any addiction, that to cheap oil is hard to overcome, and even individuals and governments with the will to change are held back by habit. Even though the end of the oil era is now in sight, the transition to alternative energy sources is far behind schedule. The fading of the nuclear dream and the potential climatic constraints on the future use of coal further underline the urgency of developing renewable resources.

Coming to terms with ecological stress and dependence on petroleum may require rationing threatened resources among societies. Sustaining the supplies of essential commodities may be possible only if global limits on their use are established. These will need to be divided among countries either formally through national quotas or through the marketplace. The latter is attractive to the richer countries with greater purchasing power, but this method will not work without the cooperation of the poor countries. Indeed, when national allocations fall short of national demands, price rationing or other more formal rationing mechanisms will have to be adopted at the national level as well. Needless to say, national political leaders are not eager even to discuss, much less to put into effect, such controls.

The question before us is not whether we will accommodate ourselves to the earth's natural systems and resources, but how we will do so. The question is not whether the offtake from oceanic fisheries will be limited. It will be—if not by us, then ultimately by nature. There is no question whether the overcutting of forests will eventually halt. It will—either because we consciously decide to do so or because no forests remain to be cut. There is no question whether we will soon reduce our consumption of oil. We will.

The changes involved in accommodating ourselves to the earth's natural capacities and resources suggest that a far-reaching social transformation is in the making. The origins of the change are ecological, but the change itself is social and economic. The processes for achieving it are political.

Coming to Terms with Nature

When global consumption of food commodities and industrial raw materials of biological origin exceeds the sustainable yield of biological systems, consumption must be curbed. If it is not, the productive resource base itself will eventually disappear. In economic terms, we are now consuming not only the interest from biological systems but some of the principal as well.

We know that overfishing is commonplace in the late seventies, but we can only speculate about how much the world catch would fall if the catch from all fisheries were reduced to a sustainable level. We do know that it would drop precipitously, even while world population and demand continue to climb. We lack the information to estimate precisely either the extent of the decline if stock depletion were halted or the impact this cessation would have on the price of fish and of food in general. In the northeast Atlantic, where a fifth of the global catch is taken, a reduction in catch to the sustainable level would sharply reduce protein supplies in Europe. This, in turn, would lead to higher food prices and a reduction in food intake, an increase in food imports, or, more likely, to some combination of the two. In England, fish and chips would become dearer and individual portions smaller. The overall economic effects in Europe would be greater inflationary pressures and a worsening of the balance of trade. In other, less well-studied fisheries, reducing the catch to sustainable levels could have equally devastating effects.

Like overtaxed fisheries, overcut forests begin to shrink once their regenerative capacity is exceeded. Although at least some forests on every continent are now overcut, we do not have enough information to calculate how much the price of forest products would rise if the offtake were everywhere limited to the sustainable yield. Even with overcutting and a reduction in the forested area, firewood prices in some countries have doubled or tripled since 1970. Eliminating overcutting would undoubtedly lead to worldwide rises in the prices of newspapers, magazines, textbooks, and housing that would make recent increases seem modest.

On grasslands too, overgrazing is fast becoming the rule rather than the exception. The reduction in herds that occurred during recent drought years in the Soviet Union, the Sahelian countries of Africa, the East African plateau countries, the U.S. northern Great Plains, and Australia indicates how close existing livestock populations are to the maximum numbers the land can sustain. How much the world's herds of cattle and flocks of sheep and goats would shrink if overgrazing were eliminated is not known, but we do know that the scope for increasing their numbers is limited and that future gains in the production of beef, mutton, and wool will perforce depend more on getting greater output per animal and less on expanding herds.

With oil, a nonrenewable resource, the key question is not whether global oil production will decline but whether alternative energy sources will be available when the decline occurs. As oil reserves are gradually depleted, production will eventually taper off. If substitute fuels are not on hand, overall energy consumption will decline.

Historically, the prospect of running short of a particular commodity was not especially troubling. If commodity A became scarce, commodity B was substituted for it. But substituting the plentiful for the scarce is no longer always an option. As Professor Willis Harman of Stanford University and the Stanford Research Institute explains, "because all of these interdependent factors are approaching planetary limits together, the solutions that resolved scarcity problems in the past —geographic expansion and technological advancement—do not promise the same sort of relief in the future."[1]

Once the limits of a particular biological system have been reached, the burden of demand is shifted to other systems. For example, as the world fish catch leveled off, the demand for soybeans rose. When the price of soybeans, which averaged $2.45 a bushel during the sixties, climbed to the $5-to-$12-per-bushel range after 1973, many Brazilian coffee growers tore out their coffee trees and planted soybeans.[2] When a severe frost hit Brazilian coffee growing areas in late 1976, coffee stocks were inadequate to cushion the crop shortfall and prices soared to unheard-of levels.

As the cost of petroleum and the cost of synthetic fibers rises, the demand for natural fibers, particularly wool and cotton, climbs. But where grasslands are grazed to the maximum or beyond, markedly expanding wool production is difficult. Moreover, two of the principal cotton exporting countries with growing food deficits, Mexico and Egypt, are under pressure to use their limited land and irrigation water for cereal crops. Indeed, between 1974 and 1976 Mexico cut its cotton acreage by half so as to reduce its growing dependence on imported food.[3]

As pressure on resources builds, scarcity spreads from sector to sector. Competition for resources between the food and energy sectors is becoming especially keen. In Brazil, where a program is being launched to produce the automotive fuel ethanol from sugar cane and cassava, the energy and food sectors are also vying for land, water, and fertilizer. If the goal of producing most automotive fuel from agricultural sources by 1995 is realized there, vast areas of cropland will be tied up in fuel production.[4] If the move to energy crops spreads to other countries, demands for cropland, irrigation, water, and fertilizer could run far above projected levels. In effect, spreading use of the private automobile is almost certain to drive food prices upward.

Scarcity is no longer a local or temporary phenomenon. Like the more virulent strains of flu, it spreads quickly from one country to another. In a world that has always been ecologically interlinked and is now economically interlinked as well, inflation has become a global matter that only a cooperative, coordinated global effort is likely to control.

The Inner Limits

The unavoidable adjustments made necessary by the overtaxing of biological systems and the depletion of oil reserves have received far too little attention. This oversight is due in part to a common tendency by analysts to assess the physical limits of a particular system while completely overlooking the social limits to growth. Usually even the economic optimum of any productive system is well below the physical maximum. Only rarely does the productivity of a corn field or an oil field closely approach its physical limits. For example, the oil that can be profitably extracted from an oil field may only be 30 percent of the total. Beyond that the energy required to extract a barrel of oil may exceed the energy content of the oil itself. Similarly, the amount of fertilizer needed to produce the highest possible yield of corn is well above the economic optimum. At some point, fertilizer will still raise the corn yield, but its cost will exceed the value of the additional yield.

While coming to terms with nature, we must also come to terms with ourselves, frankly recognizing our own limitations as we attempt to stabilize our relationship with nature. While it is tempting to couch discussions of growth prospects in physical terms because they are measurable, the more severe constraints are invariably human ones—the limits on the human capacity to change, the slowness and occasional irrationality of political processes, and the glacial pace at which institutions adapt.

The gap between the outer and inner limits can be demonstrated by examining specific situations. A properly managed forest can, for example, be depended upon to produce a fixed amount of wood. But proper management usually means the careful selection of the trees to be cut—not the clearcutting done by some lumber and newsprint firms and by some governments. It means that the trees cut must either be replaced by nature or replanted by hand, and it may mean that the forested area must be preserved at all costs. In the real world, few countries have even closely approached this level of forest management. West Germany and a handful of other nations have managed a relatively high sustained yield of their forests for several decades. Pakistan, in contrast, has lost most of its forested area over the past two generations. Apart from the conversion of forests to croplands, a rapidly expanding population's demands for firewood and lumber have totally overwhelmed forest-management schemes there. As a result, Pakistan's forest lands today yield only a small fraction of what they could.

The contrast between the limits set by nature and those set by humans is starkly evident in agriculture. Average rice yields in Japan approach the yields attained under ideal experimental conditions, while those in Bangladesh are scarcely a fourth as high.[5] It is not unreasonable to assume that Bangladesh could match Japanese levels, but it is important to keep in mind what such an achievement would require. All Japanese rice is grown under carefully controlled irrigation, while most Bangladesh rice is rain-fed by the monsoons. Over centuries, Japanese farmers have devised ways of constructing meticulous terraces and elaborate water-control devices that permit them to control precisely the amount and timing of water (and of fertilizer) used in the rice fields. No magic technique will permit a Bangladesh economic planner or political leader to bring about irrigation development comparable to Japan's with a snap of the fingers; decades and perhaps generations of back-breaking toil might. Attaining such yields would also require of Bangladesh farmers technological understanding and management ability on a par with those of the Japanese farmers, nearly all of whom are literate. But even such superlative farming skills cannot significantly narrow the gap in the absence of support services—the technical advisory services on pest control, soil fertilization, planting techniques, and water management. Moreover, without an effective price-support system for rice, and without confidence in the government, even advanced agriculture and first-rate support services would not be enough.

In global resource management, too, social limits can also operate long before physical ones come into play. For example, the greatest gains to be realized today from additional fertilizer use exist in the developing countries where fertilizer usage is low. At a time of global food scarcities, available fertilizer should be channeled to those farmers who can use it most productively. But political pressures applied by farmers in fertilizer-exporting countries act to restrict fertilizer exports in times of scarcity and, consequently, to keep world food production substantially below what it would otherwise be. Production, in this case, is obstructed by politics, not nature.

Another social limit to resource management, the failure of the users of "the commons" to organize so as to use resources for their long-term mutual benefit, occurs at all levels of social organization. At the village level in Benin, failure to manage local forest resources contributes to a firewood shortage. At the global level, failure to control pollution leads to the deterioration of oceanic life.

A particularly troublesome social limit is the wide difference between the length of political terms of office and the time required by the elements of accommodation—population stabilization, the reforestation of denuded lands, or the switch from fossil to other energy sources. With two-, four-, or six-year terms of office, politicians cannot hope to solve any of these problems. At best, they can launch programs that will pay dividends only years or decades hence.

Countless examples could be cited of how "inner limits" prevent the realization of full physical potential. Any realistic assessments of the human prospect must consider both. We delude ourselves dangerously if we think only in terms of the outer or physical limits.

The Limits of Technology

Recent history divides into two distinct technological periods —the period from 1940 to 1970, and the period since then. The first was a period of unrestrained optimism—the second, one of disillusionment. After a generation of landmark advances in technology that began with the splitting of the atom and culminated with the landing of American astronauts on the moon, science seemed capable of doing almost anything. Comments such as "today's science fiction is tomorrow's reality" and "if we can describe it we can do it" were freely passed around along with the quintessential expression of optimism: "There are no problems, only solutions."

The three-decade span from the forties to the moon landing in 1969 was the golden age of science. It brimmed with technological optimism. In an excellent article on the limits of technology published in the *Washington Post* in mid-1977, Stewart Udall, Secretary of the Interior during the Kennedy-Johnson years, chronicled the evolution of this optimism.[6] A seemingly shatter-proof faith in technology guided the entire scientific and public-policy establishment. This cornucopian vision of the future derived in large part from the assumption of an inexhaustible energy supply. One of the first documents to describe this future of abundance was *The Next Hundred Years*, by geochemist Harrison Brown. It promised that "we will finally sustain ourselves with materials obtained from the rocks of the earth's crust and gasses of the air and the waters of the seas." The mining industry, said Brown, will be replaced by "vast, integrated multipurpose chemical plants supplied by rock, air, and sea water from which will follow a multiplicity of products ranging from fresh water to electrical power, liquid fuels, and metals."[7]

Brown was not alone in this view. The influential series of Rockefeller panel reports published in 1959 and 1960 and drawing on the work of such respected intellectuals as Dean Rusk, Henry Kissinger, and Arthur Burns continued in the same vein. "Even now we can discern the outlines of a future in which," they reported, "through the use of the split atom, our resources of both power and raw materials will be limitless. . . ."[8]

In 1962 the National Academy of Sciences produced a report for President Kennedy that recommended a new natural-resources policy. Udall describes this report as fascinating because it represented an official sanction by the scientific community of the supertechnology hypothesis. Relying heavily on the work of atomic scientists, it asserted that this new technology could provide "dramatic increases" in the supplies of energy and food. In the words of Udall, who was then Interior Secretary, "It was a landmark study, and its recommendations were unanimous. It cemented the concensus about technology and implied that, if we ran out of petroleum or iron ore—or any other mineral—technology would soon come forth with a better, cheaper substitute."[9]

These promises of technological miracles notwithstanding, many technological solutions to problems remain elusive. Udall noted that the desalting of sea water undertaken by his own Interior Department was one of the great promises of the early sixties, but that a desalinization technique that "would make it feasible to turn the world's deserts into irrigated gardens" is as distant today as it was fifteen years ago. A few years later a crash program to find a cure for cancer was launched with much money and fanfare. A decade has now passed and hundreds of millions have been spent, but no sure way to prevent or cure most forms of cancer has been found.

In the seventies, once-promising fields of technological endeavor have been abandoned. The promised abundance of energy and food has not materialized. Instead, the decade has been marked by hunger-induced rises in death rates and by soaring energy costs. The promised breakthroughs in food and energy supplies have not occurred. The risk of heavy dependence by industrial countries on imported oil notwithstanding, scientists have not come up with any cheap, abundant alternative to petroleum. Most of the numerous commercial efforts launched in the late sixties to develop single-cell protein from petroleum have since been abandoned. Few, if any, of the research efforts to produce fish protein concentrate (FPC) from trash fish are being continued. Fish farming still accounts for only a small fraction of the world's catch. Two decades of intensive efforts by agricultural scientists have not achieved a breakthrough in soybean yields.

This review of the failures and the unfulfilled promises of science is not intended as a criticism of those who were infused with optimism. It was part of an era; we were all involved. Nor is it intended to downplay the role of science and technology in coping with problems now before us. Indeed, in some instances technology has delivered even more than was promised: the excellent global telecommunications network exceeds even that envisaged by science-fiction writers, and the computational capacity of today's pocket calculators exceeds that of the desk calculator of a generation ago. Rather, this review is an attempt to demystify science and technology and to put them in a realistic perspective.

Technology's future contributions in moving toward a sustainable economic system may lie largely in a reorientation of scientific research toward high-priority basic human needs. The need for new energy systems may now exceed that for new weapons systems. Yet, the development of the latter still claims the lion's share of the world's scientific talent. Other areas of research are sorely neglected. Fast-growing varieties of trees to supply firewood for Third World villages would be invaluable. Likewise, the need for a cheap, efficient solar cooker and simple efficient wood stoves would be a boon to Third World villages and of far greater value than further research on nuclear reactors. Pest-resistant cereals would add to man's food supply.

The Analytical Gap

The social response to the ecological stresses and resource scarcities of the seventies has lagged partly because their scale has not been well documented and their significance has not been well understood. The decade has been marked by a chain of analytical failures, as well as by unanticipated, convulsive changes in the global economy and political structure. The spectacular rises in commodity prices caught commodity analysts off guard.

Economists are bearing the brunt of the criticism, partly because they have traditionally been responsible for undertaking such analyses and making projections. Professor Gary Gappert of the University of Wisconsin describes the dilemma insightfully by paraphrasing Dickens: "These are the best of times and the worst of times for economists. We know everything and yet we know nothing. Most of all, these are the times that challenge the aggregate analysis of the neo-Keynesian economist. . . . Economics requires a thorough-going reorientation if its relevance for policy-making is once again to be established."[10]

Economists are no longer able to recommend policies that will satisfactorily cope with both inflation and unemployment. Few would argue that economic theory as it exists today is adequate, but as yet there is no replacement, no Keynes in sight. As T. S. Kuhn notes, in many fields of knowledge the passage of time brings anomalies that the existing theory can no longer explain.[11] As the divergence between theory and observed reality widens, questions begin to arise, and a new theory or explanation that is consistent with reality eventually evolves. Resistance by those who may have to abandon familiar theories or analytical tools is naturally strong. Galileo advanced a new paradigm and paid dearly for it. When Robert Wegener, German astronomer and meteorologist, first proposed in 1912 the theory of continental drift that was eventually to revolutionize geology in the sixties, he was scorned by fellow professionals everywhere.[12] While geology was being revolutionized by an astronomer, genetics was being invaded by chemists, physicists, and microbiologists. Together their work led ultimately to discovery of the double helix, the seminal concept needed to unravel the genetic code.[13]

What the source of the new paradigm needed in economics will be remains to be seen. It could come from ecology, systems analysis, or, as some have suggested, from political philosophy. Whatever its origins, it is certain to be resisted by many established economists. But the period following the emergence of the new paradigm could be marked by excitement and intellectual ferment comparable to that in geology and genetics in recent decades.

Failure to anticipate the major shifts and discontinuities of the seventies is not attributable to any single discipline or any single shortcoming in analysis, but rather to many. Asking the wrong questions; confusing causes with triggering events; and, perhaps most important, overspecialization are all involved.

In a world where ecological, economic, and political systems interact, even asking the right questions has become difficult. For example, the question "How much food can the world produce?" is not very illuminating. The critical question is "How much food can the world produce at a price people can afford?" Only when price is specified can a meaningful answer be given. Bland assertions that world food output could double or triple can mislead rather than inform.

Analysts of current affairs also run a risk of seeing symptoms as causes and of confusing triggering events with the long-term causal factors. This problem particularly bothers broadcast journalists, who must often interpret news events on the spot. Unfortunately, analysts with more time for research and reflection sometimes make the same mistakes.

A dramatic illustration of how too-hurried analyses can mislead occurred in late 1971 when the news media covered a typhoon in the Bay of Bengal that literally washed away some five hundred thousand islanders who lived just a few miles off the coast of what is now Bangladesh. Reporters described this event as one of the largest natural disasters on record in terms of lives lost. Yet, as Garrett Hardin pointed out in an editorial in *Science,* what happened should more appropriately be attributed to intense population pressure.[14] Since people would not move onto land that was only a few feet above sea level unless they were desperate, what appeared to be a natural disaster was a manifestation of intense population pressure.

Another case of misreporting followed the African droughts of the late sixties and early seventies. During this period the Sahelian-zone countries of Africa experienced crop failures, food shortages, severe nutritional stress, and the loss of perhaps two hundred thousand lives to outright starvation.[15] Most reporters and commentators attributed this tragedy to the drought itself. But the drought should be viewed as a triggering event rather than as a causal factor. The conditions leading to the disaster were decades in the making: overgrazing, deforestation, and the creation of desert-like conditions over a vast area followed the doubling of human and livestock populations during the thirty-five years before the drought hit.

As these examples illustrate, the point at which a biological or social system under stress begins to deteriorate rapidly or to collapse is not well understood and therefore not widely anticipated. The U.S. Dust Bowl era of the thirties had few heralds. Fewer still anticipated social and economic changes that the partial collapse of the Great Plains wheat-producing ecosystem was to set in motion—changes that were chronicled by John Steinbeck in *The Grapes of Wrath.*

Assigning the right weight to the various factors that make up a crisis is another analytical pitfall that slows the process of progressive change. For example, the rich and poor countries are divided over whether population growth or rising affluence is the principal source of pressure on the earth's resources. While both factors contribute to ecological stresses and resource scarcities, their relative contributions can be precisely weighed only with respect to a particular resource, country, and time period. Moreover, some political leaders apparently prefer to avoid the facts for fear of compromising their positions. It was this denial of reality that allowed so much energy at the World Population Conference in Bucharest in 1974 to be channeled into meaningless rhetoric.

Perceiving the origin of ecological stresses and resource scarcities is no easier for individuals than for governments. American housewives who boycotted beef in April of 1973 were asked by a TV interviewer to explain who caused the high beef prices that they were protesting. These consumers didn't think farmers were solely at fault, they didn't think that the markups in the supermarkets made much difference, and they didn't have a clear idea of who the middleman was, though his take exceeded that of the farmer and supermarket combined. What never occurred to these protesters was that they might somehow be responsible. As parents, they had contributed to a 63-percent increase in the country's population since 1940. As consumers, they had more than doubled their per-capita consumption of beef from 25 kilograms in 1940 to 52 kilograms in 1972. Together, these two factors increased national beef consumption by 342 percent in a generation.[16]

Loss of vision due to overspecialization may be the analyst's chief weakness today. Specialists are often somewhat facetiously described as those who know more and more about less and less, until eventually they know everything about nothing. Humorous though this statement may be, it only modestly overstates the dilemma. As knowledge advances, mastery of any particular field leads to ever-narrower specialization. All principal disciplines have broken into innumerable subdisciplines. Economics, for example, has splintered into labor economics, agricultural economics, transportation economics, and at least a half-dozen other branches. Within law, medicine, and engineering, specialization and fragmentation have evolved to comparable levels.

The central problem associated with specialization is that the important problems facing humanity do not fit within the confines of any individual discipline, much less a subdiscipline. Thus, in what educators have called the "expert society," more and more problems remain unsolved, and more and more are proving unmanageable. Melvin Eggers, president of Syracuse University, has said that education is losing touch with the needs of society. When confronting the energy crisis, he notes, "We have petroleum and mining and nuclear engineers, but precious few energy engineers" who are capable of evaluating and advising on the overall energy situation.[17] Not surprisingly, few governments have developed coherent strategies for coping with this fundamental threat to their national economic well-being and stability. Similarly, not too many years ago, the food problem was defined almost entirely in agricultural terms. But to even begin to understand what is happening in the world food economy today, an analyst must be an economist, ecologist, agronomist, meteorologist, and political scientist rolled into one.

Specialization is a natural and necessary response to complexity. But generalists are needed to balance, synthesize, and integrate the work of specialists, bringing it to bear on public policy. Unfortunately, systems of higher education the world over produce only specialists, so projections by specialists are all too often made from a precariously narrow knowledge base. Often projections so made fail to materialize—as so many recent population, food, energy, and economic projections have. Agricultural supply-and-demand projections—whether those of the USDA in Washington, the FAO in Rome, or the OECD in Paris—are done almost exclusively by agricultural economists from their rather narrow knowledge base. This helps explain why these highly trained professionals have failed to anticipate virtually all the major new developments in the world food economy over the past decade. So too, population projections made by demographers may not accord with the complex real world; meaningful demographic projections must be based on ecological analyses and assumptions as well as demographic ones.

In analyses of global problems and trends, the extrapolation of historical trends can also lead planners astray. While extrapolation proved useful in governmental and corporate planning during the early postwar decades, it has clearly lost its value as a projection technique. Indeed, in many cases it has led to erroneous conclusions and to the misallocation of resources. For example, agricultural economists tend to assume that the rises in crop yields realized during the third quarter of the century in the agriculturally advanced countries will continue throughout the fourth. But biologists familiar with plant physiology and the limits of photosynthesis quite rightly view this extrapolation as wishful thinking.

Faulty extrapolations lead to inappropriate policies and financial waste. Viewed in a broader context, they are often obviously unrealistic. For example, UN projections on urbanization indicate that the increase in the share of world urban population from 29 percent in 1950 to 39 percent in 1975 will continue, reaching 49 percent by the end of the century.[18] But supporting a world population that is half urban would require a vast increase in the food surpluses produced in the countryside, an enormous expansion in the supply of cheap energy comparable to that occurring during the quarter-century just ended, and a great increase in the capital available for creating industrial jobs in cities. For the projected urbanization trends to materialize, all three of these conditions would have to be fulfilled. But none probably will be.

If there is anything this decade should have taught us, it is humility. Faulty analyses and unfulfilled projections are not the monopoly of any profession. Analysts, advisors, and planners in both the public and private sectors have been found wanting. Their task, to see particular problems in a broad context, is as difficult as it is essential.

The Economic Dilemma

Throughout the modern era the objective of economic policy has been growth. Only in a minority of countries has the enthusiasm for growth been seriously tempered by concerns for the distribution of its benefits. But now that human needs are outstripping the carrying capacity of biological systems and oil reserves are shrinking, growth as the dominant objective of economic policy will be forced to give way to sustainability. This is not to suggest that the growth objective will be abandoned, but rather that it will of necessity have to defer to sustainability.

A sustainable economic system will differ materially from one designed primarily to grow. Among other things, it will have to focus more specifically on satisfying basic needs. In fact, the failure of economists to recognize the need to shift from a traditional growth economy to a sustainable economic system is partly responsible for the difficulties they face in planning and policy-making.

The simultaneous existence of uncharacteristically high inflation and unemployment in virtually all of the major industrial economies during the mid-seventies poses a dilemma for which the modern Keynesian economist has no answer. From time to time, accelerating inflation or rising unemployment have upset economies, but rarely have both struck at once. Occasional bursts of inflation arising from droughts or longshoremen's strikes were usually endurable, since both droughts and strikes always end. Inflation of a cost-push nature could be managed by holding down price and wage increases. Whenever rapid economic expansion has pressed against industrial capacity and spurred temporary inflation, economists have typically recommended slowing the growth rate by manipulating either fiscal or monetary policy or both. The policy instruments traditionally used to manage inflation no longer work well. Rising real costs in key sectors are driving prices upward; diminishing returns typify the food and energy sectors of the global economy.

In effect, the real-cost curve for many basic resources, both renewable and nonrenewable, appears to be rising as production presses against some of the natural constraints inherent in the earth's resources and capacities. Technological advances could prevent or stall cost increases; unfortunately, advances of the magnitude needed do not appear to be forthcoming. With continued rapid growth in consumption, rising real costs are almost certainly inevitable.

In an interview with columnist Joseph Kraft, Prime Minister Pierre Trudeau of Canada speculated on the problem of inflation. "Inflation," he said "has not found its Keynes" (a reference to the great British economist whose insights helped relieve unemployment). I personally think the Keynes of inflation will not be an economist . . ." but will instead "be a political, philosophical or moral leader inspiring people to do without the excess consumption so prominent in the developed countries."[19] It may be possible to avoid rising real costs only by curbing the growth in global consumption. Such management—which involves both stabilizing population growth and eliminating excessive consumption—will involve governments in the systematic determination of what is excessive and what is not. Policy questions traditionally framed almost exclusively in economic terms will now enter the domain of values and ethics.

For the ills of unemployment as well as for inequity, the popular prescription has been more growth. In modern industrial economies, the common response to rising unemployment has been economic expansion. Indeed, governments everywhere have relied heavily on rapid economic growth to create jobs for the throngs of jobless young people. But this approach is becoming progressively less effective, and some new thinking is needed. Over the past generation rapid economic growth has muffled the cries for greater equity, but as growth slows, the voices of protest become louder.

No adequate means have been developed for adapting present economic systems to the changing circumstances of the late twentieth century. The economic institutions that have evolved during the industrial era in both capitalist and centrally planned economies are geared to accumulate capital and to fuel economic growth as measured in GNP. Where free enterprise exists, the accumulation usually takes the form of corporate profits; in centrally planned economies, it takes the form of a state surplus. Both kinds of industrial systems are based on the exploitation of the desire to acquire and consume. Modern economies are dependent on advertising, to generate new needs and wants. Indeed, the modern economy is virtually synonymous with growth. In the eyes of many, it is like a bicycle; it must keep moving (i.e., growing) or it will topple. The inability of most contemporary economic systems to cope effectively with questions of equity and employment while satisfying basic needs and assuring basic freedoms suggests the need for fundamental reform. As the inevitable reassessment occurs, old growth-oriented goals will begin to lose their luster.

After a point, further rises in per-capita consumption do not lead to any obvious gains in well-being. Goran Backstrand and Lars Ingelstam of the Secretariat for Future Studies in Stockholm report that over most of the past century there has been "a very clear correlation between GNP growth and indications of improvement in the overall quality of life. However, since the middle of the 1960s, this correlation seems to have broken down in several key areas."[20] They note that one Swedish social indicator, male life expectancy, now shows a negative correlation with GNP.

Using the official economic-growth projections of the Swedish economy, Backstrand and Ingelstam examine the consumption patterns for the year 2000. The projected growth rate of 4 to 6 percent per year yields an overall level of output some four times greater than at present. This expansion in the gross national product includes a sevenfold increase in steel output and a tenfold growth in the production of chemicals. With Sweden's population on the verge of stabilizing, the authors ask what the country could possibly do with such volumes of steel and chemicals, considering that consumption levels are already quite satisfactory.

The questions these futurists raise for Sweden are ones that other advanced industrial countries such as the United States, West Germany, and the Soviet Union need to raise—and answer. In addition to questions about how the vast increase in material goods will be used, questions also arise about the environmental despoilation and pollution associated with such large increases. At some point these negative impacts will more than offset the increasingly marginal social gains.

As the distinction between the volume of consumption and the quality of life becomes obvious to more and more people, so will the need to redefine national goals in terms of basic social needs. We may begin, for example, to define health goals in terms of infant mortality, life expectancy, and freedom from illness, rather than in terms of doctors, drugs, and medical expenditures. This redefinition may in turn lead to a more broad-based national effort to improve health, including the alteration of dietary and exercise habits. Similarly, in the transportation sector, we may stop worrying about how Detroit can obtain an ever-larger share of the consumer dollar and consider instead how the majority can obtain the greatest mobility.

Abandoning the historical approach to creating jobs by calling for the consumption of more and more energy, future economic planners may instead focus on ways of simultaneously conserving energy and creating employment. For instance, outlawing the use of throw-away bottles and requiring all containers to be recyclable could simultaneously save energy, increase employment, reduce litter, and cut overall costs. As another example, home vegetable gardening can reduce energy use, improve diet, and provide an opportunity to get exercise. Similarly, relying on a bicycle for short-term transport can at once reduce energy use, cut air and noise pollution, and provide some of the exercise so needed in modern sedentary societies.

In the future, a healthy economy designed to satisfy basic needs with a minimum of resource consumption may accord conservation a higher place than extravagant consumption. Such an economy may be more self-sufficient and, therefore, less vulnerable. Its hallmark may be not the rate of economic expansion but the efficiency of resource use.

The Basic Political Choice

A troublesome philosophical and political dilemma—whether to rely on voluntary adjustments in behavior or to resort to making such adjustments compulsory—stands at the center of new ecological and economic realities. The essential choice is whether to limit births and individual consumption consciously and voluntarily so as to avoid excessive pressures on the earth's natural system, or to continue pressing against the earth's biological limits until regulation becomes mandatory.

Considering the problem of regulation, political scientist William Ophuls describes the historical changes in the political context of resource distribution in the United States: "Given the cornucopia of the frontier, an unpolluted environment and a rapidly developing technology, American politics could afford to be a more or less amicable division of the spoils with the government stepping in only when the free-for-all pursuit of wealth got out of hand. In the new era of scarcity, laissez-faire and the inalienable right of the individual to get as much as he can are prescriptions for disaster."[21] In somewhat more specific terms, economist Robert Heilbroner fears that the latitude for voluntary choice may vanish rapidly under an avalanche of regulations and regimentation in response "to the slowly closing vise of environmental constraint."[22] Heilbroner believes that the alternative to compulsion, coercion, and regulation is a monastic lifestyle—a simple and frugal mode of living in which waste plays no part. In his mind, the choice is clear. He is not optimistic, however, that the earth's four billion people will curb consumption or childbearing enough to make unnecessary a degree of regulation so great that it would stifle initiative and substantially cheapen human existence.

As the pressures on a biological system intensify, they will eventually impair or even destroy the natural system, forcing governments and international agencies either to stand idly by while resources are destroyed or depleted or to regulate their use. As of the late seventies, the need for stringent regulation has made itself apparent, and increased regulation and regimentation can be felt at the local, national, and international levels. Many politicians and their constituents voice a need for less government and less governmental intervention in everyday affairs. But political campaign promises notwithstanding, there is no feasible alternative to increasing government intervention in daily life as long as the pressures on natural systems and resources continue to mount.

The use of land, once considered an inviolable and almost sacred right of the owner, is now often controlled by land-use plans and by complex zoning regulations. In some countries, cropland cannot be converted to other uses without official consent. Similarly, sewer moratoriums effectively prevent landowners from developing their property in many industrial nations. In Iowa, landowners who do not practice responsible soil conservation can be fined and even jailed.[23]

Even such personal matters as parenthood and childbearing are being influenced by governmental regulations. The Chinese government frowns on marriage for men below the age of twenty-six and for women below twenty-four.[24] Once set for social reasons, the minimum age of marriage is now being raised for ecological and economic reasons.

What people drive and how fast is no longer a strictly private matter either. Speed limits in industrial countries were initially adopted for safety reasons. More recently, they have been lowered further to conserve energy. Not only are speed limits becoming more stringent in the United States, but automobile size and design are being influenced by the conservation ethic. For example, emission-control devices are now required equipment on automobiles in many countries. In the United States, auto manufacturers are being forced to redesign automobile engines to reduce air pollution.

Ever more environmental regulations govern private and public waste disposal. Autumn leaves cannot be burned nor trash dumped indiscriminately in most American communities. Yet, half a century ago such rules would have been unimaginable. In the interest of their constituencies, local governments in the United States now have the authority to shut down plants when air pollution exceeds specified limits or when plants pollute in violation of the environmental statutes. In November of 1975, air pollution at critical levels in Pittsburgh forced Allegheny County health officials to order U.S. Steel and other smaller industries to curtail operations.[25] Elsewhere in the United States, lead and zinc smelters that failed to comply with new environmental-protection requirements have been permanently closed. In many countries costly changes have been imposed on the steel, pulp paper, and petro-chemical industries to enforce compliance with new pollution guidelines. This curtailment of industry's freedom to operate is but one sign of the importance now being accorded to ecological integrity as more and more demands are made upon the ecosystem.

In some countries rationing certain commodities and goods

may be the wisest way to combat the scarcity that occurs when too many claimants vie for the earth's resources. Efforts to reforest in poor countries may, for instance, entail the severe restriction of wood-cutting for firewood or for lumber. Villagers who could once cut trees at will may find they can cut them only in certain places, under certain conditions, and in limited numbers. Rationing by queue is often used now in the centrally planned economies of Eastern Europe and the Soviet Union to limit consumption of scarcer goods. Elsewhere, the marketplace does the rationing. But as prices for scarcer commodities rise, the world's poor will simply not be able to afford them. The quadrupling of coffee prices, for example, does not pose a serious problem for middle-class Americans, but these price hikes may keep poor Turks or Bolivians from consuming the beverage at all.

Regulation of energy consumption could become politically oppressive, but efforts to expand energy supplies using nuclear power could bring a far broader curtailment of individual freedom. As the nuclear-power industry expands, so does the amount of fissionable material moving about the world. Eventually, some is certain to find its way into the hands of terrorists. If a nuclear explosive were used to destroy a city or to hold it hostage, the public outcry for political surveillance and control that would ensue could lead to a measurable and painful loss of political freedom for Swedes and Salvadorans alike.

Coming to terms with the political dilemma outlined here will not be easy or necessarily pleasant. Historian Arnold Toynbee sees increasingly authoritarian governments emerging as economic growth slows or stops. "In all developed countries," he writes, "a new way of life—a severely regimented way—will have to be imposed by a ruthless authoritarian government."[26] Our principal hope for limiting the need for such controls is to voluntarily check our excessive consumption and procreation.

Social and Political Stresses

As economic growth slows, it is likely to fall below the rate of population growth in some countries and to lead to a decline in real income. Once the promise of gains in per-capita income begins to fade, the stress on national political systems will mount as various social groups try to increase or protect their share of the national economic pie. Conflicts over the distribution of income may divide geographic regions, ethnic groups, economic sectors, rural and urban populations, labor and management, the landed and landless, and organized labor and the remainder of the work force. Self-interested actions will heighten existing conflicts and give birth to new ones. Strikes, protests, and other disruptive activities will likely become commonplace. In some situations, the government's will may clash with the people's: faced with the need to alter attitudes and habits quickly, governments may attempt to mandate changes in childbearing (as India did) or in energy conservation (as the United States has). People everywhere will resist certain alterations, particularly when no quick gains reward sacrifice.

As inflation becomes a more dominant feature of the economic landscape, it will also exacerbate strife among societies and social groups. National governments will be sorely tempted to adopt economic policies that enable them to export their inflation. As unemployment mounts, countries will try to increase the number of jobs available at home by attracting and competing for foreign investments. A government working paper that focuses on the future of Canada flags this concern. "Severe inflation breeds recession, and periods of high unemployment and low growth, such as the one we have recently experienced, typically lead to pressure by nations to limit imports and expand exports through measures such as tariffs, quotas and export subsidies. Such rounds of national self-protection could not only harm Canada's ability to compete but in the longer run, would also present the gravest threat to an expanding and stable world trading community."[27] Canada's problem is one that scores of other countries share.

Ecological and economic pressures will force people to cross national boundaries in search of relief. The deterioration of croplands and grassland may transform great numbers of people into international ecological refugees, as they already have in the Sahelian zone. Rising unemployment in densely populated Mexico is already compelling millions of unemployed Mexicans to cross the U.S. border illegally in search of jobs, creating a highly sensitive political issue between the two countries.

As economic growth slows, the pressures to redistribute wealth will be most intense in countries where vast inequities and extreme poverty coexist. In Mexico, where a favored few have title to most of the best farm land, a slowdown in growth will generate strong pressures to redistribute land. Intense pressures of this kind could lead to prolonged instability such as that which wracked Ethiopia and Bangladesh during the midseventies. Coups, countercoups, strikes, riots, demonstrations, and the occupation of large landholdings by the landless are likely both to follow and to perpetuate such instability.

To distribute wealth more equitably, governments may be forced to impose maximum ceilings on incomes, consumption, and wealth. In societies that have disproportionately wide gaps, the poor may begin to agitate for an income-distribution pattern more comparable to that of societies in which the ratio of income of the richest one-fifth to the poorest one-fifth is four or five to one instead of twenty to one. At the same time, conspicuous consumption—particularly of food and energy—will become less and less acceptable. Increasingly, attention will have to focus on the satisfaction of basic social needs of all rather than on the all-out pursuit of material goals by the few. In this sense, the Chinese path to development will take on increased relevance.

As supplies of scarce resources dwindle, the importing countries are certain to disagree with the exporting countries about the desired exploitation rates of natural wealth. Importing countries will want producers to exploit resources rapidly to meet the former's real and imagined needs, while exporting countries will want to prolong the lifetime of such resources by exploiting them slowly and carefully. Principal food-exporting countries may wish to conserve their topsoil by fallowing larger acreages, thereby reducing the planted acreage and supplies available for export. Countries faced with severe food shortages and inflationary food prices will press for larger plantings and larger exports. If high inflation continues, the temptation to keep oil in the ground instead of exchanging it for unstable paper currencies may become irresistible.

Conflicts will arise not only among countries but between short-term and long-term needs. The need to preserve non-renewable resources for future generations has until now not been a factor in most resource calculations and economic projections. While some thought has been given to the distribution of depletable resources among groups, guidelines for sharing resources with future generations still have not been devised. The task is not one economists are well equipped to undertake. Indeed, the issue stumps philosophers and theologians.

In general, the effective functioning of a political system depends on cohesion and confidence. Periods of convulsive change arouse fears and uncertainties that demagogues can exploit. Institutions can crack and collapse under the pressures of such change. If societies lose their sense of purpose, they can become virtually ungovernable. Many cities in both the industrial and developing countries appear to have reached such a state and are now virtually unfit for habitation.

Economic depression and rising unemployment have increasingly been linked to homicide, crime, mental breakdowns, family disintegration, and other psychosocial problems. These stresses take different forms in different countries. In Scandinavia and Eastern Europe, one measure of social and economic stress is a high suicide rate. In the poorest countries in Africa and Asia, the principal stresses in the early seventies were nutritional, taking the form of increased morbidity and mortality, particularly among infants. Conflicts over how the economic pie should be divided translate into more frequent strikes by labor unions in Italy and the United Kingdom. Within the United States, social disintegration is often reflected in high crime rates. To the visitor in Latin America, one of the most obvious signs of social stress is child abandonment: in some cities, bands of homeless street children—*"los olvidados"*—wander about aimlessly.

The perpetuation of poverty within societies where wealth is conspicuous encourages kidnappings and terrorism. Long a tool of those seeking power, it has now become a survival tactic for poor people in some countries. In Colombia, police officials estimate, as many as ten thousand kidnappings took place in 1975, with the ransoms demanded often less than a hundred dollars. One local spokesman notes, "What is so terrifying is that one is not dealing with well organized political groups, but with bands of desperately hungry or diseased people who believe they have little to lose."

Increasingly, governments will be up against intractable problems. Following a 1977 Summit Conference of leaders of the principal industrial countries, Prime Minister Trudeau of Canada summed up the prevailing mood: "We all face problems that we cannot easily solve. So there is popular disaffection. But the opposition parties are also tested on these problems. They do not show up any better."[28]

Governments of poor countries already find the management of chronic social problems trying in the extreme. As problems become unmanageable, ever more governments become unstable. Frequent changes in governments make the sustained, effective addressing of problems even more difficult, setting in motion a downward spiral of upheaval and confusion. Shortages, inflation, unemployment, and cumulative declines in real consumption all combine to breed unrest and political instability.

II

The Elements of Accommodation

Accommodating our needs and numbers to the earth's natural capacities and resources will affect virtually every facet of human existence. In terms of its effect on human values and institutions, the coming transformation could ultimately approach the Agricultural and the Industrial Revolutions. Like these earlier momentous changes, it will surely give rise to new social structures and to an economic system materially different from any we know today. While its scope may resemble these earlier transformations, its pace will be far swifter. The agricultural revolution took several thousand years and the industrial revolution began two centuries ago, but the coming transformation must be compressed into a few decades.

Stabilizing World Population

At the center of this global accommodation will be the efforts to bring population growth to a halt. The double-edged effect of population growth in our global lily pond leaves little time to act. In a speech at MIT in early 1977, Robert S. McNamara noted the widespread decline in fertility under way, but then went on to say that "as welcome as this is, the fact remains that the current rate of decline in fertility in the developing countries is too slow to avoid their ultimately arriving at stationary population far in excess of acceptable levels."[1]

Obvious and urgent though the need to stabilize population may be, there are few areas of public policy that governments have so consistently shied away from. Only during the current decade have many countries begun to deal seriously with the issue. In its 1972–76 Five-Year Plan, the government of Sri Lanka announced that "the continued growth of population at the present high rates will pose problems which would defy every attempt at solution. . . ." A year later President Nyerere of Tanzania pointed out that "whatever we produce has to be divided between an increasing number of people every year. . . . [I]t is no use saying that these extra 380,000 people have hands as well as mouths. For the first 10 years of their lives, at the very least, children eat without producing." In 1975, Peruvian President Francisco Morale Bermudez Cerrutti stated that "the growth of our economy, as it is today, will not be able to absorb the high levels of unemployment and growth of the population."[2]

As global economic growth slows, the wide variations in population growth rates become far more conspicuous. Those countries whose populations are stable or growing slowly can weather a slowdown in global economic growth, whereas those with rapid population-growth rates are highly vulnerable. Any rate of economic growth, however modest, leads to per-capita income rises in those countries (such as East Germany or Belgium) where population has stabilized. These countries are protected from the adverse per-capita effects of declining economic-growth rates, whereas those with rapidly expanding populations are not. A 2-percent rate of economic growth would lead to steady per-capita advances in East Germany and Belgium, but to a steady deterioration in Ecuador or Senegal.

Like many other trends that must be arrested, the growth in human numbers has momentum behind it. In a paper commissioned by the United Nations for its Conference on Population at Bucharest, Paul Ehrlich and John Holdren report that this momentum "has its origins in deep seated attitudes toward reproduction and in the age composition of the world's population—37 percent is under 15 years of age."[3]

In considering these factors, the Conference at Bucharest resolved that all couples have the right to plan their families and that it is the responsibility of governments to ensure that they have the means to do so. But the world is still far from achieving the goal set forth there. Requests for assistance with family-planning programs have escalated sharply since 1974, not so much because of the conference, which helped focus attention on the problem, as because governments are now being forced to face the ecological and economic consequences of a generation of rapid population growth. This sharp increase in requests for help has overwhelmed the three principal sources of assistance—the United Nations Fund for Population Activities (UNFPA), the U.S. Agency for International Development, and the International Planned Parenthood Federation. Director of the UNFPA Rafael Salas reported in 1975 that his agency could not accept any new requests for assistance until early 1977.[4]

Despite the inadequacy of resources, many governments have boldly adopted explicit demographic goals. Bangladesh, frequently identified as the country in which the Malthusian nightmare is most likely to unfold, is striving to stabilize its population within the next twenty-five to thirty years. China and India, the world's two most populous countries, have both officially adopted population stability as a national goal.

Once a government recognizes the need to halt population growth and decides to do so, tactical decisions remain. It may slow population by taking five distinct actions: by providing family-planning services, by satisfying basic social needs, by improving the status of women, by educating the people about the consequences of rapid population growth, and by reshaping national economic and social policies to encourage small families. The two countries that have moved on all five fronts simultaneously, China and Singapore, have both been spectacularly successful in reducing their birth rates.

Growing evidence as well as common sense indicates that fertility levels usually fall most rapidly in societies that satisfy people's basic needs. Adequate nutrition, health services (particularly those that lower infant mortality), and education all influence fertility. The social indicator that correlates most closely with declines in fertility appears to be education for women, particularly the attainment of literacy. Such data as are available on the relationship between literacy and birth rates suggest that raising literacy levels would lower fertility levels.

Understanding the consequences of rapid population growth is an essential prelude to bridling it. Unfortunately, few governments, and thus few citizens, have a thorough grasp of population arithmetic and of the many dimensions of the population problem. Few, if any, governments have attempted to determine the population-sustaining capacity of their countries in the post-petroleum era when they must depend largely, if not entirely, on renewable energy sources. If more governments comprehended the arithmetic of population growth and if more understood that having too many children too close together adversely affects the health of both mothers and children, more countries would have effective family-planning programs. Population education is everywhere sadly deficient, everywhere in need of more attention and resources than it is now getting.

Expanding employment opportunities for women can also help curb birth rates. If women are not to spend most of their productive years bearing and rearing children, then they must be provided with alternative jobs and other means of self-fulfillment. As attractive career opportunities become available to women, these options often compete with the traditional role of motherhood. Europe, the Soviet Union, North America, and China have gone farthest in recognizing and utilizing women's abilities and talents outside the home.

Without risking sizable capital outlays, governments can help lower birth rates by revamping economic and social policies. In many countries, economic and social incentives and structures were originally designed to encourage large families. In others, the pressure to reproduce is inadvertent. In all, beneficial social changes can flow from new laws and incentives. Effectively raising the minimum age of marriage, for example, can both reduce family size and improve the health of mothers and infants. A steep rise in the age of marriage in Ireland following the potato famine of 1847 led to a population decline there that lasted for nearly a century. Today, the combined ages of a Chinese couple at marriage should, the rule of thumb goes, total at least 50 years. In Sri Lanka, some evidence indicates, young people are beginning to delay marriage for economic reasons, particularly because job opportunities are scarce.

Tax policies that limit the number of "tax-deductible" children serve the same end. In Singapore, tax relief is granted for the first three children only. In 1975, Nepal passed a law eliminating tax deductions based on the number of children.[5] U.S. Senator Bob Packwood of Oregon has introduced legislation in the U.S. Congress that would limit income-tax deductions for children to two.

Policies governing social security, maternity leave, and access to education, as well as to governmental jobs, can be molded to promote small families. The government of Pakistan provides an insurance policy to couples who have no more than three children and who voluntarily undergo sterilization. In Tunisia, child allowances are limited to four. The state of Bihar in eastern India limits the number of children's food-ration cards for use in the concessional "fair-price shops" to three per family.[6]

Increasingly, the notion that world population can expand to the ten to fourteen billion that UN demographers have projected is being questioned. Governments are beginning to recognize the need to adopt stabilization as a national goal. China has instituted the local birth-quota system, wherein the responsibility for family planning is delegated to small local groups in factories, neighborhoods, and villages. Bruce Stokes describes the procedure for localizing responsibility. "Schooled by the need to plan locally for production, income distribution, investments, and social welfare, these local groups fully understand the cost to the community of excessive childbearing and coordinate their birth plans with the targets set by community, regional, and national agencies. Once the number of births for a factory or neighborhood group has been set, the members allocate the births among themselves."[7] According to American demographer Pi-chao Chen, "Couples are given priority in the following order: first are the newly married who are free to have their first child without delay; second are couples with only one or two children; and third are couples whose youngest child is nearest to five years of age."[8] In India the central government approaches the issue less directly, by apportioning public funds to the states on the basis of their 1972 population, thus encouraging state governments to promote and sponsor family-planning activities.[9] The slogan "stop at two" could well become a global norm as the many manifestations of population pressure make themselves felt. Quite conceivably, pressures could so intensify in some countries that a one-child family could become the norm until population growth is tamed.

In the United States, Zero Population Growth seemed quite novel a decade ago. Today, the objective of population stability is espoused by Americans in every walk of life. In the United Kingdom in 1972, a group of leading activists argued forcefully in *Blueprint for Survival* for a long-term gradual reduction of one-half in national population size.[10] As the ecological and social costs of continuing population growth become more visible, more and more governments are likely to adopt population stability as a national goal.

The Energy Transition

The world has undergone two energy transitions and is about to undergo a third. The first two, the shift from wood to coal and that from coal to oil, wrought profound social changes. The shift from wood to coal set the stage for the Industrial Revolution, and the substitution of oil for coal gave birth to the Auto-Industrial Age. There is no reason to believe that the shift from oil to other energy sources will not bring changes of a comparable magnitude.

The end of the age of oil was being contemplated as early as the mid-twentieth century, but it was not a source of alarm because nuclear power was waiting in the wings, along with vast reserves of coal. But during the mid-seventies the outlook began to change. With oil wells going dry, nuclear power in limbo, and the heavy use of coal threatening to alter the global climate, the urgency of developing renewable energy sources was becoming obvious.

The dominant characteristic of the transition now beginning is its urgency. Only some ten to fifteen years remain before the projected downturn in world oil production. Many years are required to bring new energy sources onstream. A technology such as large-scale wind-powered electrical generation must first be developed, then tested and refined. Once a satisfactory prototype exists, means to bring it into commercial use must be found. Time is required to mobilize investment capital, to build plants, to manufacture the generator, to train construction crews to install equipment, and to prepare environmental-impact statements.

A huge collector converting solar heat into steam can generate enough electrical power to satisfy the needs of a middle-sized city. Smaller and simpler collectors can cheaply heat water for a single home. But even installing solar collectors on individual homes can take a country many years. No one knows how many hundreds of millions of solar collectors would be needed worldwide by 1990 to offset or perhaps even postpone the downturn in petroleum production.

Circumstances suggest the need for a crash energy-conservation program and for a broadly based global effort to develop the entire range of renewable energy resources. An all-out conservation program would help stretch remaining oil reserves as far as possible and thus buy time to shift to renewable energy sources. The challenge is to husband scarce petroleum resources while designing an economic system that will be sustainable without petroleum. The risk is that petroleum supplies will be squandered frivolously on nonessential uses before a non-petroleum agricultural system can be developed.

The conservation component of a global strategy for the energy transition applies particularly to the United States, which wastes more energy than the poorest one-half of the world uses. This energy waste appears to reflect carelessness and to bear little relation to the quality of life. Indeed, energy consumption in the United States may now be so excessive as to adversely affect health and well-being. For example, using cars to travel distances that are easily walked or bicycled not only wastes energy but also makes staying physically fit and healthy harder. Similarly, eating excessive quantities of fat-rich livestock products, which are highly energy intensive to produce, wastes energy and undermines human health. The time has come to recognize that energy conservation is nothing less than a survival tactic. Within another generation, relatively little petroleum will remain. By that time, energy demands that are not readily satisfied by renewable resources may not be satisfied at all.

There may not be any easy solutions to the energy crisis. Escaping its grip may involve curtailing the petroleum-dependent automobile in favor of the bicycle; it may mean walking up or down a few flights of stairs rather than using an elevator; it may mean reversing the urbanization process that has so deeply influenced society in the third quarter of this century.

Some conservation tactics can be used without affecting lifestyles noticeably. Others require moderate changes in lifestyles. Still others would entail sacrifice and hardship. Among those measures that need not upset daily life are a switch from a large car to a small one and the use of home insulation to reduce fuel needs. At this level alone, the potential for conservation is great.

An effective conservation strategy would eliminate the more frivolous uses of energy—such as automatic transmissions in automobiles, a technology that sacrifices 10 percent in fuel efficiency in exchange for a trifling reduction in human effort. It would also eliminate first-class air fares, single-car suburban commuting, and short-distance air travel between cities such as Washington and New York or Paris and Brussels, which are served by rapid-rail systems. Electrical rate structures would be revised to discourage rather than encourage consumption.

The potential for energy conservation in industrial societies cannot be measured until an all-out effort has been made. However, some industrial countries have already taken first steps toward effective energy conservation. The Canadian government is imposing a heavy tax on automobiles that weigh more than 4,000 pounds and a flat tax of 100 dollars on every new car sold with an air conditioner.[11] This measure both penalizes those who waste energy and drives home the government's concern about Canada's energy budget.

The post-petroleum, energy-frugal world will differ markedly from the one we now know. Renewable energy sources such as wind, sun, and water power are widely dispersed. Reserves of oil, by contrast, are heavily concentrated in a few countries in the Middle East. Consequently, a solar-powered world offers promise of a decline in economic and political interdependence. An international economy that depended heavily on renewable energy sources would also be far less vulnerable to wars and strikes than an oil-hungry one.

But though the global transition to renewable energy resources must be made quickly, nothing even vaguely resembling a global plan for making this transition has been put on paper. No national timetables, much less a coordinated global timetable, for shifting the economy from petroleum to renewable energy sources have been drafted. The rate of transition from petroleum to solar-energy sources, the number of solar collectors to be installed each year by country, the number of windmills to be erected where use of wind power is economically feasible, and the area of farmland to be devoted to the various energy crops all need to be calculated. Such a global plan would specify deadlines for developing new building standards that would promote energy conservation. It would, at a minimum, put solar-energy sources on an equal financial footing with other sources in terms of tax breaks and public investments in research and development.

The need to formulate and launch a transition program, including devising a timetable, is paramount. The entire world needs to move ahead. Yet only a few countries—such as China with its reforestation programs, methane generators, and small-scale hydroelectric generators; and Brazil with its ethanol automotive-fuel program—are systematically developing their renewable energy sources. Without a timetable, the world may well wake up one day to find that the oil is gone and that adequate alternative sources of energy are not available.

Recycling Raw Materials

The consumption of both energy and raw materials has become extravagant in the United States over the last few decades partly because a "throwaway" economy has evolved. Together with the planned obsolescence of consumer goods, this evolution has led to an indefensible squandering of the earth's resources. But while this waste may appear essential to our economic system, nothing could be farther from the truth. Such a system, in fact, is so vulnerable that it cannot long survive without modification.

Although recycling has been widely discussed in the United States in recent years, little real progress has been made. Of the United States, the National Commission on Supplies and Shortages has this to say: "Sizable amounts of some major materials already are recycled, but as a percentage of total consumption, recycling has been static or declining in America, and only a small portion of post-consumer waste is recycled. . . . A number of government practices effectively (if inadvertently) discourage recycling. . . ." The Commission then goes on to outline some of the new legislative initiatives needed from Congress "to eliminate discrimination against recycled materials in procurement specifications, possible discrimination against recyclables in regulated freight rates and a variety of institutional barriers which cause localities to miss recycling opportunities." It recommends that "further action should be taken in furtherance of the true-cost-of-materials principle—for example, repeal of tax subsidies to producers of urgent materials and the imposition of disposal charges and refundable deposits on containers and paper products."[12]

The U.S. economy consumes vast quantities of paper, the great bulk of which is simply discarded after use, contributing to waste-disposal costs. The Commission reports that "the rate of paper recycling in the United States has declined from 35 percent to 21 percent since capital gains treatment for timber was enacted (over President Roosevelt's veto) in 1944." Each year the newsprint needs of the *New York Times* total some 265,000 tons—thousands of hectares of timber. If an efficient recycling system were developed, *Times* readers could recycle their copies, limiting the need for tree cutting to that required for replacement of losses in the recycling process. If this system were also widely practiced by newspapers throughout the world, including many who use even more newsprint than the *New York Times*, the savings in both newsprint and energy would be impressive. Recycling paper is one important way of lightening immediate pressure on the earth's overtaxed forests. Other claims, such as those for firewood and lumber, are not so easily reduced.

The all-around savings associated with the use of ferrous scrap are most impressive, but the U.S. government nonetheless subsidizes the use of iron ore with a 13-percent depletion allowance, and railroad freight charges permitted by the Interstate Commerce Commission are three times as high for scrap as for iron ore. Consequently, a backlog of six hundred million tons of ferrous scrap is strewn about the countryside, much of it in automobile hulks. Using data from the Environmental Protection Agency, David Hill writes that when steel mills use ferrous scrap in lieu of iron ore, "there is an 86 percent reduction in air pollution, a 76 percent reduction in water pollution, and a 40 percent reduction in water use." There is also of course a net reduction in the metallic waste stock pile. Energy savings too are impressive. In 1976 alone, Hill reports, even the limited use of scrap by the U.S. steel industry "saved 14 million tons of coal and the equivalent of 5.7 billion gallons of gasoline —enough to power one-tenth of America's cars for the entire year."[13]

All used metals can be recycled at great savings once they are collected. The vast quantities of steel used in a modern industrial society such as the United States can, for example, be recycled indefinitely with only modest losses due to rusting and other kinds of material attrition. A ton of steel manufactured from scrap requires only a third as much energy as a ton produced from virgin resources (for aluminum, the comparable figure is one-twentieth). Much of the steel produced in the United States over the last several decades was used to fashion the automobiles that now litter the countryside. To guard against this blight, Sweden put into effect "a mandatory deposit system for automobiles similar to that for bottles."[14] A tax of three hundred Swedish kroner, or sixty-five U.S. dollars, is placed on every car and is refunded when the car is turned in to a scrap yard. Such a policy makes good sense and should be adopted universally.

The advantages of recycling glass containers are obvious. Oregon's mandatory deposit on carbonated-beverage containers has greatly stimulated recycling and reduced the amount of roadside litter while leaving beverage prices essentially unchanged. Two other states—Michigan and Vermont—have followed Oregon's lead.[15]

Recycling has several ecological and economic advantages. Once an extensive stock of a given material—metals, glass, newsprint or other materials—is in circulation, less fresh raw material is needed. Another advantage is the vast saving in energy. Savings in material and energy reduce pollution and other forms of environmental disruption. In addition, as studies of the switch from throw-away to returnable bottles consistently show, the use of returnable containers creates additional jobs. Energy saved by recycling can be used to create jobs elsewhere in the economy. Such double-acting policies are precisely those an energy-short society beseiged by unemployment should embrace.

The planned annual obsolescence of clothing and automobiles also sanctions waste. The existing U.S. economic system depends on products that are designed to wear out quickly so that consumers will perpetually have to purchase replacements. By subordinating durability and practicality to style, consumer-goods manufacturers make a mockery of human intelligence and social values even as they waste precious energy.

One way to shake the throw-away mentality, and we surely must, is to shake the "there's more where that came from" mentality. For there may not be, at least not at the same price. To accord the recycling of materials and the design of durable goods high priority is merely to recognize that our supplies of energy and raw materials are limited. Exactly how much we can save will not be known until the vast array of sophisticated scientific and engineering know-how of an industrially advanced country is brought to bear on the problem.

Reform in the Countryside

The pressing need for rural reform now evident in a great many countries has its roots in the failure of indigenous agriculture to satisfy even minimal food needs and in the grossly inequitable distribution of income and social services. Rural reform may be the principal means available for creating jobs and arresting the worldwide rise in unemployment. The first step is to redress the imbalance between countryside and city, giving the capital-starved countryside its due. But redressing the urban bias in public policy may be as difficult as it is essential. Only a handful of countries have achieved a balanced allocation of public resources between the countryside and city. Government policies and programs that overwhelmingly favor the cities are still the rule.

The second reform needed is a redistribution of land so that those working on the land will own it and will have the incentive to improve it. Powerful Latin American landholders have monopolized the fertile tillable soils in the valleys, while the less influential have been forced up the hills and mountainsides in their quest for land. The ecological consequences of this socially regressive land distribution pattern are evident in the gullies that scar the farmland on the hillsides and in the silt that clogs streams and reservoirs in the valleys.

In Mexico, the large landowners control the highly productive irrigated land in the northern part of the country, while growing numbers of peasants are being squeezed onto marginal land, much of which will not support sustained cultivation. As population pressures mount and the ranks of the landless expand, failure to redistribute land could lead to political unrest. Indeed, when Mexican President Echeverria's term of office was nearing an end in late 1976, thousands of peasants occupied large landholdings with the intent of claiming title to them. In this case, the forced evacuation of these squatters may have prevented a major upheaval and land grab.

The buildup of population pressure on the land and the growing numbers of landless unemployed provides a formula for social and political unrest, if not revolution. Roy Prosterman, a law professor and land-reform specialist, notes that "In virtually all the societies that have undergone major revolutions in this century, the bulk of the rural population has consisted of non-landowning peasants who rarely were less than a third of the total population of the country." He then cites among others pre-1941 China, pre-1952 Bolivia, pre-1959 Cuba, and pre-1961 South Vietnam, where the landless peasants accounted for 32 to 60 percent of the population.[16]

Once those who actually work the land own it, or share in its ownership, the key to rapid progress becomes access to credit, technical advisory services, and markets. The basic formula for effective agricultural reform is rather straightforward and simple. What is lacking is the willingness of existing power structures to undertake the needed reforms.

By far the most successful agricultural systems are those built around the family farm. Those of Japan, Taiwan, and the United States fall into this category. Small family farms were formed in Japan and Taiwan as part of a broad land reform undertaken after World War II. In these East Asian countries, few large farms exist, nearly all farm families own their own land, and tenancy is limited. In the United States, landowner-ship was rather concentrated, particularly in the South, until Abraham Lincoln's presidency, when the end of slavery and the passage of the Homestead Act led to a breakup of the large estates. Granting free land in the Midwest and West to those willing to live on it and work it, the Homestead Act helped strengthen family farms. Average size for a viable family farm can vary widely—from scarcely one hectare of cropland in Japan to a hundred or more in the United States. The impor-tant thing is that the size of farms reflect the ratio of the agricultural population to farmland.

A country's labor force is most effectively utilized under a family-farm system. Large landowners employ additional labor only as long as the value of the additional output ex-ceeds the prevailing wage. In contrast, families who till their own land invariably invest more labor per hectare, since the criterion for employment of family members is that their efforts merely increase output. Moreover, the link between effort and reward are much greater on the family-based farm. Not only will people work harder and longer, but they also have a strong incentive to devote idle time during the off season to land improvement—to terracing, to constructing irrigation or drainage facilities, to tree plant-ing, and to other land-conservation and improvement prac-tices. Not surprisingly, countries with family-size farms con-sistently out-perform those in which landownership is concentrated in a few hands or in which vast state farms are the norm. Production per hectare on the one-to-two hectare farms prevalent in East Asia is the highest in the world.

Food shortages, rising energy costs, and soaring unemploy-ment suggest the need for rural reforms in countries at all stages of development. Reports from Moscow in mid-1977 indicate an unprecedented initiative by the Soviet government to provide greater public support for the small private family plots that provide such a disproportionately large share of Soviet meat, milk, eggs, and vegetables. Party leader Leonid Brezhnev described the private plots as a "reserve of no small importance" and instructed state officials to help farmers with their private plots.[17]

In the United States, meanwhile, the courts were ruling in favor of the long-ignored 1902 Reclamation Act that limited water rights from publicly supported irrigation projects to one hundred sixty acres per family. The principle on which the act was based was the same as that underlying the Homestead Act; namely, that the distribution of public resources should be related to the amount of land a family could farm. In a world where fertile land is scarce and where the family farm has consistently been the most efficient production unit, public policy should be used to support family-size holdings. Indeed, the time may now be ripe for restricting eligibility for commodity price supports to the amount produced by family farms. In the United States this would certainly be consistent with such landmark legislation as the Homestead Act. Adoption of such a policy could everywhere strengthen family farms and, consequently, agricultural productivity.

Land redistribution alone cannot alleviate food shortages and correct gross income inequities. Farmers also need not only credit and technical supporting services but also social services on a par with those offered in the city. Those countries that have succeeded in these efforts in the countryside have derived broad social benefits. While no common geographical, political, or cultural factor unites Japan, China, Taiwan, the United States, Canada, Australia, and New Zealand, they all have successfully created vital rural sectors in which both social conditions and worker productivity compare favorably with those in the urban sector.

The Changing Roles of Women

The need to accommodate human needs and numbers to the earth's resources has special significance for women. Combined with the feminist push for equal rights and responsibilities, it promises to alter female social roles fundamentally. Although far more advanced in some societies than others, the contemporary women's rights movement is a worldwide social phenomenon. Women everywhere are pressing for a more equitable role in social affairs and for the removal of age-old legal and social constraints.

Women's attempts to alter their social roles are being reinforced by two powerful forces—the mounting pressures for a reduction in births and a growing reliance by government planners on expanded female employment as a means of increasing the overall production of goods and services. These forces are themselves closely related and mutually reinforcing. For example, women's desire to take more active roles in economic and political affairs is closely associated with a declining birth rate, which in turn enhances the prospect for employment outside the home.

Female college students in the United States are beginning to think of their professions and careers in ways that are virtually indistinguishable from those of their male counterparts. In a poll taken in 1973 among women seniors at Stanford University, fewer than one in twenty-five said that she expected to become a full-time housewife within five years of graduation.[18] Because both Stanford's academic standards and its tuition fees are high, its students should not be considered a cross-section; nonetheless, the response does reflect a pronounced attitude change among young U.S. women. Many female graduates of American colleges today simply do not accept the traditional roles assigned to their mothers.

Stirrings of the women's liberation movement can be felt in developing and developed societies alike. Rumblings are heard even in some of the most traditional ones, in which women's roles have always been carefully circumscribed. Women's organizations are being formed in such restrictive societies as Afghanistan and Morocco. The First National Women's Congress in Brazil was convened late in 1972. Held publicly in a traditionally male-dominated society, this week-long conference attracted a great deal of attention and covered many issues. On two of these issues—the need for planned parenthood and for day-care centers—there was strong agreement.

As women exchange old roles for new, they are often torn between the privileges of the passing order and the responsibilities and opportunities of the coming one. Increasingly, they will experience the psychosomatic stresses of the executive suite or the loss of the custody of their children after a divorce. Women in virtually all societies are caught between two worlds. As Charlotte Saikowski writes of Chinese women, they are "vigorous contenders in a tug of war between Confucianism and Maoism. Confucius said women must subordinate themselves to their husbands. Chairman Mao says 'women hold up half of heaven.' It is not hard to know which side the women are on. . . . There is no doubt that Mao Tse-tung by preaching that women can do the same things men do has brought women into the mainstream of Chinese life and given their lives new dignity and meaning."[19] The changing roles of Chinese women is of particular interest, since China represents a fifth of humanity and may be the first agrarian society in which women's principal energies have shifted from childbearing and rearing to employment outside the home. For thousands of generations, bearing and rearing children was the main social task of women. For much of their comparatively short adult lives, women were almost continuously pregnant or nursing. If a woman weaned her infant at two years or so or lost it during its first months of life, then she would quickly become pregnant again. The combination of a short life expectancy and the need for large numbers of children meant that no female role other than that of nurturant parent was consistent with human survival.

The modern reductions in mortality to a fraction of historical levels leads perforce to changes in women's roles. On a crowded planet, women cannot concern themselves primarily with childbearing and child rearing. Within the more hard-pressed societies, couples may soon be forced to forego having more than two children. Accordingly, the great number of females who will reach reproductive age during the final quarter of this century may not choose to realize more than a small fraction of their collective reproductive potential.

The third emerging factor that will multiply women's options and reinforce the movement of women into the paid labor force is environmental and economic change. As energy becomes more costly and as gains in labor productivity diminish, as now seems likely, raising a nation's production of goods and services may mean increasing female participation in the labor force. Women have already been effectively drawn into the paid labor force to expand the economy in the industrial countries and in China. But relatively few women have found gainful employment in other agrarian societies.

The female share of the paid labor force varies from a low of several percent in some countries to nearly half in a few socialist countries such as the Soviet Union, East Germany, and Rumania. In virtually all industrial societies, female participation has risen over the past generation. In Western Europe, women constitute roughly a third of all employed workers. In Canada, the female share of the labor force increased from 27 percent in 1960 to 33 percent in 1970. As of 1977, women hold two of every five jobs in the U.S. economy.[20] Between 1950 and 1975, the number of employed females increased from just seventeen million to thirty-four million, while the male labor force increased from forty-two million to fifty-one million.[21] During this period, the male labor force expanded by less than a quarter, while the female labor force doubled. Female employment patterns in the United States over the past twenty-five years in many ways typify those of other industrial societies.

The socialist countries have made a particularly strong effort to employ women by creating jobs and by providing support services such as child-care centers. As Svetlana Turchaninova rather idealistically writes in the *International Labor Review*, "The typical Soviet woman today is not a housewife permanently chained to her kitchen sink, nursery, or garden plot, but a full citizen active in productive employment and interrupting it only for a while to bear and look after her children."[22] Within the Soviet Union, however, participation rates vary substantially among regions of the country: those in the Central Asian Republics, where birth rates are high, are much lower than those in the European portions of the country, where birth rates are low.

The metamorphosis of women's roles, one of the adjustments required to accommodate ourselves to a small planet, will weigh most heavily in the poor countries. In Third World countries, childbearing will of necessity decline precipitously, and so will the need for childbearers. In the industrial societies changes in prospect are more a matter of degree than kind. The increasing employment of women outside the home is already leading to a major shift in economic status, and childbearing is already considered by many an option rather than a calling.

In production brigades in China and on university campuses in the United States, women are beginning to perceive and assume new social roles. Given both their desire for more equitable roles and the pressing need to reduce fertility everywhere, society is sure to be transformed in ways that affect all. Changing women's roles will necessarily change those of men as well. In the future more and more women can be expected to strive for the same opportunities and responsibilities that men value.

Redefining National Security

As the deteriorating relationship of man to nature is put into perspective, and as the necessity of accommodation becomes more obvious, governments will inevitably have to redefine the traditional concept of national security. The concern for the security of a nation is undoubtedly as old as the nation state itself, although only since World War II has it acquired an overwhelmingly military character. Yet concern about military threats from other nations has become so dominant in the deliberations about national security that other threats are being ignored. The deterioration of biological systems, the progressive depletion of fossil fuel resources, and the economic stresses due to resource scarcities all represent threats that derive less from the relationship of nation to nation than from the relationship of man to nature.

The policy of continual preparedness has led to the militarization of the world economy. Military expenditures now account for 6 percent of the global product. Worldwide, the military claims of national budgets exceed health-service appropriations. Most countries spend more on "national security" than they do on educating their youth. The development of new, "more effective" weapons systems now engages fully a quarter of the world's scientific talent.[23]

This competition between the military and social sectors of the world is not new, but the overwhelming cost of maintaining modern military forces is without precedent. In a time of growing scarcities, the military can continue to absorb an ever larger share of the world's limited resources only at great social cost. As science-fiction writer Isaac Asimov has pointed out, "Even a non-nuclear war cannot be fought because it is too energy-rich a phenomenon." We cannot afford such extravagance, contends Asimov, "and are going to have to use all our energy to stay alive" with none "to spare for warfare."[24] In a speech to a group of business executives in the fall of 1977, U.S. Secretary of Defense Harold Brown stated that "the present deficiency of assured energy resources is the single surest threat that the future poses to our security and that of our allies."[25]

Perhaps the best contemporary definition of national security is one by Franklin P. Huddle, director of the massive U.S. congressional study *Science, Technology, and American Diplomacy*. In *Science,* he writes, "National security requires a stable economy with assured supplies of materials for industry. In this sense, frugality and conservation of materials are essential to our national security. Security means more than safety from hostile attack; it includes the preservation of a system of civilization." Dr. Huddle goes on to say that each country should design a way of life that is acceptable to its people and compatible with the needs and choices of the rest of the world.[26]

Increasingly, national security must be tied to the condition of the world's economies and political systems. The stability of these systems is in turn dependent on assured energy supplies and on the stability of the earth's biological systems. National-defense establishments are useless against these new challenges. Neither bloated military budgets nor highly sophisticated weapons systems can halt the deforestation or solve the firewood crisis now affecting so many Third World countries. Nor can they ameliorate the worsening food shortages or arrest the rise in unemployment levels in some of the same countries.

The new threats to national security are extraordinarily complex. Ecologists understand that the deteriorating relationship between four billion humans and the earth's biological systems cannot continue. But few political leaders have yet to grasp the social significance of this unsustainable situation. Intelligence agencies are organized to alert political leaders to potential military threats, but there is no counterpart network to warn of the collapse of a biological system. Energy analysts understand the need to arrest ecological deterioration, but few individuals are trained or able to weigh and evaluate such a diversity of threats and then to translate such an assessment into the allocation of public resources that provides the greatest national security.

Unfortunately, these nonmilitary threats are much less clearly defined than military ones. They are often the result of cumulative processes that ultimately lead to the collapse of biological systems or to the depletion of a country's oil reserves. These processes in themselves are seldom given much thought until they pass a critical threshold. Thus, it is easier in the government councils of developing countries to justify expenditures for the latest-model jet fighters than for family planning to arrest the population growth that contributes to food scarcity.

In a world that is not only ecologically interdependent but economically and politically interdependent as well, the concept of "national" security is no longer adequate. Though national governments are still the principal decision makers, many threats to security require a co-ordinated international response. The times call for efforts to secure the global systems on which nations depend.

The continuing focus of governments on military threats to security may not only exclude attention to the newer threats, but may also make the effective address of the latter more difficult. The heavy military emphasis on national security can absorb budgetary resources, management skills, and scientific talent that should be devoted to the new nonmilitary threats. Apart from the heavy claim on public resources, the continuing exorbitant investment in armaments contributes to a psychological climate of suspicion and mistrust that poisons the well of international co-operation.

The purpose of national-security deliberations should not be to maximize military strength but to maximize national security. In the late twentieth century the key to national security is sustainability. If the biological underpinnings of the global economic system cannot be secured, then the long-term economic outlook is grim indeed. If new energy sources and systems are not in place as the oil wells begin to go dry, then severe economic disruptions are inevitable.

Neither individual security nor national security can be sensibly considered in isolation. In effect, the traditional military concept of "national security" is growing ever less adequate as nonmilitary threats grow more formidable. At some point, governments will be forced either to realign priorities in a manner responsive to the new threats or to watch their national security deteriorate.

Coping with Complexity

Since World War II, interdependence among nations has so deepened that political or economic decisions taken in one country often affect far more people outside that country than within it. A decision to change the exchange rate in the United Kingdom, for example, can profoundly alter Britain's trade relationships with countries throughout the world. A governmental decision to offset a crop shortfall in the Soviet Union by importing grain rather than by belt-tightening can send up food prices everywhere. A decision by OPEC to raise the price of oil can influence economic growth, inflation, and employment in every country.

Although a single country or group of countries now has more power than it once did over the fate of other nations, no global political institutions offer the citizens in these other countries any hand in the decision making that so directly affects them: the institutions required to manage these new relationships have not yet evolved. Indeed, in *Awakening From the American Dream*, an analysis of the social and political limits to growth, Professor Rufus Miles of Princeton University questions whether humans can effectively manage these vast and complex interdependencies. He hypothesizes that "there are limits to the human capacity to design and manage, by the political process, huge complex interdependent economic and ecological systems, and that we are now pressing against those limits."[27]

Nations can respond to the deepening interdependence among countries in two ways by managing it or reducing it. The creation of new supranational institutions represents an attempt to effectively manage it. In finance, the International Monetary Fund already serves as such an institution, but a need is emerging for parallel institutions to manage other major areas of international interdependence. Just as the International Monetary Fund attempts to regulate national actions or interventions that affect the international monetary system, so an institution is needed to control national influences on the global climatic system. Another regulatory institution is needed to oversee the use and exploitation of oceanic resources that are beyond national jurisdiction.

At the national level, countries are beginning to resent their growing dependence on external resources and assistance and to worry about the vulnerability bred of such dependence. In particular, food-deficit countries are beginning to realize how their reliance on external supplies leaves them susceptible to political pressures and to the vagaries of climate in the supplying region. Similarly, industrial countries heavily dependent on petroleum imports have been both frustrated and humiliated since the Arab export embargo of late 1973 revealed their own vulnerability. "World systems of interdependence are more remote, precarious, and inefficient than national (or subnational) systems," says Rufus Miles, "and have probably exceeded their sustainable level of complexity and dependability."

The second way of coping with interdependencies is to reduce them. Some countries may now be willing to sacrifice some amenities and prestige in exchange for greater security. Without the illusion that international trade, investment, and tourism will continue to expand indefinitely, they will attempt to reduce their dependence on externally supplied raw materials such as food, energy, and minerals. National decisions on energy policy will be particularly critical. Countries that opt to turn to nuclear power as their principal source of energy will find themselves at least as vulnerable to external powers such as the uranium cartel as they were to OPEC's leverage. Those that decide to turn to solar sources, on the other hand, will greatly reduce their dependence on outside energy sources.

As petroleum reserves dwindle and energy grows costlier, the high degree of specialization of production in the world economy and the associated high levels of international trade will be reduced. Countries that have become heavily dependent on imported food supplies may take action to increase domestic food production substantially and to lower their birth rates.

If the various economic and political forces now at work do reverse the long-standing growth in interdependence among countries, as they almost surely will, some economic bonds between countries will be loosened, if not severed. Indeed, the economic interdependence among nations may even now be approaching its zenith. Frustrated over being constantly buffeted about by external forces beyond their control, nations may act to reduce their exposure to these forces. More and more, national self-reliance may be the order of the day.

12

The Means of Accommodation

Once we recognize that the issue is not whether we accommodate ourselves to the earth's natural capacities and resources but how, other questions arise. Will the adjustments be made sensibly, co-operatively, and with foresight, or blindly and catastrophically? If we know what we must do, will we be able to muster the political will and organization to do it? In an era of profound change, who will be the prime movers? Will they be individual activists and enlightened government leaders, or the indiscriminate, sometimes brutal, forces of nature and the marketplace?

A Planetary Bargain

The call for a new international economic order is justified and overdue, but it is not in itself sufficient. It needs to be pursued as part of a broader effort to create a sustainable, just society. In today's world sustainability has both an ecological and a political dimension. If the biological foundations and energy supplies of the economic system cannot be secured, then the system itself is not sustainable. If gross inequity leads to social upheaval and political turmoil at the national level, as it inevitably must, then the international order will not be a stable one. The transformation called for has three components—reform of the international order, social reform at the national level, and the overall accommodation of human needs and numbers to the earth's resources. All can take place within the framework of what Harlan Cleveland of the Aspen Institute has termed the "planetary bargain."[1]

A planetary bargain should embrace efforts to address the entire range of threats to humanity. Falling logically within its compass are such diverse threats as food insecurity, nuclear-weapons proliferation, export embargoes, human rights violations, youth unemployment, oceanic pollution, terrorism, illegal migration, the buildup of atmospheric carbon dioxide, and depletion of the ozone layer. Many of these threats can be managed only through international cooperation.

Working toward a new international economic order requires the co-operation of rich countries and poor. But, as former U.S. Secretary of Commerce Peter Peterson has noted, the strident demands made by the poor countries "contain an irksome assymmetry whereby 'we' are assigned the duties while 'they' acquire the rights."[2] If rich countries are to help design an international order that will lead to a shift in resources toward the poorer countries, they must be convinced that this new order will improve the lot of the poor within those countries. Otherwise, they will continually raise the question posed by President Carter, "Why should the poor in the rich countries help the rich in the poor countries?"[3] If, however, resource redistribution at the international level can be linked with national redistribution and reform, and if the parallel changes can be seen as part of the broader human accommodation to the earth's resources, then the interest and support of all countries might be enlisted.

One of the principal obstacles to the sorely needed internal reform has been the inability of governments to finance the redistribution of land. However, if land reform is linked with international reforms, then it could be financed with the additional resources made available to the poor countries through the restructuring of the international economic system. Some of the resources thus made available could be used to compensate the large land-holders, who stand to lose much of their oversized holdings, while the rest could be used to create the rural services so desperately needed if the small farmer is to succeed. Moreover, if an international organization which had the confidence of the large landowners, such as the World Bank, could administer the broad financing of the reform, those who would be exchanging land for bonds might be more willing to support an orderly land redistribution.

Land reform is not the only problem challenging the capacities of governments. Stabilizing human population at a level that natural systems and resources can sustain will not be easy. Countries that have delayed too long in slowing population growth may find that they will be forced by circumstances to reduce average family size below two children in the short run. Equally difficult will be the adoption of limits on individual consumption so as to avoid overconsumption by the rich. The affluent everywhere, whether the minorities in poor countries or the majorities in the rich ones, should be urged to view unbridled consumption as a denial of resources needed to satisfy others' basic human needs. Some, such as Swedish economist Gunnar Myrdal, have gone so far as to urge the rich countries to declare a growth moratorium.[4]

302: The Twenty-Ninth Day

The initial difficulty with such a proposal is that existing growth strategies for developing countries are keyed to the expansion of exports to the affluent industrial economies. In effect, this is the international version of the national "trickle-down" approach to development that has been widely discredited. The theory of international trickle down, too, is bound to be discredited because rapid growth in the industrial societies is beginning to deprive developing countries of the energy and other resources they need for development.

This inherent conflict in the international trickle-down theory and inevitable shift in the relationship between rich countries and poor suggests that the latter should look more to each other for export markets and less to the industrial countries. Indeed, the goods they would import from each other, and the technologies inherent in them, are likely to be more appropriate to local conditions than those coming from the advanced industrial societies. Third World rhetoric emphasizing greater national self-reliance would, if translated into effective policy, reduce the ultimately self-defeating heavy dependence on the further growth of the affluent economies. A vigorous move toward greater self-reliance, such as that followed in China, would also be consistent with the broader global transition from oil to locally available renewable energy resources. This inevitable change in the nature of the economic relationship between rich countries and poor necessitates a long-overdue re-examination of the foreign economic policies of both groups.

Internal reforms and development strategies should be structured around efforts to satisfy basic human needs rather than the more traditional objective of economic growth alone. To measure progress in this direction, the Overseas Development Council has devised a new indicator, the Physical Quality of Life Index (PQLI), to augment per capita income, the more traditional measure. The PQLI is a composite of three key social indicators—infant mortality, life expectancy, and literacy. Its great advantage is that it reflects both gains in income and improvements in its distribution. Some countries with low incomes have a high quality of life, such as Sri Lanka with a per capita annual income of 130 dollars and a PQLI of 83 (against and ideal of 100). Iran and Brazil have per capita annual incomes of 1,250 and 940 dollars respectively but PQLI's of only 38 and 66. Algeria and Cuba, middle-income countries with incomes of 710 and 640 dollars respectively but PQLI's of 42 and 86, provide a vivid contrast in the capacity of governments to satisfy the basic needs of their people.[5]

Social goals should incorporate such basic needs as literacy, clean water, adequate nutrition, access to family planning services, and the opportunity to participate in social and political processes. In countries where the quality of life is still abysmally low despite rapid economic growth, the PQLI could be exceedingly helpful in reorienting development planning. The timetables for achieving these goals could be based on the time it has taken some of the more successful developing societies to make similar advances. In no country would the satisfaction of basic needs require a performance of governments that several have not already achieved.

At the international level, the creation of a sustainable economic and political order may, paradoxically, require both a reduction in the potentially unmanageable interdependencies among societies and a strenghening of international cooperation in several key fields. The contemporary overwhelming dependence of the entire world on one geographic region for food and on another for energy makes the international economic system extraordinarily vulnerable to natural disasters such as droughts and to international conflicts. The shift to renewable energy sources, which are invariably local in nature, as well as the rural reforms that could stimulate agricultural production in food-deficit countries would lessen this dangerous degree of vulnerability. In effect, nations would increasingly seek local solutions to problems that are global in scale.

Even while efforts to reduce the dangerously high levels of food, energy and monetary interdependence among countries are under way, efforts to strengthen international co-operation on other fronts are needed. The spectacular achievements in such fields as health and communications provide solid evidence of the benefits such co-operation can yield. The age-old scourge of smallpox is on the verge of being eradicated because the World Health Organization skillfully coordinated an international attack on this disease. The creation of Intelsat and of a highly efficient international electronic communications network is the product of close co-operation among countries interested in sharing U.S. telecommunication technology.

In the most basic sense, the security of food supplies can come only from local production increases and a slowdown of population growth. But there is also a need for emergency reserves to offset harvest shortfalls. If each country attempts to maintain a food reserve sufficient to offset the largest likely shortfall in its own harvest, then the worldwide cost of maintaining adequate food reserves will be inordinately high. If, however, a shared international food reserve is established to cover national emergencies, the amount of grain (and the cost of procuring and storing it) would be no more than a fraction of that needed if each country were to assume the responsibility unilaterally. Creation of such a reserve with a floor price at which grain would be acquired and a ceiling price at which grain would be released would provide both stability for producers and security for consumers.

A rising awareness of the extent to which national security now depends on the stability of the international economic system may make governments more willing to reduce military expenditures than they were in an earlier age of lesser dependence. Thus arms reduction could be linked to a concerted effort to satisfy basic human needs: resources could be channeled from the manufacture of tanks to the production of small tractors. This will not come easily, but conditions are riper for change than at any time in recent history.

Putting together a planetary bargain will require long-term continuous negotiation, leadership, and vision. Since major new international policy initiatives often come from the United States, the election in 1976 of a president with a global vision and a deep social concern augurs well for the new bargain.

Long-Term Global Planning

In a complex and interdependent world faced with profound change, decision makers at every level need all the guidance they can get. Since planning at the national level is most effective if undertaken within a commonly perceived global framework, planners need to do more than simply allocate public resources in the short term; they need to undertake long-term "indicative planning" of the sort the French have pioneered. As management consultant Jack Friedman notes, such planning "indicates where the economy and government policies will be heading but does not coerce industry into fulfilling plan objectives."[6] Using this approach, French economists project the national economy many years into the future, trying to foresee the future of each sector as well as of France's economic relationships with the rest of the world.

Planning is not a mysterious unfathomable process; rather, it is, as Professor Kirby Warren of Columbia University indicates, essentially a process for "making today's decisions with tomorrow in mind."[7] Investment decisions in all major multinational corporations, for example, are guided by detailed long-term planning. As change and the need for change accelerate, the consequences of both good and bad decisions are compounded. The more rapid the change, the greater the premium on planning at all levels.

Indicative planning at the national level involves the projection of economic trends into the future with as much detail by sector as possible. It includes, of course, the basic national economic indicators of capital formation, growth, income, and employment, as well as the overall capital and trade relationships with the rest of the world. Planning is often undertaken within two different time frames—a long-term period of perhaps twenty years at a rather general level and a short-term period of perhaps five years for detailed planning purposes. Planning does not automatically ensure success in policy making, but properly done it can be an exceedingly useful means of reducing uncertainty.

Unlike the planning practiced in centrally planned economies, which allocates virtually all investment capital, indicative planning merely attempts to sketch out the long-term trends and thus provide a common framework for the decision makers in both government and business. Although governmental planners would actually prepare the indicative plan, they would look to a broad-based public dialogue for information and insights. Because it facilitates astute decision making, the common store of knowledge embodied in such a framework would allow a nation to reduce the misallocation of resources. The need for indicative planning is heightened when such key variables as energy costs and population trends are in rapid flux.

The deepening economic interdependence among nations has now reached the point where indicative planning is needed at the global level. Inflation illustrates well the global dimension of contemporary problems. Since national economies are integrated, inflationary pressures spread quickly from one economy to another, especially when they are generated by global scarcities. Narrowly conceived national efforts to cope with inflation may succeed only in shifting the brunt across national borders, aggravating the global inflationary threat. Co-operative planning and action, on the other hand, are more likely to address the root causes of inflation and, therefore, to successfully curb it.

Global planning is needed to incorporate economic, demographic, resource, and biological variables in a global model with regional and national components. The model developed at MIT by the Meadows team that wrote *The Limits to Growth* in 1972 was only a beginning.[8] Produced by systems analysts, it was widely criticized by economists who preferred to view the world in terms of economic models only.

More recently, a team of economists directed by Professor Wassily Leontief of Harvard devised a general global economic model and used it to make economic projections to the year 2000. The team's report, *The Future of the World Economy,* is designed to shed light on the "environmental aspects of the future world economy."[9] Unfortunately, the study overlooks or dismisses serious environmental stresses such as overgrazing, deforestation, soil erosion, cropland loss, and oceanic pollution. It makes some rather specious assumptions about agriculture—namely, that agricultural production in the developing countries will expand at more than 5 percent yearly. Nowhere does the study so much as mention the need to restrict population growth. This model is a beginning, but it desperately needs to be strengthened and brought closer to reality by inputs from other fields such as ecology, agronomy, and energy.

Even while ongoing efforts are improving these models, individual sector analyses and projections are under way. One promising initiative in this direction was the Workshop on Alternative Energy Strategies (WAES) directed by Carroll Wilson at MIT. The workshop and its report, *Energy: Global Prospects 1985–2000,* were born of Wilson's "belief that more effective mechanisms were needed to study critical global problems."[10] This particular effort involved thirty participants from 15 industrial countries that together account for four-fifths of world energy consumption. In Professor Wilson's own words, the workshop was "effective in harnessing the efforts of a diverse multinational group to develop a methodology for the study of global energy problems." The workshop report has obvious weaknesses, but it does provide the beginnings of a comprehensive global framework within which to view long-term energy problems. Its principal finding, that the demand for petroleum will probably overtake supplies as early as 1983, should influence literally millions of government, corporate, and individual decisions over the next few years.

The advantage of using such a model is that its explicit assumptions can be altered as newer information becomes available or as energy technologies advance. For example, population growth trends are being revised downward for three key continents to reflect falling birth rates. Projections of nuclear-power use should also be adjusted downward, since the economic prospects of nuclear power have deteriorated markedly since the study was undertaken. Although the study was labeled a global study, it omitted the centrally planned economies in Europe and Asia. These should be incorporated into the analyses as soon as data become available.

Although the WAES report (the product of a two-year effort) has just been released, there is already a need for a revised, updated version. In addition to including new information and incorporating the centrally planned economies, the next edition could go beyond the first by establishing priority uses of energy, distinguishing between those that are essential and those that are merely convenient. When the serious shortages projected for the eighties develop, governments will then be better prepared for them.

The world food economy also urgently needs a model or plan that encompasses ecological, demographic, and economic variables. In addition to the usual projections of the effect of technological progress on future production trends, it could also incorporate such ecological factors as soil erosion and its contribution to cropland abandonment and to deteriorating land productivity. Such a model should be explicit about probable future trends in real prices and their impact on both malnutrition and death rates. A model of the world food economy would also allow for the growing competition from other sectors for resources, particularly land and water. Such sectoral studies should project at least a quarter-century into the future, since lead times for the development of new agricultural technologies and new food sources are so long.

A detailed analysis of ways to reverse rising unemployment is sorely needed. Although the International Labor Office has made some exceedingly useful long-term projections of labor-force growth, effective guidelines to help governments reduce unemployment by any means other than promoting rapid economic growth do not exist. Given the steep rise in unemployment during the seventies in so many industrial and developing economies, an ILO report that drew on the organization's unique international perspective to describe both successful and unsuccessful attacks on unemployment would be exceedingly useful to hard-pressed governments.

The need for indicative global planning can no longer be questioned. Unfortunately, the United Nations, which should be providing the leadership in such planning activities, has been slow to act. Indeed, most of the important initiatives have come from private organizations such as the Club of Rome, which consists of some seventy members drawn from a score of countries. Under the leadership of Aurelio Peccei, an Italian corporate executive, the Club of Rome has sponsored several global studies, three of which have been widely read and discussed. In addition to the landmark work *The Limits to Growth*, it has sponsored *Mankind at the Turning Point* by Mihajlo Mesarovic and Eduard Pestel and *Reshaping the International Order*, coordinated by Jan Tinbergen, the Nobel Prize–winning economist from the Netherlands.[11] The first two of these studies emphasized the issues associated with continuing economic and material growth, while the third focused on the need for a more equitable global distribution of wealth.

One way to appreciate the need for global planning is to take stock of the problems caused by miscalculations or by a lack of planning. In the food sector, for example, individual food-deficit countries have typically related their projected import needs unilaterally to the capacity of the United States and a few other countries to supply food. Unfortunately, the combined claims of all countries had by the mid-seventies temporarily exceeded the available exportable supplies. Had countries cooperatively projected and totaled their combined needs, this resulting wave of global food scarcity and the associated rise in malnutrition and death rates might have been avoided.

The concept of indicative global planning should be viewed not as an extension of short-term national economic planning but as a means of organizing information and projecting the future so as to increase the effectiveness of decisionmaking at all levels. As Tinbergen has pointed out, no "rational choice between alternative courses of action is possible without some understanding of their consequences."[12] Perhaps most important, an interdisciplinary effort to create a global indicative plan would draw governments and interested individuals and groups into a long-overdue global dialogue on human goals and priorities.

The Role of Government

The speed with which biological systems are deteriorating and oil reserves are being used up calls for an immediate response. Since voluntary behavioral changes alone are unlikely to transform priorities, institutions, and economic systems quickly, government will of necessity play a major role. Attractive though reduced government intervention in our lives might seem, it does not appear to be a realistic prospect.

It is tempting to rely on the marketplace to bring about the changes required. But the marketplace can be as inhuman and destructive as it is efficient. Although a rise in the price of oil can promote energy conservation and thus help balance long-term supply and demand, a rise in the price of whale meat can lead to extinction of the giant mammals. A rise in the price of wheat can stimulate production, but it can also cause starvation.

While analysts can define the elements of accommodation and draw up the timetables for making the necessary changes, only governments have enough power to implement these changes. The tools at the disposal of governments—legislation, budgetary and fiscal policies, taxation, and the analytical and educational capacities of government institutions—have no rivals. By spending less on military hardware and more on efforts to preserve biological systems, a government can save an ecosystem that all the environmentalists in the world cannot. By taxing large automobiles, a government can realize energy savings that voluntary efforts cannot easily match. By diverting research funds from nuclear power to renewable energy sources, a government can effectively accelerate the move into the solar era in a way that others cannot.

To direct change sensibly, governments need information and knowledge. The needed analyses can be undertaken by the United Nations agencies, governments, or private groups with appropriate analytical resources. When one country conducts a study on an important global ecological, social, or economic problem, the results should be shared systematically with other countries, particularly the smaller ones.

The value of such studies is partly determined by the quality of the particular analysis and partly by the degree of public confidence in governments attempting to implement their findings. Unfortunately, government technocrats have over-sold many technologies, among them supersonic air transport and nuclear power, leading to a loss of public confidence. In a society or organization under stress, mutual trust is essential. Rufus Miles of Princeton describes mutual trust as "the cement which holds the organization together. It is the mortar between its human bricks." He then adds, "Where trust is high, an organization can stand an unbelievable amount of buffeting; where it is low, a seemingly innocuous incident may set off a chain reaction of crumbling human relationships."[13] In the United States, the combination of the Vietnam war and the Watergate experience drove successive presidents from office and reduced public confidence in political leaders to a low in modern times. As a result, there has been a loss of the capacity to bring about economic and social change, a loss that is all too evident in the Carter Administration's efforts to get its 1977 energy program through Congress.

Given the prominent role of public funds in research and development, governments can determine the direction technological progress takes. Indeed, one reason nuclear power is so much more highly developed than solar power is that government research funds for the former have dwarfed those for the latter. With comparable commitments to more worthy goals—health, agriculture, transportation, communications, and education—governments can guide the evolution of technology to socially constructive ends.

The capacity of individual societies to mobilize to pursue specific goals varies widely. Societies organize for many purposes: to achieve food self-sufficiency, to win a war, to tame a frontier, to conquer disease, to raise living standards, or to slow population growth. Some manage to achieve some objectives but fail utterly at others. Some move more swiftly than others. In many ways, societies with centralized leadership are much better equipped than pluralistic societies to adapt to rapidly changing circumstances. On the other hand, centralized societies governed by one political party or individual may lack the flexibility to change direction quickly, whereas those with a more pluralistic system can be more adaptable. Some societies have many public-interest organizations that can rally support for innovative action, while those lacking such independent groups may not even perceive the need for change.

From time to time social mobilization has resulted in singularly impressive achievements: the construction of pyramids in ancient Egypt, the massive restoration of the Chinese countryside (particularly reforestation, water-conservation works, and terracing) since 1953, and the U.S. landing of astronauts on the moon. But for each success story there are tales of social failure.

Three important instances in which set goals were not met come quickly to mind. Twenty years ago, India adopted one of the world's first official family-planning programs. Since then, its birth rate has fallen—but only modestly. In 1964, following Khruschev's demise, the Soviet Union launched an all-out effort to increase food production and eliminate the need for food imports. A decade later, the Soviet Union is more dependent on imports than ever before. In 1973, the United States inaugurated Project Independence in energy. Four years later, it imports far more oil than it did when the project began. This pattern of successes and failures suggests that it is leadership, motivation and strategy—rather than a particular political system—that determine whether societies can mobilize to achieve specific social goals.

These examples hold particular interest because the scale of change now called for probably will require social mobilization to degrees hitherto unknown outside of wartime. And, as always, some societies will be more successful than others. The ingredients of success appear to be a clear understanding of the problem and of how to respond to it, and the ability to convince at least the critical segments of society that change is necessary.

The personal examples set by political leaders can be central to success. What leaders do is often as important as what they say. When Jerry Brown, California's young governor, declined to occupy the new mansion approved by his predecessor, Ronald Reagan, and moved into a modest apartment instead, he "voted" through his actions for an end to the wasteful use of public funds and associated himself with his state's electorate. In Washington, D.C., the number of gas-guzzling government limousines assigned to high-ranking officials has been sharply cut. If a political leader personally demonstrates concern for energy conservation by riding a bicycle or for the population threat by getting a vasectomy, this may influence constituents far more than any amount of exhortation would.

Leadership is a complex, often subtle process, involving far more than just getting elected to political office. Those who choose to lead in the dynamic period ahead are assuming far more responsibility than they would in more tranquil times. The greater the change needed, the greater is the need for effective leadership. Those who would lead must be able to see the big picture. In an Aspen Institute paper on governance, Joseph Slater notes, "Many bright people can analyze situations with great skill, but many of them also tend to leave the pieces of the analytic mosaic scattered uselessly on the top of the table. It is truly great persons who show us how we can put these pieces together—indeed, that ability is the hallmark of greatness."[14] Given the complexity of contemporary ecological, economic, and social issues, it is much easier to describe this capacity than to acquire it.

Individuals and Organizations

The world is on the threshold of an era of concentrated adjustment and change. As economist Robert Heilbroner sees it, an extended period of "sustained and conclusive change" is the "inescapable lot of human society."[15] If we stand idly by, assuming that nothing can be done to get off a collision course, then change will almost certainly be painful and chaotic. But, to cite Heilbroner again, we need not be "reduced to the impotence of astronomers watching the imperturbable mechanics of celestial objects." We need not retreat into helpless passivity, watching a biological system deteriorate or nuclear weapons proliferate. We can alter trends and avert catastrophes if we recognize and exercise our own power to make a difference.

Times that call for rapid, revolutionary change place a premium on leadership. Indeed, times of ferment and change often seem to draw forth leaders and qualities of leadership. Historically, religious leaders have sometimes set the moral tone for the response to crisis situations. Unfortunately, such leadership appears to be on the wane as religious leaders and theologians sidestep the troublesome philosophical questions associated with ecological stresses, resource scarcities, and global poverty. To the extent they are prepared to deal with contemporary issues, many address the symptoms of social problems rather than their causes.

Jørgen Randers and Donella Meadows believe churches have a central role to play in shaping values and behavioral patterns and therefore in shaping the new ethic of accommodation and sustainability. They note that Western social values evolved in a seemingly infinite world where consuming more in the short run was not inconsistent with consuming more in the longer run. Their analysis indicates that contemporary man's "ethical system is poorly suited for guiding him in a period when short-term gains often entail long-term sacrifices and vice-versa." If a sustainable society is to come into being, "It will be necessary to develop new ethical principles, a goal that will inevitably involve religious institutions."[16] Accepting this analysis sets the stage for an interesting convergence between theology and ecology, one that holds out the prospect of church leaders and environmentalists joining hands and engaging in joint projects in public education and political action on theological-ecological causes.

Heilbroner sees in the current situation a new role for institutions of higher learning. To his mind, the educational system with its research capacity at the upper echelon and the need to quickly shift priorities are closely linked. He proposes that colleges and universities "add a new orientation to their traditional goals and programs. I urge that they deliberately set out to become the laboratories of applied research into the future. I urge that they direct a major portion of their efforts toward research into, training for, and advocacy of programs for social change."[17] This proposed role would, for example, have these institutions working on such local issues as materials recycling, land-use planning, and public transportation. They would become a source of analysis and information for such public policymakers as the governor, members of the town council, or even national legislators.

For better or worse, the current age of "charisma" and mass communications is one in which individuals can affect critical issues at the global level. Prior to World War II, very few individuals provided global leadership on any important issue. Since then, a group of intellectuals and activists has been at the forefront of social change. One of the first was Rachel Carson; her book *Silent Spring* alerted the United States and the world to the dangers inherent in the careless use of chemical pesticides.[18] Shortly after, Betty Friedan launched the modern feminist movement with *The Feminine Mystique.*[19] The burst of social activism that followed these early works found many outlets.

Other global problems have benefited from the efforts of particular individuals. Through his continuous exploration, film-making, writing, and lecturing, French oceanographer Jacques Cousteau has been instrumental in publicizing the plight of the oceans. Norwegian explorer and writer Thor Heyerdahl has also been a tireless champion of marine ecology. Norman Borlaug has effectively exploited the influence he won along with the 1970 Nobel Peace Prize, which he received for wheat breeding, to rally governments in support of critical programs to increase food production and curb population growth.

The consumer-protection movement, now international in scope, can largely be traced to Ralph Nader's work. Nader's personal dismay over the exploitation of the American consumer by corporations, often abetted by government regulatory agencies, found a constructive channel in the small organization he put together to examine issues related to consumer product quality and safety. This organization then gave rise to other groups that now address a wide range of consumer and environmental issues; it also inspired similar efforts abroad.

Barbara Ward has become a political force in her own right. Writing, speaking, and prodding various key leaders on environmental and developmental issues, she has ready access to numerous political, religious, and international leaders. Her influence springs from her deep concern, articulateness, and tireless advocacy.

Before his death in 1977, English economist E. F. Schumacher almost single-handedly forced a basic re-examination of the technological thrust of modern society. His book *Small is Beautiful* both affected policymaking in developing countries and led to a basic reassessment of technologies employed by the industrial societies themselves.[20]

Global change does not begin at the global level. It starts with individuals and then expands to ever-larger groups. These citizen movements—a response to the perceived need for change—provide a useful counterweight to the more traditional organizations such as corporations, government agencies, legislative bodies, labor unions and religious organizations. Hazel Henderson notes that the traditional organizations "tend to institutionalize past needs and perceptions and are ill-designed to perceive new needs and to respond to new conditions."[21]

The anti-nuclear movement began with a few individuals asking probing questions, some of which the nuclear-power establishment could not readily answer. The unease generated by their inability to provide satisfactory answers led to the formation of anti-nuclear groups first in the United States, then in France, Sweden, Australia, the United Kingdom, West Germany, and Japan. The movement spread until groups unsettled by the prospect of widespread nuclear power have now formed in almost every major industrial country that either has nuclear power facilities or is contemplating building them.

Of all recent American social movements, the environmental movement has probably been the most successful. The

organizational roots of the United States environmental movement lie in such long-standing groups as the National Audubon
Society, the National Wildlife Federation, and the Sierra
Club. These early groups, with a strong commitment to wildlife preservation, have been joined by a younger generation of
politically active environmental organizations and research institutions, such as Friends of the Earth, Environmental Action,
the Environmental Law Institute, Natural Resources Defense
Council, the Environmental Defense Fund, and the numerous
Public Interest Research Groups. Their focus has broadened to
encompass air and water quality, environmental influences on
health, land-use policy, and the conservation of scarce natural
resources. The environmental movement now includes legal
research groups, some of which resemble middle-sized law
firms. Total membership in all such groups in the United
States now exceeds four million, and an estimated three hundred to five hundred lawyers now work full time representing
various environmental organizations.

Counterparts to the environmental organizations have
grown up around other public-interest issues. Zero Population
Growth has a U.S. membership of some ten thousand. Non-
membership population groups such as the Population Crisis
Committee and the Population Institute play an important
educational role. The Population Reference Bureau has a vigorous education program that is now expanding beyond the border's of the U.S.

Groups formed to help protect the environment exist outside the United States too. Some, such as Friends of the Earth,
have chapters in several countries, and indigenous environmental groups are sprouting up in industrial societies everywhere.
Political analyst Neal R. Peirce notes that "in Japan's major
cities 'quality of life' issues have become a burning concern.
Grass roots ecological movements—a brand of local citizen
protests previously unknown in this central, traditionally obedi-
ent society—have grown up."[22] The extent of the reassess-

ment under way is reflected in a comment by Tokue Shibata, head of Japan's Environmental Research Institute: "Autos, the symbol of modern civilization and social status, have now switched to a demon-like symbol of tragedy."[23] The vigorous localism now sprouting on Japanese soil is seen by Peirce as a way of protecting local interests at a time when "national government bureaucracies are often far too distant and oblivious to local needs."

In West Germany, Peirce notes, the traditional reverence for authority "has been shaken by some 15,000 grass roots protest groups." These "Buergerinitiativen" are "battling nuclear-power plants and new auto-bahns, fighting to save city neighborhoods and historic buildings, combating air and water and noise pollution."[24] Cynthia Whitehead of the Conservation Foundation has identified several factors that have converged to generate these citizen-initiative movements. Among them are the example provided by the earlier student-protest movements, the desire to look beyond material goods, concerns about the environment, resentment of bureaucracies, and "deep-rooted feelings of impotence and helplessness against powerful government and business interests."[25]

A mid-1977 article in *Business Week* described the growing muscle of French ecologists generally and the antinuclear group specifically. Describing the French movement, the article stated that this "new sophistication is reminiscent of Western Germany's anti-nuclear movement which has brought reactor construction to a virtual halt."[26] Candidates for political office who ran on the "green" ticket in France have garnered a steadily growing share of the vote in recent elections.

As the ranks of citizen-action groups swell, such organizations will acquire even greater influence. Growing dissatisfaction with ecological deterioration and the materialism that contributes to such abuse is certain to fuel this movement. Exactly where these public-interest citizen groups are headed no one can say, but they are sure to be a prominent part of the political landscape for decades to come.

Education and the Media

Traditionally, the formal educational system has played a central role in bringing about change by inculcating new perceptions and values. But with so little time to accomplish so much, this leisurely route is no longer open. Educating a generation of teachers to new realities so that they may then educate a generation of students who will a generation later become the principal decison makers takes more time than we have. Many critical changes will occur within a single generation—ours.

Thus, the staggering educational challenge before us is not merely a matter of acquiring new values but of discarding many existing ones. Many values, attitudes, and assumptions assimilated during a historically unique period of economic and demographic growth will have to be jettisoned. New analyses and information will play an important role in the shift toward a sustainable society. In assessing the role of information, Hazel Henderson notes that "the rise of new participatory citizen movements for consumer and environmental protection, peace, and social justice is grounded in an almost intuitive understanding of the persuasive power of information."[27]

Access to information may permit a more objective assessment of technology, disabusing ourselves of the "technological fix" as an easy solution to our problems. Even though petroleum reserves are rapidly being depleted, scientists may not be able to pull a cheap new energy source out of the proverbial magician's hat. Commercial fusion power may never materialize. At least since Jules Verne's time, we have wanted to believe that the oceans might one day feed humanity, but the limits of many important oceanic food sources are being reached before those of land-based food supplies.

Since necessary changes in attitudes, values, and lifestyles are called for quickly, the educational task at hand involves "reschooling" many mature adults. Because value changes can precipitate identity crises, such education can put great stress on the individual. Informal educational networks are needed to deal with emerging problems. Business executives may need to be briefed on environmental issues, and civil servants on population dynamics.

As rapid behavioral changes become imperative, the burden of responsibility for informing people of the need for change shifts from the formal educational system to a nonformal one —especially the communications media, both print and electronic. Within the communications media, book publishers and books perform a critical function. Most of the complex problems confronting society cannot be adequately analyzed by those whose fullest forums are newspaper feature articles. Book-length analyses often form the only reliable basis for reaching conclusions that can subsequently be reported and disseminated in two-minute television or radio news commentaries or in newspaper articles. For example, publication of *The Population Bomb* by Paul Ehrlich in 1968 raised public awareness of the population threat.[28] Like *Silent Spring* and *The Limits to Growth*, it has been translated into many languages and has spawned a continuing public dialogue not only in the media but in academic, political, and other spheres as well.

Although the educational challenge facing humanity is formidable, existing communications networks have an impressive educational capacity. The international news networks—Associated Press, United Press International, Reuters, Agence France-Press, and government-supported organizations such as the British Broadcasting Corporation or the United States Information Service—quickly and effectively disseminate information and ideas around the world. These information networks are augmented by internationally circulated periodicals such as the news magazines *L'Express*, *Asiaweek*, and *Newsweek* and by more specialized periodicals such as *The Econo-*

mist or *Science.* Internationally distributed newspapers such as the *International Herald Tribune* also play an important role. Together these information networks and sources, along with the newspools being formed by the Third World countries, are quite capable of elevating global concern for a particular problem or issue.

Important issues such as environmental deterioration, population growth, the changing roles of women, and the threat of nuclear power are given life by print and broadcast journalists. And so it will be with more and more issues. Our awareness, our understanding, and our actions will be influenced more and more by information we acquire from the communications media.

Those working in the communications media thus find themselves carrying an ever-heavier responsibility. Although journalists, editors, and media executives have not asked for this new responsibility, may not wish to assume it, and indeed may not be prepared for it, they may have little choice in the matter. They are the authorized and licensed purveyors of the information that influences decision making and shapes our lifestyles. This emerging educational role of the media suggests that journalists and editors, like teachers, may need to be better educated in the complex ecological, economic, and social issues facing society. The question is what form the education should take and who should bear the cost. In many cases the needs of those in the media might be better served by intensive short-term workshops on such subjects as energy, population, or environment than by supplemental education in a more formal academic sense.

A Social Transformation

The changes in attitudes, institutions, and lifestyles required in our global lily pond amount to nothing less than a social transformation. The prospective changes in consumption and reproductive patterns are without precedent. The former will cause the greatest change in industrial nations; the latter, in developing countries.

The ultimate convergence of lifestyles within and among societies may be inevitable. Social pressures to accommodate consumption habits and fertility behavior to the earth's resources are likely to erode the extremes in consumption levels and family size. Public transportation will become more prevalent everywhere as the oil wells begin to go dry. Dietary considerations will lead to a reduction in per-capita grain use among the world's affluent as the health risks associated with the heavy consumption of fat-rich livestock products become more apparent.

The principal dynamic that has shaped society since the beginning of the Industrial Revolution has been the growth ethic. If material growth as we have known it cannot continue indefinitely, then a new ethic—an ethic of accommodation— will take its place. Although the changes originate in the physical realm, they ultimately manifest themselves in new values. Soedjatmoko, former Indonesian ambassador to the United States, points out that "once growth ceases to be our reason for being then we have to ask basic questions about the purpose and meaning of life."[29]

The demise of unrestrained materialism will scarcely be cause for mourning. As Heilbroner has noted, "Material advance, the most profoundly distinguishing attribute of industrial capitalism and socialism alike, has proved unable to satisfy the human spirit."[30] Dwayne Elgin of the Stanford Research Institute agrees: "By defining our identities through the material goods that we consume, we limit and distort our human potentials—we are possessed by our possessions, consumed by that which we consume." We are left with "an inner poverty and alienation."[31]

The period ahead will undoubtedly be difficult, but it can also be extraordinarily exciting. René Dubos views the human future with confidence, noting that "crises are practically always a source of enrichment and of renewal because they encourage the search for new solutions."[32] There can be little doubt that humanity is on the verge of a profound social transformation, at the edge of a new social frontier. It has fallen to our generation to shape the new social order. Only those who view materialism as the ultimate in human social evolution will be apprehensive about moving beyond it.

New ways of thinking of growth—a new paradigm—are called for. The fact that physical or material growth as we have known it in the industrial societies may not continue much longer should not shock or scare us any more than maturity does a teenager. The physical growth of early life gives way to intellectual, cultural, and moral development that lasts a lifetime. And so it could be with societies. A change in the nature of growth may well be a blessing, not a disaster.

The forthcoming changes will permeate every dimension of human existence: lifestyles, landownership patterns, economic structures, family size, international relations, and the educational system. An economic system that must continually create new material needs through advertising and then new products to fill those needs is not sustainable. Its days are numbered. Change will be either mandatory or voluntary— some change will be guided by the marketplace, some will be the result of regulation, and some will come about through voluntary changes in behavior. The basic choice will be between voluntary simplicity and enforced austerity.

For some, the turn to voluntary simplicity in lifestyles may be the result of concern over the effects of overconsumption on the earth's ecosystem. Another motivating force is summed up on a bumper sticker seen on a small car: "Live simply that others may simply live." Those advocating voluntary simplicity and urging an outwardly more simple lifestyle often have achieved a personal maturity and sophistication that leads to an inner richness as well.

Another social strand feeding into the movement toward voluntary simplicity is the desire for greater self-reliance. In a modern society the individual's role is often a highly specialized one. Individuals are beginning to resent this specialization and the associated psychological and economic dependence on "the system." Among the more visible signs of this move toward greater self-reliance are the increase in bicycling, the return to home vegetable gardening, and the growing interest in solar energy.

The coming shift to renewable energy sources will foster a decentralization of economic activity. Heavy reliance on renewable energy sources will almost certainly feed the back-to-the-land movement. Urbanization—dependent on an ever-larger food surplus in the countryside, on capital-intensive modes of employment, and on generous supplies of energy—seems certain to slow and in some situations even to be reversed.

Economic activity promises to become not only more localized but also more participatory and less hierarchical. At the individual level, attention will shift toward efforts to create a simpler, healthier, and less economically and ecologically vulnerable lifestyle. As the transformation of society progresses, individuals will begin to differentiate between basic needs and those contrived by the world's Madison Avenues. The "bigger is better" mentality will continue to give way to "small is beautiful."

Frugality and conservation will increasingly dominate our daily concerns. Research and development efforts are likely to be reoriented to concentrate on technologies designed to do more with less. Population stability will become a social goal in virtually all societies as more and more countries actively strive to join those six countries where population growth has already come to a halt. Efforts to achieve these goals will likely lead to a wholesale reorientation of economic and social policies to encourage small families and discourage large ones. The role of women, particularly in high-fertility countries, may also change abruptly. Less time and energy will be devoted to childbearing and rearing and correspondingly more to work outside the home.

The new ethic of accommodation has already gained a foot-hold. In some circles the bicycle is now a symbol of enlighten-ment, and parents with more than two children are viewed as socially irresponsible. In the future, the social conversation piece may be a thriving vegetable garden or an ingeniously designed solar-heating system. Physical fitness will be more highly regarded than the expanded girth of the successful Ger-man businessman or senior Soviet bureaucrat. In all, society may come to value more highly whatever contributes to human welfare and to eschew material acquisitiveness as such.

The social capacity for such rapid and pervasive change is untested. It is certain to put great stress on both individuals and institutions. Willis Harman, director of the Center for Study of Social Policy at the Stanford Research Institute, won-ders whether society can "bring about the transition without shaking itself apart."[33] Political leaders must strike a balance between panic and complacency. Leaders need to be in con-stant communication with their constituents, always explain-ing the reasons for change. Change must come, but a loss of confidence in public leaders would be disastrous.

The world stands on the threshold of a basic social transfor-mation. Of that there can be little doubt. Like earlier "revolu-tions," this one could raise us to a higher level of humanity. But unlike others, it must be reckoned with in advance. Whether the impending transformation will be orderly or convulsive depends on our foresight and will.

Notes

Chapter 1. Introduction

1. I am indebted to Robert Lattes, who earlier shared this riddle with Donella H. Meadows *et al.*, *The Limits to Growth* (New York: Universe Books, 1972).
2. Denis Hayes, at a press conference, March 31, 1977, for the publication of *Energy: The Solar Prospect*, Worldwatch Paper 11.
3. Walter Heller, "What's Right With Economics," Presidential Address presented to the 87th Annual Meeting of the American Economics Association, San Francisco, December 29, 1974.
4. Cited in Henry Allen, "The Economists," *Washington Post*, December 8, 1974.
5. Cited in Hazel Henderson, "Ecologists Versus Economists," *Harvard Business Review*, July–August 1973.

Chapter 2. Ecological Stresses I: The Dimensions

1. W. F. Lloyd, *Two Lectures on the Checks to Population* (Oxford, England, 1833), reprinted in part in Garrett Hardin, ed., *Population, Evolution, and Birth Control* (San Francisco: W. H. Freeman and Company, 1969).
2. Garrett Hardin, "The Tragedy of the Commons," *Science*, December 13, 1968.
3. William Ophuls, *Ecology and The Politics of Scarcity* (San Francisco: W.H. Freeman and Company, 1977).
4. *Yearbook of Fishery Statistics* (Rome: Food and Agriculture Organization, annual).
5. Edward Goldberg and Sidney Holt, "Whither Oceans and Seas?," presented to the Second International Conference on Environmental Future, Reykjavik, Iceland, June 5–11, 1977.
6. Economic Research Service, U.S. Department of Agriculture, private communication.
7. *Ibid.*
8. *Ibid.*
9. *Annual Report,* International Commission for the Northwest Atlantic Fisheries, Dartmouth, Nova Scotia, 1975.
10. Erik Eckholm, *Losing Ground: Environmental Stress and World Food Prospects* (New York: W. W. Norton & Company, 1976).
11. J. P. Lanly, "Régression de la Forêt Dense en Côte d'Ivoire," *Boits et Forêts des Tropiques,* September–October 1969.
12. S. Kolade Adeyoju, "Forest Resources of Nigeria," *Commonwealth Forestry Review,* Vol. 53, No. 2.
13. H. C. Rieger, "The Himalayas and the Ganges Plain as an Ecological System," in *Mountain Environment and Development* (Kathmandu, Nepal: University Press, 1976).
14. Otto Soemarwoto, "The Soil Erosion Problem in Java," presented to First International Congress of Ecology, The Hague, September 1974 (Bandung, Indonesia: Institute of Ecology, Padjadjaran University, 1974).
15. Eckholm, *op. cit.*
16. United Nations, Economic Commission for Latin America, *El Medio Ambiente en America Latina* (Santiago, Chile: May 1976).
17. Quoted in "Back to the Trees," *Development Forum,* April 1976.
18. Eckholm, *op. cit.*
19. *The Economist,* May 21, 1977.
20. United Nations, Economic Commission for Latin America, *op. cit.*
21. Eckholm, *op. cit.*
22. Harlow J. Hodgson, "Forage Crops," *Scientific American,* February 1976.
23. *Production Yearbook 1973* (Rome: Food and Agriculture Organization, 1974).

24. *Environmental Quality: Sixth Annual Report* (Washington, D.C.: Council on Environmental Quality, 1975).
25. Eckholm, *op. cit.*
26. Ibrahim Nahal, "Some Aspects of Desertification and Their Socio-Economic Effects in the ECWA Region," Report of the United Nations Conference on Desertification, Regional Preparatory Meeting for the Mediterranean Area, Algarve, Portugal, March 28–April 1, 1977.
27. Eckholm, *op. cit.*
28. K. K. Panday, "The Livestock, Fodder Situation and the Potential of Additional Fodder Resources," in *Mountain Environment and Development, op. cit.*
29. Agricultural Statistics 1970 (Washington, D.C.: U.S. Department of Agriculture, 1970).
30. Hilaria Valladares Antica, "Experimentos Para Determinar la Influencia de la Topografia del Torreno Sobre el Grado de Erosion de los Suelos," cited in R. F. Watters, *Shifting Cultivation in Latin America* (Rome: Food and Agriculture Organization, 1971).
31. R. Schmid, "The Jiri Multipurpose Development Project," in *Mountain Environment and Development, op. cit.*
32. *Master Plan for Power Development and Supply* (Kathmandu, Nepal: His Majesty's Government, with Nippon Koei Company, 1970).
33. Quoted in Jack Shepherd, *The Politics of Starvation* (Washington, D.C.: Carnegie Endowment for International Peace, 1975).
34. Quoted in Watters, *op. cit.*
35. Eckholm, *op. cit.*
36. Quoted in Eckholm, *op. cit.*
37. Kenneth Grant, "Erosion in 1973–74: The Record and the Challenge," *Journal of Water and Soil Conservation,* January–February 1975.
38. Quoted in "Chemical Pollution," *Christian Science Monitor,* July 14, 1977.
39. "The Lasting But Partial Influence of Silent Spring," *New York Times,* January 9, 1977.
40. Kevin P. Shea, "PCB," *Environment,* November 1973; Dr. Kimbrough quoted in "Industrial Pollution May Be Worse Threat Than DDT to Ecology," *Wall Street Journal,* October 10, 1975.
41. "Chemical Pollution," *Christian Science Monitor,* July 14, 1977.
42. *Pollution: Kuala Juru's Battle for Survival* (Penang, Malaysia: Consumers' Association of Penang, 1976).
43. "Blue Only a Memory; The Danube is Filthy," *New York Times,* February 6, 1977.
44. "Clean Thames, Dirty Rhine," *Washington Post,* January 4, 1976.
45. Quoted in "Is a Biological Nightmare Endangering the Chesapeake's Future?," *Washington Star,* April 29, 1977.
46. Michael B. McElroy, "Threats to the Atmosphere," *Harvard,* February 1976.
47. Quoted in McElroy, *op. cit.*

48. U.S. House of Representatives, Interior and Insular Affairs Committee, *Land Use and Energy,* Committee Print, January 1976.
49. Quoted in "Far-off Ozone Emissions Imperil Grape Crop in Western New York," *New York Times,* December 5, 1976.
50. U.S. House of Representatives, *op. cit.*
51. "The Acid Fallout that Rains on California," *Business Week,* July 18, 1977.
52. National Academy of Sciences, *Mineral Resources and the Environment,* Washington, D.C., 1975.
53. "Deadly Rain Imperils Two Adirondacks Species," *New York Times,* March 28, 1977.
54. "London's 'Pea Soupers' Only a Fading Memory," *Washington Post,* January 28, 1977.
55. "Clean Thames, Dirty Rhine," *Washington Post,* January 4, 1976.

Chapter 3. Ecological Stresses II: The Consequences

1. H. N. Le Houérou, "North Africa: Past, Present, Future," in Harold E. Dregne, ed., *Arid Lands in Transition* (Washington, D.C.: American Association for the Advancement of Science, 1970).
2. H. F. Lamprey, "Report on the Desert Encroachment Reconnaisance in Northern Sudan, 21 October to 10 November" (Nairobi, Kenya: UNESCO, undated).
3. Science Council of Canada, *Population, Technology and Resources* (Ottawa, Ont., Canada: July 1976).
4. *Ibid.*
5. *Agrologist,* Agriculture Institute of Canada, Autumn 1975.
6. David Pimentel *et al.,* "Land Degradation: Effects on Food and Energy Resources," *Science,* October 8, 1976.
7. *Country Report by the Indian Government to the United Nations Conference on Human Settlements* (Vancouver, B.C., Canada: June 1976).
8. John Waterbury, "Egypt's Staff of Life," *Common Ground,* July 1975.
9. *Country Report by the Japanese Government to the United Nations Conference on Human Settlements* (Vancouver, B.C., Canada June 1976).
10. R. A. Brink, J. W. Densmore, and G. A. Hill, "Soil Deterioration and the Growing World Demands on Food," *Science,* August 12, 1977.
11. Pimentel *et al., op. cit.*
12. "Soil Erosion: The Problem Persists Despite the Billions Spent on It," *Science,* April 22, 1977.
13. Quoted in "Soil Erosion: The Problem Persists Despite the Billions Spent on It," *Science,* April 22, 1977.

14. United Nations, Economic Commission for Latin America, *El Medio Ambiente en America Latina* (Santiago, Chile: May 1976).
15. *Ibid.*
16. Economic Research Service, "26 Years of World Cereal Statistics by Country and Region," mimeographed, U.S. Department of Agriculture, Washington, D.C., July 1976.
17. "Symposium Weighs Effects of Oceanic Oil Pollution," *BioScience*, October 1976.
18. Quoted in "Huge Fish Kill Found Off Jersey," *New York Times*, July 8, 1976.
19. Cited in "Radioactive Material Found in Oceans," *New York Times*, June 21, 1976.
20. "Symposium Weighs Effects of Oceanic Oil Pollution," *BioScience*, October 1976.
21. "Declining Fisheries," *Christian Science Monitor*, December 11, 1975.
22. Noël Mostert, *Supership* (New York: Alfred A. Knopf, 1974).
23. George M. Woodwell, "Managing the Earth's Surface," *Natural History*, December 1976.
24. Thor Heyerdahl, "How to Kill an Ocean," *Saturday Review*, November 29, 1975.
25. Norman Myers, "An Expanded Approach to the Problem of Disappearing Species," *Science*, July 16, 1976.
26. Thomas Lovejoy, "We Must Decide Which Species Will Go Forever," *The Smithsonian*, July 1976.
27. "H.E.W. Plans New Way to Alert Public to Cancer-Causing Agents," *New York Times*, November 16, 1975.
28. *Fifth Report on the World Health Situation 1969–1972* (Geneva, Switzerland: World Health Organization, 1975).
29. Ernst L. Wynder and Gio B. Gori, "Contribution of the Environment to Cancer Incidence: An Epidemiologic Exercise," *Journal of the National Cancer Institute*, April 1977.
30. "Statement of Dr. David Rall," U.S. House of Representatives, Subcommittee on the Environment and the Atmosphere, Committee on Science and Technology, Hearings, November 11, 1975.
31. "Immunological Defects Found in People in Michigan Who Ate Food Contaminated by PBB," *New York Times*, August 2, 1977.
32. I. J. Selikoff, "Cancer Risk of Asbestos Exposure," presented to Meeting on the Origins of Human Cancer, Cold Spring Harbor Laboratory, Cold Spring Harbor, New York, September 7–14, 1976.
33. Erik Eckholm, *The Picture of Health: Environmental Sources of Disease* (New York: W. W. Norton & Company, 1977).
34. World Health Organization, "Occupational Health Program," Pan American Health Organization Seminario Regional de Silicosis (Washington, D.C.: 1970).

35. *Ibid.*
36. Eckholm, *op. cit.*
37. *Understanding Climatic Change* (Washington, D.C.: National Academy of Sciences, 1975).
38. *Energy and Climate* (Washington, D.C.: National Academy of Sciences, 1977).
39. *Ibid.*
40. Helmut E. Landsberg, "Man-Made Climatic Changes," *Science*, December 18, 1970.
41. Nuclear Energy Policy Study Group, *Nuclear Power, Issues and Choices* (Cambridge, Mass.: Ballinger Publishing Company, 1977).
42. "Rainmaking Effort Triggers Battle over Cloud Rustling," *Washington Post*, March 1, 1977.
43. Kenneth Hewitt, "Earthquake Hazards in the Mountains," *Natural History*, May 1976.
44. R. F. Watters, *Shifting Cultivation in Latin America* (Rome: Food and Agriculture Organization, 1971).
45. Arthur Candell, "Haiti Is an Object Lesson in Ecological Disaster," *World Environment Report*, September 1975.
46. Jonas Salk, in Dom Moraes, ed., *Voices for Life* (New York: Praeger Publishers, in cooperation with the United Nations Fund for Population Activities, 1975).
47. Private communication.
48. Salk, *op. cit.*

Chapter 4. Population: Understanding the Threat

1. Population Reference Bureau, Washington, D.C., press release, March 28, 1976.
2. Lester R. Brown, *World Population Trends: Signs of Hope, Signs of Stress*, Worldwatch Paper 8, October 1976.
3. *Monthly Bulletin of Statistics* (New York: United Nations, monthly).
4. *World Population Data Sheet 1977* (Washington, D.C.: Population Reference Bureau, annual).
5. Lester R. Brown, Patricia McGrath, and Bruce Stokes, *Twenty-Two Dimensions of the Population Problem*, Worldwatch Paper 5, March 1976.
6. Erik Eckholm and Kathleen Newland, *Health: The Family Planning Factor*, Worldwatch Paper 10, January 1977.
7. Bruce Stokes, *Filling the Family Planning Gap*, Worldwatch Paper 12, May 1977.
8. Brown, *World Population Trends.*
9. W. Parker Mauldin, "Fertility Trends: 1950–75," in *The Population Council Annual Report 1975* (New York: Population Council, 1975).

10. Population Reference Bureau, *Intercom* (newsletter), June 1976.
11. *Monthly Bulletin of Statistics.*
12. United Nations Fund for Population Activities, "One Child Family Gaining Popularity," *Population* (newsletter), September 1976.
13. The Population Problems Research Council, *Summary of Thirteenth National Survey on Family Planning* (Tokyo: The Mainichi Newspapers, August 1975).
14. "A Feeling of Crisis is Rising in Poland," *New York Times,* September 19, 1976.
15. A. K. M. Alauddin Chowdhury and Lincoln C. Chen, *The Dynamics of Contemporary Famine* (Dacca: Ford Foundation, 1977).
16. United States Department of Agriculture, Foreign Agriculture Circular FR–1–76, May 1976.
17. Chowdhury and Chen, *op. cit.*
18. Dr. Colin McCord, "The Companiganj Project," presented at the annual meeting of American Public Health Association, Miami Beach, Florida, October 17–21, 1976, as updated in a personal communication from Dr. Ray Langsten of the Johns Hopkins Center for Medical Research and Training in Dacca.
19. "Island of Hunger," *Time,* July 7, 1975.
20. Dr. Michael C. Latham, "The U.S. Role in African Development with Special Reference to the Sahel," *World Hunger, Health, and Refugee Problems,* record of the United States Senate Committee on Labor and Public Welfare Meeting, June 10–11, 1975.
21. Jack Shepherd, *The Politics of Starvation* (Washington, D.C.: Carnegie Endowment for International Peace, 1975).
22. Kevin M. Cahill, M.D., "Report on Somalia," *World Hunger, Health, and Refugee Problems.*
23. United Nations, Secretariat, "World Population Prospects Beyond the Year 2000," mimeographed, New York, May 16, 1973.
24. "Mexican Families Wary of Birth Control Clinic," *New York Times,* November 27, 1975.
25. Science Council of Canada, *Population, Technology and Resources* (Ottawa, Ont., Canada: July 1976).
26. Stokes, *op. cit.*
27. Quoted in Kaval Gulhati, "Compulsory Sterilization: The Change in India's Population Policy," *Science,* March 25, 1977.

Chapter 5. Energy: The Coming Transition

1. "White House Says Weather-Crisis Layoffs Totaled 1.8 Million at Its Peak," *New York Times,* February 8, 1977.
2. *Statistical Yearbook* (New York: United Nations, annual).
3. *Ibid.*
4. Joel Darmstadter, "International Energy Sources," Resources for the Future, Washington, D.C., July 1970.

5. Denis Hayes, *Rays of Hope: The Transition to a Post-Petroleum World* (New York: W. W. Norton & Company, 1977).
6. "World Report," *Oil and Gas Journal*, December 27, 1976.
7. Workshop on Alternative Energy Strategies, *Energy: Global Prospects 1985–2000* (New York: McGraw-Hill Book Company, 1977).
8. Quoted in "World Oil Shortage Is Called Inevitable," *New York Times*, May 17, 1977.
9. "Schlesinger Warns West U.S. Energy Plan Is Vital," *New York Times*, October 6, 1977.
10. "Will Energy Conservation Throttle Economic Growth?," *Business Week*, April 25, 1977.
11. Hayes, *Rays of Hope*.
12. Denis Hayes, *Nuclear Power: The Fifth Horseman*, Worldwatch Paper 6, May 1976.
13. Nuclear Energy Policy Study Group, *Nuclear Power, Issues and Choices* (Cambridge, Mass.: Ballinger Publishing Company, 1977).
14. "Reneging on Uranium at Westinghouse," *New York Times*, February 1, 1976.
15. Nuclear Energy Policy Study Group, *op. cit.*
16. Quoted in *Energy Finance Week*, September 10, 1975.
17. Hayes, *Rays of Hope*.
18. "Nuclear Man at Bay," *The Economist*, March 19, 1977.
19. Nuclear Energy Policy Study Group, *op. cit.*
20. "German Official Sees Nuclear Power Halt," *Journal of Commerce*, August 5, 1977.
21. Denis Hayes, *Energy: The Case for Conservation*, Worldwatch Paper 4, January 1976.
22. Amory Lovins, *Soft Energy Paths: Toward a Durable Peace* (Cambridge, Mass.: Ballinger Publishing Company, with Friends of the Earth International, 1977).
23. Roger Sant, former Director, Office of Conservation, Federal Energy Administration, private communication, September, 1977.
24. National Academy of Sciences/National Research Council, *Resources and Man* (San Francisco: W. H. Freeman and Company, 1969).
25. *Statistical Yearbook*.
26. *Statistical Yearbook 1974* (New York: United Nations, 1975) and *Yearbook of Forest Products 1973* (Rome: Food and Agriculture Organization, 1974).
27. P. D. Henderson, "India's Energy Problems," *Finance and Development*, December 1975.
28. Hayes, *Rays of Hope*.
29. "Solar Heat Competitive with Electric, Agency Finds," *New York Times*, December 30, 1976.
30. Denis Hayes, *Energy: The Solar Prospect*, Worldwatch Paper 11, March 1977.

31. "France Inaugurates a Solar Power Plant," *New York Times*, January 26, 1977.
32. *Statistical Yearbook.*
33. Vaclav Smil, "Intermediate Technology in China," *Bulletin of the Atomic Scientists*, February 1977.
34. "Small Dams—Enough Power for New York City," *Christian Science Monitor*, July 29, 1977.
35. Cited in "Giant Windmill Farms Seen as Power Source of Future," *Province* (Vancouver B.C., Canada), May 31, 1976.
36. Cited in "U.S. Funds Four Giant Wind-Generators," *Christian Science Monitor*, May 5, 1976.
37. Cited in "This Power Source Is No Breeze to Use," *Washington Post*, June 11, 1977.
38. "Windmill's Owners Tilt with Con Ed on Urban Energy Plan," *Washington Post*, December 4, 1976.
39. National Academy of Sciences/National Research Council, *op. cit.*
40. *Ibid.*
41. Hayes, *Rays of Hope.*
42. "Energy from Waste Projects Moves Ahead," *Journal of Commerce*, March 21, 1977.
43. P. D. Henderson, *India: The Energy Sector* (Washington, D.C.: World Bank, 1975).
44. Vaclav Smil, "Energy Solution in China," *Environment* October 1977.
45. Hayes, *Rays of Hope.*
46. *Ibid.*
47. "Alcohol: A Brazilian Answer to the Energy Crisis," *Science*, February 11, 1977; Allen Hammond of *Science*, private communication.
48. Hayes, *Rays of Hope.*
49. Charles J. Hitch, "Taking the Blinders Off," *Annual Report 1976*, Resources for the Future, Washington, D.C.

Chapter 6. The Food Prospect

1. Erik Eckholm, *The Other Energy Crisis: Firewood*, Worldwatch Paper 1, September 1975.
2. Economic Research Service, "26 Years of World Cereal Statistics by Country and Region," mimeographed, U.S. Department of Agriculture, Washington, D.C., July 1976.
3. Lester R. Brown, Patricia McGrath, and Bruce Stokes, *Twenty-Two Dimensions of the Population Problem*, Worldwatch Paper 5, March 1976.
4. Economic Research Service, *op. cit.*
5. *Agricultural Statistics* (Washington, D.C.: U.S. Department of Agriculture, annual).

6. Lester R. Brown, *World Population Trends: Signs of Hope, Signs of Stress*, Worldwatch Paper 8, October 1976.

7. *Agricultural Statistics.*

8. Lester R. Brown, *The Politics and Responsibility of the North American Breadbasket*, Worldwatch Paper 2, October 1975.

9. U. S. Department of Agriculture, Foreign Agriculture Circulars FR–1–76, May 1976, and FG–7–77, July 1977.

10. Population Division, United Nations Secretariat, "Trends and Prospects in Urban and Rural Population, 1950–2000, As Assessed in 1973–1974," mimeographed, New York, April 25, 1975.

11. Brown, *Politics and Responsibility.*

12. Lester R. Brown, *Man, Land & Food* (Washington, D.C.: U.S. Department of Agriculture, 1963).

13. Lester R. Brown and Gail W. Finsterbusch, *Man and His Environment: Food* (New York: Harper & Row, 1972).

14. Lester R. Brown with Erik Eckholm, *By Bread Alone* (New York: Praeger Publishers, 1974).

15. Charles C. Bradley, "Human Water Needs and Water Use in America," *Science*, October 26, 1962.

16. C. C. Delwiche, "The Nitrogen Cycle," *Scientific American*, September 1970.

17. David Pimentel *et al.*, "Food Production and the Energy Crisis," *Science*, November 2, 1973.

18. Brown with Eckholm, *op. cit.*

19. *Ibid.*

20. Economic Research Service, *op. cit.;* U.S. Department of Agriculture, Foreign Agriculture Circulars FR–1–76 and FG–7–77.

21. Lester R. Brown, "Nobel Peace Prize: A Developer of High Yield Wheat Receives Award," *Science*, October 30, 1970.

22. "U.S. Cranks Up New Moves to Stem Illegal Immigration," *Christian Science Monitor*, April 19, 1977.

23. *Agricultural Statistics.*

24. U.S. Department of Agriculture, Foreign Agriculture Circulars FR–1–76 and FG–7–77.

25. *Agricultural Statistics.*

26. U.S. Department of Agriculture, Foreign Agriculture Circular FLM–12–77, August 1977.

27. U.S. Department of Agriculture, Foreign Agriculture Circular FG–7–77, July 1977.

28. *Agricultural Statistics.*

29. *Yearbook of Fishery Statistics* (Rome: Food and Agriculture Organization, annual).

30. *Agricultural Statistics.*

31. *Ibid.*

32. "Brazil's Soybean Expansion Seen Shifting to New Areas," *Foreign Agriculture*, March 21, 1977.

33. Erik Eckholm, *The Picture of Health: Environmental Sources of Disease* (New York: W. W. Norton & Company, 1977).
34. *International Financial Statistics* (Washington, D.C.: International Monetary Fund, monthly).
35. L. M. Thompson, "Weather Variability, Climatic Change, and Grain Production," *Science*, May 9, 1975.

Chapter 7. Economic Stresses

1. U.S. Department of Agriculture, Foreign Agriculture Circulars FR-1-76, May 1976, and FG-7-77, July 1977.
2. *Review of Fisheries in OECD Member Countries 1975* (Paris: Organization for Economic Cooperation and Development, 1976).
3. *The International Market for Iron Ore: Review and Outlook*, Working Paper No. 160, World Bank, Washington, D.C., August 1973.
4. *OECD Economic Outlook*, Organization for Economic Co-operation and Development, Paris, July 1976.
5. Quoted in "The Inflation Role of Commodity Speculation," *Business Week*, March 22, 1976.
6. "Alaska Oil's Wellhead Price Being Studied by the FEA to Ensure Its Competitiveness," *Wall Street Journal*, March 10, 1977.
7. Colin Jones, "Inflation: The Global Virus," *Saturday Review*, November 21, 1972.
8. Quoted in "Seeking Antidotes to a Global Plague," *Time*, April 8, 1974.
9. *The Capital Needs and Savings Potential of the U.S. Economy, Projections Through 1985*, New York Stock Exchange, Inc., September 1974.
10. "The Capital Crisis: $4.5 Trillion America Needs to Grow," *Business Week*, September 22, 1975.
11. *Ibid.*
12. *Ibid.*
13. "Adverse Impacts Seen in Antipollution Outlay," *Journal of Commerce*, September 17, 1975.
14. *Ibid.*
15. "U.S. Airlines Get Timetable to Cut Noise of Planes," *New York Times*, November 19, 1976.
16. "World Job Losses Put at 40-Year High," *New York Times*, November 30, 1975.
17. Harry T. Oshima, "The Time to Change to Labor-Intensive Policies Is Now," *Ceres*, November–December 1970.
18. "How Millions of Illegal Aliens Sneak into U.S.," *U.S. News and World Report*, July 22, 1974.
19. "Coping with the Invisible Immigrants," *New York Times*, May 16, 1977.
20. Jonathan Power, "Europe's Immigrant Population," *Washington Post*, July 20, 1976.

21. "Cuba, Swallowing Promises, Now Shapes Modest Aims," *New York Times*, January 25, 1976.
22. "South Korea Faces Slackening Growth," *New York Times*, January 25, 1976.
23. *International Financial Statistics* (Washington, D.C.: International Monetary Fund, monthly).
24. U. S. Department of Agriculture, Foreign Agriculture Circular FR-1-76, May 1976.

Chapter 8. Wealth Among Societies

1. *The United States and World Development: Agenda 1977* (New York: Praeger Publishers, for the Overseas Development Council, 1977).
2. Erik Eckholm, *The Picture of Health: Environmental Sources of Disease* (New York: W. W. Norton & Company, 1977).
3. *International Financial Statistics* (Washington, D.C.: International Monetary Fund, monthly).
4. Arthur F. Burns, "The Need for Order in International Finance," *The Columbia Journal of World Business*, Spring 1977.
5. "Quotation of the Day," *New York Times*, November 29, 1976.
6. *International Financial Statistics.*
7. "Aluminum Research Pushed As Bauxite Levies Jump; Economic, Political Risks," *Wall Street Journal*, April 2, 1976.
8. Lawrence A. Mayer, "Climbing Back From Negative Growth," *Fortune*, August 1975.
9. Task Force on Technology Transfer, *Technology Transfer and the Developing Countries* (Washington, D.C.: Chamber of Commerce of the United States, April 1977).
10. "The Chinese in Houston—In Neckties," *New York Times*, November 30, 1975.
11. Lester R. Brown, *The Interdependence of Nations*, Headline Series No. 212, Foreign Policy Association, New York, October 1972.
12. "Apolitical American Consultants," *New York Times*, September 28, 1975.
13. Lester R. Brown, *Seeds of Change: The Green Revolution and Development in the 1970s* (New York: Praeger Publishers, for the Overseas Development Council, 1970).
14. Juliet Clifford and Gavin Osmond, *World Development Handbook* (London: Charles Knight & Co., for Overseas Development Institute, 1971).
15. Brown, "Interdependence of Nations."
16. "Oil Riches Change The Middle East," *New York Times*, January 30, 1977.
17. *Ibid.*

18. Roger D. Hansen, *A "New International Economic Order"? An Outline for A Constructive U.S. Response,* Overseas Development Council, Development Paper 19, Washington, D.C., July 1975.
19. *The Latin American Banana Crisis,* U.N. Development Program, Development Issue Paper 1, New York, 1977.

Chapter 9. Wealth Within Societies

1. Quoted in John G. Gurley, "Rural Development in China 1949–72, and the Lessons to Be Learned from It," *World Development,* July–August 1975.
2. Income-distribution figures in this section are from *The U.S. and World Development: Agenda for Action 1975* (New York: Praeger Publishers, for the Overseas Development Council, 1975).
3. Mahbub ul Haq, *The Poverty Curtain: Choices for the Third World* (New York: Columbia University Press, 1976).
4. Edgar Owens, "Development with Social Justice," presented to the International Seminar of Economic Journalists, New Delhi, December 5, 1972.
5. *Towards Full Employment: A Programme for Colombia* (Geneva, Switzerland: International Labour Office, 1970).
6. James P. Grant, "Marginal Men: The Growing Global Job Crisis," presented to Development Issues Seminar No. 10, *Unemployment and Development,* Overseas Development Council, Washington, D.C., June 15, 1971.
7. William Rich, *Smaller Families Through Social and Economic Progress* (Washington, D.C.: Overseas Development Council, 1973); *World Bank Atlas* (Washington, D.C.: 1976); *World Population Data Sheet 1977* (Washington, D.C.: Population Reference Bureau, 1977).
8. *World Population Data Sheet 1977.*
9. Rich, *op. cit.*
10. Haq, *op. cit.*
11. "Concorde Decision Imminent," *Christian Science Monitor,* March 8, 1977.
12. Private communication.
13. Michael Lipton, "Urban Bias: Or Why Rural People Stay Poor," *People* (London), Vol. 3, No. 2, 1976.
14. Gurley, *op. cit.*
15. Keith Griffin, *Land Concentration and Rural Poverty* (New York: Holmes & Meier Publishers, 1976).
16. *Ibid.*
17. Keith Griffin, *The Green Revolution: An Economic Analysis* (Geneva: United Nations Research Institute for Social Development, 1972).

18. *The United States and World Development: Agenda 1977* (New York: Praeger Publishers, for the Overseas Development Council, 1977).
19. Ibrahim Nahal, "Some Aspects of Desertification and Their Socio-Economic Effects in the ECWA Region," Report of the United Nations Conference on Desertification, Regional Preparatory Meeting for the Mediterranean Area, Algarve, Portugal, March 28–April 1, 1977.
20. "Cut in Shellfishing Ordered in Suffolk," *New York Times,* May 7, 1977.
21. *World Bank Atlas.*

Chapter 10. The Inevitable Accommodation

1. Willis W. Harman, *An Incomplete Guide to the Future* (Stanford, Calif.: Stanford Alumni Association, 1976).
2. *International Financial Statistics* (Washington, D.C.: International Monetary Fund, monthly).
3. U.S. Department of Agriculture, Foreign Agriculture Circular FC-9-77, May 1977.
4. "Alcohol: A Brazilian Answer to the Energy Crisis," *Science,* February 11, 1977.
5. U.S. Department of Agriculture, Foreign Agriculture Circular FR-1-76, May 1976.
6. Stewart L. Udall, "The Failed American Dream," *Washington Post,* June 12, 1977.
7. Quoted in Udall, *op. cit.*
8. *Ibid.*
9. Udall, *op. cit.*
10. Gary Gappert, "Post-Affluence: The Turbulent Transition to a Post-Industrial Society," *The Futurist,* October 1974.
11. "Thomas S. Kuhn: Revolutionary Theorist of Science," *Science,* July 8, 1977.
12. Philip W. Guild, "Discovery of Natural Resources," *Science,* February 20, 1976.
13. Donella H. Meadows, private communication.
14. Garrett Hardin, "Nobody Ever Dies of Overpopulation," *Science,* February 12, 1971.
15. Dr. Michael C. Latham, "The U.S. Role in African Development with Special Reference to the Sahel," *World Hunger, Health, and Refugee Problems,* record of the United States Senate Committee on Labor and Public Welfare Meeting, June 10–11, 1975.
16. *Agricultural Statistics* (Washington, D.C.: U.S. Department of Agriculture, annual).
17. Melvin A. Eggers, "Where Education Is Losing Touch," *Business Week,* September 15, 1975.

18. Population Division, United Nations Secretariat, "Trends and Prospects in Urban and Rural Population, 1950–2000, as Assessed in 1973–1974," mimeographed, New York, April 25, 1975.

19. Joseph Kraft, "A Talk With Trudeau," *Washington Post*, May 17, 1977.

20. Goran Backstrand and Lars Ingelstam, "Should We Put Limits on Consumption?," *The Futurist*, June 1977.

21. William Ophuls, "The Scarcity Society," *Harper's*, April 1974.

22. Robert L. Heilbroner, "Second Thoughts on the Human Prospect," *Challenge*, May–June 1975.

23. Laura Lane, "Will You Go To Jail Over Erosion?," *Farm Journal*, mid-February 1976.

24. Dorothy Nortman, *Changing Contraceptive Patterns: A Global Perspective* (Washington, D.C.: Population Reference Bureau, August 1977).

25. "Pittsburgh Area's Air Pollution Reaches Emergency Levels; U.S. Steel Slates Curb," *Wall Street Journal*, November 20, 1975.

26. Quoted in "A Crowded World: Can Mankind Survive in Freedom?," *Christian Science Monitor*, February 10, 1975.

27. Government of Canada, "The Way Ahead: A Framework for Discussion," mimeographed, Ottawa, Ont., 1976.

28. Kraft, *op. cit.*

Chapter 11. The Elements of Accommodation

1. Robert S. McNamara, "Population Growth Needs 'Far More Attention,'" speech delivered at the Massachusetts Institute of Technology, Cambridge, Mass., April 28, 1977 (Washington, D.C.: World Bank, 1977).

2. Quoted in Dorothy Nortman, *Population and Family Planning Programs: A Factbook*, Reports on Population/Family Planning, Population Council, New York, October 1976.

3. Paul R. Ehrlich and John P. Holdren, "Human Population and the Global Environment," Symposium on Population, Resources and Environment, United Nations Economic and Social Council, Stockholm, August 14, 1973.

4. Rafael M. Salas, statement at the 19th session of the United Nations Development Program Governing Council, New York, January 1975, cited in *Populi*, Vol. 2, No. 1, 1975.

5. Nortman, *op. cit.*

6. *Ibid.*

7. Bruce Stokes, *Filling the Family Planning Gap*, Worldwatch Paper 12, May 1977.

8. Pi-chao Chen, "On the Chinese Model of Group Planning of Birth," presented at the Conference on IEC Strategies: Their Role in Promoting Behavior Change in Family and Population

Planning Programs, Honolulu, December 1–5, 1975.

9. "National Population Policy," statement by Dr. Karan Singh, Minister of Health and Family Planning, New Delhi, April 16, 1976.

10. Edward Goldsmith *et al.*, "The Blueprint for Survival," *The Ecologist,* January 1972.

11. Canadian Embassy, Washington, D.C., private communication.

12. *Government and the Nation's Resources,* Report of the National Commission on Supplies and Shortages, Washington, D.C., December 1976.

13. Quoted in "Fighting Over Scraps: Steel Mills vs. Recyclers," *Washington Post,* September 4, 1977.

14. *Government and the Nation's Resources.*

15. "Bottle-Bill Wins Busy Environmentalists," *Christian Science Monitor,* November 4, 1976.

16. Roy L. Prosterman, "Land Reform As Foreign Aid," *Foreign Policy,* Spring 1972.

17. "Facing Food Problems, Moscow Is Encouraging Private-Plot Farmers," *New York Times,* July 10, 1977.

18. Lester R. Brown, *In the Human Interest* (New York: W. W. Norton & Company, 1974).

19. "In China, Women Fight for Equality," *Christian Science Monitor,* August 20, 1975.

20. Kathleen Newland and Patricia McGrath, *The Sisterhood of Man* (New York: W. W. Norton & Company, forthcoming).

21. Bureau of Labor Statistics, U.S. Department of Labor, private communication.

22. Svetlana Turchaninova, "Trends in Women's Employment in the USSR," *International Labour Review,* October 1975.

23. Ruth Leger Sivard, *World Military And Social Expenditures 1974* (Leesburg, Va.: WMSE Publications, 1974).

24. "Dr. Asimov: The Future is No Fun," *Washington Star,* April 27, 1975.

25. "Brown Says Lagging Fuel Supply Is Largest Threat to U.S. Security," *New York Times,* October 27, 1977.

26. Franklin P. Huddle, "The Evolving National Policy for Materials," *Science,* February 20, 1976.

27. Rufus E. Miles, Jr., *Awakening from the American Dream: The Social and Political Limits to Growth* (New York: Universe Books, 1976).

Chapter 12. The Means of Accommodation

1. Harlan Cleveland, "Introduction: Toward an International Poverty Line," in John McHale and Magda Cordell McHale, *Basic Human*

Needs: A Framework for Action (Houston: Center for Integrative Studies, April 1977).

2. Peter G. Peterson, "Sharing the Bounty," *New York Times*, May 12, 1977.

3. Quoted in Peterson, *op. cit.*

4. Gunnar Myrdal, "On the Equality Issue in World Development," *World Issues*, October–November 1976.

5. *The United States and World Development: Agenda 1977* (New York: Praeger Publishers, for Overseas Development Council, 1977).

6. Jack Friedman, "A Planned Economy in the U.S.?," *New York Times*, May 18, 1975.

7. Quoted in Walter D. Hill, "Foreword," in W. W. Simmons, *Exploratory Planning: Briefs of Practices* (Oxford, Ohio: The Planning Executives Institute, April 1977).

8. Donella H. Meadows *et al.*, *The Limits to Growth* (New York: Universe Books, 1972).

9. Wassily Leontief *et al.*, *The Future of the World Economy* (New York: Oxford University Press, 1977).

10. Carroll L. Wilson, "Foreword," in Workshop on Alternative Energy Strategies, *Energy: Global Prospects 1985–2000* (New York: McGraw-Hill Book Company, 1977).

11. Mihajlo Mesarovic and Eduard Pestel, *Mankind at the Turning Point* (New York: E. P. Dutton & Co./Reader's Digest Press, 1974); Jan Finbergen, *Reshaping the International Order* (New York: E. P. Dutton & Co., 1976).

12. Quoted in Leontief, *op. cit.*

13. Rufus E. Miles, Jr., "The Pathology of Institutional Breakdown," *Journal of Higher Education*, May 1969.

14. Joseph E. Slater, *Governance* (New York: Aspen Institute for Humanistic Studies, 1976).

15. Robert L. Heilbroner, "Second Thoughts on the Human Prospect," *Challenge*, May–June 1975.

16. Jørgen Randers and Donella H. Meadows, "The Carrying Capacity of Our Global Environment: A Look at the Ethical Alternatives," in *Toward Global Equilibrium*, D. L. Meadows and D. H. Meadows, eds. (Cambridge, Mass.: Wright-Allen Press, 1973).

17. Robert L. Heilbroner, "Priorities for the Seventies," *Saturday Review*, January 3, 1970.

18. Rachel Carson, *Silent Spring* (Boston: Houghton Mifflin Company, 1962).

19. Betty Friedan, *The Feminine Mystique* (New York: W. W. Norton & Company, 1963).

20. E. F. Schumacher, *Small Is Beautiful: Economics as If People Mattered* (New York: Harper & Row, 1973).

21. Hazel Henderson, "Information and the New Movements for Citi-

zen Participation," *Annals of the American Academy*, March 1974.
22. Neal R. Peirce, "Japan: From Atomic War to Garbage War," *Washington Post*, April 29, 1977.
23. Quoted in Peirce, *op. cit.*
24. Neal R. Peirce, "Grass-Roots Protests on German Soil," *Washington Post*, August 22, 1977.
25. Quoted in Peirce, "Grass-Roots Protests."
26. "French Antinuclear Forces Get Rough," *Business Week*, July 25, 1977.
27. Henderson, *op. cit.*
28. Paul R. Ehrlich, *The Population Bomb* (New York: Ballantine, 1968).
29. Soedjatmoko, "Meeting Human Needs in a Sustainable Society," Workshop Meeting at Alternatives to Growth 1977 Conference, The Woodlands, Tex., October 2–4, 1977.
30. Heilbroner, 'Second Thoughts on the Human Prospect."
31. Duane Elgin, "The Evolution of Consciousness and the Transformation of Society," mimeographed, Center for the Study of Social Policy, Stanford Research Institute, Menlo Park, Calif., December 1974.
32. René Dubos, "The Humanizing of Humans," *Saturday Review*, December 13, 1974.
33. Willis W. Harman, "The Coming Transformation," *The Futurist*, April 1977.

Selected References

Chapter 2. Ecological Stresses I: The Dimensions

Bormann, F. H. "An Inseparable Linkage: Conservation of Natural Ecosystems and the Conservation of Fossil Energy." *BioScience*, December 1976.

Byerly, T. C. "Ruminant Livestock Research and Development." *Science*, February 4, 1977.

Eckholm, Erik. *Losing Ground: Environmental Stress and World Food Prospects*. New York: W. W. Norton & Company, 1976.

Ehrlich, Paul R.; Ehrlich, Anne H.; and Holdren, John P. *Ecoscience: Population, Resources, Environment*. San Francisco: W. H. Freeman, 1977.

Hardin, Garrett. "The Tragedy of the Commons." *Science*, December 13, 1968.

Hodgson, Harlow J. "Forage Crops." *Scientific American*, February 1976.

Holt, S. J. "Marine Fisheries and World Food Supplies." In *Man/Food Equation*, edited by M. Rechcigl. New York: Academic Press, 1975.

Mountain Environment and Development. Katmandu, Nepal: University Press, 1976.

Shepherd, Jack. *The Politics of Starvation*. Washington, D.C.: Carnegie Endowment for International Peace, 1975.

Chapter 3. Ecological Stresses II: The Consequences

Ashford, Nicholas. *Crisis in the Workplace.* Cambridge, Mass.: MIT Press, 1976.
Brink, R. A.; Hill, G. A.; and Densmore, J. W. "Soil Deterioration and the Growing
    World Demands on Food." *Science,* August 12, 1977.
Eckholm, Erik. *The Picture of Health: Environmental Sources of Disease.* New York:
    W. W. Norton, 1977.
Lovejoy, Thomas. "We Must Decide Which Species Will Go Forever." *The Smith-
    sonian,* July 1976.
Myers, Norman. "An Expanded Approach to the Problem of Disappearing Species."
    Science, July 16, 1976.
Nahal, Ibrahim. "Some Aspects of Desertification and Their Socio-Economic Effects
    in the ECWA Region." Prepared for the Regional Preparatory Meeting for
    the United Nations Conference on Desertification. Algarve, Portugal, March
    28–April 1, 1977.
National Academy of Sciences. *Energy and Climate.* Washington, D.C., 1977.
Pimentel, David, *et al.* "Land Degradation: Effects on Food and Energy Resources."
    Science, October 8, 1976.
Schneider, Stephen H. *The Genesis Strategy: Climate and Global Survival.* New York:
    Plenum Press, 1976.
Watters, R. F. *Shifting Cultivation in Latin America.* Rome: Food and Agriculture
    Organization, 1971.
Woodwell, George M. "Managing the Earth's Surface." *Natural History,* December
    1976.

Chapter 4. Population: Understanding the Threat

Brown, Lester R.; McGrath, Patricia; and Stokes, Bruce. *Twenty-Two Dimensions of
    the Population Problem.* Worldwatch Paper 5, March 1976.
Chowdhury, A.K.M.A., and Chen, Lincoln C.. *The Dynamics of Contemporary Fam-
    ine.* Dacca, Pakistan: Ford Foundation, 1977.
Levi, Lennart, and Andersson, Lars. *Population, Environment and Quality of Life.*
    Prepared for United Nations World Population Conference. New York, 1976.
Orleans, Leo A. "China's Experience in Population Control: The Elusive Model."
    World Development, July–August 1977.
United Nations, Secretariat. "World Population Prospects Beyond the Year 2000."
    New York, May 16, 1973.

Chapter 5. Energy: The Coming Transition

De Marsily, G., *et al.* "Nuclear Waste Disposal: Can the Geologist Guarantee Isola-
    tion?" *Science,* August 5, 1977.
Hayes, Denis. *Energy for Development: Third World Options.* Worldwatch Paper 15,
    December 1977.
———. *Rays of Hope: The Transition to a Post-Petroleum World.* New York: W. W.
    Norton, 1977.
Lovins, Amory B. *Soft Energy Paths: Toward a Durable Peace.* Cambridge, Mass.:
    Ballinger, with Friends of the Earth International, 1977.
McKelvey, V. E. "Energy Sources—An Overview of Supplies—Known and Fore-
    casted Reserves." U.S. Geologic Survey, May 6, 1977.

National Academy of Scienes/National Research Council. *Resources and Man.* San Francisco: W. H. Freeman, 1969.
Nuclear Energy Policy Study Group. *Nuclear Power, Issues and Choices.* Cambridge, Mass.: Ballinger, 1977.
Revelle, Roger. "Energy Use in Rural India." *Science,* June 4, 1976.
Schipper, Lee. "Raising the Productivity of Energy Utilization." In *Annual Review of Energy,* edited by Jack M. Hollander. Palo Alto, Calif.: Annual Reviews, 1976.
Widmen, Thomas F. "Energy Conservation and a Healthy Economy." *Technology Review,* June 1977.
Workshop on Alternative Energy Strategies. *Energy: Global Prospects 1985–2000.* New York: McGraw-Hill, 1977.

Chapter 6. The Food Prospect

Brown, Lester R., with Eckholm, Erik. *By Bread Alone.* New York: Praeger, 1974.
Chancellor, W. J., and Goss, J. R. "Balancing Energy and Food Production, 1975–2000." *Science,* April 16, 1976.
Lipton, Michael. *Why Poor People Stay Poor.* Cambridge, Mass.: Harvard University Press, 1977.
National Academy of Sciences. *Agricultural Production Efficiency.* Washington, D.C., 1975.
Steinhart, John S., and Steinhart, Carol E. "Energy Use in the U.S. Food System." *Science,* April 19, 1974.
Thompson, L. M. "Weather Variability, Climatic Change, and Grain Production." *Science,* May 9, 1975.
Weatherly, A. H., and Cogger, B. M. G. "Fish Culture: Problems and Prospects." *Science,* July 29, 1977.
Wittwer, Sylvan H. "Maximum Production Capacity of Food Crops." *BioScience,* April 1974.

Chapter 7. Economic Stresses

Bosworth, Barry; Duesenberry, James S.; and Canon, Andrew S. *Capital Needs in the Seventies.* Washington, D.C.: The Brookings Institution, 1975.
"The Capital Crisis: $4.5 Trillion America Needs to Grow." *Business Week,* September 22, 1975.
Hawkins, Augustus F. "Full Employment to Meet America's Needs." *Challenge,* November–December 1975.
New York Stock Exchange, Inc. *The Capital Needs and Savings Potential of the U.S. Economy, Projections through 1985.* New York, September 1974.
Villard, Henry H. "Economic Implications for Consumption of 3 Percent Growth." *American Economic Review,* May 1968.

Chapter 8. Wealth Among Societies

Bergsten, C. Fred. "The New Era in World Commodity Markets." *Challenge,* September–October 1974.
———. "The Response to the Third World." *Foreign Policy,* Winter 1974–75.

Cooper, Richard N. "A New International Economic Order for Mutual Gain." *Foreign Policy*, Spring 1977.

Gardner, Richard N. *New Structures for Economic Interdependence*. Proceedings of an International Conference at the United Nations and The Institute on Man and Science. Rensselaerville, New York, May 1975.

Goulet, Denis. *The Uncertain Promise: Value Conflicts in Technology Transfer*. New York: IDOC/North America, 1977.

Graves, Frank Malcolm. "International Distribution of Income Among 188 Countries, 1971." Washington, D.C.: Institute of Public Administration, June 30, 1974.

Hayden, Eric W., and Nau, Henry R. "East-West Technology Transfer: Theoretical Models and Practical Experiences." *Columbia Journal of World Business*, Fall 1975.

Timmer, C. Peter, *et al. The Choice of Technology in Developing Countries*. Cambridge, Mass.: Harvard College, 1975.

Tinbergen, Jan, coordinator. *Reshaping the International Order*. New York: E. P. Dutton, 1976.

Chapter 9. Wealth Within Societies

Grant, James P. "Asian Agriculture in the Seventies and the Role of U.S. Private and Governmental Aid." Paper presented at Ramon Magsaysay Award Foundation Seminar. Manila, December 12–18, 1971.

Griffin, Keith. *Land Concentration and Rural Poverty*. New York: Holmes & Meier, 1976.

Gurley, John G. "Rural Development in China 1949–72, and the Lessons to Be Learned from It." *World Development*, July–August 1975.

Haq, Mahbub ul. *The Poverty Curtain: Choices for the Third World*. New York: Columbia University Press, 1976.

Chapter 10. The Inevitable Accommodation

Backstrand, Goran, and Ingelstam, Lars. "Should We Put Limits on Consumption?" *The Futurist*, June 1977.

Ehrlich, Paul R., and Holdren, John P. "Human Population and the Global Environment." Paper presented at Symposium on Population, Resources, and Environment. United Nations Economic and Social Council, Stockholm, August 14, 1973.

Harman, Willis W. *An Incomplete Guide to the Future*. Stanford, Calif.: Stanford Alumni Association, 1976.

Heilbroner, Robert L. *An Inquiry Into the Human Prospect*. New York: W. W. Norton, 1974.

———. "Second Thoughts on the Human Prospect." *Challenge*, May–June 1975.

Hirsch, Fred. *Social Limits to Growth*. Cambridge, Mass.: Harvard University Press, 1976.

Meadows, Donella H. *et al. The Limits to Growth*. New York: Universe Books, 1972.

Mesarovic, Mihajlo, and Pestel, Eduard. *Mankind at the Turning Point*. New York: E. P. Dutton/Reader's Digest Press, 1974.

Miles, Rufus E., Jr. *Awakening from the American Dream: The Social and Political Limits to Growth.* New York: Universe Books, 1976.

Ophuls, William. *Ecology and the Politics of Scarcity.* San Francisco. W. H. Freeman, 1977.

————. "The Scarcity Society." *Harper's,* April 1974.

Schumacher, E. F. "The Nature of Problems: An Argument Against Final Solutions." *Quest,* September–October 1977.

Wagar, Alan J. "Growth versus the Quality of Life." *Science,* June 5, 1970.

Udall, Stewart J. "The Failed American Dream." *Washington Post,* June 12, 1977.

Chapter 11. The Elements of Accommodation

The American Rural Small-Scale Industry Delegation. *Rural Small-Scale Industry in the People's Republic of China.* Berkeley: University of California Press, 1977.

Ferkiss, Victor. *The Future of Technological Civilization.* New York: George Braziller, 1974.

Gardner, Richard N. "The Hard Road to World Order." *Foreign Affairs,* April 1974.

Grant, James P. "The Changing World Order and the World's Poorest Billion: A Fresh Approach to Meeting Essential Human Needs." Paper presented at the Twenty-fifth Pugwash Conference. Madras, India, January 1976.

Huddle, Franklin P. "The Evolving National Policy for Materials." *Science,* February 20, 1976.

Keesing, Donald B. "Economic Lessons from China." Research Memorandum No. 63. Williamstown, Mass.: Center for Development Economics, Williams College, January 1975.

————. "Income Distribution from Outward-Looking Development Policies." Research Memorandum No. 59. Williamstown, Mass.: Center for Development Economics, Williams College, April 1974.

Lisk, Franklin. "Conventional Development Strategies and Basic-Needs Fulfillment: A Reassessment of Objectives and Policies." *International Labour Review,* March–April 1977.

Newland, Kathleen, and McGrath, Patricia. *The Sisterhood of Man: Women's Changing Roles in a Changing World.* New York: W. W. Norton, forthcoming.

Orleans, Leo A. "The Role of Science and Technology in China's Population/Food Balance." Washington, D.C.: Science Policy Research Division, Library of Congress, September 1977.

Prosterman, Roy L. "Land Reform as Foreign Aid." *Foreign Policy,* Spring 1972.

Schultze, Charles L. "The Economic Content of National Security Policy." *Foreign Affairs,* April 1973.

Science Council of Canada. *Canada as a Conserver Society: Resource Uncertainties and the Need for New Technologies.* Ottawa, Ont.: September 1977.

Sivard, Ruth Leger. *World Military and Social Expenditures 1977.* Leesburg, Va.: WMSE Publications, 1977.

Stokes, Bruce. *Filling the Family Planning Gap.* Worldwatch Paper 12, May 1977.

Taylor, Maxwell D. "The Exposed Flank of National Security." *Orbis,* Winter 1975.

Terrill, Ross. "China and the World: Self-Reliance or Interdependence?" *Foreign Affairs,* January 1977.

The United States and World Development: Agenda 1977. New York: Praeger, for the Overseas Development Council, 1977.

Chapter 12. The Means of Accommodation

Aspen Institute for Humanistic Studies, Program in International Affairs. *The Planetary Bargain.* Aspen, Colorado, July 1975.

Barney, Gerald O., ed. *The Unfinished Agenda: The Citizen's Policy Guide to Environmental Issues.* New York: Thomas Y. Crowell Co., 1977.

Birch, Charles. *Confronting the Future; Australia and the World: The Next Hundred Years.* Middlesex, England: Penguin Books, 1975.

Daly, Herman E. "The Stationary State Economy." *The Ecologist,* July 1972.

Elgin, Duane. "The Evolution of Consciousness and the Transformation of Society." Menlo Park, Calif.: Center for the Study of Social Policy, Stanford Research Institute, December 1974.

Goldsmith, Edward, *et al.* "The Blueprint for Survival." *The Ecologist,* January 1972.

Henderson, Hazel. "Ecologists versus Economists." *Harvard Business Review,* July–August 1973.

Leontief, Wassily, *et al. The Future of the World Economy.* New York: Oxford University Press, 1977.

McHale, John and McHale, Magda Cordell. *Basic Human Needs: A Framework for Action.* Houston: Center for Integrative Studies, April 1977.

Meadows, D.L., and Meadows, D. H., eds. *Toward Global Equilibrium.* Cambridge, Mass.: Wright-Allen Press, 1973.

Schumacher, E. F. *Small Is Beautiful: Economics As If People Mattered.* New York: Harper & Row, 1973.

Slater, Joseph E. *Governance.* New York: Aspen Institute for Humanistic Studies, 1976.

Index

abortion, 79, 209
accommodation, 242–326
  elements of, 272–98
    coping with complexity,
      296–98
    energy transition, 278–82
    recycling, 282–85
    redefining national security,
      293–96
    rural reform, 285–88
    stabilizing world population,
      273–78
    women, changing roles, 289–92
  inevitability, 242–71
    analytical gap, 253–59
    basic political choice, 263–66
    economic dilemma, 259–63
    limits set by nature, 247–50
    limits of technology, 250–53
    scarcity, 244–47
    social and political stresses,
      267–71
  means of, 299–326
    education and the media,
      320–21

    government, 310–14
    individuals and organizations,
      314–20
    long-term global planning,
      305–10
    planetary bargain, 300–305
    social transformation, 322–26
"acid rain," 42–43, 55
adult illiterates, 76
aerosols, 17, 41
African droughts, 90–92, 255
Agence France-Press, 321
Agency for International Develop-
    ment (AID), 90, 213–14,
    225, 274
agriculture:
  family farm systems, 286–87
  food prospects, 128–60
  impact of industrial pollution on,
    42
  loss of croplands, 46–50
  new-money needs of, 179
  overplowing, 33–37
  population growth and, 72–73,
    78, 136–137

agriculture *(continued)*
  slash-and-burn, 27
  technologies, 209, 213
  types of, 143–44
Ahelson, Philip H., 63
air pollution, 40–44, 58, 63, 263
  automobile industry and, 265
  crop yields and, 41–42
aldrin (pesticide), 38
aluminum, sources of, 207
American Economic Association, 9
American Electric Power Corporation, 111
analytical gap, 253–59
Antica, Hilaria Valladares, 35
anti-nuclear movement, 317, 319
Arab export embargo (1973), 297
Arab-Israeli War of 1973, 204
Argo Merchant (oil tanker), 52
arsenic, 39
Arthur D. Little, Inc., 212
asbestos, 59
Asiaweek (news magazine), 321
Asimov, Isaac, 293–94
Associated Press, 321
automobiles, 230, 231
  air pollution and, 265
  energy-conservation efforts and, 115
  speed limits, 183, 265
Awakening from the American Dream (Miles), 296–97

Backstrand, Goran, 261, 262
bauxite, 207
Bay of Bengal typhoon (1971), 255
beef prices (1973), 256
benzene hexachloride (pesticide), 39
Bethe, Hans, 109
biochloromethyl ether, 58
birth rate, 72, 227

population stabilization, 81–86
  relationship between literacy and, 275
  world (1976), 74
  see also population growth
black lung disease, 59
Blueprint for Survival, 278
Boeing Corporation, 211
Borlaug, Norman, 316
Brezhnev, Leonid, 288
British Broadcasting Corporation, 321
Brown, Harold, 294
Brown, Harrison, 250, 251
Brown, Jerry, 313
Bureau of Land Management (BLM), 29–30
Burns, Arthur, 251
Business Week (magazine), 107, 178, 319

cadmium, 39, 40, 59
cancer, 41, 59
  environmentally induced, 57–58
capital scarcity, global economy and, 177–82
carbon dioxide, 64, 118, 300
  in the atmosphere, 62–63
CARE, 90
carrying capacities, biological, 3, 6, 12–13
  concept of, 13–15
  earth's productivity and, 14–15
  reflections on, 67–70
    S-shaped growth curve, 68–70
Carson, Rachel, 38, 316
Carter, Jimmy, 5, 121, 301, 312
Carter, Luther, 49
Center for Disease Control, 39
Center for Earth and Planetary

Sciences (Harvard University), 40–41
Center for Study of Social Policy, 326
cereal hybridization, 168
Cerrutti, Francisco Morale Bermudez, 273
Cervantes, Miguel de, 122
Chase Manhattan Bank, 206
Chateaubriand, François Jean de, 26
Chicago Board of Trade, 129
child abandonment ("los olvidados"), 270
chlordane (pesticide), 38
chrome, 208
chromium, 40, 51
Clean Air Act (Great Britain), 44
Cleveland, Harlan, 300
climate and climate change, 61–65
Club of Rome, 309
coal energy, 116–18
  thermal output of, 64
Coddington, Alan, 9
coffee prices, 246, 266
commodity cartels, 205–8
common resources, shrinkage of, 15–17
Concorde (jetliner), 231
condoms, 79
Confucius, 290
Congress Party (India), 96
conservation, 113–16, 279–81, 313
Conservation Foundation, 319
Consolidated Edison, 123
consumer-protection movement, 316–17
Consumers Association of Penang (Malaysia), 39–40
continental drift, theory of, 254
contraception, 79
Cook, Donald, 111

copper, 51
Cornell University, 43
Council for Agricultural Science and Technology (Iowa), 49
Council of Economic Advisors, 9
Cousteau, Jacques, 316
cow dung, uses of, 124–25, 129, 201
Crittenden, Ann, 212
croplands:
  carrying capacity, 15
  food prospects and, 139–43
  loss of, 46–50
  yields, 149–52, 163
crowding, consequences of, 77
Cushing, D. H., 20

death rate, 73, 93, 227, 251
  landowning status and, 236
  population stabilization, 81–86
  rise in, 86–92
  see also population growth
deforestation, 23–27, 63, 66
development planning:
  global, long-term, 305–10
  role of (within societies), 223–29
dichlorodiphenyl-trichloroethane (DDT), 38
Dickens, Charles, 253
dieldrin (pesticide), 38
diminishing returns, global economy and, 162–69
distribution of wealth:
  among societies, 193–98
  within societies, 212–23
Don Quixote (Cervantes), 122
Drake, Colonel E. L., 102
Dubos, René, 323–24
DuPont Corporation, 158
dust, airborne, 63
Dust Bowl era of 1930s, 255
Dyer, Robert S., 51–52

earthquakes, 13, 65–66
earth's heat, 61–62, 118
Echeverria, President, 286
Eckholm, Erik, 26, 27, 31, 36, 59–
       60, 77, 199
ecological refugees, 238–39
ecological stresses, 12–70
    consequences of, 45–70
        biological carrying capacities,
            67–70
        climate, 61–65
        endangered species, 54–57
        illnesses, environmentally in-
            duced, 57–61
        loss of croplands, 46–50
        natural disasters, 65–67
        oceanic pollution, 50–54
    dimensions of, 12–44
        biological carrying capacities,
            13–15
        deforestation, 23–27
        overfishing, 17–23
        overgrazing, 27–33
        overplowing, 33–37
        pollution, 37–44
        shrinkage of common re-
            sources, 15–17
economic gap, defined, 194
economic stresses, 161–91
    capital scarcity, 177–82
    changing growth prospects,
        188–91
    diminishing and negative returns,
        162–69
    global inflation, 169–77
    labor productivity, 182–84
    unemployment, 184–88
economic system:
    inevitable accommodation with,
        259–63
    objective of, 259

Economist, The (periodical), 27,
       111, 321–22
education system, media and,
       320–22
Eggers, Melvin, 257
Ehrlich, Paul, 274, 321
electricity, 114, 119, 120, 121, 234,
       250
    hydroelectric generation, 121,
        123, 281
    nuclear-generated, 112
    wind power, 121–23, 167, 278–79
Elgin, Dwayne, 323
embargoes (to advance political ob-
       jectives), 204–5
employment, income distribution
       (within society) and, 225–26
endangered species, 54–57
endrin (pesticide), 38
energy, 5, 7, 97–127, 252, 311
    coal, 116–18
    conservation, 113–16
    consumption of (between coun-
        tries), 201–2
    food prospects and, 143–45
    nuclear, 108–12
    oil, 100–107
        Middle East dominance, 100–
            102
        transition to post-petroleum
            era, 102–7
    shortages, 97–98
    and social evolution, 98–100
    solar, 118–27
    "throwaway societies," 99–100
    transitions, 278–82
Energy: Global Prospects 1985–
       2000, 307–8
Energy Research and Development
       Administration (ERDA),
       111–12

Environmental Action, 318
Environmental Defense Fund, 318
Environmental Law Institute, 318
environmental movement, 317–20
Environmental Research Institute, 319
Essay on the Principle of Population, An (Malthus), 75
ethanol automotive-fuel, 281
Ethiopian famine of 1974, 35–36
expansion, economic, slowdown in, 188–91
extinction, threats of (fauna or flora species), 54–57

family-planning, 79, 81, 95–96, 275–78, 313
Federal Energy Administration, 173
Federal Home Loan Bank Board, 176
feedlot waste, gas produced from, 125
female-sterilization, 79
Feminine Mystique, The (Friedan), 316
fertilizer, 41, 144, 145, 146, 152, 163, 171, 234, 246
  grain production and, 163, 164–66
firewood, 118, 119, 201, 252
  scarcity of, 23–27
fish and fisheries, 2, 13, 40, 51, 239, 244
  decline of catches, 129, 246
  gross tonnage of vessels, 166
  oceanic pollution and, 53
  overfishing, 17–23
  population growth and, 18
fish protein concentrate (FPC), 252
Fitzpatrick, Dr. Thomas, 41
floods, 65

Floyd, Barry, 36
fluorocarbons, 41
Food and Agriculture Organization (FAO), 36, 67–68, 257
food prospects, 128–60
  balance between supply and demand, 128–29
  croplands and water, 139–43
  dependence on North America, 135–38
  effect of energy shortages on, 98
  energy dimension, 143–45
  final quarter of century (1975–2000), 156–60
  Green Revolution, 145–49
  past quarter-century (1950–75), 129–35
    consumption per person, 133–35
    grain production, 129–32
    instability, 132–35
  protein supply, 152–56
  yields, 149–52
Ford Foundation, 64, 110, 146
Fortune (magazine), 208
fossil fuels, burning of, 38, 43, 57, 62
Freon, 41
Fresh Water Biology Institute, 38
Friedan, Betty, 316
Friedman, Jack, 305
Friends of the Earth, 318
Future of the World Economy, The, 307

Galileo, 253–54
Gandhi, Indira, 147
Gappert, Gary, 253
gasoline, price of, 115–16
gasoline crisis of 1974 (U.S.), 97
General Agreement on Tariffs and Trade (GATT), 203, 204

glass containers, recycling, 284
government, role of, 310–14
grain production:
  and fertilizer use, 163, 164–66
  per capita, 129–32, 199–200
  per person (1950–77), 130
  yields, 149–52
  see also agriculture; croplands
Grant, James P., 226
Grant, Kenneth, 37
grasslands, 2–3
  carrying capacity, 13–14
  overgrazing, 27–33
Great Depression, 9, 103, 161
greenhouse effect, 62
Green Revolution, 145–49
  Mexico net grain trade (1961–78), 149
  wheat production in India (1950–77), 147
Griffin, Keith, 235–36, 237
Gross National Product (GNP), 224, 261
  per capita in populous countries (1974), 196
Group of 77, 217
Gurley, John, 234

Haile Selassie, Emperor, 92
Hammond, Allen, 125
Hansen, Roger, 217
Haq, Mahbub ul, 224, 230
Hardin, Garrett, 17, 255
Harman, Willis, 245, 326
Harvard University, 40–41
Hayes, Denis, 5, 108, 126
health hazards, occupational, 59–60
heart disease, 60
Heilbroner, Robert, 264, 314, 315, 323
Heller, Walter, 9

Henderson, Hazel, 317, 320
Henderson, P. D., 119
heptachlor (pesticide), 38–39
Heronemous, Dr. William, 122
Hewitt, Kenneth, 65, 66
Hewson, Dr. Wendell, 122
Heyerdahl, Thor, 54, 316
Hill, David, 283
Hitch, Charles, 126
Hodgson, Harlow, 28
Holdren, John, 274
home insulation, 113
Homestead Act, 288
housing industry, capital requirements of, 179–80
Hubbert, King, 123
Huddle, Franklin P., 294
Huggett, Robert J., 40
hunger, 86–92, 93, 251
hydrocarbon pollution, 51
hydroelectric generation, 121, 123, 281

illegal immigrants (U.S.), 187, 268
illiteracy, 76
illnesses, environmentally induced 57–61
Immigration and Naturalization Service (INS), 187
income distribution:
  ecological deterioration and, 237–39
  national versus international inequities, 239–41
Industrial Revolution, 73, 183, 193, 194
inflation, 178, 246, 259–60, 271
  generated by excessive demand 170–71
  global economy and, 169–77
Ingelstam, Lars, 261, 262

instability, food-price, 132–33

Inter-American Committee for Agricultural Development, 235

International Business Machines Corporation (IBM), 211, 212

International Cholera Research Laboratory, 87

International Corn and Wheat Improvement Center, 213

International Council of Copper Exporting Countries, 207

International Energy Agency, 106

International Labor Organization, 226

International Labor Review, 292

International Labour Office (ILO), 186, 309

International Monetary Fund, 219, 297

International Planned Parenthood Federation, 274

International Rice Research Institute (IRRI), 146, 213

Interstate Commerce Commission, 283

intrauterine device (IUD), 79, 209

Japan Times, 112

Jellife, Dr. Derrick B., 77

Johns Hopkins University, 88–89, 236

Johnson, Lyndon B., 250

Jordan, Dr. Trenholm D., 42

Journal of Commerce, 180

Kellogg Engineering, Inc., 211

kelp, 125

Kennedy, John F., 9, 250, 251

Kettering Foundation, 158

Keynes, John Maynard, 253

Khruschev, Nikita, 313

kidnappings, 270

Kimbrough, Dr. Renata D., 39

Kissinger, Henry, 251

Kraft, Joseph, 260

Kuhn, T. S., 253

labor force, projected growth in (1970–2000), 186

labor productivity:
global economy and, 182–84
inflation and, 170
and unemployment, 184–88

land distribution, 235–37, 301
need for reform, 285–88

land prices, 175–76

Landsberg, Helmut, 63

landslides, 66

Latham, Michael, 91

lead, 39, 51, 59, 208

Le Houérou, H. N., 47

Leontief, Wassily, 307

Lewis, Arthur, 214

L'Express (news magazine), 321

Lilienthal, David, 109

Limits to Growth, The, 306, 309, 321

lindane (pesticide), 39

Lipton, Michael, 232, 233

livestock population, overgrazing, 27–33

Lloyd, William Forster, 15–16

Losing Ground (Eckholm), 26, 31, 36

Lovejoy, Thomas, 56

Lovins, Amory, 114

McElroy, Michael B., 40–41

McHugh, Dr. J. L., 40

McNamara, Robert, 206

magnesium oxide, 59

malathion (pesticide), 38
male sterilization, 79, 96
Malone, Thomas F., 63
Malthus, Thomas R., 6, 75, 162
Mankind at the Turning Point
    (Mesarovic and Pestel), 309
Mao Tse-tung, 227, 290
Marine Pollution Bulletin, 51
Marshall Plan, 193
"maternal depletion syndrome," 77
Mattholfer, Hans, 112
Meadows, Donella, 70, 315
mercury, 39, 53, 59, 208
Mesarovic, Mihajlo, 309
methyl butyl hetone, 58
Miles, Rufus, 296–97, 311
Mostert, Noël, 53
"Most Severely Affected" (MSA)
    countries, 198
Myers, Norman, 56
Myrdal, Gunnar, 301

Nader, Ralph, 316
National Academy of Sciences, 43,
    61, 62, 63, 251
National Audubon Society, 318
National Commission on Supplies
    and Shortages, 282
National Institute of Environmental
    Health Sciences, 58
national security, redefining, 293–96
National Wildlife Federation, 318
National Women's Conference
    (1972), 290
natural disasters, 65–67
natural habitats, physical destruction
    of, 55–56
Natural Resources Defense Council,
    318
Needham, James, 177
Newland, Kathleen, 77

newsprint, 176, 283
Newsweek (news magazine), 321
New York Stock Exchange, 177
New York Times, The, 176, 187,
    212, 216, 283
Next Hundred Years, The (Brown),
    250
nickel, 51
nitrogen fertilizer, 41
noise pollution, 263
North American food, dependence
    on, 135–38
North Sea oil, 172
nuclear power, 108–12
    relationship between nuclear
        weapons and, 110
    thermal output of, 64
Nuclear Power: Issues and Choices
    (Ford Foundation), 64
nuclear power plants, 111, 112
nuclear reactors, 108
    fuel supplies for, 110–11
nuclear waste, 108

obesity, 60
oceanic pollution, 50–54
offshore drilling, 51, 52
oil, 7–8, 111, 203, 245
    barrels per day (1970s), 103
    deforestation and, 26
    depletion of reserves, 247
    fall-off in production, 103–4
    imports (U.S.), 101
    Middle East dominance, 100–102
    need for conservation, 113, 114,
        115, 116
    prices of, 173, 197, 205, 206, 218,
        246, 296
    proven reserves, 104–5
    recoverable, from conventional
        sources (1942–1975), 105

tanker transport of, 17
transition to post-petroleum era,
102–7
transporting, 17, 172–73
world price of (1953–77), 173
Oil and Gas Journal, 104
oil shale deposits, 107
oil spills, 51, 52
Okun, Arthur, 9
Ophuls, William, 263
Oregon State University, 122
Organization for Economic Cooperation and Development
(OECD), 166, 169–70, 257
Organization of Petroleum Exporting Countries (OPEC), 101,
172, 173, 193, 197, 218, 296,
298
as a cartel, 205–8
export revenues (1973), 205
influence of, 215–16
success of, 205
Oshima, Harry T., 185
overfishing, 17–23
northeast Atlantic region, 20
Peruvian anchovy catch, 20–21, 22
overgrazing, 27–33
overplowing, 33–37
Overseas Development Council,
198, 226
Owens, Edgar, 225
ozone layer, 17, 40–41, 300

Panday, K. K., 32
parathion (pesticide), 38
parenthood and childbearing,
264–65
Peccei, Aurelio, 309
Peirce, Neal R., 318–19
Perai Industrial Estate (Malaysia),
39–40

Perez, Carlos Andres, 206
Pestel, Eduard, 309
pesticides, 38, 51
Peterson, Peter, 300
petrochemical industry, 58
petroleum, *see* oil
phosphate rock, 206–7
photosynthesis, 55, 119, 124, 158,
165
Physical Quality of Life Index
(PQLI), 302–3
Picture of Health, The (Eckholm),
59–60, 199
pill, the, 79, 209
Pimentel, David, 48, 49
planetary bargain, 300–305
meaning of, 300
plankton, 54
Ploesti oil fields (Rumania), 101
plutonium, 52
pollution, 37–44, 63, 239, 263
control expenditures, 180–81
see also types of pollution
polybrominated biphenyls, 59
polychlorinated biphenyls (PCBs),
39, 53
Population Bomb, The (Ehrlich),
321
Population Crisis Committee, 318
population growth:
agriculture and, 72–73, 78,
136–37
countries achieving stability,
81–86
increase (1970 and 1975), 79
per-capita fish catch and, 18
preagricultural era, 72
in preindustrial societies, 75
stabilizing, need for, 273–78,
301
understanding, 71–96

population *(continued)*
 arithmetic and dynamics, 72–75
 hunger, 86–92
 multidimensional problem, 75–77
 supply and demand for resources, 77–78
 trends (1970s), 78–81
 urgency of stabilization, 92–96
 see also birth rate; death rate
Population Institute, 318
Population Reference Bureau, 318
potato famine of 1847 (Ireland), 276
poverty, 196–97, 268, 315
 dimensions of, 198–202
Project Independence, 313
Prosterman, Roy, 286
protein supply, 152–56

radioactive waste, 52, 110
rainmaking technology, 64
Rall, Dr. David, 58
Randers, Jørgen, 315
raw-material exporters, 206–8
Reagan, Ronald, 313
recession of 1970s, 185
Reclamation Act of 1902, 288
recycling, 282–85, 315
 advantages of, 284–85
Reshaping the International Order, 309
Resources for the Future, 126
respiratory diseases, 59–60
Reuss, Henry, 122
Reuters (news agency), 321
Ricardo, David, 162
Rieger, Hans, 25
Robinson, Joan, 170
Rockefeller, David, 206

Rockefeller Foundation, 146, 214, 251
Roosevelt, Franklin D., 283
rubber, 208
rural reform, need for, 285–88
rural-urban relationships, 232–34
Rusk, Dean, 251

Saikowski, Charlotte, 290
Salk, Dr. Jonas, 69
Santa Barbara oil-well blowout (1969), 52
Santorelli, Leonard, 44
scarcity, global politics of, 202–5
schistosomiasis, 60
Schlesinger, James, 106
Schmid, Robert, 35
Schmidt, Helmut, 177
Schneider, Erick, 52
Schumacher, E. F., 317
Science (magazine), 17, 48, 49, 125, 126, 255, 294
Science, Technology, and American Diplomacy (congressional study), 294
Science Council of Canada, 47, 94–95
Secretariat for Future Studies (Stockholm), 261, 262
Selikoff, Dr. Irving, 59
Shibata, Tokue, 319
Sierra Club, 318
Silent Spring (Carson), 316, 321
silicosis, 59–60
slash-and-burn agriculture, 27
Small is Beautiful (Schumacher), 317
smallpox, eradication of, 304
Smith, Adam, 182–83
Soemarwoto, Dr. Otto, 25
Soil Conservation Service, 37

solar energy, 63, 118–27, 167, 279
    captured by plants, 124
    for heating and cooling, 119–20
    indirect source of, 125
    land and marine plant use of, 55
    tidal, 123–24
    water power, 120–21
    wind power, 121–23
Soviet wheat purchases (1972), 5, 173–74
soybean-production, 154–56
    world prices (1958–77), 175
specialization and overspecialization, 256–57
speed limits, automobile, 183, 265
S-shaped biological growth curve, 68–70
SSTs, release of nitrous oxide by, 41
stabilization, population:
    countries achieving, 81–86
    need for, 273–78, 301
    urgency of, 92–96
stagflation, defined, 161
Stanford Research Institute, 245, 323, 326
Stanford University, 289
Stokes, Bruce, 95
stresses:
    ecological, 12–70
    economic, 161–91
    social and political, 267–71
strip-cropping, 35
strip-mining, 118
sturgeon industry, 53
sugar cane, 125, 126
sulfuric acid, 58
Supership (Mostert), 53
supply and demand:
    food prospects and, 128–29
    population growth and, 77–78

synthetic fuel, production of, 117–18

tariff structure, 214–15, 218
tax policies, 276
technology, 208–14
    exports (U.S.), 210
    foreign investors, 211–12
    from foreign students, 213
    licenses and patents, 210–11
    limits of, 250–53
    nonproprietary, 213–14
    role of, 229–31
terrorists, 109–10
thermal pollution, 64
Thompson, Louis, 157
tidal power, 123–24
Tinbergen, Jan, 309
Titusville oil well, 102
toxaphene (pesticide), 39
Toynbee, Arnold, 266
Trudeau, Pierre, 260, 270
trypanosomiasis, 140
Turchaninova, Svetlana, 292
2, 4-D (pesticide), 39
"Two Lectures on the Checks to Population" (Lloyd), 15–16

Udall, Stewart, 250, 251
unemployment, 178, 183, 268, 269, 271, 287–88
    economic expansion and, 260–61
    global economy and, 184–88
United Nations, 12, 21, 27, 31, 35, 49, 57, 70, 92, 119, 137, 198, 213, 238, 258, 311
United Nations Conference on Desertification, 12, 31
United Nations Conference on Human Settlements, 48

United Nations Conference on Population, 95, 274
United Nations Conference on Trade and Development, 203, 217
United Nations Educational, Scientific, and Cultural Organization (UNESCO), 47
United Nations Environment Program, 46
United Nations Fund for Population Activities (UNFPA), 274
United Nations Special Session on Raw Materials, 212
United Press International, 321
U.S. Army Corps of Engineers, 121
U.S. Department of Agriculture, 257
U.S. Department of the Interior, 250, 251
U.S. Energy Research and Development Administration, 122
U.S. Environmental Protection Agency (EPA), 52, 180, 283
U.S. Federal Power Commission, 125
U.S. Food and Drug Administration, 239
United States Information Service, 321
University of Massachusetts, 122
University of Wisconsin, 253
uranium, 111, 298
urbanization, 325

vasectomies, 79
Verne, Jules, 320
Vietnam War, 311
vinyl chloride, 58

Ward, Barbara, 317
Warren, Kirby, 305
Washington Post, 250
waste energy, 114–15
water, food prospects and, 139–43
Watergate, 311–12
water pollution, 39–40, 43
water power, 120–21, 167
Watts, James, 99
wealth, 134, 192–241
    among societies, 192–219
        commodity cartels, 205–8
        dimensions of poverty, 198–202
        dissatisfaction, 217–19
        global distribution, 193–98
        new-found influence, 214–17
        politics of scarcity, 202–5
        technology market, 208–14
    within societies, 220–41
        ecological deterioration and income distribution, 237–39
        inequities, 239–41
        land distribution, 235–37
        national distribution, 221–23
        role of planners, 223–29
        role of technology, 229–31
        rural versus urban areas, 232–34
Wegener, Robert, 254
wheat, world price of (1951–77), 174
Whitehead, Cynthia, 319
Wilson, Carroll, 106, 307–8
windmills, 122
wind power, 121–23, 167, 278–79
    drawbacks of, 123
women, 76–77, 276
    changing roles of, 289–92
women's liberation movement, 289–90

Wood, Dr. John, 38
wood shortages, 23–27
Woodwell, George, 54
Workshop on Alternative Energy
    Strategies (WAES), 307–8
World Bank, 167–68, 206, 219, 301
World Health Organization
    (WHO), 60, 213, 304
World Population Conference of
    1974, 256

World War II, 73

Yanaton, Pat, 51
yields, cropland, 149–52
    per hectare (1950–77), 151

Zero Population Growth, 278,
    318
zinc, 51
zoning regulations, 264

GF
41
D818
1978

82078

DATE DUE

DEC 1 6 1988			